# THE
# MAGIC
# MAN

M000210102

For everything, thank
you. Your help last year
has given me life; a life
to spend with my children

my parents, my family; i the
ones i love. From the
bottom of my heart, thank
you.

with love.

Keith

# Will Reece

# THE
# MAGIC
# MAN

**TATE PUBLISHING**
AND **ENTERPRISES**, LLC

Published by Tate Publishing & Enterprises, LLC
127 E. Trade Center Terrace | Mustang, Oklahoma 73064 USA
1.888.361.9473 | www.tatepublishing.com

Tate Publishing is committed to excellence in the publishing industry. The company reflects the philosophy established by the founders, based on Psalm 68:11,
*"The Lord gave the word and great was the company of those who published it."*

Book design copyright © 2013 by Tate Publishing, LLC. All rights reserved.
*Cover design by Arjay Grecia*
*Interior design by Honeylette Pino*

Published in the United States of America

ISBN: 978-1-62854-134-2
Fiction / General
13.10.08

# ONE

He could jump so high that he seemed to float. And maybe, just maybe, he was floating right down the street to the corner where a row of seats sat empty under a cloudy sky. Mister Jones chose the seat in the middle. A shadow with shoes—shoes that needed shining.

With his towel on his shoulder, the blind man sat in front of the smiling man on his stool with two brushes, a small and a long brush, and a can of his own brown polish at his feet. He had chosen that brown polish because he knew that the long shoes in front of him were brown, though he could only see shadows. But he could see the shadows clear, sharp, see them like the moon crossing in front of the sun. And this here shadow right before his eyes made him cry—only he didn't know why.

"Mister Jones," the shoeshine man's voice was a gravely thing, "you don't mind if I spit on your shoes?"

"How come you always ask me that?"

"Just 'cause some folk don't like another man's spit on their shoes," the shoeshine man said. "So I always ask."

"And I always say I don't mind."

"Yes, sir, you always say that."

"Besides, it's the only way these shoes ever shine." Mister Jones smiled. "You sure make 'em shine bright."

"Yes, sir." The old man patted the step on the stool. Mister Jones put his foot on the step, and the shoeshine man took the towel from his shoulder and wiped down the shoe, cleaning it. He said, "How long you been coming here now?"

"Tell me."

"Well, every day for fifty years now."

"That long, huh?"

"That long." The shoeshine man nodded. "Yes, sir, fifty years I've been shining your shoes. Shining your same shoes, too. Same laces, same brown leather, same soles. Tell me, how can that be?"

"Why"—Mister Jones smiled—"it's your spit."

The shoeshine man's hand stopped. "My spit?"

"Yessiree, your spit. Like I said, nothin' makes these shoes shine like your spit."

"That might be so, but that still don't explain how these shoes have lasted fifty years without new soles or sides or laces. What's your secret?"

Mister Jones laughed. "My secret?"

"Yes, sir, your secret."

"Tell me, how much do I give you every day?"

"You know as well as I do."

"Humor me," Mister Jones said. "How much, one bit? Two?"

"No, sir, you give me a ten spot."

"Ten dollars to shine my shoes." Mister Jones nodded away. "I pay you ten dollars a day, six days a week, sometimes seven. Sixty dollars a week, almost three hundred dollars a month, now don't I?"

"Yes, sir, you do."

"And you want to know my secret?"

"Yes, sir, I do."

"The secret to my shoes."

"You might say it's 'cause I'm in the business, sir."

"You could say that, but we both know that you'd be lyin'," Mister Jones said. "Still, why not. Why not tell you a little secret of mine. It'd only be fair 'cause I know all of yours. I know it just ain't your spit like you say. It's those coffee grounds in your polish, used ones, 'cause new ones are too strong. Don't want your patrons smelling like a fresh pot now, do ya?"

"No, sir, that'd be too obvious. Looks like you do know all my secrets."

Mister Jones laughed. Laughed so hard and loud that people passing by turned to look and then looked away even quicker. "But that ain't all your secrets now, is it?"

The shoeshine man took his brush and scrubbed.

Mister Jones said, "Nosiree, not by a long way. You are a regular snake oil man, an alchemist, so to speak. There's a little bourbon in that can of yours, a little ash too, now ain't that right?"

"Yes, sir, that's right."

"Yes, sir, that's right." Mister Jones laughed to himself and leaned back in the chair. "Mix it with that spit of yours and nobody shines a better shoe than you. And you know, it only seems fitting that I tell you a little secret of mine on account of us being in the magic business and all that. But you got to promise now, on your word, on your life, that you won't tell a single soul. No, sir, not a soul."

"You can count on me." The shoeshine man nodded. "Your secret's safe with me."

"Don't I know it." And Mister Jones leaned forward and whispered, "You see, my feet never touch the ground. Not ever."

For a moment, just a heartbeat, the old man's hands stopped, his eyes looked up at the shadow in front of his face. Mister Jones breathed in, sucking the old man's breath right from his mouth. He felt like he was dying, he was sure of it, but the old man wasn't. No sir, he wasn't dying 'cause Mister Jones leaned back and let out his air with a deep laugh. The shoeshine man bent over and breathed heavily until he caught his breath. Mister Jones asked, "Now where's that dog of yours?"

The old man spit on Mister Jones' shoes. "He's home today. Too damn cold for him."

"You don't worry 'bout him, he's gonna live for a long, long time. Live 'till the day you die."

"How do you know that?"

"'Cause I can see. Just like you, I can see. Except the difference between me and you is that you just don't want to see. You're afraid of what you'll see 'cause you saw it with your wife, didn't you. Funny thing about that too, they say no one knows the hour of their death, but you knew hers. Knew it down to the second, and yet here you are on a street corner, shining shoes. How come?"

"You talkin' nonsense now, like you always do."

"Am I?" Mister Jones stared at the man. "You know when that dog of yours is gonna die, and yet you keep him home 'cause it's cold. Fact is, you knew when your wife was gonna die, stayed home with her too, held her as she died. And you felt it. Felt her going like she was some balloon, something on a string that you held in your hand until it slipped from your fingers. And no matter how hard you tried to grab it, no matter how hard you held onto her, she just died. That door opened and closed, and then she was gone. And the thing about it all was that you felt it, you knew it, and still you couldn't do a damn thing about it. Scary, ain't it?"

"How come you come here?" The man wiped at his eyes. "How come you tell me all these things and then just walk away?"

"'Cause you want me to."

"Hell if I do."

"You do." Mister Jones nodded. "I'm the only one that'll talk to you 'bout these things, and that makes you feel good 'cause otherwise you would have lost your mind a long time ago. Yessiree, a long, long time ago. Fact is, you is as old as me. Well, almost. Besides, when I talk to you, you sleep a little better at night 'cause you think at least you ain't as crazy as me. But then, you'll just get to sleep, and that thought will come in your head. That one thing that bothers you about me, that something big."

"And what's that?"

"You know what it is." Mister Jones smiled. "Yessiree, you sure do. But it looks like today is my day for talking so I'll tell ya. Every day you see all them people passin' by you, shadows the way you see them, and every day you have a good idea of just when they all gonna expire. But here's the kicker, every day I come and sit here and what do you see?"

"Give me your other shoe."

"Come on," Mister Jones urged as he sat his right foot on the step. "Tell me what you see."

He didn't want to say, didn't want to breathe either.

Mister Jones said, "Don't make me say it for you."

"Nothing," the shoeshine man said. "I don't see nothing with you."

And Mister Jones laughed—laughed so hard that even the shoeshine man shook like an old leaf clinging on a branch in winter.

"Yessiree, you don't see a thing. And you want to know why?"

"No, sir, I don't."

"'Cause I'm just like you."

*Not another word*, the shoeshine man thought, *just shine this shoe. Just this shoe, just a little spit now, just the towel, buff it good.* But for some reason, the shoeshine man opened his mouth, "So what are you gonna do now?"

"Magic." Mister Jones stood, his feet never touched the ground, and dropped a twenty in the man's jar. "And don't you worry about that dog of yours none 'cause it's like I said, he gonna live a long, long time. Yessiree, he's gonna live just as long as you do."

15 –

Just black numbers on a white sign held high above the head of a girl in a swimsuit. Some girl in high heels strutted around a smoke-filled ring as a bunch of no-goods whistled from the crowd.

The old man was in front of the fighter, yelling in his face, but Matt never heard a word he said, just spit flying from half-dead lips. Across the ring, one face held Matt's attention, the one that kept changing round after round.

As he sat on that little stool in his corner of the ring, the only thing he heard was the sound of breaking bottles. Tall bottles with long necks held high above the world on a fire escape five floors up. Easy fingers held spirits inside a brown bottle.

The face changed again.

The old man leaned down, he was livid now: a former champ from a forgotten time. He was old, so damn old that if he were a horse he would have been white paste on the tip of some school girl's brush. Matt loved the old man.

And hated him too.

Matt turned from the face as it changed again and found the long legs of the woman with the black 15. They weren't moving anymore. The swank, the push of her hip was stuck in midstride. Her face was frozen with a hopeful smile because tonight might be the night she got her ticket out of the city. The night she might get noticed. But she was just a face, just eyes and a mouth, a little nose too, a face that changed in front of Matt's eyes again.

Matt looked away and found the old man in front of him; a finger knotted with age pointing right at him. A finger that hung in midair. All around the ring, out in the crowd where the pimps sat with their fur coats sweating like the pigs they were, the whole world was still except for the face—the one that smiled.

*Does it scare you, Matt?*

It laughed, its head snapped back, its mouth split wide, teeth stuck up as if they were a trap—a trap that was waiting for some poor rabbit's foot.

The bell rang.

A slap, the old man's hand on Matt's face. "What's a matter with you?"

"Nothin'." Matt shook his head. "I'm fine."

Art turned and stole a quick look at the other fighter—the cock of the walk, the big son of a gun with a long left jab, the ladies' man who wasn't looking so pretty anymore. Too damn bad, Art thought, Matt could have beaten this fool.

Art leaned down. "Do me a favor."

"What's that?"

"Make him remember you." Art smiled a lie, a thing he had worn a thousand times. "Just like you always do, win or lose. Make this fool remember you."

A half-hearted grin from a split lip.

Matt got to his feet and started across the ring. The man who had never gone down, Marvelous Matthew Gore, was gonna give Joseph one more round of hell.

Now Matt was moving, gloves held high, still the face changed in front of his eyes as everything came to a stop. The fighter breathed in one last time and threw a left, a wicked shot. There was the crunch of bone.

It was Monday. Or maybe it was Tuesday.

Matt didn't know, didn't care either; he was alone again—alone and hurting in the middle of the night. Sometimes it seemed that life never did change. The streetlight shone in through the window the size of a warehouse.

Matt looked out through his swollen eyes and up at the night sky. There wasn't a single star, just clouds—thick, ugly clouds that smothered the city like a disease. A city without grass and trees and little parks where kids could play. Just bricks and blacktop, metal hoops on broken walls, and even if there had been a tree, it would have been dead.

Fifteen rounds and six hundred punches, forty every round—always forty a round. Punch 587 and the crack of bone. Matt smiled even though it hurt, smiled real wide because he knew that Joseph would remember him.

Matt reached for his glass and groaned. His ribs pinched, but Matt still grabbed the damn thing. *They're only bruised*, he convinced himself as he sipped warm water, *just bruised, that's all. I should have won*, Matt stared at the glass, *I should have won*.

*Tomorrow*, he thought, *tomorrow I'll get out of this cot and start over again. I'll walk down those stairs and into the gym, and all of those other fighters will stare at me. They won't say nothin', not one of them, but their eyes will say it.*

*Still, I'll walk to the showers and turn on the water. Ice-cold water in the middle of winter. I'll wish for hot water, but it'll be cold. It's always cold*. Matt stared at the glass in his hand: warm water to drink, cold water for a shower; ain't life just nice.

*I'll shower and get moving again, walking even if it's with a limp, lifting those crates, all those boxes all day long, fighting the pain in my ribs, truck after truck, day after day, and in a week or two, three at the most, I'll start training again.*

*Running before work, sparring too, a little bag work, jumping so much damn rope it could stretch to the moon before I head off to work. And after a long day, I'll run home and catch five hours of sleep—six if I'm lucky. I'll do it*, Matt told himself, *just like I've been doin' day after day, year after year. I ain't ever gonna give up.*

"Matt?" Matt looked across the room where a shadow stood in the doorway. "You awake?" it said.

"What you doin' here, Art?"

"Just thought I'd check on you." Art stepped forward, holding his knit cap in his hands and nervously working its black cloth. "How you feelin'?"

Matt tried to laugh, but it hurt. "Like hell."

"Listen." Art walked across the room, slipping his cap into his pocket and sat down on the metal folding chair. He took the glass from Matt and cupped it in his hand. It was half-empty. "I wanted to talk to you about somethin'." Art fiddled with the glass. "Actually, I got somethin' I want to ask you. Call it a favor of sorts."

"Anything for you, Art. Just say the word."

"Anything for me, he says. God, he's a good kid. I like you, kid, like you was my own. Ever since you came here, I felt that way about you. Me and you, you know, family. Anyway"—Art paused—"I was thinking tonight, you know, that maybe after all this is done, that maybe you'd like to work with me."

"Sorry." Matt shook, trying to clear it, but all he could hear was the sound of breaking bottles. "What did you say?"

Art sat so far back that darkness hid his face. "You know, when all this is done and over, I want you to come work for me, be my partner and everything. What do you say, kid?"

"What are *you* sayin', Art?"

"I'm getting old, kid, real old. I hurt like you do. When I go, someone's got to take over for me. You know, teach these kids to fight and everything. You can do that, kid. You'll even take one to the top."

Matt stared up at the window, dirty snow falling. "Are you saying I'm done?"

"No, I ain't sayin' that." Art shook his head, regretting his words. *I should have waited for another fight or two. Waited until the writing on the wall was just as plain as day.* "I just couldn't sleep and got to thinkin', that's all. It ain't you, it's me. Like I said, I'm old and when you old like me you want to make sure everything's all right before that final bell."

*It's over.*

"Did you say somethin', kid?"

"You, you ain't ever gonna die." Matt tried to smile, and the old man leaned forward and stretched his arms. "Not ever."

"I was always right about you, kid. Knew it from the first day you walked in here when you had nothin'. Just like I always told you, you is special." Art smiled now, seeing the future before his eyes. "It'll be nice, kid, just you and me working here, training together."

Matt stared out at the dirty snow. *He's telling me everything, ain't meaning to kill me, but he's telling me I'm done. One, two, maybe three fights left. How long is that? A year, two, maybe three if I'm lucky.* Matt closed his eyes, closed them tight. Outside the window, snow turned to rain.

"Get some rest." Art groped for words. "You got work in the morning?"

"Yeah." Matt nodded.

The old man stood and shuffled on his feet. "By the way"— Art tried to smile as he set the empty glass back on the chair— "you broke Joseph's jaw, kid. They operated on him last night. Nobody's ever fought him like you did. Be proud of yourself."

"Thanks, Art."

"'Night, kid."

The old man shuffled across the room and disappeared down the stairs. Matt lifted his hands and stared at his knuckles: big and swollen, a broken finger, a pinky that was permanently crooked to the left. The hands of an old fighter, hands like Art's.

Art stood at the bottom of the stairs. *I'm sorry, kid, I should have told you sooner, should have told you lifetime ago, you ain't got a shot. Not no more.* Art shut off the lights and walked across that cold floor toward the boxing ring. The floor creaked under his worn-out shoes. *You just ain't got the tools.*

Art looked through the monster roped in red at the front door where dings and knocks had laid since forever. *I remember the day you came in. You was all wide-eyed, real quiet too. Guess some things never do change. I remember how you kept staring up at all those banners.*

They still hung there above the ring, pictures of the greats that Art had trained, pictures of two kids that became champs—one a lightweight, the kid with hands and feet just as quick as lightning; the other a welterweight—Art himself. Welterweight champ back in the day, those days when boxers didn't make a thing.

*Remember how I told you about Dink and Dizzy, Old Leon too? You was the first kid who really listened. I could have sworn that day that you was different. I thought you was gonna hang up here with us. Maybe you was never meant to be the champ.*

*Maybe I only wanted to believe that you could be the heavyweight champ 'cause you're like my own. A son I never had. But it don't matter none 'cause now it's too late.* Art put his beanie back on his head. *It's just too late. Maybe I should have never made you fight all them older boys.*

*I was a fool,* Art thought. *Then again, maybe all that fighting made you what you are now—a survivor. A man who's never gone down. No, not once. Never a champ though, just a survivor. How come that is, kid? You got sweet feet, good hands and a jaw that's made of iron. What's wrong inside that head of yours?* Art looked away from all those banners and shook his head. *Life, this is it.*

*Just a ring and ropes and spit buckets. And if you're lucky, someone in your corner to lift your drink.* Art walked from the ring into the office and shut off the gym's light. Dead men hovered above the ropes.

The old man sat behind an old metal desk and laid his head down. It was a cold metal thing that he bought for nothing twenty-five years back. And as Art closed his eyes, as sleep snuck up on him like the shadow at his feet, he wondered if winter would ever pass. Outside, the snow fell, black and ugly.

# TWO

It was cold and still dark. There wasn't an alarm, no clock that told Matt it was time to get up and get going. No, Matt just woke up like he always did. Day after day, year after year, Matt woke up at four thirty in the morning because it was time to train.

He sat up, threw off his old wool blanket, which was a GI surplus from a forgotten war, and swung his feet onto the floor. It was cold. *One of these days*, he thought, *I'm gonna sleep in. Sleep in when I'm strong and healthy and not just lying in bed after a fight.* It was three weeks later, three weeks after his loss to Joseph.

For a minute he sat there, his body still sore, his head still aching; he could almost feel the blows from the ring. But it was time to put in the miles because Matt hoped that a call would come, a call that would throw him back into the ring. Matt stood and stretched; it only took ten minutes to loosen up, so he could bend down and put on his Converse trainers. Matt wrapped a white towel around his thick neck, zipped up his sweatshirt, and hurried down the stairs. Down the stairs and out through the back, locking the door behind him, setting off into the snow. Five miles this morning, two more tonight before bed.

The snow was wet, his Converse instantly soaked, his feet stomping up the slush, but Matt didn't care. It was good to get out and let his lungs burn, let the body warm up and loosen up while the mind drifted away. Drift like the thick black smoke that billowed up from those high smoke stacks, red lights flashing at their tops.

Crumbled sidewalks, hard streets littered with potholes, Matt's feet splashing the slush as he ran under broken street lights. He was in and out of the dark, his eyes always watching, and he rounded a corner to Mikey's window that stood a foot from his broken porch. He stopped and knocked. Glass that was patched with cardboard. It was only then that he noticed a crack in the other bedroom window—Margaret.

"Mikey." Matt's voice carried in the dark, still running in place to keep warm. "It's me, Matt."

"I know who it is." The voice came back cranky. "Don't you think that I know who it is? You don't have to say your name every damn morning."

Matt shrugged to himself and threw a lazy jab. "Let's go."

"Yeah, yeah."

"It's wet."

"I know."

He wasn't a bad kid. Matt threw a lazy left, a lazy right. A moment later, the front door opened. Tall, lean, seventeen: someday Mikey might be a heavyweight, but not now. Now he was just a string bean. Mikey stood on the porch, stretching his arms and legs.

"Ready?"

Mikey rolled his eyes. "How far this morning?"

"Five miles."

"Damn."

"You don't have to, you know."

"I know."

Matt didn't wait for the kid. He was off and down the street while Mikey stood on that porch.

"Son of a…" Mikey muttered to himself and took off running.

The kid caught up to Matt, watching his feet, imitating the lefts and rights that the heavyweight threw. The two ran side by side, along corner bars, brick apartment buildings, warehouses and smokestacks, snow falling as they headed towards the river.

"Heard you got a fight." Matt glanced sidelong at Mikey.

"Harris," the kid said.

"Work hard and you'll beat him."

"I know."

"You scared."

"I ain't ever scared."

Matt smiled as the two ran onto the crumbled sidewalk by the river. "Never?"

"No, never."

"I felt like throwing up before I fought Joseph."

"You did?"

"Felt the same way when I fought Junior, too."

"You beat Junior good."

"So?"

Cold air, Mikey's breath in front of his face. "I didn't think you was ever scared."

"They was scared, too." Matt took a deep breath, his ribs pinching from a big-time left. "Even Art was scared when he fought."

"Yeah, of course he was scared. Fighters back then, they was no good."

"You think so, huh?"

"I mean I see his belt and all those pictures of him and those old guys and everything, but they were no good."

"They were better."

"Tch."

"Mikey, we got everything. Gyms and weights and all that equipment, those guys didn't have all them things. And Art, he teaches us everything he knows. You know, all his secrets and everything. Stuff he learned from getting hit in the face. Were they good?" Matt looked at the kid. "Yeah, they was real good. Better than us."

Footfalls in the snow.

"Damn, it's cold. I hate winter."

"Me, too."

"Mom wants to know if you and Art want to come over for dinner. She said to tell you that she was makin' your favorite, meat loaf. How come you like that junk, anyways?"

"I don't."

"What you mean?"

"Your mom, she works real hard, right?"

"Yeah, so?"

"She's on her feet all day down at the grocery store and everything and then comes home and cooks you dinner. So when she cooks for me, it's my favorite, you know?"

"Man, that's stupid. Why don't you just tell her that you hate it?"

"Cause it'd hurt her feelings. People should be nicer to each other in the city."

"Nobody's nice in the city."

Matt stared out over city, pink clouds hung low. "They should be."

"But they ain't."

"There's a lot of nice people here, Mikey. Your mom, Art, Leonard, they all nice people. Lot of other people are nice, too, you just got to look."

"Tch." His face puckered up like he just ate something sour, Mikey shook his head. "Man, they all poor people. People who can't do nothin'. It don't matter anyway 'cause nobody cares nothin' for us. Nobody. Why the hell are we talkin' about this anyways for? It's too damn early and too damn cold."

"How 'bout we race then?"

"You old."

"You young."

"My legs are longer."

"Mine stronger."

"Sucka.'" Mikey took off running. "You gonna lose."

"Never." He ran, catching up with the kid where the black river broke from the ice and snow, passing him by, leaving him far, far behind.

*Never.*

# THREE

The lights weren't antique, they were just old and yellow. Yellow from years of smoke that hung in the little apartment. They sat in the living room around a small card table. Art having a beer, Matt's bottle already empty, and Mikey had excused himself a long time ago and slipped out into the dark mean streets.

"I hear, Mister Matt, that meatloaf isn't your favorite." She sat casually back in her chair and lit up a long, white cigarette. "Is that true?" Margaret crossed her arms and blew that smoke up into the yellow light. "You don't like my meatloaf?"

"No, ma'am." Matt grinned. He couldn't help but notice that Margaret looked good tonight: pretty face, lips all shiny, and damn good body like a brick house. "I love your meatloaf. It's other people's meatloaf that I don't like."

"Don't you 'ma'am' me. I ain't no old woman yet. I'm only thirty-three and folks tell me every day that I look twenty. But we wasn't talkin' about that now, we was talking about my meatloaf." Margaret took another drag off her cigarette and Matt looked away. "About how you don't like meatloaf, but that you just love mine? How does that work, exactly?"

"I don't know. Why don't you ask Art."

"Ask Arthur, why?"

Matt smiled at the old man. "'Cause he hates it, too."

"Arthur! Is that true?"

"Oh no." Art glared at Matt. "I love meatloaf. Just love it. And yours is the best I've ever had."

"Now I know the two of you are lyin'." Margaret smiled and took another drag. "Tell you what, *if* I ever have you two over again, what would you like?"

Matt looked at Art, Art at Matt.

"Meatloaf."

They laughed.

"Men, they like anything that a woman puts in front of them. Meatloaf it is." Margaret turned to Art. "So tell me, Arthur, what's on your mind? And don't tell me nothin' 'cause you been frettin' all night. I saw the way you was lookin' at Mikey. You finally come here to tell me that he ain't got no heart? Cause if that's it, I could have saved you the trouble a long time ago."

Art took a drink. "The kid's got skill."

"He's a lazy bum." Margaret crushed her cigarette. "Just like his father. Here one minute, gone the next, that was him. Like father like son. No, Mikey don't got what Matt's got." She looked at Matt, soft eyes, soft smile—the picture of a thousand words. "I heard you fought good. You never do quit, do you?"

He hated hearing it, "Nope."

"You'll just keep workin' hard, too. All your life you will, even when you're done with boxing and working a real job. You is a hardworking man, Matt, a good man. Tell me now, how come some woman hasn't snatched you up yet?"

"Never met a woman who can box."

Margaret's eyebrow lifted. "How 'bout a woman who can fight?"

"Fight fair?"

"Matt, honey, no woman fights fair. You of all people should know that. Still, it must be nice not havin' to worry about anything but boxin'. I guess you got the whole world at your feet. So tell me, who you fightin' next?"

"Probably some bum." Art halfway laughed. "And don't let him fool you either, he don't like women who fight fair. He's too old for games."

Matt breathed out. "Just like you, huh, Art."

"That's right, kid." Art smiled wide. "We're old-time fighters, ain't we?"

"Yeah." Matt lifted his bottle, but it was empty. "Old time."

"Don't you listen to that old pain in the ass, Matt, you just a pup. You got your whole life right in front of you. Trust me, you gonna have somethin' more to fight for one of these days." Smoke slipped from Margaret's mouth and hid her eyes. She said, "You just keep workin' hard and everything will work out. You'll see."

Matt breathed out and set his empty bottle aside. "Yeah."

"You know, I really appreciate what you do for Mikey. He looks up to you, Matt. He ain't got a lot of men he can look up to, you know? You too, Art, I appreciate both of you working with him. I had hoped that boxing would keep him off the streets, but it don't look like that's gonna happen now. So you gotta let him go?"

Art killed off his beer. "Well, that's up to you."

"The way I see it, it really don't matter now, does it?" Margaret struck a match and lit up another cigarette. "I mean, he ain't here, is he?"

"No." Art stared down at his plate. "I guess he ain't. I'm sorry, Margaret."

"He'll up and leave one day just like his daddy did. No goodbyes, no nothing, just up and gone. Seems like it's in his blood."

"Don't write the kid off yet," Matt said. "There's time, he's still young."

"So was his father." Margaret let out a long breath. Smoke curling up, hanging on the ceiling. "I think I need a drink. How 'bout you two, something else to drink?"

"Oh, Margaret"—Art stood and patted his stomach—"I'll never make it home if I do."

"You sure? You're welcome to stay for a while if you'd like."

"I'd just fall asleep on the couch if I did. Dinner was nice as always, Margaret, thank you," Art said and Matt started to get up. "I'm fine, kid. No need to walk me back tonight. Tell you what, why don't you help with dishes or somethin', have another drink, relax a little for once. You could use it."

The kitchen was small, nothing more than a long closet with a window. Cold rain falling outside. They were doing dishes, Matt washing; Margaret drying. She brushed past him, touching him, loving him like she did every night when she cooked for him. Saving money during the week, pinching pennies, cutting coupons, sweet-talkin' the butcher into a little more hamburger just so she could wash dishes with Matt. Hot water running from the tap.

*Damn, he feels good.*

She bent over, legs straight, Margaret putting a pan away right before his eyes. Of course, she peeked, just a quick glance back to see if he was watching. Matt looked away.

Washing, scrubbing, a little perspiration on his forehead. Margaret smiled as she stood and leaned against the counter—a damn fine hip. "Tell me something, Matt, do you remember the first time you saw me?"

"It was when you brought Mikey to the gym."

"It was, but do you remember me?"

"Yeah."

"Really?" Margaret hit him with her towel. "Tell me, what was I wearin'?"

"A coat."

*He don't,* Margaret looked away, *he don't remember me or that dress I was wearin'.* The one that turns every man's head, every man's but his.

"It was cold," Margaret breathed and Matt could smell the ash on her breath. "Cold and both me and Mikey were downright scared. I thought that maybe there was gonna be a bunch of thugs there, too. But the moment I walked in, I knew that everything was gonna be just fine. Do you know how I knew that?"

"Not a clue."

"You." Margaret's voice was soft. "You was in the ring, moving like I ain't seen no man ever move before, and I thought to myself, 'If Mikey could be like that man, then he'll end up just fine.' Well Mikey, he's just Mikey, and you is you. I was right about you, Matt."

"Seems like the whole world knows me." Matt kept on scrubbing the dishes. "Guess I'm the only one who don't."

"You a good man." Margaret smiled. "I mean you could have ended up like Mikey, but you didn't. Instead, you work hard, damn hard. I can tell Arthur's being rough on you, but he loves you, that's all. He's just lookin' out for you."

"You think so? 'Cause I don't know," Matt said. "I mean he's always been good to me, but lately, I just think he's done."

"Have a little faith, Matthew. Things always work out in the end, even if that end isn't exactly how you thought it'd be. You'd do yourself good to remember that. Besides, a man can't always think about boxin'. There are other things out there." Margaret smiled and moved close. "Better things."

Matt smiled and scrubbed the dishes harder.

"Matt, you already are the champ." Margaret touched him. "When I saw you that day, I knew you was. I knew you was a good man. A man who would fight for everything he wanted, for all the people he loved, and I was right. But there's one thing that you're not seein'."

"Oh yeah?" He turned, Margaret's hand falling from his shoulder, eyes meeting. Matt said, "What's that, 'cause all I see is a lot of dirty dishes."

"Matthew Gore" —she hit him with her towel again—"I'm being serious here."

"I'm sorry." He smiled. "I'm listening. What am I missin'?"

She wanted to say it, needed to tell him, but she couldn't. There was another part of Margaret, a strong part of her that just wouldn't let the world stop spinning. "Cake"—Margaret smiled—"you is missing your cake."

"Well, I don't see no cake."

"That's 'cause men is blind. If you would just open that breadbox and look inside, you might find something."

"Sounds sweet." Matt grinned. "Like that red dress you was wearin' that day when you came in with Mikey."

*He remembered*, Margaret's hands trembled, *he remembered*.

The same sky; the same damn sky. Matt was halfway home from Margaret's, halfway to his room above the gym where his old cot with the surplus GI blanket waited for him. Halfway back when he stopped and stared up at the sky.

The

same

damn

sky.

And the street, how many times had he walked down this street? How many times had he run down this street? How many mornings had he woken up early to run? How many days had he spent in the gym? How many years had he danced in the ring? How many faces had he fought? How many days, how many months, how many years were exactly like this one? Years that ended with meatloaf.

Matt stared down the street and saw the buildings with their crumbling bricks. He saw the broken sidewalk with all its cracks, and for the first time, he felt the millstone around his neck. Ash fell from the sky. Ash that looked like dirty snow.

Nothing had changed. Not one thing. Meatloaf. It was all meatloaf. He couldn't do it anymore. He just couldn't. Something, anything, had to change.

Just one thing, one little thing to show him, to tell him that his life would all work out. Work out the way he wanted it to. That's what he needed. That's all he needed, Matt thought, so he could keep on going, keep on working, keep on running, training day after day, year after year until…Matt breathed out and looked away.

He would have sworn that it wasn't there, not before tonight, but the gaping black mouth of the alley waited. As he stared into the alley, as he looked into its darkness, Matt heard a laugh track playing from a broken window five stories above.

Ash fell heavy inside the alley, ash from books: pages and pages of his mother's books. Ash that crunched with the glass of so many broken bottles. Brown bottles that hid spirits inside. And Matt wondered why he was here. He hated this place.

The ash, the bottles, they piled under his foot, growing deeper by the minute. Ash that rose to his ankles, ash that stood at his knees. The world was burning again.

In the hush of the fall, the laugh track looped, running around and around. Matt turned and brushed the ash from his head and walked from the alley back onto the street.

Margaret lay on her bed, staring at the crack in the window. A little crack that laid between the pane and the frame, a crack that let the air from the alley in. Margaret breathed out, smoke slipped from her mouth as the sound of sirens mixed with the falling rain. Some things never do change.

She had worried about Mikey ever since he was eleven and it was 1968. Nineteen sixty-eight and Vietnam and the draft were going strong. And now, it was wonderful 1974 and nothing had changed. Mikey was older, closer to the draft, one year from being eighteen and dead.

*But he remembered,* Margaret thought, *Matt remembered my dress.*

She had worn that dress that day because she had a job interview at the corner grocery store. A checker position had opened up. Someone had died and left an opening in a sagging economy. People from all over the city applied. Margaret dressed nice, desperate for a break, putting on her red dress and heels, painting her nails, having her hair done nice and, for some reason, leaving it down. It was long then, longer than it was now.

She had sat in a long line of applicants, all of them hoping, praying for the same break because they had a kid or two or three, or a wife who was sick, or a no-good for a husband. All of them dressed nice, as nice as they could dress, all of them waiting for their name to be called. Every head turned as the door opened and the man called her name. Margaret stood and almost tripped. Tripped as the woman next to her stuck out her foot.

She remembered the manager turning, shaking his head, walking back into his office as the stupid woman smiled and feigned her apology. Margaret didn't snap, didn't call the woman every name in the book. Instead, she had just said, "That's okay."

And smiled.

Smiled and walked into that office with her head held high and sat where the man told her to sit.

"You always do that?" James had asked her, and Margaret remembered staring at his mustache. It was big, bushy, and moved as he talked.

"You mean trip? No, that was just an accident, that's all."

"No." James had shaken his head. "I mean do you always act like that with people? That woman, I saw her trip you, you didn't say nothing. You didn't even give her a look."

"I try to, yes."

"What's your name?"

"Margaret."

"Do you have a last name, Margaret?"

"I've had two." She smiled. "One I'd like to forget."

James had sat back in his chair and smiled real wide. "Would you like a job?"

"Yes, sir."

"Can you make it to work on time?"

"I don't live far, only eight blocks," Margaret had said. "And I am always a little early to work."

"Do you always dress nice?"

"I try."

"You ever worked in a grocery store?"

"I helped my brother out."

"Where?"

"Across town, Mister Johnson's store," Margaret said. "Sometimes I would help out on the weekends. Never got paid though."

"Johnson's a tightwad." James shook his head and then he smiled again. A real honest smile. "So am I, but I'm nice. You work hard, I'm fair, and I'll pay you good. You don't work, I fire you. It's that simple."

"I work hard."

"What's your brother's name?"

"It *was* Ben."

"Vietnam?"

"Yes, sir."

"My name's James," he said. "Don't call me sir, don't call me Mister Henderson, and don't call me boss either, it makes me feel old. Just call me James."

"Sure."

"I'm sorry about your brother."

"So am I."

"Lost my son, his name was Michael."

"I'm sorry about your son."

"Me too," James looked away. Looked out the big window where people walked up and down the aisles putting groceries in their carts. "Do you drink, do drugs?"

"No drugs," Margaret said. "And I only drink occasionally."

"When?"

"When my son isn't home."

"How old is he?"

"Not old enough for the draft yet."

"Then I'll pray for him and hope to God this war is over before he's eighteen," James said. "Hope there's no more wars either."

"Thank you."

"What about his father?"

"He's gone."

"Vietnam?"

"I wish."

And then James had laughed. Laughed good and hard again. "I like you, Margaret, you're no nonsense and so am I."

"I try."

He had stood then, walked to the door and opened it to hopeful faces and told them that he was sorry. "The position has been filled."

They stood, some old, some young, some with tears in their eyes. Stood as tears filled Margaret's eyes. There were still tears in her eyes as she walked home, knowing that she was lucky, that she had to do something with Mikey too, passing the gym and seeing Matt inside, seeing him spar—seeing a good man fighting.

She had hurried home and dragged Mikey back, not bothering to change her dress, thinking about the good, fighting man. Thinking about him all the way there as Mikey whined and complained and said that he didn't want to go. Said he wanted to watch television instead. But Margaret had said no. Said no again and again, hoping that the good, fighting man was still there. It was the first time in a long time that she had thought about a man. So she told herself. Outside the gym, Mikey had nearly broken free, but Margaret dragged him in.

Mouths dropping, whistles blowing, heads turning—every head but Matt's. Matt, who was sparring, who was working hard, Margaret falling right then and there. For some reason, Margaret had looked up at the clock on the gym's wall, the one with a yellow face and black hands.

11:11.

But that was then.

"Where's that damn boy?" she said to herself now and thought about having another smoke but forgot just as quickly as she thought about tonight.

He was still in the kitchen with her, she imagined, still talking, still laughing with her, just doing dishes. She would always dry because he was always too nice, too much of a gentleman to let her wash. Too much of a gentleman to brush against her.

Sure, Margaret had let him dry the dishes a couple of times, but never once had he touched her. He never bumped her, never did brush up against her; somehow he'd danced all around her as if he was in the ring.

To hell with gentlemen, Margaret had thought, and from then on she insisted on drying. Drying like she had tonight, working around him, leaning against him, putting her body against his, touching him. All he needs is—

The front door opened.

"Mikey?" Margaret hurried from her bed, wearing just a T-shirt that barely fit, and hurried out into the hallway. "Mikey?"

Mikey stood in the dark. "What?"

"Where you been?"

"Tch," he breathed and Margaret caught the smell of beer on his breath. "I was out."

"I know you was out, I asked where?"

"On the corner."

"With who."

"With the guys."

"*Mikey!*" Margaret snapped. "They ain't no good. How many times have I told you them friends of yours is no good. Do you want to end up like them?" Margaret folded her arms. "Do you?"

"I will, anyway. We poor, remember?"

"Don't matter if we poor or rich, you don't hang around trash."

"What the hell am I suppose to do?"

"Anything."

"Tch." Mikey just shook his head. "There ain't nothin' to do. Nothing.'"

"Why don't you get a J-O-B then!?"

"There ain't none."

"You're drunk, ain't you?"

"I ain't drunk."

"You don't talk to me like this, Mikey, you never have. You're drunk and actin' like a fool, just like your father."

"How the hell would I know? He ain't here. Besides, I never met him."

She sat there, eyes fully open—just a wounded thing. "Go."

He felt bad, he really did. He hated hurtin' her because she would limp around wounded for days. "Mom, please. I'm sor—"

"Go."

Mikey lifted his hands helplessly. "Mom, I didn't mea—"

"Just go." Margaret's eyes spilt over. She whispered, "Please."

Mikey walked into his room and closed the door behind him, leaving Margaret alone in the dark hallway. She wrapped her arms around herself and whispered again, but this time she made a wish; a wish that couldn't be heard.

Margaret walked into the kitchen and opened a drawer. She took a cigarette from its pack and a book of matches. The strike of a match, Margaret's face lit for a moment; invisible tears that fell from her eyes as she blew smoke.

# FOUR

"Okay, kid"—Art motioned to the heavy bag as he sat down on the bench—"twelve rounds, three minutes each and only thirty seconds in between. I want three punch combos, good punches too, and then I want you to move. Combo, move and all good shots, got me?"

"Anything else?" Matt smiled, a sarcastic thing, and hit his gloves together. "Maybe you'd like me to do your wash or something?"

"Yeah, instead of a three-punch combination, let's do four. I want you to lead with a right jab, a good jab too, nothin' sloppy. I want it to snap. Right jab, left hook to the body, then a right uppercut, a hard one, really drive up into that bag, and then finish off with a beautiful right hook to the head. I want you to decapitate that bag. Okay, wise guy?"

"Twelve three-minute rounds, thirty seconds rest, four-punch combo, right jab, left hook to the body, right uppercut, right hook to the head, decapitate, do your wash, make dinner, shine your shoes—"

"Just hit the damn bag, will ya?"

Matt smacked his gloves together and moved. He danced, slipping to his left, bobbing his head, weaving his body, hands held high in front of his face peek-a-boo style. The jab came quick, Matt's shoulders didn't move. He didn't give his punch away, no man would have ever known what was about to hit him.

A hard jab smacked the bag, the hook an instant later, Matt's legs drove up, his torso twisting, delivering that uppercut into the bag, the damn thing thudded deep in its guts as Matt's right hook concaved its top. It was nothing short of vicious.

But Art never saw it.

*Just me in that damn apartment,* the old trainer thought, *sitting in front of that black and white TV, watching something stupid. Watching something I won't even watch. Just noise to fill the house. TV dinner, TV tray, TV blaring away while I sit alone.* "Time!" Art yelled. "Catch your breath, kid. Good job."

Matt nodded, sweat dripping off his nose, Art still staring down at the stopwatch. He never looked up. The sound of the jump rope, speed bag, two kids in the ring sparring, seconds ticking. "Ding," Art said. "Round two."

*It's just the same,* Art stared down as Matt bobbed and weaved, *hitting that bag good today, every day's just the same. Train kids in the morning, kids in the afternoon, lunch in my office, brown paper bag with the same damn thing inside, bologna between two slices of bread, train kids in the evening, sit at home alone with that damn TV. He should just move in with me.*

*Matt ain't ever gonna beat that Dancing Man from Detroit. He ain't got a shot in the world. He's good, but just good, that's all. He ain't great like I thought he was gonna be. But he'll make a fine trainer*—Art smiled to himself—*a damn fine trainer. Like me.*

*Me and him working, me teaching him all my tricks, we can spend all our time together, training some kid, talking the night away about what we gonna do with him. Matt should just hang it up and move in with me. Jump rope, speed bag, sparring in the ring, Matt hitting the bag, seconds ticking by, just the same thing.*

A hook, Matt threw it, a finishing right to the head that would have decapitated the Dancing Man from Detroit. The sound of the punch, that hook, it cut through the gym: the speed bag hanging dead, every eye on Matt. He slipped to the left, right jab, left hook to the body, uppercut, hook to the head, and the bag bled stuffing. Matt moved. Again to the left, the same four-punch combination coming, each punch devastating.

"Time!" Art yelled. "Catch your breath."

"That was good." Matt bent over, sweat dripping from his nose. "Real good, don't you think?"

"Yeah, that was good, kid. Three beautiful punches in a row."

"I could have took Herns's head off with any one of them," Matt said. "I want to fight Herns."

"Then do it again." Art looked down at his stopwatch. "Ten seconds."

"I said, I.Want.A.Shot."

"Show me that you can throw that punch every time, kid." Art looked at his fighter. "Every time. Round three."

For a moment Matt stood there, staring down at the old trainer. He nodded and danced, moving to the left, right jab, left hook to the body, a mean uppercut, hook to the head. No stuffing, no pop from the punch that shot through the gym, the bag just wobbled.

*You nothin'.*

Matt moved to the left, throwing the combination, hitting the bag hard, but only hard. No decapitation. Again and again, three minutes of work in round three, throwing that four-punch combination, never hitting that shot—not once.

"Time." Art stared at the stopwatch: seconds, minutes, the speed bag popping, jump rope clicking, sparring in the ring. "Ten seconds," the old trainer said; he never looked up. "Watch your breathing, kid."

Matt laid in the dark on his metal cot, staring out the oversized window. Rain fell through the streetlight on the corner. He could see himself in that ring, belt around his waist, arms lifted above his head, the cheer of the crowd coming loud. Red and blue lights flashing, a siren wailing; Matt stared at the window.

*Tomorrow*, Matt breathed in, *I'll train harder. Train like never before in my life. I'll put the hours, the miles on the road, jump rope like nothing, lift and spar and work the bags and I'll get better, stronger.* Matt turned and looked at the clock: two in the morning. *I ain't ever gonna sleep, not tonight.* He breathed in and got out of that cot.

He walked across the floor to a dented refrigerator and swung open the door. Light fell from the empty shelves onto his feet. For a moment, Matt stared at nothing. *I know I'm the champ.* He swung the door shut and wandered back to his metal cot, sitting on the edge with his head in his hands.

*Two in the morning and I ain't never gonna sleep.* Matt stared at the floor where his old Converse laid: broken laces, broken rubber, a hole in the toe.

Margaret lay on the couch, listening for her son. Mikey had been out late every night for a week. She didn't know what he was doing except that he was drinking, not coming home drunk, mind you, but not coming home sober either. Just coming home. Maybe tonight he wouldn't even come home at all. Margaret breathed out, rain falling outside; just like this morning.

Every morning just before five, she would wake and listen for Matt. Listen for his feet banging on the sidewalk, sometimes splashing rain, sometimes slushing snow, sometimes hot pavement and nearly soulless shoes.

He'd stop at Mikey's window and knock as quietly as he could, making Margaret feel better, knowing that Mikey was with somebody decent for a change. Sometimes she would wish as he ran in place that Matt was coming inside, climbing onto her bed, sharing her warmth.

Sometimes.

How long has it been since I've shared my bed? Too long, way too damn long. It was a lie. Probably just as long as it had been since Matt had shared his bed with a woman. Margaret sat up: another woman?

She had never thought of it, maybe there was another woman in Matt's life. Maybe his heart was wrapped around some no good's finger. Margaret tried to picture her, tried to see that woman clearly in her mind: pretty, almost beautiful, ready to swoop in and love him after a fight and take what little Matt had earned. And what happened to all his money, anyway?

Sure, he didn't make a lot from his fights, but he made something, right? Made enough at least to live in a hellhole like this if he wanted to. *Where did all his money go? There had to be another woman,* Margaret thought, *had to be, especially after that night in the kitchen.*

After all her brushing and bumping, after all that touching, Matt still hadn't made a move. But then again, men were dumb. She lay back down on the old couch as a touch of cold air drifted in through the cracked window.

"Red," he said in that strong, deep voice of his. A voice that always touched her. *Why the hell didn't he kiss me then? He should have taken me in his arms and held me. Should have kissed me and made me forget everything. Forget Art and Mikey and boxing and training and that tramp, if there is a tramp, just me and him. Damn, I sound like a woman dying of thirst, and there's a beautiful, clear glass of cold water right in front of me. I need a smoke.*

Margaret was up, off the couch, hunting through drawers, looking on shelves, sticking her hand in the cracks of the couch to pull out a few nickels and dimes; a quarter too. Pulling out everything but a smoke.

"Damn."

She looked up at the yellow-faced clock; just after two in the morning. *Just after two and no Mikey, and I'm all alone on the couch and there ain't a cigarette to be had. Ain't a man to be had either. And if I go into the kitchen and open the fridge then that cake is gonna start looking real good, too good, and the last thing I need is a big butt when that little tramp is stealing all of Matt's money. Eat,* Margaret thought, *or go get some smokes?*

Smokes.

She was up, into her bedroom, trying not to think about the bed, just sitting on it, tying her shoes. *I need new shoes. Nice shoes,* she thought, *something Matt might like.* Coat, purse on her arm, down the hallway to the front door. She opened it, stepped out onto the porch, rain falling—burned-out porch light.

She was two steps down when she stopped at the sound of feet running in the rain. She turned and looked down the street. Matt was running hard, shadow boxing—nothing but shadows.

Margaret's heart skipped a beat—*I'll be damned.*

"Matthew Gore"—Margaret smiled—"I was just thinkin' about you."

Matt stopped at the porch and ran in place. "What you doin' up?"

"I haven't had a smoke in a week, can't sleep. You know, trying to quit and everything," Margaret lied. "I almost gave in there."

"Glad you're quitting. I hate smoke."

"So do I, but it was either a smoke or the cake. I like my backside just how it is." Margaret winked. "You, uh, you wouldn't want some cake now, would ya?"

Maybe it was the fact that there was nothing in his fridge, maybe it was the fact that Margaret was asking him in for something other than meatloaf, maybe it was a little of both. Matt said, "I'd love some." And he stopped running in place.

Margaret was cooking, standing over the stove, sweat beading up on her forehead, even though the burner was off. The pork chop was done, just needed to be heated, potatoes too: it was Mikey's dinner that he never ate; that he wasn't home for. Nineteen seventy four and there was a war out on the streets. Still, Margaret was hot, hot from the steam, hot from what was in the shower. Margaret had insisted that Matt clean up before cake.

Steam poured down the hall because Margaret had opened the bathroom door. Opened it and left it open, sneaking peeks at the silhouette of a fine man. Now in the kitchen she wiped her forehead, thinking that she wanted to peek again, fighting against her urge, losing to her desire.

Margaret snuck to the edge of the kitchen and peeked around the corner. At the end of the hall, the bathroom stood open to her eyes—Matt naked behind the cream curtain.

"Damn," she muttered.

"Margaret?" Matt called as hot water ran over his body. "You say somethin'?"

Margaret popped back into the kitchen. "What?"

"Did you say somethin'?"

"No," she called. "I thought you did."

"Nope."

"Ain't a thing. Food ain't quite ready yet, so just take your time," Margaret lied, looking at the pork chop, hoping it wouldn't get cold. "Is the water hot enough?"

"Yeah."

"You tellin' me," she muttered to herself. "You need anything? Anything at all?"

"No, I'm fine."

"Damn."

"What?"

"Nothin'." Margaret needed a cigarette.

She took the pork chop from the pan and put it on the plate with the potatoes. The shower shut off, the curtain ran open, and before Margaret could peek around the corner again, before her brain could suggest that she should do such a thing, the door shut.

She stood, looking down at the plate, wishing it could be more, wishing it could be like this every night at three in the morning. She wasn't gonna get any sleep tonight, maybe an hour or two, maybe three if she was lucky. But she could sleep all day if she wanted to, didn't have to be at work tomorrow. Maybe she'd see if Matt wanted to do something.

Like what?

Like anything, Margaret thought. They could go for a walk along the river or in the park or maybe catch a movie or something; not that there was anything good to see. Not that either of them had the money to catch a no-good movie, anyway. *Maybe I'll cook him dinner again. I can afford it 'cause Mikey ain't eating here.*

The bathroom door opened and Margaret listened as Matt walked down the hall to the kitchen, stopping as he saw Margaret fussing with the plate, fussing with nothing. She turned and looked up.

She tried not to smile, tried not to let her satisfaction show, but she couldn't—he looked too damn good. Good in the small white undershirt, one of Mikey's, that stuck to his body like skin. Stuck and showed every bump, every line, every muscle of his body. "Perfect timing." Margaret picked up the plate,."I'm all ready for you," she said and brushed by him.

Brushed by, stepping into the hall, feeling his body against hers, avoiding his eyes, missing his look, walking into the living room where she had set up a TV tray. Margaret set his plate down and turned—Matt was right behind her.

"Thanks," he said. "Looks real nice."

"You're welcome. Anytime." She meant it from the bottom of her heart.

They stood under the yellow light like two teenagers at a school dance. Finally, Margaret sat down and so did Matt, taking his fork and knife, cutting into the pork chop. Margaret didn't know why she did it, but she sat and watched him eat, feeling good about feeding him, taking a little pleasure in the fact.

"Ain't gonna be able to run now." Matt set his knife and fork on the plate, leaned back in his seat, and touched his stomach; Margaret stared at his hands. "No, not for awhile."

"I don't mind." Margaret smiled, still staring at his hands. Broken hands, beaten, his pinky permanently bent to the side, his knuckles the size of golf balls. Margaret seeing the hurt in that perfect body, scars around his eyes, cuts in his brow, that missing tooth in a handsome smile. "How you feelin', Matt?"

"Great now, thank you."

"Just couldn't sleep, huh?"

"Couldn't stop thinkin'." Matt tried to smile. "Just one of those nights, you know?"

"Do I ever. Sometimes I get to thinking too much and I can't go to sleep for the life of me. I get all worried about something: bills, rent, Mikey or something else and then I get thinkin' and thinkin' and then I know I ain't ever gonna sleep." Margaret pulled her feet up on the couch, folding them under her, curling up. "But that's just life, Matt. There's always stuff to think about or worry about, but usually there ain't a thing you can do about it. But you"—she smiled at him—"you got options."

"Yeah." Matt looked away. "Options."

"This is nice, ain't it? I sure do enjoy having you over. I know it ain't much, but it's the company, don't you think?"

"I appreciate it, Margaret. It's the first hot shower I've had in awhile. Showers at the gym are always cold."

"Matt?"

"Yeah?"

"How come?"

"How come what?"

"Boxing." Margaret shook her head. "I mean I see you and everything, see your hands there, for instance. I know you hurt, Matt. I hate to see you hurtin', so how come boxing?"

"I'm a fighter, Margaret, that's all."

"A fighter, huh?"

"Yes, ma'am." Matt smiled, missing tooth. "An old-time fighter. I swear, Margaret, that was the best pork chop I've ever had."

Margaret stared down at the hardwood floor. "You just want that cake."

They sat, both quiet under that yellow light. Finally, Matt looked up at the clock, it was just after four. He gathered his plate, the fork and the knife, took them into the kitchen and stood at the sink—rain hitting the window.

"Matt." He turned, Margaret stood, her hands fidgeting, "I'm glad you came by."

He nodded, not really knowing what to say. "Yeah, me too."

"I meant what I said." Margaret looked up into that broken face: flattened nose, beaten cheeks, scars around his eyes. "If you need to get away from the gym or something, you can always come by here. Besides, I don't know how you can stand it there all the time. I would go crazy if I was in the gym 24-7, but that's me. Anyway, you're always welcome here. Things ain't so crazy here anymore. And I want to tell you"—Margaret looked away—"I need to tell you that I really appreciate all that you've done for Mikey. Thank you."

"Anytime." Matt leaned back on the counter, away from her perfect body. "I guess I should get going. I'm supposed to pick him up in an hour to train."

"Yeah." Margaret breathed. "Mikey."

On the corner across the street from the gym, Matt stood in the dark, leaning against the streetlight, staring up at the second floor where his window sat like a gaping mouth surrounded by red, crumbling bricks. He wasn't thinking. He wasn't praying either. He was just standing there, wanting to scream.

Open his mouth and let it all out: anger, frustration, all the why's and why-not's, just scream and get rid of it all. But he couldn't. Matt couldn't open his mouth. Something inside wouldn't let him. Hands in his pockets, eyes fixed to that black mouth, Matt felt his mind numbed.

Of course it was cold, but it was the clouds—those thick heavy things that hung over the city—dirty pink that made the whole world seem small. Clouds that seemed to press right down on Matt's head. Clouds that tried to smother the last shred of his identity. Matthew Gore needed an opponent—not options.

He could have told her tonight that he would rather live under a bridge and die without a penny in his pocket than ever give up, but Margaret deserved to be treated good. Her life, he thought, was hard enough already. Besides, she would never understand, not in a thousand years, no one would. He found it strange that tonight, after years of indifference, she had finally invited him in. Maybe that's why he always stared at her mouth: the smoke seemed like a screen.

Not that he meant to do it, but Matt would find himself staring at that beautiful mouth of hers as she stuck that long white thing between her lips and lit up. The inhale, that red glow, then came the moment where Margaret would hold that smoke inside her body. And then, she would let it out. Smoke filling the air in front of her face, covering it like a burial shroud.

It was a damn shame too, because part of him wanted to like her. He could imagine himself with her. Theirs would be a comfortable life—poor but happy. Just him and her sitting in that apartment, doing the dishes, and then the kiss would come, along with all that smoke.

Smoke pouring from her mouth, hanging on the ceiling: smoke all over the place. It was enough to make Matt stop himself from sweeping her off her feet. Matt blew in his hands. The streetlight went out and he looked up.

Clouds pressing down, the light hung above him, dead. Matt shoved his hands back in his pockets. Tomorrow, he thought, just another day like today. Cold air, Matt breathing out, steam rising up in front of his face.

Margaret lay in bed, staring up at the dark ceiling, hearing the sound of his feet again in her head, hearing them run away. *It ain't there*, she thought as she stared up at the little sweeps in the plaster, *he just don't love me. Maybe it's not supposed to be. Maybe I'm just too damn old for him. Maybe he found out about Carlos. Or Nate. Maybe tall Jim too.* Margaret smiled, *Jim.*

*Don't matter now 'cause no man wants to be a father to a wreck of a kid. A kid that's more of a man; seventeen. It's my fault,* she thought, *I've ruined everything.*

*Ruined everything the first time I saw Mikey's father. Sixteen and thinkin' I knew it all, sixteen and stupid, not seeing the world around me—not seeing a man for what he was. Sixteen and married and Mikey halfway here. The man only married me because he said that was what you was supposed to do.*

*But that was a lie too.*

*Sixteen and thinking that life was gonna be perfect, sixteen and already alone even though I was married. Stupid,* Margaret thought, *young and dumb.* She rolled over, pulling the blanket over her shoulders, staring at the window, at the crack; cold air seeping in. *End of November and it's still dark even though folks will be getting up to go to work soon. Still dark and cold, especially in my bed.*

*I never thought I'd grow old, but I will. Never thought I'd be an old maid either, but I already am. All I got left to do is die—that's life.*

There were feet coming down the street, feet moving towards her door, walking up the steps, standing at the porch. Mikey, Margaret thought, the prodigal son, the son of a no-good. Like father, like son. Home and most likely drunk. Margaret got up out of bed.

She was down the hall, stomping as she went, wearing nothing but a tight t-shirt. Her breasts rounded the number on the front—a big old sixty six. Storming past the kitchen in a t-shirt and panties that barely covered her backside. Moving towards the front door—a knock.

The stupid kid lost his key again.

Down the hall, past the living room, to the front door where she undid those damn locks. She threw open that door, her mouth already open, words coming in a torrent. "Where the hell you—"

He was leaning tall against the rail. "Hello, baby." He smiled, gold teeth shining in the night. "Daddy's home."

# FIVE

Same old clouds, pressing down on life. Late afternoon and still it was dark. Inside the gym, the old hanging lights hummed 'cause they were on. Still, they didn't light a damn thing. But the gym was full, light coming from all those fighters, sweating, breathing hard, throwing punches. In the ring, Mikey sparred with an old bald man of forty-two, old for boxing.

Old Forty Two's face was beaten, his nose broken, missing two front teeth. But Old Forty Two was still big and strong, fighting with a younger kid, using the tricks that only age can bring. Sparring with Mikey 'cause he loved it. Fighting was deep down in his soul. Old Forty Two threw a left, just jabbing at the kid, urging him on. "Come on, Mikey, move! Move like you mean it or I'll move your head for you."

It was a hook, just a hook. Nothing special, a punch thrown by Mikey that the kid would regret. Old Forty Two moved, dancing like Fred Astaire, slipping to the side, catching Mikey with a hook of his own that kissed the kid's chin. A hook that if thrown harder would have knocked him cold.

Mikey stood and dropped his gloves; spit his mouthpiece across the ring.

"What gives, Mikey?"

"Just thinkin'."

"That's just it, Mikey." Old Forty Two grinned a wide, toothless thing that even made Mikey lighten up. "You don't got to think. Boxin' is like music, you hear it, you feel it and you move. Sure, you got to keep your head down, but that don't mean that you got to think everythin' out. Sometimes you just got to go with the flow, dance to the music, if you hear what I'm sayin'."

"You can't dance." Mikey was kidding, just a jest with Old Forty Two. "You're too old to dance. You'd probably break your hip if you did. Besides, they didn't have no good music back when you was a kid."

"It's better than that stuff you call music now."

"Sticks and stones?" Mikey lifted his eyebrow, just like his mom did. "Please. I don't think so."

"Sticks and stones, huh?"

"That's all you had." Mikey tried not to smile. "Just old sticks beatin' on stones, that's all."

"Tell you what, I'm gonna show what an old man can do. You go on and try hittin' me with whatever you like. Throw it hard too, 'cause it ain't gonna matter. I'm gonna go with the flow."

"Okay, your funeral."

"Get your mouth piece, son." Old Forty Two smiled. "You gonna need it."

Mouthpieces, gloves touching, Mikey and Old Forty Two backing away from each other. "Ding ding." Old Forty Two was dancing, moving like he was on air, but so was Mikey. He was mimicking Old Forty Two, even if he was a step behind. But Old Forty Two didn't care, not one bit, 'cause he was feeling it. It was his move, his dance, Mikey just imitating the thing he was. Mikey planning ahead, thinking of two left jabs followed by a vicious hook.

Hands high, elbows in, the two fighters circling in towards each other, the ring shrinking between them. Mikey lining up Old Forty Two in his sights, steering the dancing man into place, throwing meaningless jabs. Another left, another right, Mikey just throwing, and sure enough Old Forty Two danced right into place.

Got him!

Two left jabs and Old Forty Two stopped dead cold—a big old hook laying on Mikey's chin. A fat glove that would have taken the kid out. "Gotcha." Old Forty Two was smiling wide, his mouthpiece hanging from his mouth.

Mikey shook his head. "Tch."

"Just like I said, kid, you got to go with the flow. Ain't no thinkin', just goin'. You get me?"

"Leonard?" Mikey was trying to forget, trying to put the past two weeks behind him. "Never mind."

"Never mind what?"

"How can you do that? I mean, you know someone's comin' at you, you know I was tryin' to hit you, but how can you just forget that?"

Leonard Hill, Old Forty Two, just smiled. "Who says I forgot?"

"But you just said go with the flow." Mikey shook his head. "I don't get it."

"That's just it, Mikey, sometimes, it makes no sense at all. But then one day you find yourself in the ring and maybe you're dancing or maybe you're charging like a crazed bull, or maybe someone's doin' that to you, but it don't matter cause you're goin' with the flow. No matter what's comin' at you"—he showed a toothless smile—"You gonna see it just like I saw that hook you were gonna throw. You'll know it's comin', it'll be staring at you as plain as day, and you'll just move out of the way. And when you do, you let your feet dance, let those hands of yours go and bingo! Now you try it."

"I don't know, Leonard."

"Come on, just try."

Mikey nodded. "Okay."

"That's my boy. Now don't think, don't imitate me, you just be you. That's all, just you. You want to dance, dance. You want to charge me, get inside me and hit me good, do it." Leonard smacked his gloves together, making them fit nice and tight. "Got it?"

"Yeah."

Leonard moved, but he wasn't dancing. He was a big cat stalking its flat-footed prey. But Mikey was trying to let go, trying to move, thinking about too many damn things. Some of them inside that ring, some things outside those red ropes. Throwing a jab, forcing another as Leonard bobbed and threw an uppercut—a square connection.

"Come on, Mikey." Leonard danced back from the kid. "You can do it. Don't think, just go with the flow. The only thing you got to think of is what you is doin' right now. Nothing else matters, nothin'. You just here in the ring with me, sparring, that's all. Let everything else go. Got it?"

"Got it."

"Then do it."

Leonard came like a china-crazed bull, not giving the kid a chance to think; just react. Jabs coming a million miles per hour, Leonard now throwing a hard right, meaning to take Mikey's head off, but the kid moved, slipped away like running water.

The bull turned too late.

It caught him, a hard right to the head followed by a mean body shot that made Leonard lose his breath. But as Mikey's mind started to think, as the kid stood proud, Leonard popped back a step.

Just a step combined with a hook that fell right into place. The kid's head snapped back, but he was in the flow, dancing like he had never danced before. Springing on his toes. Left and right jabs probing, looking on their own for an opening, seeing a toothless grin. A left, followed by another, Leonard's head popping back, his gloves opening, his smile even wider, and Mikey slipped a right into that mouth.

Old Forty Two laughed and dropped his gloves. "How'd it feel not to think?"

"Good." The kid smiled. "Thanks, man."

"What's this? Mike Jones thanking me? What a damn good day. You're welcome, kid. And by the way, if you can do what you just did outside the ring, you'll learn the trick to life."

"What you mean?"

Leonard leaned his arms on the ropes and looked out across the gym. "Ten thousand things are gonna come at you, but you can't fight them all. Not at once and some not at all. You ever hear folk say 'pick your battles'?"

"Yeah."

"They're wrong. Just take the fight that opens up in front of you and beat it, beat it good, and then move on. Don't think about it, don't gloat, just go on living and getting ready for the next fight. That's life, Mikey." Leonard turned and looked the kid in the eye. "But you can't always win. Every boxer, every champ, every president, every single man and woman on this planet is gonna lose sometime. Want to know why?"

Mikey stared at the other man. "Why?"

"Cause we all die."

And Old Forty Two tried to smile.

She was in the bathroom, standing in front of the medicine cabinet, staring at herself in the little mirror. Margaret could only see part of herself, only her shoulders, her breasts, her long neck, and that face of hers. It was beautiful. Margaret wasn't thinking that, of course, not right now, but she had. She reached into the shower and turned the water on hot. Steam filled the room.

There were always whistles, always men who came through that grocery line, smiling all big and wide at her. Most never said a word; a few did. Embarrassed, shy, all of those men would act the same way. Scratching their heads, rubbing the back of their necks, eyes never looking at her until after they had said it: beautiful. And then she would smile, eyes heavy, lips soft, until the old woman next in line would complain that she didn't have all damn day. Margaret wiped the mirror with her hand, little streaks ran down her breasts. And then those men would walk out that door. Every one of them, except Jones.

Margaret would let him in every time. She opened the medicine cabinet and took two aspirins from a bottle. Head back, swallow, something sticking in her throat. Year after year, didn't matter if it had been two months or ten, three years or five like now, she always let Mister Jones in through that door.

He'd stay for a while of course, they'd eat well, maybe have a few laughs together, and then he'd walk away, leaving Margaret to wonder why. Even though it hurt, even though she should have shut the door on him, she never would because a woman has to have options.

Margaret stepped into the shower, hot water touching her body. Besides, Matt had just walked away, hadn't he? It didn't matter anyway cause Good Old Jones had come knocking at her door.

Mikey had wandered in that next morning only to find Mister Jones standing in the hallway, smiling with all those teeth of his—gold. It wasn't good between them, Mikey and Mister Jones, it never was. But Mikey was a good boy, Margaret was sure of that, sure he'd understand. He'd try and get along, but when Mister Jones called him son, Mikey would say he wasn't his son. Inevitably, it would come, that one question from Mikey.

"Do you love him?"

"There ain't nothin' inside me for him. Nothin' but what probably shouldn't be there."

"How come you let him in then?"

"It was late, I was tired…"

*I was alone.*

She squatted down in that shower and hugged her knees. Long perfect legs, breasts, hot water falling on the back of her head, running into her face, around her mouth, pouring on those perfect lips of hers, full lips, slipping into the drain. Things would work out, Mikey would understand. Water slipped down the drain.

"Well, I'll be damned. Mister Jones?" He stood behind the bar, seeing what he saw, not believing what his eyes were telling him. Maybe TJ just didn't want to believe. "Mister Roy Jones."

"The one and only." Mister Jones grinned a mouthful of gold from ear to ear. He walked into that bar, a dark thing that sat below the street, and stretched his long legs across the old wood floor, missing every board with every step. "How you been, TJ?"

"Good, good. And you, Roy?"

"Never better."

"Damn, it's good to see you."

"The feeling's mutual."

"Please, Roy, have a seat."

He sat, elbows on that old wooden bar, smiling like the world was his—and maybe it was. Mister Jones looked around the bar, only a few folk sittin' at lonely tables. "Place looks the same, and so do you, TJ."

"Now I know you're lyin'." The old man smiled and wiped the bar; a hand-carved thing that was made from the finest of cherry—an old wood that had been cured for years on end; TJ caring for it like it was his baby. "Still, I thank you just the same."

"How 'bout a drink?"

"That's what I'm here for," the old man brightened. "Now let me think, if I remember right, you used to drink somethin' terrible, somethin' only you would drink." TJ rubbed his bald head and stooped down under the bar. Bottles rattling, a skinny arm reaching into the back, coming up with something in a caramel colored bottle. "Scotch." TJ set the dusty bottle on the bar. "An awful scotch, too. How 'bout it, Roy, this one's on me."

"You the man." Mister Jones tipped his hat, even though he wasn't wearing one. "The same man I remember. And TJ…"

"Yes, Roy."

"Don't be insulting my favorite drink"—Mister Jones smiled—"'cause this is the best damn drink there is."

"If you say so, Roy."

"I do."

"Well then, it is." TJ smiled and poured the caramel liquor over ice. "Guess some things never do change." He laid a napkin on the bar and set Mister Jones's drink down before his eyes. "This here scotch is probably a whole hell of a lot better than you remember. Fact is, it's been sittin' for ten years now. You know, come to think of it, that ain't right. Hell, Roy, how long have you been gone?"

Mister Jones stared at that glass, tasting the liquor though he hadn't touched a drop yet. "Fifteen years."

"Fifteen years…" TJ stared at that bottle of scotch. "You know, I could sell that bottle for a whole hell of a lot of money, but it's yours, Roy. All of it. It's been waiting for you. Tell me, honestly now, between old friends, how've you been?"

"Same song, same dance." Mister Jones laughed. "But you already know that, don't you. You always know your customers, even if they're just sitting down at your bar for the first time. You know what baffles me?"

"What?"

"You."

"Me, Roy?"

"Yes, you. You see, the last time we had a good talk over scotch, I set you up fine. You remember that, don't you, TJ?"

"I do, Roy. And I'm grateful."

"I figured you'd stay with all them rich people, stuffing your pockets with all their money. Tell me, TJ, what happened?"

"Well, I was there for a while. Worked in the top of one of them high skyscrapers serving drinks to all kinds of folk. You know, big important people in their suits and fine business dresses who were always workin' day and night. Real-salt-of-the-earth types, or so someone said. But you know what?"

"Tell me."

"Not one of them was important. They were just people like me and you. Sure they might have a Cadillac or a nice LTD, but they got problems too. And you couldn't talk to 'em, Roy. You couldn't get in a word edgewise, even though you knew what their problem was. They was just too caught up in all that fuss around them. You know, important, high and mighty money."

"So you came back here."

"Not right away, I didn't. I'm no fool. Those people had money and they tipped well if you gave them a little extra when they was down and out or sky high. Tipped real well. I saved me enough to buy this here joint and now she's mine. She's all mine, Roy. I live here, sleep here, work here too. I'll probably die here, but I don't care. I own her and she owns me. Thank you, Roy. From the bottom of my heart."

"Damn good for you, TJ. Let me buy you a drink."

"Don't drink no more."

"Hell, TJ, you know me. I don't give a damn if you do or don't. Like I always say, you get to choose. Still, let me toast you and your lady here. A perfect match."

"Aw, hell, Roy, you don't need to do that."

"I insist."

"You don't mind if I just have water, do you?"

"Not at all."

TJ nodded, poured himself a glass of city water and lifted that dirty thing as Mister Jones raised his scotch. "Here's to a damn fine man, a good man, a man who made a choice. You deserve it, TJ. You deserve all you got, and all you're gonna get."

"Hear, hear."

They drank together, scotch and water over rocks. TJ set his glass under the bar and picked up his bar rag. He wiped the wood, staring down at that high gloss shine as Mister Jones set his empty glass down with a fine smile. "Damn, you was right. A man sure could get used to a drink like that."

TJ refilled his glass. "Who would have thought that something so terrible could have aged so well. It just don't usually happen like that, does it?"

"Nosiree, it sure don't. The place looks good, TJ, just like it used to. Feels like it used to too."

"I should have stayed a little longer at that fancy bar and earned a few more dollars. Could have fixed the old lady up a bit more. Still, she's fine as she is, but you should have seen her back in the day. Tramp had her fixed up all nice and everything. But things were good then. You know, there was money even for poor folk. They'd come in and have a few drinks, few laughs too, forgettin' all their worries for awhile. Forgettin' the war. You know, Roy, the big war, W-W-Two." TJ stared down at that old wood. "Tell me, how come folks don't do that anymore? How come folks have changed? Seems like they've forgotten how to have a good time."

"That was two wars ago, TJ." Mister Jones looked past the old man at the big mirror that filled the wall behind the bar. Bottles in front of that mirror, rows and rows of bottles, colored bottles and clear bottles that were all filled with something; Mister Jones's reflection lost somewhere in between. "Things are always changin', TJ. They changin' every day."

"Guess you're right, but it don't make me miss it any less. Wish things would come around again. You know, fill this place up with laughter."

"Funny thing about life, you think you gone and buried something and then the next thing you know it's staring you right in the face. Kind of like me today." Mister Jones smiled. "Here I am."

TJ laughed. "Guess so, Roy. Tell me, what brings you back?"

"A fight."

"A fight? What kind of fight?"

"A boxing fight."

"Really now?"

"No lie."

"Who's fightin'?"

"King David."

The old man looked up at Mister Jones. "Really? I hadn't heard."

"Of course you hadn't. How could you? Anyway, that's what brings me back. A big fight with the king. And that so-called wife of mine."

"How is she, Roy?"

"Margaret? Well Margaret is Margaret now, ain't she. You know, TJ, some things never do change, and sometimes that ain't so great." Mister Jones lifted his glass and smiled as he drank. Chills ran down the old man's back—somebody dancing on a grave. "Nosiree, some things never do change."

It was late, the gym was nearly empty, only a few fighters left, dressing by their lockers. Leonard sat on an old wooden bench, a thing that had been around since the gym was built up around it. Old Forty Two was trying to put on his socks, groaning though he didn't know it, just too damn tired to notice the pain. Pain in his hands, pain in his back, old knees that knew something was coming.

*Just bad weather,* Leonard thought, *ice and snow, a lot of wind that'll blow. But that's winter, even though it ain't winter yet. December ain't here and Thanksgiving's still a week away, but it ain't in front of me. No, not yet; not for a week. Just like I told the kid, I'll dance and wish she was here.* Old Forty Two groaned and pulled on his sock. *Dance and wish I was dancing with her.* Somehow he tied those shoe-shined shoes.

*But that's gone, right Leonard? It ain't in front of you no more. Just biting at my heels. There's just today, just now and I fought good, fought hard, even though I'm getting old.* Leonard turned and looked down to that row of lockers and a mirror that hung cracked on the wall.

*White hairs mottled in the stubble on his face. White hairs coming and deep lines that gonna be wrinkles. Lines that gonna look like all them scars from fighting. Damn, I look old. Starting to feel it, too. Body don't heal like it used to when I was young. When I was Mikey's age, Matt's too. I could fight the world back then, take a good beating, and then do it all over again the next day. But now,* Leonard laughed, *I'm forty two and I don't heal so fast anymore. What used to take a day now takes three or four. Life, just as mean as hell.*

*But today I'm strong, today I fought hard. Just like I told the kid, today I won.* Yes, Leonard smiled at himself in the mirror, *today I won.* "Hey, Matt," Leonard called out. "You still in here?"

From the shower, a voice came. "I'm here."

"You got plans tonight?"

"Nope."

"You seen the Herns–Harper fight?"

"I watched it, but you know, the picture was all snow."

"Tell you what, I'm all hungry as hell. What you say I go grab us something to eat and then we watch that bum beat up Harper?"

Matt walked around the corner of the lockers, towel around his waist. "Really? You got the reel?"

"I sure damn do."

"You're on."

He was the Dancing Man: sweet feet, quick hands, a head that moved on a swivel. Matt and Leonard sat in Art's office, lights off, door halfway closed, the projector clicking on that old metal desk as the frames ran by: moving pictures on a cracked wall.

"Look at him move."

And he could. The Dancing Man from Detroit had the sweetest feet either fighter had ever seen. Even Harper, the other fighter, the number one contender in the world, stared at the Dancing Man's shoes. Red shoes that were as bright as his smile. Red shoes, even though that film was just black and white. No color, no sound, no bell that announced the rounds, just two men toe to toe.

"Look at him, Matt." Leonard leaned forward on his cold metal chair. "We halfway through round two and Herns already got control of the fight."

Matt sat three feet from the old white wall—three feet away from the champ. "He's gonna wear Harper out. Damn, he's good."

"He is. He sure is. How many punches has Harper thrown?"

"Maybe two dozen jabs and half as many hooks. But none of them hooks have connected."

Leonard turned to the other man. "I know you know. How many, Matt?"

"Twenty-eight jabs, twenty-nine now, and thirteen hooks."

"Thirteen hooks that caught nothing but air." Leonard shook his head. "Herns slipped 'em all. If Harper doesn't connect with a few of them, he gonna wear that right arm of his out mighty fast."

Matt stared at the wall, pictures running by. "It's just a mouse trap."

"Hell, yes it is. Herns is just egging him on."

"Setting him up."

"And then comes the fall."

"Ain't that life."

"Sometimes." Leonard nodded. "Sometimes."

On the wall between the cracks, Harper stalked left and right, left and right, always moving forward, pressing the champ back into a neutral corner, throwing meaningless jabs, trying to get in close. And he did. Harper got in close, real close, like a man and lady between the sheets. The hook came, a hard punch, aimed high, elbow high too, sailing for the champ's head. But the Dancing Man from Detroit moved.

It was like magic: Herns slipped under Harper's hook, that punch sailing high as the champ moved out of the corner. Harpers' hook hung in mid air, his face open to the hard left that kissed his cheek, the hard right that followed on its heels, Harper's neck snapping to the side, cracking like a sail catching the wind. One after another, punches quicker than lightning, striking again and again as Harper tried to turn, but to no avail.

He fell, a ton of bricks hitting the floor, Herns already in a neutral corner, dancing on his toes as the referee counted; sand slipping through Harper's hands. Somewhere in his mind, Matt heard a bell. "He ain't gettin' up."

"Damn right he ain't." Leonard stopped the reel and ran it back, Harper rising up from the mat like it was resurrection day, rising up only to fall again by Herns's hands. "You was right when you said it was a mousetrap. Herns just led him in. You see how he did that?"

"He just stopped. Just stood in the corner and let Harper come in."

Leonard let the reel roll—Harper falling all over again. *Damn*, Leonard thought to himself, *he's a monster. A real monster. I'd hate to fight him.*

*Liar. You'd love to fight him.*

Leonard smiled, *damn right I would.*

"He's one scary cat."

"Harper's no slouch either."

"No"—Leonard stared at the wall—"he ain't. He's a damn good fighter. An inside guy, a brawler for sure."

"Just like me."

"Just like you." Leonard nodded. "Tell me something."

"You're not my type."

"I'm serious now."

Matt smiled. "So am I."

"You crazy."

"Just like you."

They laughed, both men smiling, both men wiping at their eyes. Leonard said, "You young and everything and there're plenty of ladies out there who would jump at the chance of dating you. Don't ask me why, but that's what I hear. All over the damn neighborhood too. Why don't you find yourself a good woman and have yourself a family?"

"And end up like you?"

"What you talkin' about." Leonard looked Matt in the eye. "We've both lost people."

Matt looked away. "I don't know if it's worth it."

"Worth what?"

"Going through everything you went through."

Leonard stared at the wall; Harper lying on the ground. "I miss her, Matt. Miss her something terrible, but I'd do it all over again."

Matt looked at the other man as if he was crazy. "You would?"

"In a heartbeat. One day, you'll know what I mean. You'll find yourself a woman that makes the world come together for you, just like I did."

"Just to lose her?"

"Jackie ain't gone." Leonard turned to his friend. "Look, Matt, every damn day I thank God for her. Thank him that she was part of my life. She still is. I feel her, even now."

"Then if it was so good, how come you is preachin' to me about finding someone when you don't?"

"'Cause there are some things in life you just can't replace. Besides"—Leonard smiled like a fighter after fifteen losing rounds—"if I got married again, Jackie would haunt my ass. Probably come back and kick it. Hell, maybe I should get married again just so she would come back." They laughed, both men smiling again, laughter dying now as they stared down at nothing. Leonard said, "I've watched you, Matt, watched you from the very first day you came in this place with that old man of yours. You gotta hear me when I tell you that life is what you make it. You hear me?"

"I hear you."

"What *you* make it, Matt, not anyone else. Not me, not Art, not that old man of yours either. No one, Matt, just you. Just you. There's a world around you, and all you got to do is listen."

"I'm listening, but I can only hear one thing."

"Okay." Leonard nodded. "What's that?'"

Matt looked down at his feet, down at his old shoes. "Time's going by."

"But I bet it's sayin' something else too. Am I right?"

"Maybe." Matt smiled, "May-be."

"You ain't gonna tell me, are you?"

"Nope, I ain't."

"I see how you are. Here I am, both of us talkin' and everything, me telling you stuff I ain't ever told nobody and you ain't gonna tell me what that voice is tellin' you? But you will. Sooner or later that mouth of yours is gonna open up and spill it all."

"Maybe."

"Huh"—Leonard shook his head—"maybe. He says may-be."

Matt smiled. "You done?"

"With you, yes. You want to watch it again?"

"It's a date."

"Hell, no, not with you, it ain't."

# SIX

There were cracks in the concrete, some big, some so small that they couldn't be seen. But they were there, touching the soles of Matt's feet as he walked across that parking lot toward those two big doors. They were glass doors, clean doors with metal bars on the inside running up and down like a prisoner's cell. Doors that opened and shut but not on their own. No, there were no automatic doors in this part of the city. Not even at grocery stores like this one.

Hands in his pockets, mouth muttering something, words that Matt had rehearsed ten thousand times. And as he neared those doors, somehow they opened, smiling wide as he walked inside, something glinting behind that fighter. Something that looked like teeth.

But there was nothing there, not now; the doors swung shut. Matt stood for a moment, something like a shadow at his feet, music playing from an elevator a million miles away. She was there of course, standing at her checkout, taking people's groceries from their carts, looking at the price, punching in the numbers on an old fifty-pound thing. He almost left, right then and there, Matt turned toward those doors, those long metal bars, looking outside at the cold. He didn't know it, but somewhere inside he wished for summer. For June or July but not August because August meant that September was just around the corner and the days would grow shorter, colder, and winter would come.

*Winter. Man, I hate it.*

He walked down the aisle, passing a dozen men with the same brawny mustaches and plaid red shirts. Men who smiled at Matt, smiled as he passed by, smiled at nothing except an empty aisle. Matt walked to the back where the butcher stood behind glass that bled. It was just hamburger—fresh, bleeding hamburger—a few other cuts of meat too old and too expensive that laid in that bubble case. Cuts that the butcher would take home for himself before they went bad. Wiping his hands on his apron, a once-white thing, the butcher looked up and recognized Matt. A smile, a nod, no autograph. After all, he just lost his last fight. Matt didn't buy any meat.

Fact was, he hadn't planned on buying anything. But he had to, he couldn't go up there empty-handed, had to buy something. There was juice, cold juice that would go down nice on a hot summer day. Grape or Orange or even Red Juice—what the hell was Red Juice, anyway? With just a shrug, Matt grabbed the carton, walked to the front of the store, to the checkout—to Margaret.

He stood in line, feeling nervous just like he did before a fight. Staring at his feet, feet that wanted to dance all them butterflies away, looking up every now and then at his opponent. Nothing felt right. But she was beautiful, that mouth, those eyes, a foxy lady. Seemed like a nice lady too. Head falling, butterflies swirling, Matt looked to his corner, but there was no towel to throw in. *Maybe I should just walk out.* Matt looked up and caught her eye.

Or maybe she caught his.

She could feel the burn in her cheeks, that flush that came with excitement. But it was more than that, it was—Margaret punched in a number—electric. She set the sack of potatoes aside and picked up the milk. Numbers, fingers dancing on heavy lead keys, the fifty-pound thing ringing. And Margaret wished she was in the kitchen. *Just him and me at home doing dishes, washing, drying, touching. Juice*, she thought, *he came all this way for juice? I don't think so. So what is he here for? Mikey?*

They all came at once, voices and reasons, some loud, some quiet, saying the same damn thing. *Mikey, he came here cause of Mikey. What the hell has that kid done now? Maybe he opened his mouth. Please, God, no. Don't let him have said a thing. But that can't be it, it just can't be, look at him standing there.*

*He's nervous*, Margaret thought, *nervous and sneakin' peeks at me. No, Matthew Gore wants something from me.* It came again, that flush in her cheeks. Margaret looked down the row of registers toward the office—into the one-way mirror. She could see herself, her face, her hair, top half of her body, but Margaret was blind to it all except her eyes.

She stood, staring across the store into her own eyes. Light-brown eyes, almost the color of caramel, windows to the soul shut. Apples, milk, a carton of cigarettes, Margaret punched in their price without ever looking. The line moving, Matt standing next—the cash register rang.

"Hey."

"Hey, yourself," Margaret said, smiling too, unable to help herself. "What you doing here, and don't just tell me you wanted some juice. It's a long way to come for juice. That brat of mine ain't caused you no trouble now, has he?"

"No," Matt said and almost kept his mouth shut after that. But he couldn't, he didn't, he had to try something. "I just wanted to ask you somethin'."

*He knows*, Margaret thought, *he knows about Mister Jones.* Still, she kept her cool and said, "Yeah? What's that?"

"I thought it'd be nice if we could catch a show together."

"A show...," A ton of bricks falling from her shoulders.

"Yeah, something different for a change."

"Matt. I…" *Mister Jones*, Matt, *Mister Jones. He's home, in our kitchen—dishes.*

"Miss Jones?" They both looked up. He stood, staring at them, eyes all accusing, James with his clipboard, bushy mustache moving as he talked. "Is this man bothering you?"

"Oh no, sir. This here is a friend of mine, Mister Matthew Gore."

"Matt Gore?" And James's face changed. "The fighter?"

"Yes, sir." Margaret smiled. "The one and only."

"Well, I'll be damned. It is you and here in my store too. I should've looked before I opened my mouth. I'm always doing that, Margaret can attest to that." James smiled and so did Margaret Jones. "Nice to meet you, Mister Gore. I'm a big fan."

"Please, call me Matt."

"I will." James nodded. "I certainly will. I tell you, it must be my lucky day. It's not every day that the Heavy Weight Champion of the World walks into your store."

"Not yet." Matt smiled, loving how that sounded. "Herns is the champ."

"Not for long, son"—James tapped his clipboard—"not for long. I listen to all of your fights; see quite a few too. Your day is coming—mark my words. Don't mean to take up your time, it was real nice to meet you, champ. I'll let you get back to"—James smiled at Margaret—"to whatever the two of you were doing. Have a good day."

And Matt wanted to cry.

*Champ.*

"You too," Matt said. "It was nice to meet you too."

Margaret turned and looked at Matt. "I'd love to," she heard herself say. "When?"

Why?" Mikey rolled his eyes. He was standing in the kitchen, Margaret standing across from him with her arms folded— something that already said no. Mikey said, "Just tell me why?"

"'Cause I said no."

"Why?"

Margaret's eyes jumped to the hall. "Keep your voice down, he'll hear."

"It'd be easy. I already talked to Jimmy and his dad—"

"*You did what?*"

"His dad knows a guy who's a cop and—"

"Are you stupid? You do that and things are gonna get a lot worse around here. Son, you got to think. Use that head of yours."

"At least, I'm tryin' to do something."

"So am I."

"Like what?"

"You really think you somethin', don't you?" Margaret stared. "You think you got the whole world figured out. And what, you seventeen now?"

"Know more than you. All you do is sit around here all day and act like the whole world has done you wrong."

"If you don't like it, there's the door."

"Tsk." Mikey looked away, acting all mad. "The only reason I stay here is because of—nothin'."

"What?" Margaret's hand found her hip. "You was gonna say me? 'Cause if you were, I say you was full of it on account of you always being out and everything. You know, drinkin' and smokin' and hanging out with those thugs you call friends."

"I'm only out 'cause *he's* here!"

"And what about before that, Mikey? What was your reason then?"

"Mike. I like Mike better."

"And I like Mikey 'cause Mike is the name of a man and the way you acting, you ain't a man yet. Ain't even close." He turned to go, but Margaret grabbed his arm. "Mike, please. I'm sorry, it's just hard, you know. Listen to me for a minute, okay?"

Mikey stood, back to his mother. "I'm listenin'."

"I know this is hard on you and I'm sorry. I really am, but it's hard on me too. You got to believe me when I say that. I don't want him here either, but there ain't nothin' I can do. And the cops, hell, they ain't gonna do nothin'. They never do."

"Kick him out."

"I know him, I know your father too good. There ain't nothin', *nothin'* I can do. Nothin' you can do about it either. Not now, not yet. We try somethin' now"—Margaret shook her head—"things won't be good. But you got to trust me when I say this ain't gonna last forever. Like I said, I know him *and* I've talked to a few folk about it. Can't say nothin' now, but trust me, okay? I ain't just sittin' around doing nothin'.

"But for now"—Margaret pulled at Mikey's arm, turning him, looking into his eyes—"for now, you keep on doin' what you been doin'. Keep trainin', train hard like Matt. You get up and run with him, be good to him too. He likes you, he thinks you got talent and that's something comin' from a man like him. So you get up and train and go to school and hit the gym afterwards, okay?"

"And what about you?"

"Aw, you really do love your mother, don't you." Mikey looked away, nodding. Margaret, smiling now, said, "You don't worry about me. I'm gonna put in some extra hours at work, stay away as much as I can, just like you. So tomorrow, I won't be home till late, okay?"

He wasn't sold, not by a long shot.

"Please, Mikey, for me. Trust me."

"Okay, Mom, for you."

She held him, Mikey's arms wrapping around her, mother and son hugging for the first time in so many years. Margaret closed her eyes, tears coming. "You're a good man. A good man," she said. "I love you, Mike."

They were just keeping warm, hands out over a barrel, smoke rising up black and blue from that fire, some folks would call them thugs. Just thugs on a corner who wore sweatshirts with hoods, a few knit caps that helped keep them warm, but none of them had gloves—street thugs. Men who never looked up from that fire as the old man passed by them, muttering to himself.

Art crossed the street, walking around the potholes, moving onto the sidewalk that crumbled under his feet. *Almost Thanksgiving and the only offer I've had for Matt is a two-bit fighter coming out of retirement, a tomato can looking for a little money. Mackay*, Art shook his head, *he's nothin' but a once-upon-a-time fighter.*

Matt's too good for the bum, chew him up and spit him out, a joke of a thing. But that's how it is sometimes. Back in the day, didn't matter who you fought, you just fought. Old-time fighters, traveling by train or bus to the city or some backwoods fair just to fight whatever was put in front of you. It was easier then, harder too, just fight, win, beat enough men down until you stand in that wonderful Garden at Madison. And once you was there, you never wanted to leave.

You ate good, slept good, cause you was in a bed instead of a bus seat. Fight maybe once a week or twice a month instead of every day. Can't heal when you fighting every day. Can't do nothin' else. No drinkin', no women either, not if you wanted to make it to the top. But at the Garden, you was at the top and you could have it all. Too damn bad, some things should never change.

Art shoved his hands in his pockets, pain shooting up like fireworks. *Damn weather's gonna change. Gonna get worse, gonna snow maybe, sure as all hell it's gonna get colder; wetter too. Can't stand the cold, give me heat any day. Don't care if it's a hundred and ten and sweat running down my back, at least I won't hurt—at least not so much. But this weather*, Art looked up, *clouds that didn't give a damn, it can all go to hell. You know, sometimes hell don't sound too bad*, the old trainer smiled to himself, *not if it's hot, it don't. Cold, winter, now that's hell.*

*Just like livin' alone.*

The old trainer stopped on the sidewalk and looked down the street. It wasn't far, those steps that led inside to his apartment. That rail, black iron twisted into vines, beautiful grape leaves, just a rusty thing now. And forty years ago a real cloth canopy, green, sheltering the steps and rail. Gone, all gone. Just like Madison Square Garden, just like all those buses and trains and cities, just like all them fine dames. Art pulled his hands from his pockets and rubbed them good. Gone except for the pain. *But Matt, he'll be here for me, just like he always has been.*

*Sure, I took him in, but it was more like he took me in. If it snows, these damn steps are always cleared, and if the gym's cold in the morning, he'll put his own heater in my office. And if I need anything, groceries, or to pay a bill, or maybe I'm all out of aspirin, maybe I just can't open the cap, well then he'll make a trip. He's my own,* Art nodded, *the kid's my own.*

*What the hell do I do? Mackay wouldn't give Matt a run. Maybe I should just take it, anyway.*

*Take it and sit down with Matt, explain it all matter-of-fact. Tell him to knock Mackay out in boxing for good, tell him to make it quick, no shows, no fuss, just take the fool out to pasture and put him to rest. And then maybe, just maybe, someone will come knocking at our door. He'll understand,* Art nodded, *he's got to understand. I can't do nothin' else, can't call in a favor 'cause this one's beyond favors. Matt's lost his last two, only lost seven in his whole career, but seven too many. Seven that he could have won if only...*

If only what?

*Hell, I don't know.* Art stepped forward, walking slowly toward his apartment; it was over. *He ain't got no more, nothin' more to show, nothin' more he can do. It's over, through.*

Just ready to settle down and let life go by. Fighting, it was good, the Garden was beautiful, but now it was just winter, just cold and it all hurt. He stepped up those steps, hand on the rail, pulling his old body along, rust turning the palm of his hand red.

*It's over,* Art opened the door, *ain't no more canopy over my head.* *It's over,* the door closed behind him, *it's over.* Cold rain fell.

She was old, lying in a hospital bed as the machines around her beeped. She was still magic, blessed as she would say, given a touch that worked miracles. And before she died, she was gonna work one last bit of that magic. She was gonna reach out and lay her hands on him and give him something that he had forgotten. Give him something that he could only see when he himself was old. Something that he would look back to and smile. Johnette laughed, she saw herself shuffling down the worn-out steps of the decrepit building. Death was only a step behind.

She really wasn't there, not in the apartment where she had known him as a child. Her heart was still beatin', and it would for a while, until it was time. And then, it was gonna be hard on Matt. No doubt about it. She was the last thing that he had, the last bit of his childhood, and Johnette wondered just how deep he would sink. But that was life, give and take, birth and death, snow and rain, and in between, long summer days. And if you were lucky, you might find someone you could love, even if they die twenty years before you. Just like her John.

John, she thought and stopped for a moment on the step. Death almost ran into her. She missed John; looked forward to seein' him again. And she would see him. Even if what all them scientists said about the brain was true, about hallucinations just before it would die, she'd still see her handsome John. She had watched that program on CBS, *60 Minutes* with Harry Reasoner and Mike Wallace, seen what them scientists had claimed, but what them folk didn't know, Johnette thought, was that calculations and ticker tape computers couldn't measure love. Love held everything together. Love is like gravity. That's why the world was splittin' now, why it was such a mess; because people wasn't lovin' each other. It was as simple as that. Love could work miracles, and love would reunite her with her John.

She wasn't worried about dyin', life had been good to her. But it was short and sweet. Just one day after the birth of their first child, John's foreman had showed up on her door with his hat in his hands. That was the day that Johnette had first met Death.

She had seen Death again years later when he took their daughter away. After that, whenever he was in the neighborhood, Johnette would see him as he peeked in her window. Sometimes she had begged him to come in. He was here now in the hospital room, standing over Matt's shoulder as he sat next to Johnette's bed. In her mind, she was still in that old burnt building—her home before it had burnt down, waiting for him to come. Outside, the snow hung in the air.

"You're a good man," Johnette said. "One day, you gonna see that. See that all your fussin' was for nothin'. You gonna find yourself someone good too. Someone who's gonna love you for you. You might not believe it, but you will, and you'll be happy, Matthew Gore. I promise. You'll know when you see her."

Matt turned and looked at the snow, at the wind. She knew he wanted to believe, but how could he? "I wish," Matt was saying to her, "I wish there was another way."

"So does all mankind," Johnette said and Death stood just behind her. "It's still a long road, Matthew Gore, but I got to start. The choice ain't mine. Now be good to me and don't make it any harder than it already is. Promise me now."

Matt breathed. "For you."

"I love you, child."

They stood, in Johnette's mind, staring at each other, a last goodbye until the old woman put out her hand. "It's time."

And Matt closed the door, shut it on Death, who stared at the pair through the broken glass; he would follow, but not yet. The wind blew white.

# SEVEN

Matt was standing outside the grocery store waiting for Margaret; it was just after five. Late afternoon, early evening—didn't matter what it was called because it was dark. Late autumn, early winter, Matt just blew in his hands.

She had waved at him through the glass window, through the bars that ran up and down the door. Lifted a finger and implied that she would just be a minute, but that was fifteen of those ago. Matt looked in through the doors again. No sign, no whisper, not even a hint of the woman he was taking out tonight, just prerogative, that's all, nothing more. Matt stood in the cold.

Rocking on his heels, blowing in his hands, smiling wide at all of them folks as they came in and out, opening the door for them, trying to dispel any worries that he was a mugger just waiting for an old lady. Still, they clutched their purses. After all, it was the city. Matt pulled the door open again and smiled: time stopped, his jaw dropped.

Oh Lord, was she ever F-I-N-E, fine.

Matt looked her up and down and up and down again. He couldn't help himself. She was more than just fine, she was a looker, a head-turner, a foxy lady in designer jeans, or so they seemed. Blue jeans that snugged right over her—

"Thank you."

Matt looked up, eyes wide, hand in the cookie jar. Pretty Donna who was always smiling. He said, "Huh?"

"Thank you."

"Oh." He nodded, hoping that she hadn't noticed. But she had and she was smiling, liking what she saw, liking what she had seen him do. Matt said, "You're welcome."

"So tell me"—that damn fine thing tucked her hair behind her ear—"you just sit here all night and open doors for folks, or are you waiting for someone?"

"Just waitin' for someone."

She nodded, just a thing to herself, her words just meant for her ears. "So you're the one."

"Excuse me?"

"I just said that's a shame."

"A shame?"

"I was hoping that you would help me carry these groceries home and in return I'd sew that jacket of yours." Matt looked down at his pocket, thread running from the seam. Reaching out, she took that loose piece of thread, wrapped it around her finger and gave a little jerk. It snapped clean. "There." she smiled and Matt couldn't help but stare at the woman's eyes—something shining deep inside. "That'll hold for a while, but not long. It needs to be sewn."

He felt butterflies in his stomach. "Thank you," he said.

"You're welcome," Donna said as she played with her hair. "So tell me, Matthew Gore, what are you doing out here besides holding doors open for ladies?"

"How'd you know my—"

"Your name?"

"Yeah."

She turned and looked back inside those bars. "Because you're the talk of the town, honey. You should hear all those ladies in there going on and on about you. If I didn't know any better, I would have thought I was still in high school by the way they was acting. Glad I'm not. But tell me"—Donna smiled brightly—"are you really as nice as they all say you are?"

Matt's mouth opened, but nothing came out.

"You are." Delight shone in her eyes, her smile even wider, face brighter; Matt just staring. "You really are. I'll be. Just a word of advice, Mister Matt, Mister Big-Time Boxer, you treat her right, you hear?"

"I hear." But Matt didn't need to hear a thing because he could see the stars through the clouds tonight. Beautiful stars that had never shone brighter.

She walked right by him, Matt staring at her face: warm smile, bright eyes as she passed by, Matt staring at her backside. "I'm Donna," she called back. "Donna with the nice eyes, if you didn't notice, and nice other things too. Bye bye."

Nice jacket, handmade like her jeans, dressed to the nines in the poor part of town, crossing the parking lot with those grocery bags—she looked fine. Matt watched her as she walked away, considering things that he hadn't considered in a while. She stopped and turned around and Donna saw Matt's eyes.

She knew, knew what he was thinking, Donna smiled wide and winked at the man. "You did notice me, didn't you? Yes, you did. You sure did. You call me, Matt, and I'll sew that jacket of yours. I'll fix it right, just like brand-new." Turning and laughing to herself, Donna floated across that parking lot, not a crack underfoot, streetlights lighting her way. Streetlights that shone brighter than noontime day.

Of course she was in the bathroom, a small room in the back of the grocery store, putting on a little eye shadow that made Margaret's eyes smoky. Angie leaned against the doorframe, watching her friend get ready, watching with her arms folded.

She was a little older than Margaret, single mother too. Single like so many women in the city. "You better hurry up," Angie said.

"He can wait a little. Both me and you know that it's good to make a man wait."

"Normally I would agree with you, but not tonight, Margaret. In case you didn't notice, Donna was in the store."

"Donna?"

Angie nodded. "And she just left."

"Is she talkin' to him?"

Angie turned and looked across the store. "She sure is."

Margaret huffed. "What's he doing?"

"Talkin'."

"Just talking?"

"They smilin' too." Angie looked back at her friend. "You want me to interfere?"

"Hell with it." Margaret searched her pockets for a cigarette. "Let him."

"You sure?"

Margaret loaded her mascara brush. "If it's war, it's war, honey."

"But you already got one."

Margaret looked at her friend in the mirror. "What do you mean?"

"I've seen the way you been acting, been there too many times. What's his name?"

"Don't know what you talkin' about."

"Margaret, we've been in the same boat and when you been in the same boat, you can always tell when it's shaking. So what's up?"

"Mister Jones."

"Didn't know there was one."

"Neither did I." Margaret stared in the mirror. "Thought he was dead or something."

"Sounds like you was wishing, huh?"

"On a star. Haven't seen him in forever and then he shows up on my door. Never did bother to get a divorce either 'cause the last thing I can afford is a no-good lawyer."

"What you gonna do?"

"There's nothing I can do."

"That's where you're wrong."

"You know it ain't as easy as that."

"Look, Margaret, it ain't ever easy, but it's got to be done. The sooner, the better too. And seeing how things might go with Matt..."

"Tonight ain't about that, Angie, honey." Margaret smiled. "Tonight is just about me and Matt. He finally asked me out, didn't he?"

"That's why you gotta get rid of Jones. In fact, tonight would be best, but you don't need me to tell you all this, do you? You already know it. I bet you'd tell me the same damn thing."

Margaret stared in the mirror. "Our first date."

"You better not let Matt see you like that 'cause if you do, he's gonna know everythin' you thinkin'."

Margaret touched her face. "Is it that obvious?"

"And then some. If you go home looking like that and Mister Jones sees you looking like that"—Angie just shook her head—"you follow me?"

"Angie"—Margaret turned to her friend—"what do I do?"

"Call the cops."

"He'd go mad."

"Let him."

"Angie, it takes time for the police, you know? Especially in our part of town."

"So?"

"I got Mikey to think about."

"Mikey's seventeen, Margret. The boy can take care of himself. Besides, he's a boxer, right?"

"Yeah."

"I imagine that he could probably take Mister Jones out. In fact, it might be a good thing for Mister Jones to get his clock cleaned by his own son."

"Mikey ain't that good. Maybe Matt..." Margaret turned to the mirror, dreaming. "Maybe Matt would—"

"You don't want to do that, Margaret. Matt don't need to know nothing about any of this. How's it gonna look if he finds out you married."

"I know, but still," Margaret smiled. "Matt fightin' Mister Jones for me. For me, Angie. What is he doin' now?"

Angie turned and looked; Matt staring across the parking lot. "He's just waiting for you."

"He is?"

"He sure is." Angie smiled at her friend. "Listen, if you need me to stay with you for a while, I'd be happy to. Maybe between the two of us we could get rid of Mister Jones, if you know what I mean. Besides, I got a mean hook of my own."

"Oh, Angie, I don't know."

"How long have we been friends?"

"Thanks, honey."

"You're welcome. Now, what time should I meet you at your place tonight?"

"Tonight?"

"Yes, tonight."

Matt blew in his hands and looked in past the bars on the doors—still, no Margaret. As if they had a mind of their own, Matt's eyes ran back across the dark parking lot, hurrying past all those cracks, down the sidewalk and under all the streetlights that shone like fireflies as she walked by; but she was gone. Matt looked down at his coat.

It was just a little thing, the corner of his pocket that was coming free—something that he had never noticed before. He touched it, seeing the small flap, feeling it too, fingering the end of the thread that she had so cleanly snapped. Just a little thing, but she saw it—in the dark.

Matt looked up: the lights above the door were burned out. The only light came from inside the store, out through the door, slipping past those bars, shining in her eyes. How'd she see it? Just a movement, a fighter's reaction, Matt turned to Margaret and suddenly wished that he was home in bed.

Still, he opened the door and held it for the lady. "Hey."

"Sorry I'm late."

Matt could smell the cigarette smoke in her hair. "A lady's never late."

"If you say so."

"I did, and I do." Smiles lingering, eyes running along the ground. Matt said, "It's cold, huh?"

"Sure is, but I don't mind. Sometimes cold is nice, winter too."

"Can't stand the cold. Me, I love me summer. Spring and summer. Give me hot any day."

"Me, too." Margaret scolded herself for not saying the right thing. "You look good tonight, Matt. I like that jacket. Is it new?"

"Oh, no." Matt's finger traced the corner of his pocket. "Had it for a while now. Starting to fall apart."

"I hadn't noticed. Still, it looks good on you."

"You look nice yourself."

Soft eyes, Margaret smiling, reaching out, taking his arm, hooking hers through his. "So, what's the big plan?"

"Lady's choice."

"Really?"

Matt nodded. "Yeah."

"You're sure now?"

"Anything you want."

"Even if it's one of *those* movies?" Margaret nudged him. "You know, the ones that us women always cry at?"

"Sure, if you want me to fall asleep."

"You wouldn't?"

"In a heartbeat."

"Matthew Gore, what am I ever gonna do with you?"

"Guess we'll see."

"Tell you what, I could go for a cup of coffee. So what do you say we sit down, have some, maybe get a little something to eat too. I imagine you hungry."

"I am."

"It's a date."

"It sure is."

"You weren't bored waiting for me, were you?"

"Nope, not at all."

They walked across that parking lot, Margaret holding his arm, both of them stepping on cracks under those dim lights. Margaret said, "Tell me, what did Donna say to you?"

"She said"—Matt touched that loose hanging thread—"she said to treat you good."

Mister Jones sat on the couch in the living room, staring at the ancient thing, at the black and white television set—snow on the screen. He looked up at the clock, looked at that yellow face with black hands. "Boy, where's your mother?"

"Tsk." Mikey lay on his bed in his room, staring up at the ceiling, wishing that he had stayed at the gym. "She workin', that's where she is."

"She supposed to get off at five. It's almost seven now."

"So what?"

"I'm hungry, that's what, you damn fool! What we got to eat?"

"What you askin' me for?" Mikey was glad that he said it, glad that he had stood up to the fool—Mikey smiling on his bed. "Why don't you get up and look!"

It stretched across the ceiling, the shadow of Mister Jones. "What did you say?" Mikey turned—nothing at his door. "I asked you"—a smile, teeth glinting now, Mister Jones standing over Mikey, staring down at the boy—"what did you say?"

Mikey stared up at that face, stared into eyes just as cold as coal. "Nothin'." his mouth was dry. "I didn't say nothin'."

"You know, son, maybe it's time for you and me to have one of those father to son talks. I know we ain't never had one before, but you know what they say, some things ain't ever too late. This is one of them things." Mister Jones's teeth glinted—sharp gold. "Now, don't you worry none, 'cause we ain't gonna have one of *those* talks. You know, one of them bird and bees kind of talks. You too damn old for that. I imagine you've already seen some birds in your day. Probably not, but that ain't what we talkin' about, are we? Nosiree, we ain't. What we talking about is you and that mother of yours."

Mikey wanted to sit up, but he couldn't move.

"Now, your mother works hard every day, cooking, cleaning, taking care of everything, and then she goes to work. That's a good woman, son, a woman who knows what she's supposed to do. But you"—Mister Jones shook his head, eyes stretching past their corners, looking down at Mikey—"you don't seem to know what you should be doin'. Do you know what you should be doin', son?"

Mikey found himself nodding.

"Okay, tell me what you should be doin'."

"Helpin' my mom."

"That's my boy!" Mister Jones slapped his leg. "Now you, as a son, as a man, 'cause you are a man now, you should do everything that you can do for your mother. Yes, you already help out around here, but now that you're all grown-up and everything, there's somethin' else you should be doin'. You need to start watching out for your mother. Are you following me, son?

"You see, this here is what you would call a tough neighborhood. Yessiree, ain't no doubt about it, this here is a tough neighborhood and these are tough times. Tough times and tough neighborhoods don't mix well for women, son. No, not at all. Sometimes good folks get pushed into doing things that they would have never done if they didn't feel cornered or trapped. I'm talkin' about good people, son, the nicest people who are just dyin' to get by."

Mikey laid there staring up at all them teeth.

"Why, I heard that just yesterday, some poor lady got mugged right after she got off work." Mister Jones nodded, the honest-to-God truth. "She had her purse and her payroll check stolen, but that wasn't the half of it. Guess things went bad, son, things went real bad. They said the fool who mugged her was higher than a kite. He was on Angel Dust, but there wasn't nothin' heavenly about him 'cause he shot her dead. Shame too, the way she was beggin' and cryin' and carryin' on about how her son wasn't gonna be able to eat nothin'. Fact is, he shot her right in front of her son."

Rain beat on the bedroom window.

"He was just standing there all scared and everythin', holding on to his momma's coat while she begged and begged and begged and *bam!*" A long finger stretching down toward Mikey—finger gun. "There's only so much begging a man can take before it gets on his nerves. Anyway, that's gonna haunt that boy for the rest of his life. But things happen, Michael, happen all the time. Happen everywhere, on the streets, in parking lots, by alleys, right in broad daylight in front of a store. But you, you can watch out for your momma, can't you, son?" Mister Jones looked down at Mikey. "You can make sure that nothin' like that ever happens to her, can't you, *son?*"

His heart pounding, aching in his chest, Mikey nodded. "Yes, sir."

"That's my boy." Mister Jones smiled wide, the corners of his mouth splitting. "You can 'cause you're my son, or so your momma says. And my son can take care of himself and his family. My son can take care of his momma 'cause he knows what's best. You sure make me proud, *Michael*, you a man. Now tell me, what's for dinner 'cause I'm starvin', and your momma told you she was still at work."

"I'll, uh"—Mikey wet his lips—"I'll see what we have."

"He'll see what we have." Mister Jones clapped his hands and laughed out loud. "My boy will see what we have. And don't worry none 'cause if you need a few dollars to run to the store, I got it covered. After all"—Mister Jones pointed down at Mikey again with his finger gun—"it was payday yesterday."

The rain came cold. Margaret and Matt together, not minding the weather, not seeing the steam as it rose up from the manhole covers. They were warm together, smiles on their faces, walking the slow, lingering walk of a couple, arm in arm.

They passed by the movie house, Margaret saying that there was nothin' good, just wanting to talk, passing by Joe's and his once white coffee cups. Just the two of them wandering aimlessly—Margaret steering them toward the room above the gym.

"Am I keeping you up too late?" Matt looked up at the sky, but he couldn't see any stars through the clouds. "You got work tomorrow, don't you?"

"No, you're fine." Margaret clutched onto his arm. "Tell me, how come everything's got to be such a fight? Here we are havin' a good time and still I got to get up and go to work in the morning. I mean, it seems like that's all I do, day in, day out, the same damn thing every day. Get up, cook, clean, and then go to work and work all day on my feet, only to come home and get dinner ready, clean up and then go to bed. Just to do it all over again tomorrow. How come life's like that, Matt?"

Matt stopped and looked at her in a new light. "Is that what you do every day?"

"That...and worry about Mikey."

"Damn."

"That's life, Matt. Real life, I guess. The stories you always hear when you was a kid about livin' happily ever after, that's all they are, stories. Just stories and dreams." Margaret looked up at the sky—clouds and rain. "Tell me, what're your days like?"

Matt slowed down, his eyes running down the street—burned-out street lights. "I work, I train, you know?"

"That's it?"

"Well, I run the gym now too, train kids, do the books, clean the place, and I still work down at the warehouse unloading trucks..." Matt looked down at her. "You know, I never really thought of it like you do, like how you said, real life."

"Really?"

Matt nodded. "Really."

"Well, aren't there days that you just want to lie in bed and take it easy? Or maybe you just want to do somethin' different, you know, somethin' exciting?"

"When someone's trying to knock your head off, that's pretty exciting. It's like you said, every day's a fight. I'm a fighter, Margaret." Matt grinned. "I fight."

"Yeah, sure." She didn't hear him, not really. "But that's just boxing. I mean, you can't fight forever, right?"

Matt didn't realize it, but he leaned away. "Why do you say that?"

"'Cause it's hard, Matt. Really hard too 'cause it don't ever let up. Seems like things are always comin' at you from everywhere; work and Mikey and—" Margaret shut her mouth. "You ever feel like that? Like everything comin' at you at once?"

"All the time. Sometimes you're in a fight and you're just clutching onto the guy, holding on, trying to make it to the bell. Just live a minute more, so you can fight the next round." Matt was talking a mile a minute. "You never know what's gonna happen in the next round. Maybe the other guy's given it everything he's got and he don't got no more. By just holding on, just surviving, maybe that's enough to beat him, you know?"

"You think so?"

"I know so. I was fighting Martin a few years back and the man could punch. Hit harder than anybody I ever fought before. Third round comes and *bam*." Matt shook his head. "I thought he broke my jaw, thought I was going down too, but I wouldn't. I wasn't gonna go down no matter what."

Margaret looked away. "Really."

"See, there are different ways to fight. Some people think that fighters just use their fists, but they're wrong. A fighter uses his whole body, arms, legs, even our heads. Boxing ain't just about hitting or who hits harder, it's about"—Matt looked down the street, kids warming their hands over a fire in the garbage can—"it's about not giving up. Do you know what happened the next round?"

"You won."

"That's right, I knocked him out cold."

"I know." Margaret smiled up at the man. "I saw it."

"You did?"

"I watch all your fights, Matt."

"All of them?"

Margaret looked away, thanked God that Mikey watched all them damn things. "Every single one."

Matt stopped and looked down at her—beautiful. She could be so beautiful sometimes. "Thanks."

"But how do you do that, Matt? How do you win when it looks like you gonna lose everything?"

"Sometimes life works like that, the punch you take wins the fight."

They turned and walked, arm in arm. "I hear you, but that still don't answer my question. How come life's got to be such a fight?"

"It just is, Margaret. If any Joe off the street could waltz in and take the heavyweight title without really fighting for it, then it wouldn't mean much, would it?"

"No," Margaret huffed, "it sure wouldn't."

"I guess that's the answer then," Matt said, thinking that they were on the same page. "Maybe life is a lot like boxing. If you go down and don't get up, if you don't fight, how you ever gonna know if it was worth it? Maybe something good's gonna come your way, something that makes getting up out of bed everyday worth it."

"And if something good don't come your way?"

"Something good always comes."

"Always?"

"If you're lookin' for it."

"Are you lookin', Matt?" Margaret stopped, facing him now, stepping close. "Are you lookin' for it?"

"I am." Matt's breath streamed in front of his face. "Every day I am."

"So tell me, what do you see?"

"Something good."

Her eyes searched his. "How good?"

Matt stepped close, bodies touching, smoke in her clothes, "Margaret—"

"So what you gonna do, Matt? You gonna keep on clutching or are you gonna go for the knockout?"

Matt looked up at the sky—clouds. "What about Mikey?'"

"Matt, please, look at me." He did, Matt looked down at her, Margaret's eyes soft. She said, "I want you to know something. I'm fightin', Matt. I'm fightin' hard. I ain't ever gonna give up either, and I ain't ever gonna stop 'cause it's all worth it. Just like you said, Matt, life is a fight. I'm fightin' for you."

He wanted to kiss her, he wanted to turn and run too; Matt just wanted the whole damn world to come together.

Matt said, "You sure?"

"As sure as sure is." Margaret searched his face. "You?"

"Yes, ma'am."

"Don't call me ma'am," she said softly. "I ain't old."

"Yes, ma'am." Matt wrapped his arms around her, pulling her close. "Just one thing."

"Oh, yeah?" She breathed. "What's that?"

"What about the dishes?"

Margaret's head fell back, her eyes soft. "You can wash all the dishes you want as long as I get to dry."

Lips pressing together, rain falling in November, Matt and Margaret held each other for the first time. And Mister Jones, well, he was ten thousand steps away, staring down at something fine.

Mister Jones stood on the porch, staring down at a fine little thing: a young, pretty woman with a good body. A woman that made him smile—gold shining. Angie stood with a bag in her hand, an overnight bag, waiting for Margaret. Mister Jones said, "You're lookin' for Margaret, huh?"

"That's what I said."

"Yes"—Mister Jones nodded—"that is what you said. Said you'll wait too, didn't you now?"

"I also asked if Margaret is home."

"You did."

"Is she?"

"What's your name?"

"It don't matter what my name is." Angie bit, tired of the game they had been playing. "I asked if Margaret is home or not."

"That depends."

"On what?"

Mister Jones smiled. "On your name."

Angie huffed, her breath cold. "Angie," she said. "My name's Angie. Now, is Margaret home?"

"Angie." Jones looked up at the clouds, seeing the stars above and all of creation. "That's a nice name, a damn fine name for a woman like you. Fits you, you know. Tell me, Angie, what's a fine woman like you doing out so late, and all by yourself too? That ain't good in a neighborhood like this, you know."

"I'm out 'cause I'm here to see Margaret."

"That's right." Mister Jones nodded. "You here to see Margaret."

"Well?"

"Well what?"

"Well is she here or not?"

"Why don't you come in and look for yourself." Mister Jones stared down at her and Angie stepped back, bringing a deep laugh from the gold-mouthed man. He said, "Women, you all the same. How come that is? I mean, you're just like Margaret. I say something, she steps back just like you did there. I invited you in out of the cold, off the street, tell you that you look nice and everything, tell you your name was nice too, and what do you do? You give me that look. Margaret gives me that look too. Too bad, I thought we was getting along." Mister Jones shook his head. "What does that look mean, anyway? Since you're here and everything, maybe you could tell me what it means *exactly*."

"Nothing." Angie pulled at her coat, even though it was already zipped up. "It don't mean a thing."

"Nothing, huh?" Mister Jones smiled. "Well, it sure looks like it means somethin'. Oh well, I guess it's just one of those woman things. You know, all those secrets and all that. A woman has to have her secrets. Every woman does. So you gonna come in or stand out here all night? It's cold."

"Is Margaret home?"

Mister Jones looked back over his shoulder through the open door. "Tell you what, why don't you come on in and say hello. She'd be real happy to see you, Angie. Really happy. Maybe you could stay long enough to have a drink with us. Fact is, that'd be real nice to have a little company. Why don't you come in, take off that coat you're wearing, and have a warm drink. You like whiskey?"

"No."

"That's okay, there's plenty of other stuff. Got wine too, if you like wine. I bet you do. Besides, it'd be a damn shame to keep you out in the cold. Especially since you packed your bag." He stared down at Angie's overnight bag. "Tell me, Angie, why did you bring your bag with you, anyway? You got trouble? Maybe you need some help, some caring? You need my help, Angie?"

Angie moved her bag, hid it behind her legs, even though it was a ridiculous thing to do. She couldn't help it. She wanted to hide it—hide it from him. She said, "Look, I got manners, so I'm gonna ask you nicely one more time. Is Margaret home?"

"I tried." Mister Jones turned and leveled his eyes on her. "You asked, now what are you gonna do, huh?"

Angie turned and looked away. Looked up and down the street: no Margaret, no Matt—no one.

"Ask me nice." Mister Jones scoffed, mocking her. "Women, it's just like I said, you all alike. What? You think I'm just gonna crumble 'cause you think you're somethin'? You think you're tough? And to think I invited you into my home all nice and everything, even offered you a drink."

"Why don't you just get the hell out?" Angie bit, feeling her blood boiling. "It ain't your home, you weren't invited, and nobody wants you there either, so why don't you just leave?"

"Tell me something, Angie"—Mister Jones slid a toothpick into his mouth—"did Margaret put that into your head or something? Did she tell you that no one wants me here?"

Angie swallowed. *Stupid,* she thought, *that was just stupid. To lose my temper, to put it all out there—got to be smart.* "No. She didn't say nothing, but it don't take much to see what's going on around—"

"That's good," Mister Jones interrupted, "'cause I hate to hear a woman talking about her man, about her *husband* in a bad way, you know. It'd be real bad if that happened, Angie, real bad if you know what I mean. But you do know what I mean, don't you?"

Angie looked away.

"*I said, don't you?*"

Angie turned and looked up at him. "I ain't scared of you."

"I ain't scared of me neither." Mister Jones laughed. "Ain't that something, us not afraid of me! That's what you'd call havin' things in common, Angie. You and me, we on common ground, you know."

"I'm gonna call the cops."

"Go ahead, Angie dear, it's my home, my wife, my son. They ain't gonna do a damn thing. Fact is, nobody will, not even Margaret. But she's real happy, you know? Can't you tell? She got things going on that make her all glowin' and everything. She got somethin' on the burner. In fact, just the other day she told me how happy she was that I took her back. You know, a son needs a father, Angie, Michael needs a role model. But it's good to know that you care so much, thank you. And I mean that. You've got to have friends that watch your back. Yessiree, you sure do. It's good to have a family friend like you. Why don't you come on in, say hello to the family and have a drink, warm yourself up. What do ya say, honey?"

"I said to go away. That's what I say," Angie said. "I will call the cops."

Mister Jones just shook his head. "Look around you, honey, this ain't no fancy neighborhood. There ain't no money here. Cops don't care about people like me or you. The city don't care about us either. Now you tell me, just how long do you think it will take the police to get here after you call them? Maybe ten, fifteen, twenty minutes, honey?"

Angie looked down the street. "I don't know."

"You don't know." Mister Jones snorted.

"I said I don't know!"

"You think that in twenty minutes they gonna come rolling in here with their lights flashing and their sirens screaming, don't you? I'll let you in on a little secret." Mister Jones leaned down, resting his arms on the old porch railing. "If they come, and I said *if,* honey, they wouldn't be here for at least an hour. Maybe if you were lucky and they didn't have nothing else *and* they felt like it, maybe forty-five minutes. Do you know what can happen in forty-five minutes? Let me tell you: every and any thing." Mister Jones smiled, gold teeth shining. "Everything you can think of can happen in forty-five minutes and a few things you've never ever dreamed of. Did you know that I have the most crazy dreams? Fact is, if one of those head doctors ever got a hold of me"—Mister Jones shook his head—"damn, they'd lock me up straight. But I'd never tell anyone about my dreams unless I was sure they wasn't gonna say a word. Sure they'd never whisper a thing. You know what I mean?"

"I'll call 'em." Angie's voice was weak. "They'll come."

"Call 'em. Have 'em meet you here, have 'em take me away if they will. Maybe they will, but they won't hold me, honey. Sure, maybe they'll lock me up overnight, tell me to 'cool off' and everything and I'll say sure. But in the morning, they'll just let me go. Me, Mister Crazy Dreams, free on the street and hungry 'cause jail food ain't nothing to write home about. Let me tell you, I know. As soon as you see the light of day, your stomach starts to growl for something sweet and you got to feed it. Feed it good."

Mister Jones stared down at her, Angie looked away, trying to stand, willing her legs, her knees not to buckle. *Please, God, help me,* she prayed, *help me.* The rain starting now, falling cold across the city.

"Now you is talkin' my language." Mister Jones looked up at the sky—pink clouds hung low. "It should snow in November, you know? Look, why don't you just come on in? Be terrible if you caught cold and everythin'. Think I got something to warm you up."

"Thank you, no."

"Can't blame a man for tryin'." Mister Jones shrugged. "Especially when somethin' so fine is standing right in front of him. But I'd appreciate it if you didn't say nothing to Margaret. She's the jealous type, you know."

"You just think you're it, don't you?" The rain falling harder now, coming in great drops; Mister Jones still smiling, Angie's voice weak, trembling. "There's always a bigger dog, one that's meaner with a worse bite. You know you're gonna get bit, don't you?"

"Maybe"—Mister Jones nodded—"maybe, but if I do, it ain't gonna be by you. It ain't gonna be by Margaret either. But you just go ahead and try it if you want to. If you need to, that is."

"Maybe I will."

"Damn, I do love me a spirited woman. You know, Margaret used to be like you." Mister Jones looked off as if he was seeing Margaret so many years ago. "She was such a fine-looking woman. I had to have her. She was all young and full of fire. But things die, Angie, fire can go out real quick with a little rain. Let me tell you, I know all about the rain. But you're young and you don't know nothin' yet. Somethin' gets ugly on a woman when her fire is put out. Don't know why, it just does. Still, you don't need to stand out in the cold and get all wet." Mister Jones smiled. "Why don't you come in and we'll work on keeping your fire warm?"

"You're crazy."

"Now you seein' me right."

"Maybe I'll go get my husband."

"You ain't married." Mister Jones motioned to her hand. "You ain't wearing no ring."

"Maybe I just don't wear one."

"Oh no, you're the type of woman who would wear one. In fact, if you gettin' robbed or mugged or somethin,' I bet you wouldn't give it up. You'd probably get shot over it, wouldn't you?"

Angie couldn't see his eyes.

"Look, Angie, I don't know how we've gotten off to a start like this, but I feel real bad about it. I like you and the Good Lord knows I don't want to argue with my wife's friends or anything like that. You're a fine woman, any fool can see that by just lookin' at you, so why don't we just put this all behind us," Mister Jones said, playing with his toothpick. "You ain't got no husband, no man, and you're lonely. So am I. I like you and that's something big in your favor. Come on in, honey, I'll take good care of you."

She wanted to run, turn and run and get away. Far, far away from Mister Jones. She looked up and down the street—still no Margaret. "I'm sorry. I'm just Margaret's friend, that's all."

"You just lookin' out for her, aren't you?"

"I don't want to see her get hurt or anything like that. And you. . ." Angie tried to look up at him. "You're just lookin' out for yours."

"Now you're thinking."

"Like I said, I'm sorry. Tell Margaret I stopped by."

"No need to say you're sorry, glad you did though." Mister Jones leaned back from the rail and looked inside that little apartment. "Say, why don't you come on in, it's warm and we can wait for her together. You know, to make sure everything's all right."

"No, not tonight, it's late and I got to get home." Angie picked up her bag and backed away. "Maybe some other time."

"Well, you get to choose."

"Sorry, not tonight, thank you."

"Tell you what, why don't I walk you home. Like I said, this here is a tough neighborhood."

"No!" She blurted, immediately regretting it. "I mean, thanks, but no. No need to get all wet because of me."

"It'd be no trouble at all." A mouthful of gold. "I wouldn't mind getting wet for you."

# EIGHT

Smiling and walking, feeling safe because all the pimps, the druggies and the lowlifes were out of the rain. The streets were empty. No fires in trash cans, no singing on street corners, no harmonicas, no kids out running, ignoring the calls of their mothers. Tonight, in the city, Margaret was alone—just alone. She stopped at the corner.

It was one of those nice corners, one of the few still left in this part of the city, with bricks and concrete that wasn't crumbling under her feet. Margaret looked up at the sky—pink. A sky, blushing like her, rain falling, wetting her face. It was beautiful, she thought, just beautiful. Even the city tonight, the lights, the rain's making everything clean. Life was good, she thought, damn good. For the first time in a long time, Margaret imagined the future.

She was standing in her kitchen, Matt was washing dishes, she was drying, stretching, reaching up past him, putting plates up high in the cupboard, brushing against him. Brushing against him and smiling, him smiling too, him trying to ignore her, Margaret still pushing in. Oh, was she ever pushing in. Reaching around him, bumping him, feeling that broad back of his, that strong back—a man's back with wide shoulders. And then they'd lie down in their bed. Sure, there'd be nights where they wrapped themselves up in their sheets, rolled around, trying to keep quiet because Mikey was in the next room. But not this night, not this one in her mind.

Tonight she was lying next to him, Matt snoring a little, staring at the window—the cracked window—listening to the sound of the city, the sirens, the hoods and the pimps and their strung-out girls, watching the cold stream in, keeping warm under the covers, touching Matt's skin. *Oh, God*, Margaret prayed, *I hope it's that way. I hope it's always that way: dishes, Matt and our bed, and let Mikey be okay with everything. Please, God, please.* Margaret stepped out from the corner and onto the street.

There were two working streetlights, two that lit the entire city block—an alley somewhere hidden in the middle. She walked by the alley's open mouth, never seeing the two men halfway down, standing by the dumpster, shaking hands, handing something off, hurrying back inside out of the rain. Neither man seeing the beautiful woman that passed by.

She had been walking aimlessly but always headed back toward the gym, passing it by now, looking up at the big window that opened to Matt's room. She stopped, leaning against a burned-out streetlight, hiding behind it, staring up at the green glass—the mosaic that was never meant to be—feeling like a kid, a teenage girl.

He was in there, she thought, lying in bed, sleeping, or maybe he wasn't. Maybe he was just lying there, staring at the ceiling thinking of the night, thinking of her—maybe he was—she was hoping he was. Hoping he liked her just as much as she liked him. Hoping that a good man, twenty-eight, could love a woman thirty-three and seventeen. She was scared, hoping he wouldn't get scared too, that he wouldn't run off or turn his back and pretend nothin' happened. Hoping that he could accept an older woman with baggage. A woman with a son and a—

"Husband."

The word turned to ice in front of her face. A woman with a son, a husband, with a Mister Jones. But there was time. Time because Margaret had asked Matt for a little tonight, telling him that she needed to make things right at home with Mikey. Just a lie, a little white thing that came after their last kiss. Something sealed with red lipstick.

After all, a woman's gotta have options.

For the first time in a long time, maybe even for the first time in his life, Matt wasn't afraid. It didn't matter anymore that he was just a six, didn't matter that he was getting old either, didn't matter if he never did climb that mountain, because the mountain had come to Matt. For once in his life, everything was coming together, or so it seemed.

He could dance, he could stand in front of that heavy bag and let his punches fly, and it didn't matter if they weren't perfect because he had Margaret. No more forcing it, no more pushing, just going with the flow. And tonight as Matt stood in the darkened gym, boxing gloves on his hands, that flow seemed almost easy.

He felt damn good when Margaret pressed her body against his, felt good when their lips touched. In that moment, there was only him and her, their bodies, their lips, the falling rain. Matt wasn't thinking about getting up in the morning and running, wasn't thinking about training the day away, he wasn't pinning all his hopes on something for tomorrow, something that he didn't have; there was just today. Just holding Margaret, just kissing her, just standing in the rain and letting it fall. It was just a feeling, but a feeling that Matt wanted to hold on to, maybe for the rest of his life.

Matt stood, staring at that bag: would life be worth it? *Even if I ain't the champ, even if I spend my whole life here in the gym training kids, training other fighters? I got my prize at home. Is this what Leonard had? Is this what people do? Is this what I'm supposed to do?*

*Get a fine woman with a smile that makes me smile in good times in a poor apartment and nothing else matters. Just me and her, us talkin', us lovin', just us being together every day for the rest of our lives. I can box, I can train, I can work here with Art—the man's almost like a father—work happy every day of my life being around the thing I love, going home at night to the woman I could love. Me and Margaret, Art coming over now and then, having meatloaf, washing dishes, and smoke.*

Matt hit the bag, not thinking, just throwing a punch, absolutely nothin'. *It's already like we all family, even Mikey. Don't think he'll mind a bit, don't think things will change between us 'cause I'll listen to him, I'll talk to him, I won't do what my father did.* Matt threw another punch.

He could see his old man sitting out on the fire escape, sitting five stories above the world, looking down that alley like he was the king of it all, drinking bottle after bottle, dropping them into the alley below. Day after day after day. No words between them, nothin' but shattered glass. And Mom, all she did was sit on that couch all day, reading book after book, romances, living a life inside her head. Me and Margaret, we ain't gonna be like that. It's gonna be better—better than what my parents had.

*Me and Mikey getting up early to train, running till the sun's up, training together, us talking like we do now. No, nothing's gonna change except I'll be sharing a bed.* Matt nodded to himself, danced on his toes in front of the heavy bag—just sharing a bed.

He threw a left.

It was just a jab, a hard punch, but Matt paid it no attention. *Gonna be warm at night, gonna feel her body next to mine, sleep naked every night, make dinner together, do the shopping together too, wash all them dishes.* Matt was letting his punches go, just going with the flow. *Gonna give that woman the world.*

*Birthdays and Christmas and Valentine's Day, gonna make her feel real special.* Matt smiling, moving good, hitting that bag hard— damn hard—paying it no attention, just taking his feelings out on the bag. *And maybe one day we'll buy a house. A house with a yard. And then we could barbeque and sit out on the porch and pass the day away.* He threw it, that hook, the one-that-only-comes-sometimes punch.

It hit the bag, snapping it good, snapping it almost in half, but Matt never saw it. He was still in his head. Just lost in his thoughts as he threw it again, the same hook, the same result except it was stronger, harder. Matt threw it again and again.

*Don't matter if I'm the champ 'cause I got something better. I got someone who loves me, someone who'll take care of me, someone I can love. And she'll stand by me, she'll think I'm the greatest—she's seen all my fights. And when I hang up my gloves, she'll tell everybody that I was the best damn fighter she's ever seen. And that's all that matters.*

Matt moved, down and to the left, coming up hard, throwing that punch, that hook that split the heavy bag clean. He stood, staring at the bag, realizing just now what he had done: the bag bleeding, stuffing coming out, falling to the floor, sawdust too— an old-time bag.

*I did it!*

*Every one of them punches, perfect. Gut shaking, rib-breaking punches, that hook that took Joseph's chin clean. I just threw it. Threw all of them one after another. Didn't think about it, just did it, just went with the flow.* And Matt laughed.

Laughed loud and long. Laughed so hard that all them champs hanging around that ring, hanging high in the rafters, in the shadows, all looked down. He danced over to the other heavy bag and let that punch go. It snapped just like a man's neck would, that metal chain that held that bag, snapped just like Joseph's jaw.

Margaret was soaked, but she didn't mind a bit. She opened her door, stepped inside, and fastened all the locks behind her. "You home, huh?" It was only his voice, just floating down the hall, and him breathing down her neck. "That's what I call workin' late. So how was work, Margaret? Fullfillin'?" Mr. Jones said.

"I took a walk."

He was standing behind her, just a shadow. "In the rain?"

"Just needed to clear my mind."

"What of?"

She turned, Lord knows why, and stared up at the tall, thin man and his mouth of gold. "You know"—she swallowed—"Mikey and everything."

"Oh sure." Mister Jones nodded, his head snapping back and forth like a rag doll's, "Mikey and everything. You got it cleared, Margaret? All cleared out?"

"I did."

"Well, that's good, real good too, 'cause sometimes, things get up in a woman's head. Things that shouldn't be there, you know." Mister Jones leaned down and whispered, "Things that you just can't get rid of, you know? I'm talkin' about voices, Margaret. You got voices in that pretty head of yours?"

"No."

"Well, that's good 'cause I do. Boy, do they ever talk! On and on and on, I can't get them ever to shut up no matter how many times I tell them to go to hell. And let me tell you, them voices say the damnedest things, always tellin' me to do this or that. Things no good person ought to be doin'. Fact is, they was tellin' me to do all sorts of things tonight when that friend of yours showed up here."

"What friend?"

"Angie." Mister Jones smiled. "She was the sweetest thing. You know, she's a good friend. Cares about you an awful lot. Can't have no friend better than a woman like that."

"Roy"—she felt cold, everywhere—"what did you do?"

He smiled. "What's wrong, Margaret? You gone all white on me like you've seen a ghost or somethin'."

"Please, Roy. Tell me you were good to her."

"'Course I was, Margaret." Mister Jones put his hand on his heart. "Hell, you know me. That poor thing was all alone, standing on the steps of her friend's apartment, her friend who had completely forgotten about her 'cause she needed to clear her head, rain falling, no umbrella, mind you. And so I walked that poor girl straight home and put her to bed. Wished her goodnight and everything. I'm tellin' you, Margaret, is she ever sweet."

"Roy"—Margaret swallowed—"what did you do?"

"That's twice you asked me that tonight, Margaret. What, you think I was unfaithful to you?"

"Please, Roy, not tonight. Just tell me she's all right."

"Oh"—the corners of his mouth split—"she's more than all right. She even thanked me, Margaret. You know, it almost sounded like begging. But I helped her, Margaret, I really did. Just like you, I cleared her mind right out."

She couldn't move, couldn't take her eyes off him. "You didn't, did you?"

"Ain't that sweet, you is all jealous and everything. Now, Margaret, you ain't got nothing to worry about. Yes, I must admit, and only because I believe there should be honesty in our thingy here, that your friend has feelings for me. Strong feelings too. But you have my word, I won't do nothin'."

"You promise me, Roy?"

"I promise that I won't do nothin' that you wouldn't do." Mister Jones crossed his heart, if there ever was such a thing. "Unless I have good cause."

"Good cause, Roy?"

"I'm talkin' about needs, Margaret. As long as there's a need, you can count on me. Know what I'm sayin'? Or do I need to spell it out? I can see by the way you lookin' at me that you need a little clar-i-fi-cation. You know that word, Margaret, clarification?"

"I know it."

"'Course you do. Anyway, as long as we are clear with each other and what I need and expect from you, we ain't gonna have no problems at all. I know we won't either 'cause we got a deep understanding between us. I mean, really, it's kind of scary if you think about it. Why, you know me better than anyone almost and that makes one of them unbreakable bonds. You know the types of bonds I'm talkin' about, strong bonds. The type of bonds that shatter when they're broken. The type that go ballistic and take everything out around them. That's us, Margaret, you and me—a damn, strong bond unbreakable and ballistic. Beautiful, ain't it?"

"Yeah, Roy." Margaret stepped away, her back against the door. "Beautiful."

"Now, I did promise to stop in and check on Angie every now and then, on account of her being all alone and everything. You know how that goes, right? Just a visit to make sure everything fine with her, make sure she don't need nothin', maybe have another drink with her. But like I said, we all clear on us, right?"

"Of course. Thank you, Roy."

"It ain't nothin'. For you, Margaret, I'd walk on the moon just like that Armstrong man, only I'd never dirty my feet. Fact is, I'd float right across the moon and stick a flag right into its dead gray skin just for you and all the world to see."

"I know you would, Roy." Margaret almost smiled. "I'm sorry, Roy, I should have been here earlier. Should've had dinner ready for you."

"Now don't you worry about tonight. Michael made me dinner. Took care of the dishes too, so there ain't no mess for you to clean up. Good kid, that boy. Hell of a kid. Makes me proud. And don't you worry about him neither, Margaret. Why, when you got to work late and maybe walk and clear that pretty head of yours, I'll watch him close, real close."

"You'll be good for him."

"'Course I will. I had my doubts, you know? But now I can see that we all are gonna be family or somethin'. Ain't that nice? And after all these years. I guess they're right, whoever they are, some things never do change. Some things like you."

Tears filled Margaret's eyes.

"Now look at you, all touched and everything. I could just hug you, wrap my arms around you and squeeze 'cause you let me in. After all these years, fifteen long years, you let me in. Damn, I could just celebrate. In fact, we should have a big dinner, invite all of our closest friends. A dinner celebrating life, seeing what the cat dragged in, seeing all them faces, and them jaws that is gonna drop. Sounds nice, don't it?"

"Yes, Roy." Margaret stepped into him and wrapped her arms around that man. "That sounds nice, real nice. Thank you," she breathed, "thank you for everything."

And he laughed.

Laughed real hard as Margaret tucked into him, laying her head against his chest, listening, listening to nothing. "Of course, Margaret. I always got something for you."

"Okay, kid, here we go, huh? Another day, another dollar." Art looked at the heavy bag. "Who put up the new bag, you?"

"Yeah." Eyes looking down, looking away from Art, Matt tried to hide his excitement. "The other one just fell apart."

"Damn! Them things cost money." Art rubbed his old head. "How was your run this morning?"

"Good."

"You warmed up?"

"Yeah."

"Good, kid, good." Art turned to the bench by the heavy bag and sat down slowly, using his hand to help himself down. "What do you want to work on today?"

Matt wanted to say it, wanted to show off that newfound hook of his. "Whatever you thinks best, Art. Just say the word," he said.

"How come all my fighters ain't like you?" Art smiled. "Okay then, let's work hard, real hard 'cause we gotta get you cookin'. Truth is, I've been thinkin' about you a lot lately, kid. You've always been quick, you got good feet too, but let's see if we can't get another step or two. You know, make 'em sweet. Real sweet."

"Sounds good."

"Quick combinations, don't matter what you throw, just work on hittin' that bag fast, movin' them feet of yours, and then hittin' that bag again. Don't want to see no thinkin', no stutter steps, just hit and move, hit and move, got it?"

"Hit and move." Matt smacked his gloves together. "Got it."

"All right, let's go."

Matt moved, first to right, letting three jabs go, two lefts, one right, moving to the left on his toes. He was feeling good, not thinking a bit, just moving, letting his feet move him, just going with the flow.

"That a kid." Art clapped his hands. "You're moving good. Try and step it up."

And Matt did, three lightning quick punches with pop, but he didn't throw that hook. Not yet. He was saving it, just getting warmed up, just starting to feel that sweat bead up on his body. He was just gonna let it come when it wanted to.

"I'll be! That's a step-up if I've ever seen one. Let's go for two, Matt. Two steps and you'll be dancing."

He was halfway there, one step down, two on its way, Matt's mind not even thinking, no words in his head. Just punching, moving, feet so sweet, he didn't even know it when he threw that first hook. It was the hardest hook Art had ever seen.

And he saw it good.

Saw Matt's body, saw how it dug in, how it coiled like a spring and snapped. Snapped so damn hard that the bag doubled in two. And before the old trainer knew it, Matt had moved. His feet dancing, adjusting to that bag, throwing another combination, a jab followed by two more of them right hooks. One right after the other, two in a row, two hooks that nearly broke that bag.

And the old man stood.

That bag whirled, it spun on its chain, and it didn't matter a bit because Matt had already moved; already adjusted to the damn thing. This time there was no jab, just a hook. The bag bent, the middle split, and the sound that came was a shot—a shot heard around the world. The whole damn gym stopped and looked.

Every eye of every fighter was fixed solely on Matt. He moved, quick on his feet, finding that other step that made the whole world spin. Art couldn't believe what he was seeing, but he didn't have long to think. A streak, a flash, the glimpse of a shadow moving so quick that it was nothing short of a jolt. The bag broke in half.

It was an explosion: stuffing and sawdust filled the air, the metal chain groaned as it snapped, and the bag fell like a ton of bricks. Behind it all, standing tall, Matt smiled for the whole world to come and see. And they saw, mouths wide, jaws dropped, pain in their guts from the force of the blow. No one, not Art, not Leonard, not a damn soul said a thing. They all stood in wonder until finally—

"Holy—"

"Amen." Art nodded, his mouth still hung open, and the old man stared at the fighter in front of him. He had never seen such a man. "Listen to me, Matt, listen real good. If you can do what I just saw you do in the ring"—the old trainer shook his head, he was almost manic, his old feet wanted to move, pace, dance—"I think...I think I can get you a shot. I think I could maybe even get you a fight with a top-ranked contender if you show a few folks what you just showed me there."

Matt's eyes lit like Christmas morning. "You serious?"

Art stared at the bag, "You just keep on doing what you just did and don't worry about breakin' no bags or anything. In fact, break as many of the damn things you want to, you just keep on doin' whatever it was you was doin' right there, okay?"

Matt smiled wide. "Okay."

"Would somebody get their butt in gear and hang up another damn bag!" Art barked.

And the whole gym broke.

Only God knew how long Art had sat in that chair behind the old metal desk in his office, but the sun had set hours ago. Art stared out his office door across the darkened gym at the heavy bag. It was a new bag, at least it had been this morning, but now it was nothing more than a mangled mess from a forgotten war—Matthew Gore.

There was a phone in front of the old trainer, a black thing with numbers and a dial, a thing that seemed to weigh a hundred pounds on most days to Art, but not today. Not after what Art had seen. And Lord, had he ever seen it. With his own two eyes, and felt it too as if he had been the thing standing across from his fighter. Just one of them hooks would drop any man: Joseph, Douglas, even the Dancing Man from Detroit—a straw house. But that was today.

*Just today.* The old trainer looked down at the phone. *Today the kid could have won him that belt. He could have stepped in the ring and knocked his way to the top and nobody could have stood in his way. Nobody! But what about tomorrow?*

*Can the kid throw that shot tomorrow? Can he move those feet sweet just like he did today? Can he make me stand up like I was a kid again, forgetting my old bones, forgetting the aches and pains, forgetting that when it's all said and done, I'm gonna go home tonight and sit in that same old chair and stare at that damn black and white until the snow flies on its screen—tomorrow?*

*'Cause if he can't, cause if I put in that call, if I pull every favor that's owed me and I get him a shot and he just can't do what I saw*

*him do today, it's over for the kid. Done and over—just plain dead. He won't even be a six no more. Maybe the best thing for him would be a tomato can.*

*A no-good fighter who's gonna fall quick. Just a confidence builder for Matt so I can make sure that what I saw today wasn't no fluke. And if he can do it in the ring, if he can knock some poor fool's head off his shoulders, then I'll say it was a showcase. I'll say it was an exhibition for all the world to see. Just a call out to the Dancing Man from Detroit: come and get it good.*

*And me? Well, there won't be no worry for me 'cause I'll have me another champ. Another kid I took to the top, another banner to hang up above that ring. And I'll put Matt right next to me. Even if he ain't gonna be my partner here in the gym, even if he don't move in with me 'cause I'm all alone, I'll still have me another champ who's like my own son.*

*A son who ups and leaves when the going gets good. I saw it, with my own two eyes, saw how those hooks of his got stronger, faster. Not seven out of ten, not nine neither, but every one of them hooks was a masterpiece. And those feet, just sweet. Ginger Rogers would have melted at his touch. After this, there ain't gonna be no him and me; no father, no son.*

*He's gonna have women lining up at his door, friends coming out of the woodwork, friends he ain't ever met before. People that gonna pat his back with one hand while reaching in his pocket with the other. And me, this old place, he gonna forget all about it. Sure, he'll train, he'll still smile at me, but that room up there is gonna be empty, a damn shame.*

*All we gonna be is a trainer and his fighter. Boxing,* Art looked at the ring, *that's all I am. My whole life has been spent in the gym. Just boxing, that's me. No wife, no kids, just that beautiful Garden at Madison where a man could have anything. Anything as long as I was on top. And that ride, that room with a view above it all, it felt like it was just an overnight stop. Just another train rolling into another station—fight what's in front of you, get back on and ride until it stops again. Some of them stops was nice, some was downright scary, but at least they all took me somewhere; not like this old place. No, there's only one stop coming, one stop left: dirt and six feet under.*

*God, why does it have to be so? Why can't it be like it was at the Garden? Why can't it be like New Orleans where everything and nothing happened at once? Why couldn't I have that little place by the Quarter where Betty waited for me every night? How come I had to be so stupid and leave something like that for the Garden? God, why didn't you tell me?* Art laid his head on the old metal desk. *How come the end comes so slow? How come it's so quiet?*

*Why not just let us go when we want to go? I'm tired, real tired, so how come I got to live so long. Please, God, let me sleep, let me dream of my Betty, let me wake up in New Orleans.*

He slept, that phone sitting in front of him, the old man's chest rising and falling, tears on paper thin skin.

# NINE

There's always a back door. Sometimes it's as plain as day, just like a nose on a man's face, broad daylight and everything. And sometimes that door hides in the dark behind pallets and boxes full of groceries. But it's always the same, that door, tall and rectangular, dented for sure, a doorknob with dirt around it, and a crack at the bottom that never really lets in the light. Of course, Margaret knew where that door was.

She had opened it not ten minutes ago and stepped out into the alley behind the grocery store. She was on her second cigarette. But don't take that wrong 'cause Margaret wasn't in the need, her hand wasn't shaking when she first lit up, didn't shake a bit as she pulled that smoke inside of her and felt its mellow cool. No, she was just smokin'. That was all it was.

She was just on break after four hours on her feet. Margaret didn't sit down, didn't squat down in that alley either, didn't lean against that cinder block wall. She just stood with one arm crossed under her breasts, holding up the other—cigarette. But if she had leaned against that wall, she would have seen that shadow that crept up on her. Oh, it didn't grab her, didn't pull her down that alley and take advantage of that fine thing; it just stood back and watched the world unfold around her. Margaret never saw that glint of gold behind her. There was only the smoke in front of her face, the deep mellow feeling of nicotine, those clouds that stared down on her. She didn't even turn as that door opened behind her. It was Angie, of course.

She stood by Margaret, hands in her pockets, wearing a coat that was zipped up to her neck. Zipped up high and tight, so high that there wasn't no exposing that body underneath, not even a hint of that long neck. There was no skin there to bite. Margaret stuck that unfiltered cigarette in her mouth and sucked. Angie said, "Margaret."

If someone had been watching, they would have sworn that Margaret hadn't even noticed the woman. "Angie, I didn't even see you."

"Didn't mean to startle you."

"Oh, that's all right. I was just thinkin', you know?"

"Sure do, been thinkin' a lot lately too. So where were you the other night?"

Margaret lifted that cigarette to her mouth and sucked. And the funny thing about that, her hand shook a bit. "I'm so sorry, Angie." Margaret blew that smoke. "I tried to call you, but Matt just kept on walkin'."

"Uh-huh."

Honestly, there were tears in her eyes. "I tried to find an excuse so I could get away, but all he did was go on and on about boxin' and everything. We didn't even go to the show. Just him walkin' and talkin', that's all."

"All night?"

"In the rain." Pain in Margaret's eyes. "You know, for once in my life I thought that things were gonna work out. That maybe it was all gonna be different, you know? But it seems like things is always gonna be like they is. Ain't nothin' ever gonna change. Just gonna be me and you, honey, here at this old grocery store." She smiled at Angie. "I'm glad you'll be here."

Angie stood for a moment as if considering. But being the woman she was, being a friend—and a good one at that—Angie just let it go. "So, what happened?" she said.

"Oh, Angie"—Margaret put her hand across her face—"I don't know."

"What, Margaret?" Angie's arm now around her friend. "What's wrong?"

As that hand of Margaret's fell from her face, somehow that woman's eyes seemed to be desperate. "I don't know what I'm gonna do. You ever felt that way, Angie?"

"Plenty of times, sister."

"And what did you do?"

"Well"—Angie stared at the ground—"I just did what I thought was best."

"And?"

"And what?"

"What happened? Did it all work out?"

"Sometimes it did."

"But not always, right?"

"Margaret, what you talkin' about?"

"I don't know where to start."

"Start with Matt, what happened? You gonna see him again?"

Margaret dropped her cigarette and crushed it under her foot. "Well, like I said, we walked a lot and talked too, but other than that, it was rainin'. He was a gentleman, of course."

"Well, that's good. He respects you."

"Or maybe I'm just a 'friend' type to him. I don't want to be his friend, Angie. But what else can I be if Mister Jones is at home? I mean I am married and everything, but I ain't happy. Can't remember the last time I was happy either."

"Matt know about Mister Jones?"

"Hell, no!"

"You gonna tell him?"

"Don't know."

"You don't know what, if you gonna tell him or if you like him enough to tell him? You like Matt like that, Margaret?"

It was like the sun rising up from the ocean, shining on all them waves—sparkling. "I do. All I could think about was how much I wanted him to kiss me, but…"

"But what?"

"Mikey, Angie. What about Mikey?"

"Mikey's seventeen, Margaret."

"He's still my boy."

"Not at seventeen, he ain't."

"With Mister Jones at home, he is. You know how he is."

"I know. He walked me home, remember?"

"He didn't hurt you, did he? 'Cause if he did I'll take a gun and—"

"No, he didn't." Angie shook that pretty head of hers. "Fact was, he was a gentleman. Held an umbrella for me. Got me something warm to drink too, since I was out in the cold and the rain so long."

"Oh, Angie, I'm so sorry. I know how he can be."

"We talkin' you here, Margaret," Angie exhaled. "Not me. Now tell me, you said that all you could think about was kissing Matt. Did you kiss him?"

Margaret smiling, the sun shining again. "He kissed me."

"And?"

"And what?"

Angie rolled her eyes. "How was it?"

"You can't imagine how good it was."

"Anything else happen?"

"That's all, he just kissed me." Margaret's head fell. "And then he seemed to get scared 'cause he starting talkin' about Mikey. I tried to tell him that everything would be okay, that Mikey was a man now, but Matt said he needed some time."

"Did he ask to see you again?"

"Maybe it's for the best, Angie. I mean, if he would have asked me to go home with him, I would have. I would have stayed with him too if he had wanted me to."

"Look, Margaret, you gonna have to do somethin' soon. If you don't, you gonna lose Matt. You either got to choose him or that Mister Jones of yours."

"But he's just a boxer, Angie. What's he gonna do when he's all washed up? Men like that, they gonna be poor their whole life."

Bless her, she just looked at Margaret. "So what, we already poor."

"I ain't sayin' that, Angie. What I'm sayin' is that all he could talk about doin' was boxing. Just boxing, every day of his life. Mister Jones is like that too. He just does what he wants to do, you know. Come and go, that's why we had problems."

"You in a fix." It was a smile, Angie feeling sympathetic for her friend. "I see now why you been actin' so funny, but you gonna have to do somethin', Margaret. And like I told you the other night, the sooner the better. Can't keep two fish on a pole."

Margaret nodded. "I know."

"Well, I'm sorry for you. If you need somethin', I'm here for you."

"Oh, honey." Margaret turned and hugged Angie. "Thank you. I appreciate you so much. You like a sister to me, Angie."

"You're welcome." Two woman hugging, holding in an alley, gold glinting behind them. "Look, I better get back in, but you take as long as you need. I'll cover for you," Angie said.

"Thank you."

And she left, that fine little thing, walking back in that backdoor as Margaret stuck another cigarette in her mouth. She lit it, the tremble gone in her hand, Margaret sucking in, feeling that mellow deep down inside—

Blowing smoke.

# TEN

Leonard sat alone in front of the television set; it was Thanksgiving Day. There was no turkey in the oven, no potatoes boiling on the stove, no stuffing, no pecan or pumpkin pie either. There was just that television set, just the Detroit Lions playing the Denver Broncos in Tiger Stadium, just Leonard sitting in that love seat alone.

The wallpaper was old, hanging downtrodden in the corners, and the whole place was just the same. The loveseat, the end table and her mother's lamp, the pictures on the wall, the ones that Leonard couldn't look at anymore, they were just where she had left them, even their bed.

They had made their bed together that morning before she passed, Leonard on one side, Jackie on the other, them talking about nothing in particular, just plans for the day. And since that day, Leonard had never unmade that bed, never slept on it either. Instead he slept on the floor on Jackie's side. No pad under his body, just a blanket that he pulled up around his shoulders, a wool blanket that never did cover his feet.

And in the mornings, mornings just like this one, Leonard would walk from that room and close the door behind him. Shut that bed away until the dark came, until he couldn't see where she had lain. Snow on the screen, flurries in Tiger Stadium, the Lions losing again; Leonard breathed in.

He thought about getting up, getting out of that place, grabbing his coat, heading out that door and taking a walk. And even though Leonard told himself he was going to do just that, he never did get up. Reaching out, he touched her place, put his hand just were her leg would have been as the pictures on the walls stared at him. Somewhere high up in those gray clouds, a jet engine rumbled by.

Maybe that's why Leonard didn't hear the knock at his door, but he heard it the second time it came. He sat there, staring at the door as another knock came. It was louder, maybe a voice coming with it. Maybe it was the announcer on the television set. But Leonard got up and walked to that door. He didn't bother to ask who it was, didn't matter who was behind that door good or bad. The fact was, Leonard just didn't care.

A lock, a bolt, the chain undone, and Leonard opened the door. It was Matt, Art too, both of them holding boxes. Leonard smelling something good. "What you two doin' here?" he said. "You get better reception." Matt walked in, Art right behind as Leonard stood at that door watching them.

"Where's the fridge?" Art asked.

Leonard shook his head. "You know where the fridge is."

"Who's winning?"

"Matt, please." Leonard stood, the door still open behind him. "I see what you're doing, both of you, and any other day—"

"Leonard."

"Just let me finish. Any other day I'd be—"

"Leonard"—Matt smiled—"family is supposed to be together on Thanksgiving. Sorry we is late, but we're here now."

Old Forty Two stared at the other fighter for a minute, Art walking in from the kitchen, three bottles of beer in his hands. "Family, huh?"

"Yeah." Matt nodded. "Family."

And Leonard shut the door.

Thanksgiving 1974.

He was gonna do it. Tomorrow morning when Matt knocked at his window, tomorrow when they were out on their run, Mikey was gonna tell him everything—about Mister Jones. The man who was still a boy lay on his bed in the dark, staring up at the ceiling, watching the blue light from the television set flicker. Mister Jones was out in the front room.

Mister Jones was out there, watching God-knew-what because that light was seeping under his door, stretching up to the ceiling, flashing like a storm. He never saw that shadow back behind his bed. The one that stretched blacker than black up to the ceiling where its head bobbed like a balloon full of helium. A balloon with teeth.

It leaned over Mikey, staring down at him from on high, reading his lips, hearing every unspoken word that rattled around in that boy's head—laughing all the while. And that laugh, Mikey thought it was nothing. Nothing but a laugh track on some late show. But it wasn't, nosiree, it sure wasn't. That laugh was just as wicked as they come. Cold shivers ran up and down that boy.

Mikey pulled the blanket up and around his shoulders, rolling over, looking away from that gleam on the ceiling. *Tomorrow*, he thought, tomorrow *I'll tell Matt. He'll know what to do. Tell him all about that dinner mom told me to invite him to. The one with me and her, Art and Leonard, Mister Jones too. But there ain't gonna be no dinner 'cause tomorrow I'm gonna get rid of him, even if she won't.* And as that laugh track came again, Mikey wrapped his pillow around his ears, wishing that he didn't feel so scared, telling himself he wasn't no little kid who was afraid of the dark and feeling that fear down deep in his bones.

Thank God this day is over.

Thanksgiving Day

In 1974.

# ELEVEN

Somehow Mikey fell asleep, and when he did, he dreamt dreams that kept him up all night, though he was as dead as a log. A log in a forest where trees fell right and left. Trees with no birds on their branches, no squirrels either, no deer or antelope beneath their boughs, no man, no woman, just trees that fell—trees and the sound of falling. One after the other, tree after tree, falling, lying on the ground like so many matchsticks, toothpicks stacked on top of each other. And when the last tree cracked, when its trunk splintered and the bark burst, it toppled and fell toward the ground. Mikey woke before it crashed.

Sweat ran all over his body, dripping onto his sheets, wetting them like a child. Mikey sat up, struggling to catch his breath. But it came, slowly his breath eased, and as he looked around the room, he saw his clock. It sat on his dresser, an old dresser with chipped paint, facing the window, the street light falling in. Mikey could see the alarm clock's hands, see that round face and its painted numbers, see the second hand race past the big hand that sat on nine, see the small fat hand sitting just before five. Mikey wiped his face and lay back down.

He wasn't sure if he wanted to go back to sleep. He couldn't remember his dreams, but he was glad to be awake. Didn't want to get out of bed either 'cause he was tired—dead tired. Maybe I should get up and get ready. But he didn't, even though it was a quarter to five. He couldn't get up 'cause he was safe in bed, safe beneath the covers, safe from the dark. But that shadow, it was long gone, replaced by others that crept under his bed.

Shadows that crept in his corners and behind the dresser and one that stood in the closet behind the closed door, waiting. Waiting for someone to open that door. Mikey's ears ran outside his bedroom door to the footsteps that came down the hall.

His heartbeat hard, pounding in his ears, but the footsteps passed by and the bathroom door opened and then closed. Mikey's eyes ran back and forth as he stretched his ears. The faucet turned on, the water ran and ran, and then came the sound of someone spitting. Someone was brushing their teeth.

What the hell?

A toothbrush tapping on the side of the sink, the faucet turned off, the click of a light switch, the bathroom door opening and closing. Somehow Mikey knew it was his mother. He listened as she walked back by his room, walked to her door and carefully, quietly opened it. But Mikey heard it, heard it close too, listened as she walked across the floor to her window. He knew she was looking out. Mikey's eyes ran to his alarm clock: five to five.

He wasn't afraid anymore, didn't need his covers, threw them off and hurried to the window and looked out himself—looked out from the corner. He was sneakin', didn't want to be seen; he wanted to see what his mother was doing—Mikey just being a kid. The street was empty, but it wasn't dark. A wet snow fell. It was the kind of snow that Mikey hated. The kind that always soaked him from head to toe when he went running—Mikey's mind ran wild too—when he went running with Matt.

Mom's awake.

And now they came, the sound of feet running down the street, growing closer and closer. It was all he could do to stop himself from looking, but he didn't. Instead Mikey crouched down and scooted back into the corner. He was like a shadow man himself. The sound of those running feet getting closer and closer—

Mom's window opened. "Hey, you."

"Margaret." Feet stopping. "Mornin'."

"Shhhh," Mom whispered. "Mikey's still sleeping. I miss you."

"I miss you too. Everything okay?"

"Yeah, you?"

"Yeah."

"I miss you so much."

"Me too. Can I see you again tonight?"

*Again?*

"Kiss me."

Mikey moved from that corner faster than lightning and peeked out his window. Mom leaned out her window, leaning toward Matt, her eyes big and wide, looking into his, Matt leaning into her, leaning close—and they kissed. Mikey watched as his mom wrapped her arms around Matt, her hands moving on his back, moving up to the back of his head. Margaret said, "Oh, Matt."

"Tonight?"

"Yeah."

"Where?"

Mom smiled at him. "I'll go for a walk."

"When?"

"Late. Is that okay?"

"Yeah," Matt said, smiling.

"I better go before he sees. Good night, Matt."

They kissed. "Good morning, Margaret."

Crouching back in the corner, Mikey's blood boiled as that knock came at his window. That little tap that pissed him off, that made him want to hit Matt, hit his mom, made him want to choke them both—to hell with them!

Ain't gonna tell him nothin'.

"Mikey, it's me." Feet running in place. "It's Matt."

"I know, don't you think I know? I saw you." Mikey breathed in, calming. "You don't have to say your name every damn mornin', do you?"

Matt just shook his head. "Let's go."

"Yeah, yeah."

"It's wet."

"I said I know."

They ran alongside the river, Matt and Mikey step for step as the snow fell wet on thin ice. How long? How long have they been together? How many times had they been together? How many times had she snuck out to be with him? Snuck out and left me alone? Left me with him—Mister Jones? *Matt*, Mikey thought, *does he know about Mister Jones?*

*He has to.*

*They both keepin' it a secret, from me, from Mister Jones too. Tonight she gonna sneak behind my back, behind his back too, and make love up in Matt's room. No, Matt knows. He knows everything. Knows that I'm home alone with him—with Mister Jones. But maybe*, Mikey smiled, *maybe I'll tell.* Deep down, way inside that man-boy, something smiled wide. Something that felt good, felt just like justice, just like even-stevens; something with gold teeth. *Maybe I'll tell Mister Jones.*

"You're quiet this morning."

Mikey wanted to spit in his face. "So."

"You okay?"

"Why do you always say that?" Mikey stopped cold. Behind him, the ice broke, a mouth yawned dark in the river. "Why do you think there's somethin' wrong with me? Ain't nothin' wrong with me! You the one with a problem! What's wrong with *me*?"

"Why you actin' like that?"

"You is a fool!" Mikey just shook his head, rolling his eyes. "Tch. No wonder Art says you washed up, I wouldn't get you a fight either. All you is is a tomato can."

Matt stepped towards the kid. "Mikey—"

"What?" Mikey threw out his arms, backing up, keeping his distance. "You gonna hit me? Go ahead, hit me! I don't care!"

"Go home."

"Screw you."

"Go home, Mikey."

"It's Mike, and screw you!"

"I don't know what's wrong, but I wouldn't ever hit you, Mike. I got too much respect for you." Matt looked into the man-boy's eyes. "Even when you actin' like this."

And Matt turned and walked away.

The snow fell between them, growing thicker as Matt grew smaller in Mikey's eyes. So small, so far away that soon he disappeared. And somewhere behind Mikey, the laugh track played over and over again.

Matt wasn't thinking, wasn't dwelling on this morning; he was just throwing punches. One after another, snap in them all, feet so sweet that Art just shook his head. *Don't know what it is*, the old trainer thought, *but he's different. Just plain different. What's got into his head? Will it stay?* "Bea-ut-i-ful, kid," Art said. "Just beautiful."

Matt smiled, but he didn't say a word, didn't give the old trainer a wink or a nod. Instead Matt just moved, just danced on those feet, just let that hook go as he rose up from the floor.

For some, it was like catching lightning in a photograph: the flash, the strike—memorizing. And when that surge of electricity hit, when the air crashed and thundered, all their mouths just fell open, all them eyes stared at something beautiful.

"Time, kid," Art said, even though there was still a minute to go in the round. "Time. Why don't you sit down for a minute, I want to talk to you." Matt nodded, catching his breath, wiping his face with a towel as he sat down. "You're doing good, kid. Doing better than I've ever seen you do. I don't know, maybe you finally listened to me, or maybe you quit listening to me. Whatever it is, just keep doing it, you hear?"

Matt was smiling, chuckling at the old trainer, "Sure." He nodded. "I hear."

"Good." Art took his beanie from his head and held it. "Good. I been thinking a lot, Matt, thinking what we should do, what our move should be, you know? We're in sort of a fix, me and you. I mean you've fought good, but you—"

"Art—"

"Hold on there, champ. I was—"

Matt smiled. "Champ?"

"That's what I said."

"You're getting me a shot?"

"Hold on, hold on"—Art held up his hands, asking for a minute—"let me explain. I think I can get you a shot, but after you show 'em what you got. Now I ain't suggesting that you beat some poor fool that has no business in the ring; no tomato can."

"I ain't fightin' no tomato can."

Art chose his words carefully. "Getting a fight with a top five is gonna be a hard sell, Matt. Take a year to train first, then fight someone like May or Hernandez, beat 'em good, destroy them, then no one could say nothin'. No lucky punch. You win and leave nothin' that folk can poke at."

Matt couldn't believe it. "A year?"

"You need a little time to perfect everythin', you know? Besides, I don't know if I could get you a top five fight. It could be six months or more…why not go the safe route?"

Matt looked at the old trainer, searched his eyes. *Today*, Matt thought, *today! I've worked my ass off for my whole life! Today! I know I can!*

"Trust me, champ—"

"Art, please! I know I can."

Art laid his hand on Matt's knee. "It's for the best."

He didn't want to say yes, but he did, anyway. "Okay, Art." Matt nodded. "Okay. You the boss."

"Good, good. Now you don't think about nothin', just keep working like you do, keep doing things the way you doing them, get better every day and prove to me what I'm seein' isn't just a fluke, okay."

Matt looked away.

*He still don't believe in me, it's just like Mikey said, but it don't matter. It don't matter,* Matt told himself again, trying to convince himself. *It just don't matter 'cause I'm gonna do it. I'm just gonna do it. Don't matter what Art says, don't matter what the whole world says either, I'm gonna be the champ, gonna lift that belt above my head and show them all, but I don't care. No, not one bit 'cause she'll be there, standing in my corner, wearing that red dress, looking up at me, smiling proud—Margaret. It was worth it.*

*Every fight, every day of training, after spilling my guts in the ring, the whole wide world is finally coming together. It's all gonna work out: boxing, me being the heavyweight champion of the world, Margaret, even Mikey someday, even Art, it's all gonna be in my corner. It's all gonna work out.*

It was worth it, Matt thought, the fight was worth it every step of the way. Matt tried to smile at the old trainer. "Okay, Art, okay."

"That a kid." Art put his beanie back on his head. "One other thing."

"Shoot."

"Margaret's invited me, you, and Leonard to dinner this coming Saturday. Only this time, we ain't havin' meatloaf." Art smiled. "Chinese!"

The snow was falling tonight, but Matt never saw it. She was coming. He sat on the back of a folding chair, looking out the second floor window, looking down on the street that was covered in snow, waiting for her, thinking of her; he smiled.

He smiled so wide, so bright that if anyone had been there, if they would have seen his face, they would have smiled too. He imagined her there with him, holding her, kissing her lips, feeling her body against his. He could see them together, Margaret lying on him, their faces so close, just a breath away.

Heavy breaths, whispers that turned into laughs, words so sweet that Matt just smiled as he thought of them. Thoughts of what might be. And between them, warmth. No, Matt didn't see the snow tonight as he looked out the window, he did not see a single flake. He was lost in his head. But if he had, he would have seen that the snow was like ash. Ash that muffled the city. Ash that fell like so many scorched feathers from beating wings. No, tonight there would only be her, nothing else mattered, Matt thought.

It didn't matter that it was late, didn't matter that he was going to be tired when he got up at five, didn't matter if he dragged the whole damn day because more than anything, tonight he wanted to be with her. Not only tonight. Tomorrow and the next day and next month and next year and year after year—only them. Just him and her, washing dishing, brushing up against each other, smiling, laughing, lying together for the rest of his life. And that thought, that day after day after day, it made Matt stop. Somehow, he saw his reflection in the dirty window.

He stared at that face, stared into those eyes that stared back, seeing something in there that was familiar. He saw the little nicks, the scars from all those years in fine lines, some straight, some jagged, so many lines embedded in his skin. The face in the window smiled at Matt, but Matt didn't smile back.

The ash fell in front of his face, fell past his window to the street below where footprints laid. Prints that walked from the darkness across the street and stopped at the gym door. But there was no one there.

Just footprints in the snow.

Matt stood from that chair and looked out. Hands on the panes of glass, so many different colors, separated by metal, Matt strained to see below.

"Hey." He turned from the window, Margaret stood at the top of the stairs, ash lying on her shoulders, crumbling; her face flushed from the cold. "I missed you," she said.

He stared at her, the snow falling behind him, the wind coming now. A sheet across the window—white. "You look beautiful."

"Matthew Gore, it's dark in here."

"So?"

"So how can you say that I look beautiful when there ain't even a light on? You can't see me."

Matt smiled and the man in the window looked away. "I can," Matt said. "I can always see you."

"You can, huh?"

"Just as plain as day."

She walked towards him, slow, her hips moving. "Then tell me, what do you see?"

"I told you."

"You did, huh?"

Matt nodded, Margaret standing before him, the wind blowing behind him. "I did."

"I must not have heard you. What did you say?"

He kissed her, a long kiss, slow; a kiss that made Margaret exhale. Smoke.

*Beautiful*, Matt wanted to say it, but he couldn't. *What do you feel?*

"I'm sorry, did you say somethin'? 'Cause if you did, I didn't hear it."

Matt wrapped his arms around her and pulled Margaret into his body. "I said this"—and he kissed her again. Holding, touching, and as they parted, as Matt pulled away to whisper, their lips lingered together. "Did you hear me?"

Margaret's breath came heavy, her eyes were still closed, her head still tilted, wanting that kiss. Wanting it again and again. "Didn't hear a thing."

He lifted her in his arms and carried her to his bed. Matt said, "Are you listening?"

She nodded, eyes heavy. "Yeah."

Matt laid her on his cot.

Eyes searching, she said, "Matt…"

"Yes?"

"Please."

"Please what?"

"I'm feelin' for you, Matthew Gore, feelin' it deep down inside." Margaret trembled. "And it scares me."

Matt leaned down and kissed her, his lips moving to her neck. As his mouth moved up the long curve of her nape, Margaret's skin pricked. Matt laid his head against hers and whispered into her ear, but not a word came out.

Of course it was dark, the whole damn house was dark: the living room, the kitchen, the bathroom too, and Mikey's room, it was just as dark as it comes. But Mikey wasn't in his room. No, he had opened that door and crept down the hall, sticking his ears at his mother's door, listening like he was some little kid. But Mikey wasn't a kid, he was seventeen, and in the heart of that about-to-be man, something burned.

Mikey didn't hear a thing behind that door, didn't see the curtain that hung dead, even though the wind slipped in through the crack in the window, didn't feel the chill that filled the room, didn't see the teeth behind the curtain. But it was there, waiting for him, knowing that the door would open and the boy man would peek in.

Sure enough, Mikey reached down and slowly turned that knob, letting the door fall open as he put his eye up to that crack. The room was blacker than black. It was so damn dark that Mikey couldn't see a single thing, but he felt it. Felt the cold and he shivered, but that's all it was to Mikey, just cold. You see, he thought Mister Jones was sleeping on the couch. Mikey opened the door and stepped inside, passing into that black.

He could see, not with his eyes, but in his mind. Mikey could see his mother and Matt outside his window this morning, leaning into each other, kissing, whispering, smiling at each other. And somehow he could see them now, up above the gym, lying on that metal cot, Matt on top of his mother.

*I should tell.*

*Tell Mister Jones what was going on. Turn and walk right out of this room, right down the hall and wake him up and spill the truth. The whole truth and nothin' but the truth, so help me.* And why tell? Why rat his mom and Matt out? 'Cause Mikey wanted them to feel the way he felt when they had left him here alone with Mister Jones. In the darkness, the man-boy smiled.

Of course Mikey didn't think this. It was just a feeling, hot inside of him, that wanted to reach out with its long boney fingers and wrap themselves around their necks and squeeze. Squeeze and squeeze and watch their eyes bulge as Mister Jones scared the hell right out of them. *They lied to me. They snuck behind my back and left me here alone with Mister Jones.* Shivers ran down that boy's back, *left me here alone with him like now.*

He was here.

Somewhere in the dark, he was here. And not out on the couch either, but here, close, maybe inside this room. Mikey could feel him, see those teeth glinting somewhere inside his head, feel that shadow creeping up behind him. Mikey's head turned so fast that any other man's neck would half snapped, but not Mister Jones'.

Nosiree, his neck would have twisted like some sick Jack in the Box, springing up at the last moment just when Mikey's heart was pounding in his chest and his eyes were racing around the room, looking for—

"What'cha looking for, son?" Mikey jumped, jumped so high that you would have never thought he was gonna come down, but he did. The curtains swaying in the room, cold air slipping through that crack, and Mister Jones stood like a shadow with teeth. "You lookin' for your momma?"

Mikey didn't feel so good, didn't think that his great idea was all that great anymore. The kid swallowed. "Thought I heard somethin'."

Somewhere behind Mikey, the laugh track played. "That's my, boy! Checkin' on his momma, thinkin' maybe there's trouble, and he just walks right in without a thought for himself! You is a man. Am I right, son? You're a man now, right?"

"Yes, sir, I'm a man."

"'Course you are. Any fool can look at you and see that you are. And tell me, son, what do men do?" Mikey stared at the shadow, shivers still running across his skin, wanting to shrug, too frozen to move. "Let me help you out a little here. A real man is supposed to protect his family. Now I know, I am the man of the house and so as that man, I would go through heaven, if they let me though, and strut right through hell for this family that your mother promises is all mine. You follow me, son?" Mister Jones said.

"Yes, sir."

"Good, 'cause I don't want to see this family break up. Nosiree, not yet. That's somethin' you got to do all by yourself. But if you know somethin', somethin' that I should know, maybe you should tell, 'cause all I see here is that your momma ain't in bed." Mister Jones looked at the bed. "At least she ain't in this bed."

He could tell, he could open his mouth and with a few words, make them all feel like he felt right now. Mikey looked up at that shadow, looked at all them sharp teeth that glinted in the dark, and opened his mouth.

Mister Jones smiled.

She was with him again, hanging on his arm, walking together down a cobblestone street lined with tall buildings. Bright buildings that stood side by side with long porches and wrought iron rails and people with their drinks, toasting their fellow man in the street below. Jazz music 24-7. But Art didn't give damn about all those people because he was with Betty.

Art didn't want to wake up from his dream, didn't want to open his eyes and see that old black and white television set and the snow on its screen. And somehow, Art put that hiss from the single speaker way back in his old tired mind because he was with her. Tonight, he could feel her.

Her hand around his arm, her body bumping into his as they walked down the street, Art could feel the smile on Betty's face as it burned inside of him. And just like he had been back in the day, Art was happy. Only now, unlike then, nothing else mattered. Not old New York and its new skyscrapers, not Madison and its Garden. Tonight, after living the life he had, Art regretted it all. All of it except New Orleans and Betty.

He could have been happy there. Art could have spent his days on a porch just sitting with her, sipping lemonade as he snuck peeks at her beautiful face. Day after day, week after week, letting the months roll by, the years passed in leaps. And even when she was old, even when that soft skin of hers wrinkled, Art still would have looked into her face and thought her beautiful. Deep down inside, a part of him wanted to cry.

It was too much, too painful to stay in this sleep and dream a thing of regret, but Art didn't listen. Right now he was walking with her, passing under the whole world that stood high behind those rails, lifting their drinks, toasting the pretty young thing that hung on an old man's arm. The old man who smiled at her with a crooked jaw. Somehow in his dream, Art knew that he was old.

Old like he was now, old like the winter outside his window where the snow blew and buried the world under its shroud. Old like a dog that lies by a fire, stealing the heat because it is dying.

"Art." Betty stood on her toes and whispered in his ear. "You ain't old."

Head back, mouth open wide, Art laughed in the middle of that cobblestone street as the music played. "But I am," he said. "Oh, Betty, I am."

"Ain't it nice."

"It sure damn is."

"I missed you." Betty looked down that long street; black iron lamps lighting the night. "I missed you so much."

"Well, I'll be damned, Art!" The voice came from high above. Art's eyes ran up along the rails, touching faces, searching them out, moving on to the next balcony until they stopped on a dark lean man who stood half-hidden in the back. The man said, "What you doing here?"

And the old man woke.

There were only shapes, only shadows of things to come, just a memory of a dream that died in the dark room where Art sat alone. Still, the old man felt it sting. He stood, pushing himself up from his chair, walked across the room to the window, and looked out into the night—the snow had stopped.

Smoke rose up from the floors beneath the apartment, filling the living room where his momma sat under a lamp reading a book she had already read a hundred times. Matt was just a kid, just a kid again.

A kid standing and staring at his momma, waiting for her to get up or to scream or to pull him by the arm and lead him from the fire. But she never did. She never moved from the couch as the flames licked up the wall behind her. Her eyes never strayed from the pages of the book as they curled black in her hands. One by one, she tried to turn the pages only to have them crumble. And as the couch caught fire, Momma sat as still as a statue as the flames took the back of her head and ate her body until she turned into a pillar of salt. And Matt could never turn away.

He didn't close his eyes or turn his head either, but a moment later he was standing at the window looking out at the fire escape where his father sat drinking, dropping bottles into the alley. Bottles breaking, shattering with the windows as they blew out of the burning building below. Flames reaching up the bricks, licking the mortar, stretching up to dear old dad while he still sat drinking.

Drinking and drinking, bottle after bottle, beer down his throat as the smoke poured into him like something from the Bible. Something black with long arms and gnashing teeth. Dad drank until he sat slumped like some bum that had been pancaked in an alley. A bum that wasn't breathing, a heap of nothing who would rot black until the rain washed him away. And still the boy stood.

He waited, listening, hoping that someone would burst through the door and carry him away. And for a moment, he thought he heard the old, slow steps of a neighbor with clouded eyes. He prayed for her, begged God to spare Johnette, but only the crack of the fire answered his prayer.

It spread, twisting with smoke like some beast on its belly crawling toward him. The boy couldn't back away, his feet never moved. He was stuck on the floor as if his shoes had been nailed in place. Fire chewed at his feet, but the boy never screamed; he never cried either. Matt stood, just a boy, watching as the fire ate him alive. But it was just a dream now, he told himself in his sleep, just a dream, that's all.

Matt lay on the cot above the gym where the darkness hid the Magic Man. He was breathing heavily, sweat dripping from his body, and in a moment, he realized just where he was. Thank God, it was just a dream. He was here, alone. And then Matt remembered her.

Margaret.

She was gone, her clothes, her shoes, coat and purse, all of it gone. Matt stood and walked to the window where footprints hurried away in the new fallen snow.

Maybe she had been there for hours. Hours and hours and hours, standing in the shower where the hot water never seemed to end, where the night stretched on and on in that house. In the dark where hot water fell onto her skin. Of course, she hadn't been there for hours. She had been with Matt. It felt so good, she thought, so damn good. Margaret never wanted it to end.

More than anything else in the world, Margaret wanted to close her eyes and stay there in that shower forever. To let the water fall on her, to hear it, to feel it as it trickled down her skin onto the tile and down through the drain.

Maybe her eyes were closed, but she knew they were open because she could see everything perfectly. She could see the dark, feel its warmth in the water, hear its soothing hush as the drain glinted gold. She sat, wrapping her arms around her legs, holding her knees that pressed against her breasts, sat in the corner and brushed her hair back away from her face, tasting the water. There was so much to do.

She knew what she had to do, she could feel it, see it in her mind—she knew she *had* to do it too. No one had told her what to do, not a word had been said: an idea, a thought, a dream or two, or the ten thousand that had woken her every hour of every night. For years and years and years she had woken, knowing what was coming—what she would do.

And she would do it.

No matter what, she would do it. But that too was just a dream because now, right now, there was nothing but the shower and the water falling and falling and falling into the darkness. No end, no beginning, just this moment where the water ran on and on forever. Yes, Margaret thought, this is eternity.

And she opened her mouth and drank. Drank the hot water that would never run out. And then, tipping her head back, letting it hang, letting the water drip down through her hair and onto her body, she laid her head on her knees and sat for hours and hours and hours as the night stretched forever. From somewhere in that little apartment...

A laugh track played.

The cold air burned in Matt's lungs, but he didn't give a damn. He was out early, training, running down the street in the dark of morning on a day that would only get darker. Rain was on its way.

Of course Matt couldn't feel the change —not yet, at least. But it was there. High above him in unseen currents, a gale, pushed by an unstoppable front, tore at the sky. By midday, all the white snow that now hushed the city would turn ugly and grey. And before three this afternoon, that wind would fall and rip through the streets as the rain washed that pure snow away. Only Matt didn't know it was gonna rain, no one did except for Mister Jones.

Matt was just training, running alongside Margaret's footprints, following them down the streets and round the corners, passing alleys where bums laid half-frozen. But halfway to Margaret's apartment, Matt did something funny—he began to scatter her tracks.

Maybe it was odd, but Matt kicked at her tracks, scattering the snow, wiping them from the face of the earth. The closer Matt got to Margaret's apartment, the more he blotted her out, oblivious to the sky above him and the clouds and the wind that tore at creation. There were only the tracks, only the snow, only the urge to kick them—only the cold as it poured down his throat into his lungs like so much smoke.

As Matt neared her apartment, as he destroyed her footprints, his eyes followed them up the steps and into the house. He could feel her, he knew she was there, but Matt didn't stop at Mikey's window.

Any other morning, every other morning, Matt would have stopped and knocked, but not this morning. For some reason, he just couldn't. Margaret needed the sleep, and maybe Mikey could use a little more sleep too. Or maybe his run was a little too good to be stopped; maybe he needed some time alone to think. Whatever it was, the fact was that Matt just kept on running. Passing the porch, passing Mikey's window, his eyes fixed on the broken glass as his body ran by. As he neared the river, as the reasons for not stopping finally grew quiet in his mind, Matt found himself on the long, winding walk. It was clean and dry.

The walk hadn't been swept, there weren't any heaps of snow stacked on the sides by a shovel; the walk was just clean. No ice, no salt, no snow. The sidewalk wasn't even wet. It was as if the snow had somehow fallen around it. But Matt never noticed the walk, because ahead, sitting on the bench, was a man.

He was tall, lean, hands in his pockets; hat on his head. The type of hat that every man wore back in the twenties and thirties. And as Matt neared the man, as he grew larger and larger, his legs stretching like the world before him. The tall man lifted his hand and smiled.

"Ain't it beautiful, Matt? All this ash? Just enough to bury you alive!" And that smile stretched, spreading across a face that kept on changing, until the corners of his mouth split. Matt ran past him, sprinting now, trying to leave him far behind, and still the voice came, wicked as the cold wind. "Run, Matt, run! Time's goin' by!"

Matt turned, jerked his head back, but all he saw was an empty bench. Just an empty bench covered in snow.

# TWELVE

The sky had broken, but she couldn't see the patches of blue, couldn't see the grey cloud tops; her eyes were closed. Shadows raced across the city. Matt sat in a chair next to her bed, staring out the window.

Sunlight through the window, the air swimming in front of Matt's eyes; sunlight that fell on her bed. Matt caressed her hand, gently touching her paper-thin skin with his thumbs, stumbling across veins that stuck out only because her skin had been sallow. Still, his hands looked older than hers.

So many years ago, he had held those same hands, helping her up all the stairs of the apartment building, carrying sacks of groceries for her as she pulled at the rail. Down the hall to the very last door on the right where a treat was waiting inside for a nice young man—a good helper.

A cookie—molasses, in fact—the softest cookie east or west of the Mississippi. The kind of cookie that melts in your mouth. It was the least she could do, or so she always said with a thank you; the least she could do because Matt always refused the nickel, the dime, the quarter when he got older. Ever since he was eight and she was just sixty.

Even after Matt had left that decrepit building because he had no home, no parents either—both dead and gone in the fire. He came back and helped Johnette up those stairs, holding her hand, walking slowly, smiling as she said the same things she always said. Matt didn't know why he had always come back, every week. In truth, he hated that building, hated the fourth floor, hated that charred smell. But he did, every Thursday just after noon, Matt came back because Johnette was alone and Matt understood what that meant. The clouds covered the sun, a shadow draped over a face.

In a moment, she was cold again. Matt covered her, gently lifting her arms, placing them under the blanket, keeping her old body warm. He turned to the radiator and touched it, cursing to himself that there wasn't any heat. It was just like the room, just like the tiles on the floor, just like the metal bed frame that stood on black wheels—just cold. White walls that said nothing of life's color. Life never bloomed between those walls. Walls that spoke of an end.

Matt stood and walked to the closet door, wondering why the nurses always put her blanket away. The blanket sat on a shelf behind her dress, hanging between a line of empty hangers. Matt reached in, stepping forward, accidentally kicking Johnette's shoes. They were nice shoes, her finest dress shoes, square-toed, low heels with a silver buckle. Shoes that shone in the dark before donation. Matt reached down and straightened them. Blanket in hand, Matt shut the door, covered Johnette and kissed her forehead.

"Please," he whispered. "Please don't leave me."

The old woman said nothing. Matt turned and sat down in the chair beside the bed. He stared out the window and saw a glint in the broken sky: a gull circled between the breaks, flashing like a shooting star.

As Matt watched that bird, he wondered what it felt like to fly above the city, to look down on all this filth, but it didn't matter.

Not now, not today, not even that damn punch he could throw mattered now. She was here, her eyes closed, her body cold.

"God knows why, but the sun's shining today." Matthew Gore wiped his eyes.

Art looked down at his fighter. Matt laid on his cot, sleeping. The sun hid behind that familiar blanket of grey. The rain was coming. "Kid, wake up. I got to talk to you."

Matt's eyes opened, "Art?"

"You sick or something?"

After his run this morning, after scattering Margaret's footprints in the snow, after passing by that man on the bench by the river who disappeared like Harry Houdini, after the hospital, Matt had climbed right back into bed. He said, "Somethin'."

"Maybe this ain't such a good time to talk."

"No." Matt sat up and cleared his throat. "I'm fine, really. What's up?"

Art set the alarm clock on the floor under the folding metal chair and sat down by his fighter. "You sure you're feelin' okay?" Art's hands fiddled. "'Cause if you ain't, we can talk later."

Matt breathed in, readying himself for another one of Art's talks. Ten, twenty, maybe thirty minutes or an hour of Art explaining why 'this is for the best.' "Yeah, I'm sure," Matt said.

"You ain't coming down with somethin,' are ya?"

"Couldn't sleep, that's all."

"Did you take somethin' for it?"

"Just a run."

"You ran this morning?"

"Like always."

"Of course you did." Art looked around the room: same fridge, same peeling paint, same old trash can that was missing a handle, and Matt. Matt and his old cot that sat against the wall under the window where it had been forever. Nothing, not one thing had changed in fifteen years. "It don't seem like you're feelin' well, kid, let's talk later. It can wait."

"Nah, let's get it done."

"Hey, do you smell perfume?"

"I don't smell nothin'."

"That's odd. For a minute there I could have sworn that I smelt perfume. Well"—Art sat back in the chair—"I got news. Somethin' that I think you might like to hear. Somethin' you been bugging me to get for you."

Matt sat up and his face changed. "You got me a fight!"

"A good one too. One that's gonna take us right where we want to be. You gonna look back at this day and remember it for the rest of your life."

"Douglas?"

"Nope."

"A rematch with Joseph?"

"This is better than a rematch, kid," Art said emphatically. "Like I said, this here fight is gonna take you places."

"I can't believe it." Matt was smiling now. "You did it, you got me a shot!"

"You remember our talk, right? The one about fightin' someone who's gonna help us showcase all them new skills of yours, remember?"

"You're killin' me." Matt was on the edge of his cot. "Who, Art? Who am I fighting?"

"Barns."

"Barns?" And all the air went out in the room. "Barns ain't top ten. He's twelve or something like that."

"He *was* ranked thirteenth," Art said. "As of this morning, he's eleven. He lookin' to make a big jump, you're still ranked sixth, and so he's decided that he wants a chunk of you. Not a piece, but a chunk, mind you."

"Barns?" Matt leaned back on his cot. "Barns is eleven?"

"He beat Ruiz Saturday night and beat ain't the word." Art nodded, trying to put excitement in his voice, wishing that the kid would just listen. "More like he massacred him."

"Ruiz ain't nothin' but a tomato can. Both me and you know that."

"That ain't true, kid." Art's hands worked his beanie. "Ruiz is a good fighter. The Boxing Federation had him ranked as the number eleven contender in the world Saturday night. Barns took that from him."

"Ruiz couldn't beat his own mother in a fistfight, Art."

"It don't matter, kid, 'cause Barns is now a big up and comer. Fact is, he's got folk's attention and a lot of 'em are sayin' that he belongs in the top five. Some are sayin' in the top three."

"Like who?"

"Like everyone. Some of 'em are even sayin' that he's gonna be the next champ." Art was nodding, trying to instill in Matt that this was good. Nothing but good. "This is perfect for you. You said you wanted a shot, you said you wanted to prove yourself in the ring, you know, showcase 'em new skills of yours and everything. Well, Barns is yours for the taking."

"Art, it's Barns," Matt spoke slow, emphasizing the fact. "Alfred Barns."

"I know, believe me I know. I couldn't believe my own ears when I heard it, but I gave Eddie a call. He was there, up ringside too, so he had a clear shot. I guess Barns hit Ruiz with everything in the ring except the stool and the referee."

Matt stared down at the floor where Margaret's shoes had been laid only hours ago, stared at the deep cracks that ran everywhere.

"Barn's put him away in the fourth," Art went onto say. "Knockout. More like murder, or so Eddie said. And the thing about it, after the fight, guess Barns looked as pretty as a peacock. Ruiz couldn't lay a finger on him. Guess he moves real good and everything. All sweet and silk-like. But he's yours, kid, all yours.

*And*"—Art smiled—"the money is decent. All that's left for you to do is sign your name on the dotted line."

It was like the whole world was spinning around and around and around. Matt looked at his trainer, at the old man sitting beside him.

"I can't believe it. Barns, Art? "

The old man's face bent. "What's wrong with you?"

"What's wrong with me?"

"Yeah, you!"

"You don't believe in me."

"You got cotton in your ears or something?" Art looked disgusted. "I got you a shot!"

"Barns ain't a shot!"

"To hell he isn't!"

"He's nothin' but a tomato can! He's not even ranked in the top ten! This fight does nothing for me. Nothing! Besides, both me and you know that I'll kill him!" Matt stopped dead cold. He stared at his trainer who sat with his head down, eyes diverted, kneading his beanie like it was a child's blanket. "What?" Matt felt sick. "You don't think I can beat him?"

"We being truthful here, kid?"

"Aren't we always?"

"Guess we are. With the way you've been fighting lately, no." Art shook his head. "No, I don't think you can."

It was a low blow, a sucker punch. "You don't think I can." Matt was way beyond disbelief.

"Look, kid—"

"Why do you call me that? I ain't a kid!"

"I know that! Don't you think that I don't know that? Hell"—Art breathed—"I've been trying to tell you that since your last fight, you're getting older. That's the fact, kid, there's no getting around it. Barns is a good fight for a fighter like you."

"A fighter like me?" Matt stared at the old man, anger in his eyes. "I'm the number six contender in the world, Art. Twenty-six and four and I'm *only* twenty-eight years old. Twenty-eight, Art! That ain't old! Hell, there were guys a lot older than me and they was the champ. I'm gonna be the champ, Art! One day, I know it."

"You've lost to Joseph, Douglas, and before them, Harris. Neither one of them bums could lay a finger on Herns. As for Harris, he's a joke. And if you got into the ring with Herns," Art shook his head. "He'll eat you up alive."

"I can't believe it." Matt got up from the cot and threw on his sweatpants, shaking his head the whole time – total disbelief. "I can't believe it!"

"What are you doin'?"

Matt pulled on his sweatshirt. "I'm leaving."

"Leaving?"

"Yeah, leaving."

"You asked for the truth, kid, I gave it to you. You can either take it like a man or sulk around like a little kid. I ain't here to pamper you."

"We being truthful here?"

"Just like you said." Art smirked. "Aren't we always?"

"You're quitting," Matt said. "You're old and you're quitting 'cause you're done. Everybody sees it, Art. All your fighters, everyone in this gym knows it, you're quitting. On me, on this gym, on everyone. But that ain't the half of it."

"Oh, really."

"Yeah"—Matt bit—"really. See, I always thought you had my back, but now I can see you never did. You don't believe in me. You never have."

"I gave you everything," Art roared, his face red as hell fire. "Everything! I took you in, I fed you, I trained you and I didn't take nothin' for myself! Not once! And this is the way you repay me? This is the way you thank me?"

"You get sixty percent of everything I make and I'm still living in the storage room!"

Art scowled and the old man's hands stopped working his cap. Matt stared at Art's face, at the lines that ran like fissures, at the clouds in his eyes, at the line of his mouth that looked like a crack—seeing it all for the first time.

"Everything." Matt lifted his hand and extended it, sweeping it across the room. "This is everything."

Matt turned and walked away.

Art got up from his chair. "And just where the hell do you think you're going?"

But Matt was already gone, already out the front door, already out on the street. The old trainer pulled his beanie over his skull and tore that cot apart, kicking and screaming like some seven-year-old until he stood, panting, breathing like the old man he was. "Everything." He breathed. "I did everything for him." Art's eyes fell down to the floor.

There were cracks under his feet. Cracks that ran the length of the room, cracks that ran under the alarm clock that sat ticking time away—he kicked it.

Art put his skinny old leg into it and kicked that clock across the room and into the wall where it broke. Bent numbers, shattered glass, gears bleeding from the clock's round metal body, and yet the second hand still ran. Ran and ran, time ticking by, the sound thudding in Art's ears.

The old trainer hurried from the room and down those long empty stairs where he crossed the gym, ignoring every kid, every fighter, every man, woman and child if there had been one in his gym, and stormed into the locker room.

He found himself standing in front of Matt's locker, staring at the dented door, hearing the seconds on that broken clock tick by. *Stop*, he thought, *just stop. For heaven's sake, stop.* But they didn't stop.

Not a minute, or a second, not a single moment was lost on the old man. Art opened Matt's locker and emptied it. Armful after armful, Art threw it all away. He slumped down on the bench and sat with his head in his hands. At the end of the locker room, in the mirror that sat on the wall, an old man sat crying. But Art never saw that man.

# THIRTEEN

Of course, the rain started just after noon as Mister Jones had known it would. By three o'clock, all the snow had been washed away. It was still raining as night settled in ugly on the city, and with the darkness came a bitter wind.

Matt was wet, soaked through and through, walking aimlessly as the rain fell cold. A rain that had washed away the snow. Like his body, his mind was half-dead after finding the new lock on the gym door. In fact, it was so damn numb that Matt now followed all those unseen tracks in the snow that he had scattered that morning.

Tracks that dragged him through potholes and puddles of water. Tracks that led him past an unseen pimp waiting for one of his girls. A woman with smeared lipstick that knew every trick in the book, though she was just sixteen. But Matt never saw the pimp, never saw the woman with a child's face, never saw any of the faces that looked out from their windows as he walked by. The only face he saw was hers after he knocked on her door.

"Matt?" Margaret stepped out into the rain, never feeling it, pulling the door closed tight behind her, even though Mister Jones was nowhere inside. Of course, she was smoking, the half-used thing smoldering between her fingers. "What the hell are you doin' here?"

"I was just..." Matt shifted on his feet. "I was just out for a run and was wondering if maybe you wanted to get something to eat?"

"Matt, that's real sweet and all." Margaret lifted that cigarette to her mouth and breathed in. "But I told you not to come by. Mikey's inside."

"Yeah." Matt stared at the cold wet street. "Sorry, Margaret."

"Look, Matt"—Margaret blew smoke—"I know this is hard on you and everything, but it's got to be this way. And how come you ain't wearing a coat or something? You're gonna catch cold out in this rain."

"I forgot."

Margaret looked him up and down. "You forgot?"

"When can I see you again?"

"Matt, we just saw each other last night."

"I know but—"

"I'm a mother, Matt." Margaret sucked on that white cigarette; the end glowing hot. "I got responsibilities. I can't be doin' whatever I want all the time like you can. Try and be patient. I promise it'll be worth it."

Matt looked into her eyes, trying to see just what was there. "Margaret?" he said.

"I don't got much time before he starts wondering where I am and comes lookin' for me. If he catches us out here..." Margaret shook her head and blew that smoke between her lips. "Of course, you understand."

"I'm sorry, I shouldn't have stopped by."

She leaned down from the porch, over the rusted rail, feeling the rain for the first time as she kissed him; nothin' but a peck on the cheek. "Nope. Now go home, take a shower or somethin'. Warm yourself up." She opened the door, and Matt realized that as she did, Margaret had never let go of the handle. Not even when she kissed him. Margaret threw Matt another little kiss, one that he never felt, and whispered, "Goodbye."

The door shut and Matt stood on the street.

With no place to go, he turned from Margaret's door and walked down the same dark streets that he had known as a child. It was all the same, the worn-out buildings, the same damn sky, the cold rain that fell onto the streets and ran down the gutters into grates where it washed into the city's foundation; nothing had changed. And the more he walked, the more he looked up from under his hood, the stronger that feeling of stagnation sat on him. It was just this feeling that carried Matt to his childhood home.

He stood at the steps of that five-story building, looking up its bricked side to the top floor where his old window looked out over the city. It was dark inside his room, not a hint of light came from anywhere inside that building. It was empty, abandoned, not even a rat lived inside of its putrid belly. But there were tables and chairs, couches and televisions with melted wires, pans and cupboards with food so old that even the rot had left them behind. And all of it smelt so strongly of smoke that not a thing had been plundered. They were all forgotten; left for the shadows which now used them.

And there were shadows.

In every window, at every door, standing at the top of the steps, they were there watching him as he stood in the soaking rain. Shadows with eyes and mouths that spoke with forgotten voices that Matt had sometimes heard in his sleep. Voices that whispered, others that screamed as fire consumed their bodies, voices that wailed and gnashed their teeth. And there were other things in the dark.

They all whispered to Matt, beckoning him to come and sleep, stay with them where he belonged. And as these things rose from their beds, as they slipped down the stairwell to the street, the darkness seeped back into the rooms and cowered in the corners. They all wanted him, they all called to him: *Matthew, come.*

Again and again they sang this to the man, telling him that they knew what was best for him because they knew him, they loved him, ever since he was a child. All their long lives they had watched him, though the fire had stolen their eyes. But they could still see, they could still whisper.

Breathlessly, they stood as smoke slipped from their mouths, formless arms outstretched, beckoning to their boy. And he had always come back, but only to help a friend—Johnette. He would carry her groceries up those long stairs as the formless faces watched him from below, but he would never stay. So they waited in the dark, marking the months and the hours and moments of all the days from beginning to end until this very one. He had come.

Now they would speak the words they had so long rehearsed. Both day and night, as he slept, as he sat and stared at nothing and oblivion all at once, they would tell him things. Voices that would whisper and comfort the man and then fill his soul with doubt. They would speak them all, the words of scathing hate too. An endless voice that would never cease until he broke.

The wind gusted and the door to the building opened on its own accord. The shadows noticed and smiled. Weakly, Matt stepped toward their outstretched arms, his legs carrying him to the familiars that awaited. And as he neared, they rushed him, but Matt passed through their formlessness.

The door shut behind him.

But the voice and the shadows did not care. He had come, just as they knew he would. They turned their backs on the street and rushed inside that burnt building, never seeing the man who stood behind Matt.

His eyes were fixed on the building, following the path of a man; his ears could hear, even above the rush of the wind, the sound of Matt's feet, climbing, climbing, climbing forever up.

# FOURTEEN

Art held onto the railing and pulled himself up those three small steps. He could have easily walked up those steps, one foot after another, but he felt old today. It wasn't the cold or the freezing drizzle that made the sidewalks slick or the clouds that brought the old man down; it was just the day, just Art, just how he felt.

He stood on the porch, muttering to himself as he faced the old door. Somehow his hands had found their way into his coat pockets. He wasn't sure what he was going to say, or how he would say it for that matter. Maybe he wouldn't have to say it at all, maybe Matt was here with Margaret. Maybe things would work out for the best. But if Matt was here, wouldn't Mikey have said something?

Then again, Margaret had probably told the boy to keep his mouth shut. Art thought about the woman for a moment, wondered what it would have been like if he was a bit younger. He wondered what would have happened if they had ever met up back in the day. But it didn't take much wondering to know exactly what would have happened, he smiled to himself, it would have been fire and ice. Art chuckled to himself. Sometimes, he thought, sometimes fire and ice do mix.

A little hot, a little cold, a little ice melting, cooling the fire, sometimes clashing and makin' a whole hell of a lot of steam. Sometimes that's exactly what a good fighter needed—a little wallop from something safe. A man needs a good woman, Art thought, one who can smack you around, beat you down, turn the tables and fight dirty. If she's got you off balance, she has you exactly where she wants you: right into a mousetrap. *Bam!* It doesn't matter what happens or how it happens, only that it happens. The smart fighter wins the day—sweet science. Sometimes a good woman is just like that, rope-a-dope.

And Margaret, Art thought as he stood on her porch, she would have been a lot of fun back in the day. She was the only reason why Mikey ain't ended up on the streets. Someone should hang a medal around that woman's neck.

The old trainer pulled his hand from his pocket and knocked. He looked down the street, trash in the gutters, freezing drizzle falling, still everything looked dull as yesterday. If Matt ain't here, maybe he'd already got himself out of this God-forsaken place. Maybe that would be for the best.

He shuffled on the porch, a little bit of nervousness mixed with his body trying to keep warm. There were voices inside, someone coming up the hallway toward the door. The chain rattled, locks turned, and Mikey stood before the old trainer. "Tch." The kid shook his head. "I ain't trainin' today. Got stuff to do."

"Oh." Art didn't care if the kid was in the gym or not. In fact, he hadn't even missed him. He was here for Margaret. "Listen, kid, is your mother ho—"

"Who's there, Mikey?" Margaret called from somewhere inside.

"It's Art." Mikey bit back.

"What's he want?"

"Me."

"Actually, kid, I wanted to see your mother."

"She ain't gonna make me go." Mikey stood like a punk. "I'm almost eighteen. She can't make me no more."

"Look, kid." Art wanted to slap him. In fact, more than anything right now, he wished he was younger, back in his prime, then he'd teach that kid what he'd got when he opened his mouth without thinking. "Must be nice, huh?"

"What's that?"

"Believin' the whole world revolves around you." Art stared at the kid. "Get your mom, kid. This ain't about you."

Mikey hated the old man. He turned, dirty look on his face, something that you'd see passing by a street corner with a bunch of thugs, and walked down the hall. Of course, he left the door open, heat going out, cold coming in, a thoughtless fool because he didn't pay the bills. Art pulled it halfway shut, hoping that it helped. From down the hall, he heard Mikey, "The old man wants to see you."

If there was an answer, Art didn't hear it. Margaret walked toward him, cigarette in her hand, her hips moving side to side. She was pretty, he thought, downright beautiful, a man's kind of woman with all the right assets.

"Arthur, what you doin' out in this weather?" Margaret stood at the door, smile on her face, but she never did invite the old trainer inside. "And don't tell me you walked all the way here just to see me. I ain't that special."

"That's where you wrong." The old trainer winked.

"I'm tellin' you—" Margaret sucked on that long cigarette, but she never finished the thought. Instead she just made a little noise. "Ummm."

Art smiled, hot in his cheeks, his head fell and saw that his feet were doing something funny; shuffling. "Look, I won't waste your time, but I—"

"You ain't wasting my time, Arthur. I'm glad you stopped by. It's always nice when you do."

"Oh, thank you, Margaret." Art's face got hotter. "I was just wondering if you had seen Matt."

"That's funny." Margaret blew smoke from her mouth. "I was just gonna ask you the same thing. In fact, I was gonna come by sometime."

"So you haven't seen him, huh?"

"Not for some time now. Weeks, in fact." Margaret dropped her cigarette. "Is Matt all right, Art? Is something wrong?"

"That's just it." Art took off his knit cap and held it in his hands. The old man breathed out. "I don't know. I haven't seen him since just after Thanksgiving. We, uh, we had a little disagreement and—"

"I can't believe it," Margaret said, and now the tears came.

"What's wrong?"

Tears were running down her face. "He walked out on us."

"What?"

Margaret swallowed and shook her head. "We didn't want Mikey to know because he might not take it well and everything. I told Matt I just needed some time to work things out with Mikey, but we argued about it. I ain't seen him since."

"How come you didn't tell me?"

"I didn't want to upset his training." Margaret dabbed at her nose with a tissue. "He don't know what he's done to us, Arthur. I mean Mikey's lost without him. You've noticed his attitude lately. They was good friends, real good. Matt could have been a father to him. I just can't believe it."

Matt and Margaret, Art thought, what else had he missed? Maybe this wasn't just about him and Matt, maybe there was a lot more here that Art didn't know. "What'd he say, Margaret?"

"I know it was hard on him." Margaret nodded. "Maybe I should have done more for him, you know. Just told Mikey what was what and then none of this would be happening. Arthur, do you think he's okay?"

"I'm sure things are fine." the old trainer worked his knit cap. "Look, if I, uh, if I hear anything, you'll be the first to know."

"Oh, Art." Margaret stepped out and wrapped her arms around the old trainer, hugging him tight. "I appreciate you so much." She leaned back and smiled and somehow under a gray sky, her eyes danced. "Thank you."

"It's nothing." Art shook his head and his eyes fell away.

"You're a good man." Margaret hugged him again, holding him tight, holding him for a good while before kissing him on the cheek. "A real good man."

She turned and walked back inside. As she closed the door, she said, "Let me know if you hear anything."

"I will."

And the door closed.

Art stared at the door as the freezing drizzle fell. Like a punched drunk fighter he turned and walked right down the stairs. He pulled his cap back on and muttered something that even he didn't catch. The old man set off for the gym, wondering all the while—mousetrap.

Matt didn't remember waking. He only knew that he was awake, that he was in Johnette's apartment, lying on the couch, surrounded by that sickening stench of smoke. His eyes groped in the cold darkness, his body shook; his teeth chattering like a windup toy.

There was no edge that he could cling to, no branch that stuck out from the cliff, there was only an endless pit. He was falling, he had always been falling. Ever since the fire that had eaten his mother and father, Matt's life had been nothing more than a story. A bedtime dream of one day, a someday man who would be the Heavyweight Champion of the World.

Everything that he did, everything that he had done, every word that came from his mouth was a lie. The running, the training, every hour spent hitting that damn heavy bag, dodging the double bag, they all were part of the story that Matt had told himself ever since he was a child. And in that story, a fighter was lifted on the shoulders of men, cheered for, decorated with a belt; his gloved hand lifted triumphantly above his head. But the story was a make-believe identity. Matthew Gore: fighter, boxer, contender...

Nothing.

Even his story had gone amiss because Matthew Gore was still only a six. Not a top five boxer, just a six. There in the dark, Matt couldn't hold on to a single thing: not boxing, not Art, not even the smoke that poured from Margaret's mouth, nor the little room above the gym where the radiator screamed in the middle of the night. He was...

Nothing.

But something was there, above the blackened floor and the scorched ceiling, the door on the fifth floor where it waited for him. Matt didn't want to go, he didn't want to climb those dark steps and open the door that led to his soul because he was afraid he would find nothing.

Nothing at all.

There were trees with little lights in windows up and down the street. Some big, some not so, others just a branch that bent with the weight of an ornament. Christmas in the city; why does Santa only love the rich? Christmas coming and still there was no sign of Matt.

Honestly, she had looked high and low for the man with what time she had. Of course, that's what she had told herself; that's what she believed. But with her shifts at the grocery store and Christmas coming, what time did she really have?

Sure, she heard about Matt's fight with Art. Mikey had painted the details, coloring everything that happened because deep down inside, Mikey was glad that Matt was gone. Now maybe he could be top dog at the gym. But Margaret didn't care whether it was Matt's fault or not. Matt would always hold a special place in her heart, a hole that she would memorialize and fill because he was gone. Matthew Gore would always be an icon, as long as he stayed gone.

She could see those times in a not too distant future when she would sit with a friend around a round of drinks and then the tears would come. It could be Angie or Laurel or some other girlfriend, it didn't matter who. Only the tears, that's all that mattered, the tears that would fall on the arm of a friend—a shoulder to cry on. Margaret would tell the story of her and Matt and how all the world was against them. Even her son was against her and, of course, Mister Jones, and even "Oh, Angie" tears.

Or insert some other friend's name.

And if Matt happened to come back, if he returned, well, then that was something too—an option. But now there was the grocery store and shopping to do. And, of course, she'd buy Roy something for Christmas—something real sweet. Spend her whole check on the man, worry about the rent later.

Worry about the heat and lights, water and garbage, worry about the sewer bill later too. In fact, they could all wait because he was there, sitting on that couch, bottles at his feet. Bottles with dust on the top, bottles that shone funny in the yellow light— almost like gold. And that was more than Matt.

But today was another day, just a week before Christmas. It was snowing, the clouds and the snow lay on the city like so much fog. Still, Margaret thought, it was pretty. Better than dirty and cold, blue skies and garbage in the gutters. She walked down the street, greeting some folks with a smile, avoiding others downright. And when a man passed by, one that she thought was handsome, one that could be something, Margaret would catch his eyes and tuck a little strand of hair behind her ear.

"Hi," she'd say with a flirtatious smile.

She talked to a few of these men, some were married; some not. It didn't matter if they were or weren't because they were all smiling at her and Margaret loved that—a woman's got to have options. Margaret would be ready for whatever happened. Whether Mister Jones stayed for a while, or if Matt suddenly swept in and kicked him out. Or if none of it happened, if Mister Jones left and Matt never did show up, Margaret would be ready. It was the game she had been playing since she could remember.

Life—the game of options.

Snow falling like glitter on the woman; white flakes lying on her long lashes. The grocery store wasn't far now, just a few blocks, and then the day would be spent on her feet. But Margaret didn't mind. No, not at all because there would be people, faces filing through her line. Faces with smiles, men of all kinds, and all of them options.

It was a brown bottle stamped with a cheap label that claimed that there were spirits inside. And there were spirits inside that bottle, but there was no cheer, no warmth in that liquor as the label had proclaimed. It was a cheap kind of liquor, stilled with a harsh bite. The kind of liquor that was reaped from the feet of a scarecrow. The old man lifted the bottle and drank.

He stumbled as he walked, his face colored with a week's worth of stubble, stumbling as he made his way down the dark street. They were all there, whispering to the old man, spirits of the past that shone before his eyes, blinding him to the real world around him. But the old man was used to these spirits.

He swatted at them, shooing them away, waving his hand in front of his face, and sometimes they would leave him for a while. And then the memories would come. Harder, harsher than before, memories so strong that they made a lonely old man cry.

He stumbled on a step and fell. If it hadn't been for the liquor, perhaps he would have hurt himself. But there was a looseness about his body, the kind that the old man had learned in the ring. Some said he could take a punch, but that was only partly true.

The old man had learned the skill from his father who was the master of blows. Time and time again the old man had learned from his father not to stand like a wall, not to set his feet against the thing that would break him. Later in life, those lessons were used in the ring. They became the sweet science of fighting.

A punch: the energy was coming, it was going to connect, but instead of fighting it, instead of setting his jaw and taking it, the old man would slip and move, never once taking it square. And what little energy he did take, he learned to let it flow right through him like a human conduit. In and out and let it go, move and slip, and never stand tall. As he sat on that step in the cold, Art realized that he had never once stood and taken it like a man. He wasn't like Matt at all.

Tipping the bottle back, the old man drank. He wiped his mouth with the sleeve of his coat and stared down at the sidewalk; the brown bottle hung between his knees. Matt who went straight in, both fists blazing, toe to toe, nose to broken nose; let the world be damned. That was his problem.

He never slipped, never moved, he never saw his opponent from another angle other than head on. Art had learned a long time ago how to destroy a man. A step to the left, one or two to the right, even a step backward could expose a man's weakness. Once Art saw it, he would manipulate that man until there was an opening, and then he would exploit it. That's what had made Art the champ. But not Matt. No, it was never meant to be for the kid. *If he had met me in the ring back in the day...*

He pushed himself up from the step, swayed and staggered and took another drink from that brown bottle of spirits until it was dry. The bottle slipped from his hand, or maybe Art dropped it, but it fell and shattered.

*If he had met me in the ring back in the day, I would have picked him apart piece by piece until a shell of a man lay dead in the ring. Maybe then he'd see how much I've done for him. Maybe then he'd apologize.*

The old man's feet were moving, taking him somewhere they wanted to go, his mind moving too fast inside his head, making his stomach sick. And that glass, that brown bottle that laid broken behind him, Art had already forgotten about it because he was moving, slipping down the street, never taking the brunt of the punch just like he had always done.

Just like New Orleans.

The gym door stood before him with a shiny new lock. For a minute, Art fished in one pocket before moving to the other one. He pulled his keys out and dropped them. A stoop, a swoon, still the old man didn't go down, he grabbed his keys and hunted for the right one.

He was inside now, making his way across the dark gym, muttering about how no one ever took care of the equipment. But they did. Each one of Art's fighters, all of them except Mikey, took good care of each piece of equipment because in the city, there are no trees where money can grow.

Art stopped at the ring, swaying as he looked up at the banners. The faces of dead men looked down on him. Even his own. No, Matt didn't belong up there in the rafters. He didn't even belong in the gym. The kid wouldn't listen, and if a fighter don't listen to his trainer, then it's goodbye.

He looked like a drunken sailor with his hands down at his sides, but somehow the old man made it to the stairs. He stood at the top, the world spinning around him as light from the street fell through the oversized window. It was the kind of window that stood like a gaping mouth on the side of a warehouse, but it was here where Matt used to sleep.

There were no tears now. The old man wasn't muttering to himself; his mind seemed to clear up though his body still wobbled. He walked to Matt's cot and from under it took out two boxes. Art opened the smaller of the two boxes first. It was full of the littlest things—things that smelt like fire. But there was one thing that Art took from that small box, a book.

Like the pages inside, the title had been scorched. Only words remained, snatches of sentences and paragraphs on brown and black pages with edges that were eaten by fire. Pages that crumbled under the old man's hand. Carefully, Art placed the book back inside the box and sealed it shut.

The large box was full of familiar things: trophies and metals from Matt's amateur days. There were photographs too. Some of them were on plaques, but most laid loose in the box. Art took them all one by one and peered through the dark at the images. They were all the same, nearly the same, a fighter and his trainer, standing side by side. Art's arm around the boy, his arm around the man, smiles on both of their faces.

The old man sat on the bed, hunched over the box in his hands, the big box that rested on his knees. Toe to toe, nose to broken nose, Art knew what the coming blow would feel like. His head was bent square over the dusty thing; tears in the cracks of his face. But just as that punch, just as that blow came up from the box, Art slipped and set it aside.

And somewhere behind him, forgotten on the street, the brown bottle laid broken. There was no warmth, no cheer as the cheap label proclaimed. There were only spirits that gnawed at the old man's feet.

# FIFTEEN

Matt stood in front of his childhood home, staring into the apartment through a door that wasn't there, seeing nothing but darkness. It was just a doorway, just a rectangular opening that led from one place to another. A place where Matt did not want to go, but he had to.

He could feel it, inside, waiting for him. It terrified Matt more than the voices that he had heard in his sleep, more than the awful smoke that hung in his nose and the screams on the fourth floor. It was there, inside, waiting.

And it was drawing him in. Like the reaper who pulls a soul from its body, Matt felt that cold hand inside him. His mind screamed, begged for him to turn and run from this place; but Matt didn't turn, he didn't run, his mind was smothered by the voices that had been with him in the shadows since that first night.

*Come.*

Matt stepped toward the door. Every step brought him closer to that hooded thing. His feet halted one last time before the door. The gate stood black before him, the still surface like water undisturbed; a mirror waiting for the ripple.

*Come.*

Then the pebble struck the surface, the mirror broke, and all that lay beneath was awakened. Matthew Marvelous Gore stepped through the doorway.

It was warm inside the apartment. Matt stood in the darkness, staring into the pitch, wondering at the nothingness that surrounded him. He had thought that the thing, whatever it was, would consume him as he passed through the gate, but all he found now was a gutted shell.

There were no chairs, no doors hanging on ruined hinges, only gaping mouths that faced the man standing on a floor covered in ash.

"Hello?" It was a natural thing to do. "Is anyone there?" Matt called out.

No laughter, no whispers from voices, even the shadows that had laid at his foot like faithful companions were gone. Nothing had followed him through the threshold into this place.

He breathed out, his body tensed as his eyes searched the pitch for familiars. *Maybe there's something,* Matt told himself, *something still here. Something that was left behind, forgotten like me. A toy, a chair, mother's reading lamp, a bottle—anything. Please, God, don't let there be nothing.* Matt stepped forward, his eyes always looking, searching, moving unknowingly toward his childhood bedroom. Behind him, embers filled the air like so many fireflies.

Floating and swirling, riding the hot currents in the air as little pieces of molten light fell from their bodies. He did not see the fireflies, he only supposed that it was getting lighter because he was nearing his bedroom and the light from outside was shining in through the window. But as Matt stepped through the doorway, he saw that it was dark inside his room. No light from a streetlight fell through the window, no moon, not even the stars shone through that black hole.

Confusion swirled in his mind as his eyes ran from the place where his bed had once sat on the floor, but it was gone. The pictures clipped from magazines and taped to the walls, the bed, the cardboard boxes that had served as his drawers, they had long since been turned to ash. Ash on the floor, ash on the walls; walls that had been painted with smoke.

Behind him, the fireflies grew in number like the sands of a seashore. So brilliant their light became that Matt finally turned and stared in wonder at the sight. They held him, dancing before his eyes, rising and falling on an invisible current. But as Matt stared, as his eyes looked out from his room, he saw through the embers to something on the couch.

She was reading by the light of a thousand swirling things. Cinders that fell onto the pages of his mother's book, but they did not burn the paper. Instead they lay like stars in the sky. Stars that reflected in his mother's eyes.

Hours passed into days, and Matt stood, watching his mother devour one book after another. He wanted to call to her, to look on that beautiful sad face, but her words echoed in his head.

*"Dinner's in a bit. Go play in your room. Be a good boy and let Mama read. Go ask your father. Sit down and be still."*

And he did.

Matt walked across the room and sat quietly on a chair and watched as his mother devoured book after book. Matt noticed something funny about all those books, about the covers that were painted so boldly; they were all the same. The same man, the same woman, the same passionate embrace; only their faces changed with the titles.

Still his mother read on and on, her lips moving as she took in each word; her hand tugging at the buttons of her blouse. But her face, Matt saw, his mother's face changed with every book. It twisted and contorted until it became something other than mother. It became the woman on the cover.

Matt stood and found himself backing away from the thing on the couch that was covered with embers. Backed far away until he bumped into the kitchen table. The sound of breaking glass pulled him to the kitchen window.

Father sat surrounded by bottles. Bottles without caps and lids, all of them empty. All of them except for one that dangled in his father's hand. The hand of a working man. The bottle slipped, but it did not fall. His father's thick fingers held the long neck as if he was holding the hand of a man dangling over the edge of a cliff.

He was drunk, his head nodding, the bottle clinging to his fingers, slipping ever so slowly towards the alley below as he fell into a stupor. His grip weakened, the bottle fell, and the wind moaned as it caught the mouth of the bottle before it shattered in the alley below.

His father woke, his eyes flaring for a moment, catching Matt for a moment, scathing him with one solitary look before finding the bottles around him. Father picked up another bottle, and now it was full, and he drank and drank until it was half-empty. And then the man held it between his legs once more and let it hang like the dangling man until it too slipped from his fingers and fell. Bottle after bottle, one after another, his father drank the spirits before casting them down into the pit below.

Matt was a child again. "Dad?"

But the king of that place never turned and looked at his son. Instead, his back was fixed against his family; his eyes staring out across his realm to the world where his mind had always been. The king never saw that his throne was nothing but a mountain of broken glass.

Inside the apartment, unseen by Matt, the fireflies fell to the floor and caught. Flames grew and cracked and smoke filled the air. Little beads of sweat dotted Matt's forehead. Matt reached out to his father, but the smoke billowed before him, hiding the king behind a boiling black shroud. Matt's hand began to burn.

"Dad." Matt found his mouth open, he heard the cry from his throat, only his voice was that of a child's. "Please, dad, please! Help me!"

"*A fighter...*"

"Please, help me!"

"*A fighter...*"

"Dad, pleas—"

"*You ain't no baby. Tell me, a fighter...*"

It was just a whisper. "Fights."

"*Be a man. A fighter...*"

Matt stared at the boiling curtain. "Fights."

"*Again!*"

"A fighter fights."

"*Good, good. Now, what are you?*"

Matt stood, staring at the curtain as the fire consumed the room, he just couldn't speak the word. The word that he had identified himself for as long as he could remember.

"*You can't even say it. You nothin', not even a step.*" The voice was harsh, scolding. "*You lost, fool 'cause you can't say it. You don't even believe it. You might as well curl up and die 'cause you nothin'. You hear me? You nothin'!*"

"I tried."

"*You quittin'.*"

"I work harder than anyone!"

"*You never believed.*"

"I've always believed." It was all words, no hint of conviction. "Even when no one else believed in me, I tried."

"*You dreamin', that all you is, a dreamer. You just tell yourself little lies at night so you can feel good in the morning.*"

"I believe."

"*Do you?*"

"I do."

"*Then tell me, what are you?*"

"I..." Matt breathed. "I'm a..."

*"You nothin'."*

Bottles broke in the alley, fire cracked, and the pages of a book turned one after the other. The voice laughed and laughed, looping like a soundtrack, and in that moment, Matt knew it wasn't his father.

*"You nothin', just a tomato can, just a has-been fool who got knocked down."*

"No," he muttered. "No. I ain't ever been down."

*"Fool, you on your back now."*

Matt saw the ceiling, he saw the smoke pilling up on high, pressing down, choking the room. Somehow he was on his back, lying on a heap of ash. The trickster laughed and bit at him again.

*"Matthew Marvelous Gore, you did to yourself what other men couldn't!"*

He could have lain there, he could have stayed forever and no one, not one soul, would have ever remembered, but something rose in that man. Something that shot up through his body from the souls of his feet. He was standing, his head lost in a swirl of black smoke, "No!" Matt roared. "Never! I ain't ever going down!"

*"Never?"*

"Ever!"

*"Then what are you?"*

He wanted to say it. More than anything Matt wanted to stand on a mountain top and proclaim it to all the world, but it stuck in his throat. Sure, he had trained, and yes, he had worked hard too, but he had never fought. Never had he truly fought. Douglas, Joseph—he should have fought them with every ounce of his soul. And if he had died, well then, at least he would have died as a fighter. He should have given it his all, left his heart and soul between the ropes, and died in the struggle because deep down inside, Matthew Gore was a fighter.

He smiled, wide and bright, and the clouds of smoke rolled from his head. Matthew Gore opened his mouth and said, "I am. I am."

The voice laughed and laughed, and Matthew Marvelous Gore walked through the ash and out that gaping mouth to the stairs where he descended the steps of glory. He never looked back, never once turned his head, even as the shadows clawed at him and begged at him; he never answered their call. Matthew Gore stood at the door that led out from that hell and saw a face in the shattered glass before him.

Even though he saw it for the first time, he knew the face: crooked nose—flattened too, missing teeth, cuts in the brow. And Matt smiled as he saw the face of a fighter. Smiled as he saw his face for the very first time.

He opened the door and stepped out into the night air. Above him, the clouds parted like the Red Sea and the stars shone down upon the solitary man.

A fighter fights.

# SIXTEEN

Snow fell on the city, snow mixed with rain—it was Christmas. Mister Jones opened the door to TJ's Bar and walked across the floor while singing a song to himself, snapping his fingers, passing a man who looked as old as death as he cried in his gin about days gone by. Days with his wife; the ghosts of Christmas Past.

Mister Jones sat at the bar in front of the old barkeep who stood with his soft towel, caring for his baby, wiping the bar that was already spit clean. "Merry Christmas, TJ!" Mr. Jones said.

The old keep smiled. "And a very merry one to you too, Roy!"

"How 'bout a nice glass of Scotch, if you would."

"Thought you might say as much." TJ reached under the bar, his old bones creaking as he did, and pulled out a dusty bottle. "Now then, what's got you so cheerful?"

"It's Christmas."

"Has been before"—TJ nodded—"and you ain't the yuletide type. So what gives?"

"I got me a job," Mister Jones said.

"Now that's something." TJ set a full glass of scotch before the man. "Never known you to work, Roy. Thought you were independently wealthy, so to speak."

"I am."

"Then why take the work if you don't need it?"

"'Cause this here is an opportunity." Mister Jones smiled. "Kind of like this here place was for you. Get my drift?"

"Loud and clear," TJ said. "So tell me, where you workin'?"

"It's not where, TJ, it's what."

"What..." The old barkeeper looked baffled. "What you mean what?"

"Just what I said, what."

"Okay, Roy." the old keep almost threw up his hands. "What are you working?"

"You ain't ever gonna believe it, but—" Mister Jones sat straighter than straight and smiled wider than the sky—"I'm a manager, TJ."

"A manager? Well, I'll be damned." TJ stared at the man in disbelief.

"You know what they say, TJ, it's not what you know," Mister Jones said, "but who you know and how much you know about them. And I know plenty, probably too much, and knowin' that much, well, it ain't good for the average man. But both me and you know I ain't average."

"Don't I know it." TJ stared at the reflection on the knotted wood of the bar. "So, where you managing at?"

"Excuse me?"

"Where at?" TJ spoke a little louder in case Mister Jones hadn't heard him. "What store you gonna be managing, Roy?"

"TJ." Roy scolded, giving him that disappointed look. "I said what, not where, remember? And the what has a who with it."

"Who?"

"That's right, a who, a boxer as a matter of fact, but we gonna keep that hush right now. Fact is, the who don't even know what's comin', but it's comin'." Mister Jones laughed. "Boy, is it ever comin' for him. That, my friend, is what me and you is drinking to tonight, except it looks like I'm the only one drinkin'. Me and old Harry over there. Still cryin' about his wife?"

TJ nodded. "Shame, ain't it?"

"It sure is somethin'."

"Tell me, Roy"—TJ wiped the bar—"you ain't, uh, you ain't managing your kid now, are you?"

"Hell, no." Mister Jones almost spat. "But I'd bet on him. In fact I'd bet a whole lot of money on that fool too, 'cause the thing about Michael is he does what he's told, when he's scared enough. But for him to do something on his own, to have a little spit and fire, that bag of bones ain't worth a pocket full of change right now."

"Roy"—TJ stared at the man wide-eyed—"how can you say that about your own blood."

"TJ, I'm gonna let you in on a little secret." Mister Jones leaned across the bar, his neck stretching long, stretching out from his body until his mouth was right by TJ's ear. "You can't believe everything you hear. Mikey, well, he's related to me like I'm related to you."

TJ blinked. "But we ain't related, Roy."

Mister Jones leaned back in his seat and leveled his finger at the old bar keeper in a finger gun. "Bingo."

"Oh." TJ looked away.

"Listen, TJ—" Mister Jones pushed his glass forward and TJ immediately filled it—"that room you got in the back, you usin' it, or is it available?"

"Sorry, Roy." TJ wiped the bar. "That's my room, but I do got one upstairs."

Mister Jones smiled. "You don't say."

"I do, came with the bar." The old keep beamed. "It's supposed to be for stock, or so they told me when I bought the place, but it was where Jimmy kept his girls. Damn fine place if I do say so myself, but it ain't my style. I like to be close to the bar, if you follow me. Why, you need a place to stay?"

"Do me a favor." Mister Jones swirled his glass, watching the golden liquor as it spun. "Hold onto it for me, will you?"

"Sure, Roy. Anything for you."

"One last thing. Do you know a man named Leonard? He was a boxer, pretty good fighter too. Guess he still goes the rounds down at Art's place. You know who I'm talkin' about?"

"Leonard—" TJ scratched at his head, playing it dumb, wondering just what Mister Jones was up to—"Boxer, down at Art's."

"You know, bald, missing two front teeth, don't fight no more, but helps out a lot." Mister Jones was all business. "The reason I'm askin' is 'cause I want to thank him for everything he's done for Michael. You wouldn't know where I could find him, do you?"

"Leonard." TJ smiled, satisfied with the explanation. "You mean Leonard Hill."

"That's him." Mister Jones smiled. "Leonard Hill. You don't happen to know where I can find him. I don't want to go stickin' my head around that old coot Art. Me and him, we don't mesh."

"Leonard don't live far from here," TJ said. "Just a few blocks away, in fact. Lives in the old complex." Leonard pointed across the bar, out the window and off somewhere that only Mister Jones could see. "Top floor, number six."

"Top floor, number six, got it."

"If you like, I can draw you a map."

"Oh no, that's just fine, but thank you, TJ. You're always good to me and I always remember who's naughty and who's nice. And speaking of that"—Mister Jones stood up from the bar and downed the last bit of scotch left in his glass—"it's time to go play Old Saint Nick. But I got something for you first." Jones laid a brand new, crisp fifty-dollar bill on the old bar counter. "Merry Christmas, TJ, keep the change."

TJ stared at the bill. "Thank you, Roy, and a Merry Christmas to you."

"Oh." He was halfway across the room, the door opening on its own, Harry still crying in his drink, TJ still staring at the bill, neither man seeing the snow as it flew through the open door. "It will be. I'm sure it will."

The door banged shut, the bell rang, and TJ looked up and waved. "Goodbye, Roy!"

As Mister Jones climbed those stairs and slipped from their sight, they all heard him laugh.

And laugh,

Like Old Saint Nick.

"Merry Christmas, God bless, and I know you all gonna get what's comin' to you!"

"Will you look at that." Mister Jones stood in the living room of Margaret's apartment staring at the Christmas tree. It was a full tree, an evergreen that stretched up to the ceiling; a tree that was almost taller than Mister Jones himself. Margaret had decorated it, strung old-fashioned lights from the fifties on its branches with glass ornaments and wooden ones too. And tinsel, there was enough on that tree for a Fifth Avenue Parade. Of course, there was eggnog in a bowl that almost looked like crystal. The record player's needle scratched out Bing Crosby's "White Christmas."

"If I didn't know any better, I'd have thought that you was rich, Margaret. Just look at this place, I mean presents under the tree and stockings. Not the kind of stockings I like, mind you, but still ones full of presents. I guess the other kind of stockings are like that too. I'm tellin' you, if I didn't know any better, I would have thought for sure that Old Saint Nick had broke in last night," Mister Jones said.

Margaret got up from the couch where she sat by Mikey and hurried to the tree. She was wearing a dress, the red dress she wore for special times like this, but her feet were bare, her toes painted red. And her face, it glowed through all that makeup she wore.

"I got something for you, Roy," Margaret said.

"I bet you do." Mister Jones sat down on the couch right smack dab next to Mikey and wrapped his long arm around the boy. "Do me a favor, Margaret."

"Anything, Roy."

"Let me go first, if you don't mind," Mister Jones said. "I got you both a little something special. Something I know I'm gonna like."

"Oh, Roy, you didn't have to do that."

"I know." Mister Jones smiled. "But what can I say, I'm a regular Old Saint Nick. Now, if you look in the back, way in the back there, Margaret, you'll find a red present and a blue one. You see 'em?"

"Found them." Margaret pulled the presents from under the tree.

"Careful now." Mister Jones lifted a finger. "You don't know what's in them."

Margaret stared at the presents: the one wrapped in blue was big, the red one was small. "Which one's mine?" Margaret asked.

Mister Jones's mouth stretched across his face. "Here's a little Christmas magic for you, Margaret, and you too, Michael, you get to choose which one you want."

Margaret looked like a doe caught in headlights. "Roy?"

"But there's only two presents." Mikey astutely pointed out.

"Boy"—Mister Jones whistled—"nothin' gets past him, do it, Margaret?"

"Nothin'."

"You see, Michael"—Mister Jones pulled the boy close, his arm squeezing Mikey's shoulder good and tight. Their faces only millimeters away. "I can show you a little magic if you trust me. Do you trust me, Michael?"

"I…" Mikey leaned back as far as he could, stretching. "I trust you."

"Sure you do." Mister Jones let go of the boy. "Go choose your present, red or blue, Michael."

Mikey stood up and walked to the tree. "How do I know which one to take?"

"You don't. It's just like life, you never know what's coming, but you still get to choose what you gonna do."

Mikey reached down and picked up the red present. It felt light, almost too light for his taste. Maybe it was money, maybe it was nothing but a stupid card. Maybe it was a box full of love. Mikey looked at the big present wrapped in blue paper, a metallic paper that shone under all those old bulbs. In a heartbeat, Mikey put down the red present and took the big blue. He carried it across the room to a chair that was far, far away from his mother and Mister Jones.

"Blue huh?" Mister Jones said.

"Yeah"—Mikey stared at the box—"blue."

"I knew you would choose blue. Just a big blue box, as big as the world. As least it looks like that when you compare it to that red one. But that's all right." Mister Jones turned to Margaret. "You was gonna choose red all along, weren't you, Margaret?"

"How'd you know?"

"An old, fat honky whispered something in my ear. You know, I think he was drunk." Mister Jones winked. "Okay, Michael, open your present, and just remember, you picked it."

It was a shame, Mikey tearing that beautiful wrapping paper. If the fool had known any better, he would have realized that it was antique, real special, maybe it was even magical. But there was something inside that paper, inside the box, so Mikey thought, something for him. And so the man-boy ripped every bit of that wrapping to shreds, letting it fall to the floor where it laid forgotten. In his hands, Mikey held a plain brown box.

"Go on"—Mister Jones prompted—"reach inside."

Mikey reached inside the box and pulled out a pair of brand new boxing shoes. They were white shoes with white laces and white stripes. Shoes that shone even in the low light, shoes that looked like they would dance all on their own, shoes that had even been polished by an old blind friend of Mister Jones, but Mikey didn't see that.

All he saw was a plain old pair of boxing shoes. "Tch, boxing shoes." He dropped those shoes, letting them fall to the ground where they laid on top of all that blue paper. "Gee, thanks."

"Mikey!" Margaret scolded.

"It's okay, Margaret." Mister Jones lifted his hand. "Let me talk to the boy. What, you don't like what you got?"

"They're shoes."

"Damn right they're shoes."

"I didn't want no boxing shoes for Christmas."

Mister Jones sat as cool as a cat. "No?"

"No."

"You sure, now?" Mister Jones cross-examined the boy. "'Cause once you give them shoes up, they're mine and you ain't never gonna get them back no matter how much you beg me. Think hard, Michael, do you want them shoes or not?"

Mikey stared down at the shoes. Still, he didn't see their shine.

"Do you want them or not?"

"No." Mikey folded his arms. "I don't."

"Okay, Michael. I want you to remember somethin' 'cause it's important." Mister Jones reached out, his arms stretching long, his hand groping across the room to those white shoes. "You chose this," Mister Jones said and took the shoes back.

He took the box and set the boxing shoes inside and dropped the torn paper on top of it all. Paper that wrapped itself all around that brown box until it sat perfectly at Mister Jones's side.

"Well then, Margaret, it looks like it's your turn. Merry Christmas and everything, I think you'll like it."

Margaret picked up the little red present, the color of the wrapping paper matched her dress perfectly. She fingered the paper, enjoying the briefest of not-knowing moments before her nails sliced through the clear scotch tape. Carefully, she unwrapped the red paper, even though there was nothing special about it. Folding it, she set it aside and stared at the plain envelope in her hand. "What is it, Roy?" she said.

"You'll see." Mister Jones's eyes glinted. "Go on, open it."

And she did, but this time, Margaret ripped the envelope apart and found herself holding a golden ticket. She stared at the ticket, her face reflected in the burnished color, her mind wondering at it all. "What..." Margaret shook her head and then looked up at Mister Jones. "What is it, Roy?"

"That there is a special ticket." Mister Jones held Margaret's eyes. "It grants you one wish. Whatever you want, anything in the world, you wish for it and it'll happen. So, what is it that you want, Margaret?"

She stared at the golden ticket. "Anything, Roy?"

"Anything."

"But just one wish." Margaret looked up. "Right, Roy?"

"Just the one, no more."

"I don't know." Margaret stared at the golden ticket, her eyes hypnotized. "Do I have to use it now?"

"No, ma'am." Mister Jones shook that head of his. "Whenever you want or never. You get to choose. Today, tomorrow, ten years from now. A wish guaranteed by me and a certain fat honky."

Margaret clutched the ticket to her breast. "Thank you, Roy. Thank you so much."

"Red, just like your dress." Mister Jones smiled. "You're welcome, Margaret. Enjoy."

Mikey jumped to his feet, his face all bent and pissed. "That's not fair!"

He turned, Mister Jones's head slowly turning to the side. "No?"

"Hell, no, it ain't!"

"You chose blue." Mister Jones shrugged. "You could have took red, but you didn't. Red said something like a dollar and a card so you chose blue, and now you doin' what you always do. Some damn things never do change. But tell me somethin', Mikey, what did you get for me?"

Mikey just looked away.

"What? Nothin'? You didn't get me somethin', anything at all?" Mister Jones sat mockingly shocked. "After all the trouble I went through to get you those special shoes, you didn't even get me a single thing."

"Why should I get you anything?" Mikey bit. "You ain't been around, not till now."

"Did you think that would sting?" Mister Jones laughed. "It is a good point and so I will concede to it. However"—that smile tore up his face, running like a crack that split through the ground—"tell me, what did you get for your mother there? You know, the one who works hard for you every day, the one who feeds you, who makes sure that you got a roof over your head and a nice bed with blankets to sleep in. That mother of yours sittin' so pretty under the tree. What did you get her, boy? What did you get the woman who has given you everything that you got?"

Mikey stood staring at the ground, his face flushed red.

"What's that?" Mister Jones leaned an ear towards the boy. "I didn't quite hear you. What did you say?"

"Nothin'."

"You said nothin', or that's what you got her, nothin'?" Mister Jones smiled at the man-boy. "Which is it, Mikey?"

Mikey turned, mad as all hell. "I didn't get her nothin'!"

There were tears in Margaret's eyes.

"Of course you didn't 'cause you is you, and you always do what you always do. You hurt your mother again, poor thing. Ain't you just tough as an alley cat?" Mister Jones stared into the boy's soul. "But you ain't no Tom, so sit down and shut your mouth before you ruin our family Christmas and make me do somethin' that I've been itchin' to do for a long, long time."

He was a kid—a stupid, headstrong teenager. Seventeen and grown up, eighteen soon, a kid who thought he knew it all. Mikey opened his mouth, but nothing came out. He sat down, his eyes fixed on the floor, hating Mister Jones—hating his mother more.

"Roy." Margaret looked up, her eyes still full of tears that glittered in the Christmas lights. "Can I give Mikey something I got for him? Maybe that'll make things better."

"He don't deserve it. All he should have got was a lump of coal. How come, Margaret"—Mister Jones put his hand on his chin—"how come kids don't get coal no more? 'Cause I'm tellin' you, I know a hell of a lot of little brats that should get a ton of it. And I am talkin' about black, sooty, dirty coal. It just baffles me. But oh well, they'll get theirs one day, just like Mikey here. That's the thing everyone forgets. I knew the boy wasn't gonna get you somethin', Margaret, so I splurged a little and got you somethin' extra. Somethin' I knew you've been wanting for a long, long time."

"Roy!" Margaret's face shone like the tree. "You didn't!"

"I most certainly did. If you reach back where you found your present, you'll find that there's somethin' there now that wasn't there before."

Margaret was already on her knees under the tree, digging like she was a little girl again on Christmas morning. In a moment, she brought out a big box that was wrapped in red and white paper like a candy cane. "Oh, my! What is it, Roy? Tell me!"

"You always ask that." Mister Jones smiled. "Ever since you was a child, you've always said just that to me. Why don't you open it up and see."

This time Margaret's heart was beating fast, so fast that her hands shook as her finger touched the paper. Her nail cut through the tape, but bit at the red and white paper. She was too excited to fold it although she tried, but she ended up just setting it aside. She opened that box and stuck her face inside and her eyes lit; her whole being shone. "Oh, my!" She pulled her present from the box, it was a fur jacket with a collar so big it could hide her face. "It's beautiful, Roy!" With her mouth half-open, she groped the dead animal, running her hand through the red and blacks of what was once alive, lifting it to her face, touching her cheek to the fur. "Is it mink?"

"You tell me."

"It's fox." She stared at the thing. "I know it's fox."

"Then fox it is."

"I've always wanted a fox jacket."

"I know."

"I love it." Margaret beamed and crawled inside that skin. "Thank you, Roy! Thank you so much! Oh, I got you something too!"

"How did I ever know."

Margaret reached under the tree and held a little present in her hand. It was wrapped in green paper, a hand-tied red bow. She beamed. "Merry Christmas, Roy."

"Thank you, Margaret."

Margaret never remembered him opening the present, and if Mikey had been watching, he wouldn't have either. But the man-boy was too busy this holy day, sitting in that chair across the room as others around the world wished for peace on earth and goodwill to their fellowmen, wishing that his mother and Mister Jones were dead. The present sat on Mister Jones's lap, a velvet box that opened all by itself. "Cufflinks." Mister Jones never looked down at the things. "Thank you, Margaret. I surely do appreciate it."

"They're gold, Roy."

"I know."

"White gold."

"I'd swear you was rich."

"Worked overtime." Margaret blushed. "I wanted to have the best Christmas ever this year."

"And we did, didn't we?"

"We did."

"And you got a fur."

She practically glowed. "And a wish."

"That's right." Mister Jones sat back and set the cufflinks aside. "A special wish too. One I know is gonna come true."

The front door shut as Bing Crosby sang again. Margaret turned to Mikey, but the chair was empty. Her hand found her heart, her eyes found the floor, and for a long minute, maybe even two, the woman said nothing at all. "Is he all right, Roy?"

"He never has been."

"Do you think he'll come back?"

"Does a dog eat its vomit? He won't come back for a while. At least long enough for you to catch your breath." Mister Jones stood and walked to the card table where Bing belted it out. "Eggnog, Margaret?"

"You trying to get me drunk?"

"Ain't gonna be no try to it." Mister Jones poured her a cup. "No, not with you."

She laughed and pulled the collar of her coat up, hiding half of her fox face. "Why not?" You couldn't see her mouth move. "Why not drink? I'd love some."

Mister Jones poured himself a cup and lifted it high. "Here's a toast to that red dress of yours. It look good on, but it'll always look better off. Merry Christmas, Margaret."

"Merry Christmas, Roy."

You win some, and you lose some; that's just the way it is. Art closed the gym door and stuck his key in the lock; the dead bolt slid into place. He turned and walked down the sidewalk toward his chair that sat in front of the black and white television set at home—walked toward nothing. Unreal, Art thought, life is just so unreal. It goes by so fast. One minute you're a kid, playing out back without a care in the world, playing baseball or football or playing up in a tree or on the street, and then the next thing you know is that you're eighteen. Eighteen and on top of the world, young and strong and your body's at its best and there ain't nothing you can't do—nothing at all. Fact is, you try everything 'cause you're young and dumb and don't know any better. And then you wake up one morning and you're old.

There's white in your hair, white in your beard, and now kids and pretty girls look at you different 'cause you ain't one of them no more. They call you "sir" and "mister" or some other damn thing and treat you different, and that's when you realize that time's slippin' by way too damn fast. Slipping so fast that you don't notice the changes until you look back. Still, you're in your forties, your fifties, and even then you only pause and look back when you have to, when you're forced to. Times when you lose a friend, lose someone close to a heart attack and you think, damn, we was just kids. But it don't ever last that long.

For a day, maybe two, you see life and the end and all that's coming but you're still young—only forty-two. But still, you know that time's running quick and it's taking everything you got. Taking your friends, taking your body, taking your mind too. And one day, you know it will take you—just eat you up. Eats you up and leave you for dead. But you still young, still forty-two, still fifty-something, and still you got time 'cause it's Christmas Day and you're all alone. Then comes that day when you wake up and you're blowing out all them damn candles on that imaginary cake and you know you're old.

Old and alone.

Now you got nothing, Art thought, your friends are gone, your family too, if you ever had any family, that is. And even if you do, they're all younger than you, and so they treat you like you're some ancient thing, something breakable that's supposed to sit on a shelf, stay still so you don't fall down and break your hip. They're young and you're not, so they talk loud to you because they can't see the kid who just loves baseball, who loves to box; a kid who's too old to do those things anymore.

So you sit in front of your TV with your damn TV tray and eat something that was frozen until you stuck it in the stove. And all the while you're wishing, you're praying that you could go back. Go back to the good old days and be young again and this time you'd appreciate it. Go back to New Orleans and Betty and this time you'd never take it for granted 'cause tomorrow you're gonna be old. And when you're old, you pray harder, even if you don't believe in Him.

Pray harder and tell Him that you wouldn't waste your time on stupid things that just don't matter. But still you're old and your prayers are never answered, and then you try a new angle with Him—you try to make deals.

You tell Him that you'd give your arms and legs if you could just go back 'cause what's a leg compared to Betty? Nothing, Art thought, not a thing. Both your legs too. So you tell Him that you'd love her more than yourself, love her like you love her now—now that she's gone, now that you realize what you missed—and you mean it too, because you would.

*I would*, Art thought, *in a heartbeat*. But she ain't gonna come back because He don't make deals, even if they said He does. And then you realize what you've lost.

Again he stumbled like he was drunk. In fact, he felt drunk, even though he hadn't drunk a drop. And it was the type of drunk that felt like it would never go away. The type that started off good, started fun, but as the night went on and you drank more and more, you begged for it to end over a toilet bowl. You begged for the cloud, the haze, the black hell of it all to go away. But tonight, it wouldn't go away. It seemed as if it was here to stay with rain and the cold and the dark, dirty city. Christmas night for Art. His chest tightened, Art's heartbeat fast, that uncomfortable feeling heavy in his chest. He breathed out, wishing that his heart would just stop, wishing for morning, 'cause there was always a morning.

Even if you died, even if your body was sitting in front of the black and white, the morning still came, even if you were dead.

Gone but not forgotten for a few weeks or a month or a year if you was lucky. But in the end, you'd be forgotten, even if your picture hung from a banner above a ring. You was just a picture, just a name, just a has-been of a forgotten time. *Here I am at the end of my life, wishing for something I was always afraid of, welcoming it, in fact. Ain't that funny.* Art's eyes fell to the sidewalk, to the cracks.

It was funny how some cracks, Art thought, were straight as razor's edge while some were broke and splintered, running in every direction. And then there were the cracks that were deep and dark, even though they were just cracks in the sidewalk. Cracks everywhere, Art thought, cracks in fighters too.

The crack could be in a fighter's guard, his feet or a weak chin. It could be the way a fighter stood or the way he held his hands. A crack could be in the fighter's head, in his mind, a crack like that could cost a fighter the fight, even before the bell rang. And then there were the fighters who always got hurt.

Maybe they broke their hands, maybe they bruised too easily, maybe their body was weak, or maybe their skin was paper thin. Skin that tore, that ripped, that cut too easily. Cracks like that could cut deep and nasty. Cuts like that could end a fight quick. Even if a fighter was winning, even if he was beating the other guy good, a cut could cost a fighter everything. Unless you had a good cut man.

A good cut man was worth his weight in gold 'cause he knew how to work a cut, how to stop the bleeding, how to ice the skin, work the blood away from the wound, how to gunk that cut up so good that a fighter could fight another round. And with another round came hope, came life 'cause you never knew what could happen in a fight. One minute, your fighter could get the daylights knocked out of him only to come back an instant later and knock the other fool out. A good cut man meant life. The snow came with rain, drops of silver, of white, falling in front of Art's face. *That's what I need*, he thought, *a good cut man from my day.*

Ace, Art thought, Ace was the best cut man in the day. He could work any cut—on the jut of the cheek, over the eye, the kind that dug deep in the brow and blinded a fighter—take those cuts and stop the bleeding, slow the swelling so the fight could go on. How many fights did he save, Art wondered, how many fights did he save for me? Art wished he was here, wished he could see that crooked smile and lift another round to the man. But Harry Poppleton died back in forty-four on some godforsaken island in the Pacific.

Trip and Buddy and Tango who loved to tango when he wasn't working ringside on a Saturday Night. They were all good guys, each man an A' One cut man. But they're gone, Art thought, all dead and gone and now there's only me.

*Oh, God, send me a cut man. Please, just this once, help me. Send me a cut man. A man who can stop the bleeding, slow the swelling, someone who can help me make it to the next round. God, I'm begging you, please.*

The old man walked through the snow, through the rain, and up those steps where a canopy used to hang.

# SEVENTEEN

He was whistling that same old tune, a thing he could never put a name to, wiping that beautiful bar with a soft towel as Harry's head hung over his gin. The bar door opened, the bell that wasn't there rang, and TJ stared in wonder at the man who walked up to his bar and sat down on a stool across from the old keeper. "Well, I'll be..." TJ's mouth dropped a full two inches. "You're Matthew Gore, aren't you?"

It really was a thing to see, the old barkeeper recognizing the man who sat across from him. Matt's clothes were worn thin, dirtied with soot, smelt like smoke too. And his face, a full beard now filled it, but Matt couldn't hide his eyes. No, they were bright, as they had always been, but they were stronger than before. And deep inside, a fire had been rekindled, but now it had been melded into something more.

"I am," Matt said, more than just a little surprised that the man had recognized him. He reached out across the bar and offered the old keeper his hand. "Nice to meet you."

"I can't tell you what an honor it is to meet you." The old barkeeper shook that man's hand—hands that were like stone. "I've seen every one of your fights. I tell you, Mister Gore, you sure are something. Can't wait to see you fight again."

It was Matt, a little shy, a little embarrassed, he looked around the bar, but it was empty save for one man and his crying gin. "Thank you."

"TJ"—the old keep smiled—"call me TJ. Now, what can I get you? And this one's on the house."

"Actually, I'm here for the room that you have for rent."

"Now where did you hear that?"

"Excuse me?"

"How did you hear about the room?"

"I saw the sign."

"Sign?"

"That one." Matt turned and pointed at the window where a sign hung at street level. "There in the window."

"Well, I'll be damned." TJ stared at the thing. "I wonder how that got there."

"You mean you didn't put it up?"

"Nope"—TJ shook his head—"and I'd remember if I did too."

"I'm sorry to bother you." Matt got up from his stool.

"Oh no, you ain't bothering me and if you need a room, I got one for you. Fact is"—TJ turned from the window and looked at the big man—"it's more than just a room. The previous owner and the man that I used to work for until I bought the place, he kept his girls up there. It's a real nice place, little kitchen, full bathroom with a shower and an old tub. You know the kind, cast iron, and as deep as the sea. It ain't my style, probably ain't yours, but it's real nice 'cause Jimmy always treated his women well. But if you want it—" TJ stopped dead in his tracks. "Wait a minute, I almost forgot. Guess that sign threw me for bigger loop than I thought. Sorry, Mister Gore, I promised to hold it. I don't know if he still wants it or not, I'd have to ask him."

"Ask away, TJ." He stood not more than a step behind Matt, smiling a mouthful of gold, looking down at the two of them like an old stage magician of a forgotten day.

"What, cat got your tongue?" Mister Jones said.

"Well I'll be—"

"That's the third time you've said that today," Mister Jones said. "Must be quite a day for you to go off like that."

"It sure damn is, Roy."

"Well, ain't you gonna introduce me to your new friend here?"

"Oh, gosh. What am I thinkin'? Of course I am." TJ tried to get a hold of himself. "With Mister Gore here walkin' in today and you popping up like that and then that sign up there in the window, I'm sorry, Roy."

"What sign?" Mister Jones turned and looked at the window just like TJ, just like Matt. No sign, no sun shining down on the city either. Just cold steps where the rain fell gray. "I don't see no sign."

"Well, I'll be." TJ stared at the window. "Unbelievable."

"That's four, TJ."

"It was there just a minute ago."

"Yessiree, it must be a day to remember." Mister Jones smiled. "Here I come to the bar to do a little business and what do I see? My good friend talking to the man that's gonna be the next heavyweight champion of the world! My oh my, it sure is just like TJ said, unbelievable! Tell me, Matt, you don't mind if I call you Matt, do you, or would you prefer Matthew or Mister Gore? You get to choose."

It was funny, Matt could usually get a lead on a man, see a weakness, see if he was a fighter or a talker or some stupid street thug, see if he was genuine, or lonely like Art, or if he was a preacher man with snake oil, but this man, all he could see was teeth. "Matt," he said. "Call me Matt."

"I'm Jones." Mister Jones reached out, his hand stretching, meeting Matt's in the middle. As they shook, as their hands touched, Matt heard a bell ringing, heard a crowd cheering, saw the flash of bulbs in Mister Jones's teeth; felt a belt around his waist as his hands were lifted up. "Mister Roy Jones. Pleasure to meet you, Matthew Gore."

And Mister Jones let go of the man's hand. The bell was gone, so were the flashes; gone were the cheers from the crowd and the belt Matt had felt around his waist.

"Now"—Mister Jones rubbed his sides—"if I wasn't mistaken, you two was talkin' about that apartment upstairs that I asked TJ to hold for me. Am I right or am I right?"

"We sure were, Roy," TJ said.

"Yessiree, you sure was. And before we got all sidetracked and everything, you said you'd have to talk to me first, didn't you, TJ?"

"I sure did."

"You is a good man, TJ." Mister Jones meant what he said too. "Yessiree, a damn good man. Dependable. Qualities almost every man should have. Funny thing about this is that I was holdin' that room up there for Mister Matt here."

"What?" Matt stared at the man. "How'd you know I needed a place?"

"You could say a little bird told me." Mister Jones shrugged. "Or I could tell you that I always know things like that 'cause it's my job."

"Your job?"

"That's right, Matt. You see, I'm a manager. I manage men like you. Men who need someone on their side, someone who can get them the things they want, things you want."

"You're a manager?" Matt clarified. "You manage fighters?"

"I manage men." Mister Jones smiled wide. "And yes, some of them have been fighters. And some of them fighters were mean, but not one was as good as you, and still they got what they wanted. You see, Matt, I know things. Like I said, it's my job to know things. I know that you ain't got a place to stay, I know what happened between you and that old trainer of yours. I know that you ain't got a fight comin' up 'cause you wouldn't settle for some tomato can. And if you ask me, I'd say you did right by yourself to get up and walk out of that place." Mister

Jones winked at Matt. "And I know what I can do for you *if* you hire me as your manager."

"Really?" Matt was skeptical. Still, he wanted to hear it. "What can you do for me?" he asked.

"Now don't think that. I'm on the up and up." Mister Jones put his hand across his heart. "In fact, I won't take a dime from you."

"Now I know you're full of it."

"But you didn't let me finish," Mister Jones said. "I won't take a dime from you unless you is completely satisfied. No catches, just up and up like I said, everything on the table. And I do mean everything. And by satisfied, I mean completely, one hundred percent. I'm talkin' about giving you what you want, and I know what you want, Matthew Gore."

"Everyone knows that."

"Of course they do." Mister Jones smiled wickedly. "Everyone knows that you want to be the champ, but there's somethin' else you want. Respect, belief, hope, and not only on your part. You see, that old goat Art never gave you any of them things, even though you've never got knocked down. Fact is, you don't think no one gives you that kind of respect, but I do. I know a way we can show 'em all."

"How's that?"

"By showin' the whole world that beautiful hook of yours. You know, that shot you've been waitin' to unload. I know you want a fight, not a tomato can, mind you, but a real fighter; a top five man. And one last thing here, Mister Matt, I'll gift wrap you a good fighter and drop him in your lap, and after you whoop his ass, I'll bring you the Dancin' Man himself, Mister Detroit City, Mister Franklin Herns. Tell me, Champ, how does that sound?"

He couldn't believe what he was hearing. "Like I'm dreamin'," Matt said.

"Wake up!" Mister Jones slapped Matt hard on the back. "You ain't sleepin'! Not a wink! No, you're not dreamin' no more! Fact is, you is wide awake. Wide awake! And maybe for the first time in your life too. All them faces you been seein', well, they is yours now. So how 'bout it, we got a deal, Matt? You want a shot?"

"And if I'm satisfied, then?"

"You are the cautious one, ain't you? We'll work on that. But if you is satisfied, one hundred percent, mind you, then me and you will draw us up a standard contract with one exception." Mister Jones' face was as dead as a waterless fish.

"I'm listening."

"I take a flat fee and from that fee I arrange everything that you gonna need. I'm talking room and board, which includes cooking and cleaning. From my percentage, I'll arrange for a gym, trainers and the best cut man anywhere. I'll also pay any boxing commission fees, ring night fees, the whole kit and caboodle, Matt, everything. Until then, it's all on me."

"So we're talking what here, sixty, seventy percent?"

Mister Jones laughed. "I ain't Art, Matt. Nosiree, not by a long shot. A flat forty. Nothin' more, nothin' less, nothin' up my sleeve either 'cause there ain't nothin' up it, see."

"Forty percent?" Matt couldn't believe it. "That's all."

"Oh, and one other thing." Mister Jones nodded. "You is the boss. You don't like where you're stayin,' you don't like your trainer, I'll get you a new one; you get to choose. And, for your first fight, I was thinkin' a rematch with Douglas, but if you want something else, someone like May or Hernandez, or maybe you'd prefer a man like Barns, I can do that too."

If Matt hadn't been sitting down, he would have. His head spun, his mind raced, it was all a dream, even if Mister Jones said it wasn't. "Douglas?"

"And then Herns if you like, or we can whoop 'em all: five, four, three, two, one!"

"You can do that?" Matt looked up at the man, it was like he was magic. "Douglas and then Herns?"

"And more. All you got to do is beat Douglas. That I can't do for you. One hundred percent satisfied or I'm out the door. But once you got me, you gotta keep me. So"—Mister Jones extended his hand—"do we have a deal?"

Matt stared at Mister Jones's hand. He could hear the bell again, hear the cheers, feel his arm being lifted on high; feel the belt around his waist. Matt reached out and took Mister Jones's hand. "Deal."

"I think you gonna like this place, Matt." Mister Jones took a key from his pocket, a key on a chain with a white rabbit's foot, and unlocked the door. "Yessiree, I'm sure you will. In fact, I think you're gonna sit here and wonder at everything that's comin' your way. But that's a topic for another time. Right now, I'm opening the door to your new life. Welcome home, Matt." And Mister Jones opened the door.

The apartment was clean and bright. Fresh paint on the walls but without that new paint smell, and the old hardwood floors had been stripped and sanded, polished up to a high shine. A shine that was almost as bright as Mister Jones's shoes—spit and coffee grinds.

In fact, the whole place shone like it was brand spanking new. But it wasn't. The apartment, the bar, the whole damn four stories were older than the burned-out building that Matt had grown up in. Still, Matt marveled as he took a step inside the apartment; just a step ahead of Mister Jones who loomed behind his shoulder. He had never seen so many new things in all his life.

There was a new sofa and a matching chair that sat on an area rug around a new coffee table. And just off from the living room separated by a bar was the kitchen and all its new appliances. In fact, it was all new, all redone: the bathroom and the shower and the old cast iron tub that had been sand-blasted and refinished. The kind of tub that was both wide and deep; deeper than the sea, as Mister Jones would say.

The hallway had been painted, even its closet, the light fixtures, the electrical plugs, they were all new and not only in the hallway but everywhere in that place. Even the bedroom had been redone and furnished with a dresser and a bed for two. And to top it off, there was a color television set in the corner of the living room.

"I tell ya, it sure is comfy, Matt. You ought to try it." Matt turned and looked, but Mister Jones wasn't behind him. He was sitting on the oversized chair, his legs propped up on the coffee table. "Penny for your thoughts," Mister Jones said.

Matt shook his head. "I can't believe it."

"Well, believe it, Matt! It's yours, it's all yours and even more. Come on"—Mister Jones's arm stretched, his hand patted the sofa beside him—"have a seat."

It was like he was dreaming, watching everything unfold from the ceiling, watching his body walk to the sofa and sit down. "Even when I was a kid"—Matt stared at the tall man sitting in the chair next to him—"I never imagined I'd live in a place like this."

"Matt, this ain't nothing. Why there is folks who live in houses bigger than this building. And they fill those houses, cram them with all kinds of things that only money can buy. Now you think after them kind of folk fill their houses that they would be satisfied, wouldn't you? But they ain't, not by a long shot 'cause they buy new things and move those other old expensive things into boxes and storage until they ain't got nowhere left to put anything. And then guess what they do? They don't stop buyin' things, Matt. Nosiree, they don't. They buy bigger houses and fill them all up. But we ain't talkin' about that, are we? We was just talkin' about this place and how it sure is different from that other place you've been livin' in. I think you'll find sleepin' in a real bed is a whole lot nicer than sleepin' on a rickety cot. And don't you worry." Mister Jones leaned close to Matt "That bed in your room, it's big enough for two, but not too big if you know what I mean. I'm talkin' just right."

Matt let go a laugh. Just let go a good laugh; something he hadn't done in years. "Sounds nice."

"Tell me, you like the place?"

"Love it."

"Just wait till you see it all. And if there's anything you don't like, any single thing, all you got to do is tell me and I'll fix it 'cause you're my fighter, Matt." Mister Jones kicked his legs off the coffee table and sat up straight, serious, not a hint of a glint in his smile. "And I mean it, Matt. I've hired you a cleaning lady and a cook. They is one and the same woman. She'll be here tomorrow. She can sew, mend clothes, make this place look real sweet. A little magic for you."

"Look at this place." TJ stood in the doorway. "I'll be damned."

"That's five." Mister Jones held up his hand: four long fingers and a longer thumb. "Five times you've said that tonight. But I don't blame you, TJ. Nosiree, I sure don't. The place is nice, ain't it?"

"I dare to say it's even better than when Jimmy had it. How'd you do it, Roy?"

"Oh, you know me, a little spit, a little shine, a few words here and there to a little bird I know, and bingo! Magic."

"You must have had folks in here workin' all night on this place." TJ still couldn't believe his eyes. "I didn't even hear a thing, not a peep, and I'm a light sleeper too. Fine job, Roy, damn fine."

"What can I do you for, TJ?"

"I almost forgot, you got a call downstairs. The man said you was expecting it, so I came up real quick."

"Thank you, TJ. That's mighty nice of you. If you would, ask him to hold. I know he won't mind."

One last look, one last shake of his head, and TJ headed back down to the bar where he told the other man on the other end of the receiver just what Mister Jones had said. Sure enough, the man didn't mind holding.

Back in the apartment, Mister Jones turned to Matt and said, "I'm gonna skedaddle for a minute, Matt, but while I'm gone, have yourself a good look around. Check it out. Oh, and one last thing, if you hungry, which I know you are, the cupboards are fully stocked and so is the fridge." Mister Jones was now standing at the door. "Welcome home, Matt."

And the door closed on its own.

It didn't startle Matt, the door closing, neither did the sudden appearance of Mister Jones on the sofa or at the door before he left. In fact, Matt didn't see any of it. His mind was buzzing with everything that was happening to him.

He had simply come to rent a room, and in return he had found himself a manager and the possibility of a rematch with Douglas. Now all he needed was a trainer and a gym to work out in, but Matt didn't think too long on these things, not even the rematch. He had a home. A home with a bed, his own bed. *How long has it been since I slept in a bed? A real bed?* Matt turned and looked down the hall.

He could see it, even from here, part of the frame, the thick, blue quilt that covered the bed. Matt hurried from the living room down the hallway, passing the bathroom, and walked right into the bedroom. There was a nightstand with a brass lamp beside the bed, a window that was framed with fine, white curtains, a dresser, and, of course, a closet, but Matt only saw the bed.

He walked to the bed and stood at its side. *A bed*, he thought again, *my own bed. Pillows, cotton sheets, a quilt and an extra blanket.* Matt reached down and touched it. No lumps, no bumps, no metal bars or screws that bite you when you're sleeping. And look at that, two pillows. And right down the hall, there was a bathroom.

*My own bathroom and not something that smells like one giant urinal. No more hurrying downstairs, no waiting. A bathroom with a shower and a tub where I can soak all the bumps and bruises away before I climb into bed.* Matt caressed the bed and looked at his hands for the first time.

It was like he was some chimney sweep from a forgotten time. Matt recoiled his sooty hand. He didn't want to touch another single thing. He hurried from the bedroom down the hall and into the bathroom. Sure enough, there was a cast iron tub, deeper than the sea, an oversized counter and sink, and a shower that looked like it had just been tiled; new towels hung on a silver bar. And as he turned, as he took it all in, Matt saw the face in the mirror.

He recognized the face, he had seen it in his dream now too. It was a face that belonged to a fighter who stood in a ring with his hands raised above his head. And somewhere in the crowd, a voice called to him; the voice of a woman. A woman that he loved.

Even if only in his dreams.

Steam covered the mirror. Matt didn't remember turning on the shower, but he didn't care. The man in the mirror was gone. He took off his clothes and stepped into the shower, letting the soot, black and filthy, run from his body down the drain. The big man stood under the falling water, there were no more shadows, no more doors that weren't there; just water falling onto his body, just water washing him clean.

Old clothes dropped in a pile. Matt could still smell the smoke from his old clothes as he walked down the hall and into the living room. Mister Jones sat in the big chair with his back to Matt, arms on its rests, legs stretched out before him, stretched longer than the Panama Canal.

"You kept the beard." Mister Jones didn't even turn around. "I like it. Now don't you trim it 'cause it gives you that 'beast from the east' look. And don't you worry about them old clothes of yours either, I'll take care of them before I leave. You know, wrap 'em up and take 'em away. Take it all away."

Matt walked over and sat down on the sofa next to Mister Jones. "Thanks, I appreciate it. Everything, I mean."

"No problem, Matt, no problem at all. Now tell me, how is everything? To your liking, I trust?"

"Yeah." Matt nodded. "It's perfect. Couldn't have done better if I worked at it for months."

"Damn"—Mister Jones laughed—"you is just like they said you would be, all humble and nice and everything. It sure is gonna be fun workin' with you, Mister Gore. A whole hell of a lot of fun, too. Glad you like the place. Call it a gift from me to you for hiring me as your manager. A perk, if you like. And now here's another one for you. I got news and the news is good. Yessiree, I'd say it's even better than good 'cause you is never gonna believe it till you see it for yourself. Now don't get excited or don't start thinkin' what it might be 'cause you're in need of a good night's rest. And as your manager, I insist on you gettin' it." Mister Jones stood, he was holding a bag in his hand—a bag full of Matt's clothes. "There's Chinese in the fridge, fresh sheets on your bed, and don't worry about turnin' up the heat if you is cold 'cause it's all on me."

Matt stood. "I appreciate it, but I can pay for every—"

"Oh no, Mister Matthew Gore, don't you be sayin' that. This is all on me. I know the price you gonna be payin'. What you is forgettin', what that old fool of a trainer of yours always forgot is that you is the one that's got to step into the ring. You gonna pay for it, Matt, sooner or later, you gonna pay. You is the one that's got to stand toe to toe with some gorilla and unleash holy hell on him. And"—Mister Jones leaned in close—"you got to win. If you don't win, you lose, Matt. I think both me and you know what that means. But like I said"—Mister Jones leaned back and smiled: gold—"I got faith in you, and more importantly, I got faith in me. A whole hell of a lot of it too. I don't go wrong, Mister Gore, that's other people's job. As your manager, I'm just makin' sure that you don't worry about nothin' except fightin'."

"That's it." Matt reaffirmed. "Just me fighting."

"This is all about you."

"On the level here, no strings attached. Forty percent, right?"

"No strings, nothin' up my sleeves, forty flat on the barrel head. Not a nickel more. I never go back on my word, Matt." Mister Jones stood tall. "Never. Chinese in the fridge and there's a clean bed just waiting for you. I'll be by at seven sharp to pick you up for our little date. You gonna like your surprise, all of them."

"Sounds good."

"It sure does." Mister Jones opened the front door. "Sweet dreams, champ."

The door shut and Matt stood alone in the apartment. No dark corners, no shadows, not even under his bed. He walked across the living room and into the kitchen and pulled open the refrigerator's door. White boxes, red letters: Take Out.

Matt opened the lid, Chicken Lo Mein. "I'll be damned."

His favorite.

# EIGHTEEN

The wind rose in the middle of the night, beating against Matt's window, but the fighter never woke, nor did he hear the howl. He slept deep as the warm air invaded the city. Snow and ice melted, the streets dried, trash blew into a different part of town. By morning, the city looked entirely different. Even the sunrise seemed warm for a change. But it was a lie whispered in winter, a sign of things to come: something new was moving in.

Still, Matt woke early and went for a run in this new part of the same old city. He saw the streets, saw the sky, saw that the clouds were only thin, quick things of silver. The earth turned and sun came to be. But before its rising, before the death of night, the world seemed as it was, a round miracle in the celestial sea. Matt ran, the air full in his lungs, his legs light, his feet carrying him as if they were winged. And as he stood on the steps to his new home and looked up the street, Matt could have sworn that he heard a little bird, singing in bare branches.

He showered and soaked in the falling water, ate a simple breakfast of eggs and toast. Finding a pair of pants and shirt just his size, Matt dressed and opted for the jacket that hung in the hallway closet instead of the winter coat. New socks, new shoes, dress ones too. All that he needed was there in his apartment and all of it had been provided by the wonderful Mister Jones.

Now Matt stood on the curb, waiting for the man who had given him everything in only a day—hope. *Douglas*, he thought, *Douglas. I can beat that man.* And then something odd struck Matt: last night, after his dinner, after brushing his teeth, after he had climbed between those sweet cotton sheets, all night Matt had never once thought about Douglas. It was as if that old burned-out building had spit him out from its guts and kept the fear, kept the worry, kept the very things that had always made Matt feel like he was just a step, just a six. Because he wasn't. Not anymore.

*Now*, Matt thought as he stared down at his fine dress shoes, *now I'm—maybe I should change my shoes.*

White-walled tires rolled past his shoes, an old Cadillac in perfect condition came to a stop. "It's a beautiful morning, champ. Come on." the window was down, Mister Jones was inside, behind the wheel, smiling like a cat with a canary in his mouth. "Get inside. We got business this morning. Business you gonna like."

Matt opened the door and climbed into the red seats. "Morning," he said.

"How was your run?"

"Good," Matt said. "Better than I thought it would be. How'd you know I ran?"

"Like I said"—Mister Jones smiled, teeth showing—"it's my job. Besides, I never can sleep." He pulled from the curb, cut in front of another car, and the driver thought about blowing his horn, thought about giving that fool the finger too, but he didn't. There was something about that car, something about the driver that he couldn't see, something that made him take the first left turn and speed away. Mister Jones said to Matt, "You nervous now, ain't you?"

"Yeah." Matt nodded. "But I don't know why."

"Let me let you in on a little secret. You see, you know what's going on. At least you do inside, but most folk nowadays don't listen to their insides no more. They think their brain tells them everything they need, but they're wrong. No, that old head of yours will lie to you, tell you the worst kind of things. But, it's just a brain and all a brain ever does do is think, think, think. That's it, day and night and night and day—think. But inside, you know that this mornin' is something big. In fact, you know somethin's comin' your way, don't you, champ?"

He was right, Matt thought. Ever since he had climbed out from that wonderful bed of his, even on his run, Matt could feel those butterflies in his gut boiling. Before Harris, before Ingram, before Joseph and Douglas, he had felt those same damn fluttering wings. "What is it?" Matt said.

"Before I tell you, I got somethin' for you. Have a look in the back seat, champ." Mister Jones's head twisted, turning back as his arms stayed straight on the wheel. On the seat was a package, big and bulky, wrapped in a brown paper that almost looked like butcher's paper. "That there package is for you." Matt climbed over the seat and grabbed the package. "From me to you," Mister Jones said. Matt stared at the paper, at the plain white string that held it all together. "Go on, open it."

He did. Matt pulled the string aside and tore the paper. They shone. They really shone: white, beautiful boxing shoes. In all his time as a boxer, in all his life for that matter, he had never seen such a pair of boxing shoes, let alone owned a pair.

"You like 'em?"

Matt stared at the shoes. "Like ain't the word."

"Merry Christmas, Matt." Mister Jones laughed. "Sorry it had to be late."

Matt looked over at Mister Jones, dumbfounded, "They're mine? Really?"

"Only if you want them, champ. Do you want them?"

It was a moment, a moment were there was nothing but the sound of a bell and then nothing at all; Matt was nodding, only he didn't know that he was nodding as he stared at those shoes. "Yeah," he said. "I do. I really do."

"Let me tell you a thing about them shoes." Mister Jones rounded a corner, though his hands never turned the wheel. "They is white shoes, as you can plainly see for yourself. But white shoes show off a man's feet. You ever see someone running in black shoes or brown ones? They look slow as all hell, even though they might be faster than lightnin'. And those shoes are magic shoes, Matt. Want to know why they're magic?"

"Yeah."

"'Cause you gonna be wearin' them, and on the first day you wear them, you gonna land yourself one the best damn trainers in the world." Mister Jones laughed. "Tell me, Matt, who is the best trainer out there?"

"Teddy." Matt stared at Mister Jones. "You're talkin' Teddy McNabb and James Robinson?"

"Teddy and James." Mister Jones gave his head a shake. "They here to see you."

It was like Matt was a kid again. "You're kidding!"

"Not today I ain't," Mister Jones said. "Nosiree, this morning you got a date with Teddy and James. You gonna do a little sparin' in them new shoes of yours. They want to see you, they is excited to see you too, champ, Mister Matthew Marvelous Gore."

The world spun again. "I can't believe it."

"You will, soon enough, you sure will, champ. All of this is gonna seem like a dream. But there ain't no more time for talk 'cause we here." Mister Jones smiled. "You ready?"

It was a warehouse, nothing but an old warehouse in the city. Ugly, dingy, stains running down the sides of the building, but the second Matt opened the door, the moment that he stepped inside, he felt as if he had entered a new world.

Bright lights, white walls, and in the middle of the wide floor, a boxing ring with blue and red ropes stood proudly. And there were other things Matt didn't see—heavy bags, speed bags, a double-ended bag too, jump ropes and weights. Mister Jones patted Matt on the back and pointed off to a side door. "That door there, it's your locker room. Go get changed. Let's show 'em what you got."

It felt like a fight: new shoes, boxing shorts, new protective gear, and a trainer who Matt had never seen before to tape his hands. In a moment's time, Matt was ready to spar, the butterflies multiplying in his stomach as he walked out of the locker room and into—what?

The gym.

His opponent danced in the ring, but Matt didn't recognize the man right off. Off to the side, Mister Jones stood with Teddy and James. And now Matt felt like throwing up. Matt walked up the three steps to the ring, they felt higher this morning; longer too. The ropes were parted by the referee, Matt stepped inside the ring, and then he recognized his sparring partner across the way. His name was Davis, a once upon a time top five fighter. A man many said would one day be the Heavyweight Champion of the World. A man who was more than a little dangerous.

Matt felt the mouth by his ear. "Go on now," Mister Jones said as the hammer struck a silver bell. "Show 'em who you are."

"Oh, Lord!" The old man, a man just as thin and tall as a chopstick, jumped up and down, slapping Teddy's back, Teddy who was half the old man's age. Matt stood at the center of the ring, looking down on the once upon a time fighter clutching his ribs. "Did you see that?" James said.

Teddy smiled like a regular Irish banshee as the referee knelt at Davis's side. "I sure did!"

"I knew it! I knew he had it in him." James fixed his hat, the kind of hat that a newsboy would have worn back in the thirties, as the man who had taped Matt's hands poured into the ring. "Man o' man, he is somethin' for sure. And tell me, who's been sayin' that?"

"You," Teddy said.

"For years too." James smiled. "Damn, when I'm right, I'm right, and he did it against Davis. Man o' man!"

"Jim," Teddy called up to the ring. "How's Davis?"

"A mess," the little man, who had taped Matt's hands, said. "Cracked a rib, three others a mess, or I'm a fool."

Mister Jones's mouth turned up, teeth and gold. "He's no fool."

"Teddy, you know what we're lookin' at here." James elbowed his friend as he tried to keep his grin minimal on his face. "You know it, right?"

"You think so?"

"I know so." James smiled almost as wide as Mister Jones, but it was a nice smile, a smile full of joy. And even though the trainer was old, even though he had been around the block a time or two, his eyes were clear and bright. The man could see things in fighters that other trainers never could. "Tell me, Mister Jones"—James turned to the tall, thin man—"just where has he been hidin' that hook, 'cause I'm dyin' to know."

Mister Jones smiled all cat-and-canary like. "Up his sleeve."

They laughed, the three of them; their eyes still fixed on the ring. "I think it's time we broke the good news," James said.

"Matt," Teddy called. "Why don't you come on down here, we'd like to talk to you for a minute." Matt climbed through the ropes and hurried over to the trio. "How you feeling?"

"Good." Matt nodded. "Real good."

"You can call me Teddy"—Teddy pointed to his partner in crime—"and that man there is James."

"It's an honor," Matt said. "A real honor. I mean I've watched you both forever. What you did with McCoy, it was nothin' short of genius."

James patted Matt on the back. "Believe it or not, we've had our eyes on you."

And Matt's heart soared. *It was gonna happen, things are going to go my way, Teddy and James, my trainers: unbelievable.* But Teddy was all business now. "I need to ask you something, Matt. Something important, something I need to know, to see whether or not we're on the same page," he said.

And that warm feeling sank into Matt's gut. He was nervous, downright scared. "Sure." He tried to say it with confidence, but he didn't feel sure at all. "Go ahead."

"I need to know what happened between you and Art."

Matt looked away. "We had a disagreement."

"What kind?"

"About who I should fight."

"I'm listening."

"I told him I wanted a shot, I said I didn't want to fight no has-been or no tomato can. But Art, he wanted me to fight Barns."

"Barns?" James looked like he had just stuck something sour in his mouth. "He wanted you to fight Barns? Really?"

"Yeah," Matt said. "I, uh, I don't want to talk bad about Art 'cause he gave me everything I got, you know? He's a good man, just tired, that's all. But the thing is, he didn't believe that I could beat Barns. Said Herns would kill me."

"And what do you think?"

Matt looked Teddy in the eye and nodded. *He believes,* Teddy thought. "I'm a fighter," Matt said.

"You know, Matt," Teddy said. "Sometimes a trainer can work with a fighter a little too long and when that happens, things go wrong. Art, I got nothin' but respect for the man. And you"—

Teddy nodded—"you did good respecting him like you did there. I admire that in a man. It just goes to show me what you have, and what you have is heart. That's something that you can't teach, Matt. Either a fighter's got it, or he doesn't."

And now Matt was feeling good again. "Thanks."

"You remember Martin and Smith, Ingram too."

"I do."

"And Joseph, I bet you remember him good."

"Maybe a little too good."

Teddy and James laughed. "Why don't you tell him James."

"Gladly. You see, champ, they remember you too," James said and shook that old head. "Not one of them cats want to jump into the ring with you."

"Really?"

"Gospel truth." James put his hand on his heart. "Not one of them."

"Every one of those guys respects you, Matt," Teddy said. "Let me say that again so you hear it. Harris, Ingram, that bum Smith, Joseph too, they all respect you and they all are a little more than nervous to get in the ring with you again."

"Even Joseph?"

Teddy nodded. "You see, Matt, when another fighter climbs into the ring with you, they know they're gonna take a beating. They know that they are walking into a war. I'm going to tell you a little something that's going to surprise you." Teddy smiled. "Even Herns don't want to get into the ring with you."

"No way."

"I don't lie," Teddy said in all seriousness. "Not to my fighters, Matt. Only to my wife." And they laughed, Mister Jones the loudest of the four, which gave the others a little creep. "Herns has dreaded the thought of fighting you."

"Why?"

"'Cause you keep fighting, Matt." Teddy was nodding his head, instilling his words into Matt's head.

"And"—James raised a finger—"you ain't ever been down."

"Not once," Teddy said. "You see, whenever another fighter gets into the ring with you, it's life and death. They know they aren't going to knock you out, that you won't ever quit, and that means that they have to fight not only with their hands, with their feet, with their whole damn body, but their heads, Matt. Fighting you means work, hard work. Every one of them had to train for fifteen gut-wrenching rounds of good old fashion punishment. You beat the hell out of Joseph, Matt. On the cards, he won the fight, but I can tell you he didn't *feel* like he won, and there's a lot of people out there that didn't think he won that fight either. And now you have that punch. I tell you, Matt, it's gonna scare the hell out of Joseph and Harris and—"

"And the whole damn heavyweight division." James smiled.

"The whole heavyweight division." Teddy nodded. "Fighting Barns would have been a mistake because once the world sees that shot, no one's going to want to fight you. No one."

The smile on Matt's face stretched from ear to ear. "You're gonna train me."

Teddy paused, considering. "They gonna fear that right hook of yours. If James and I teach you a little secret to your feet, then ain't nobody ever gonna be able to touch you."

And now Matt felt something else, joy mixed with hope. "I thought I was done."

"Now, when we fight Douglas—"

"Douglas?" Matt's jaw literally dropped. "Douglas? I'm fighting Douglas?"

Teddy turned to Mister Jones. "You didn't tell him?"

"I thought I'd let you."

"I can't believe it!" *I got a shot.* "I can't—when? When's the fight?"

"On Valentine's Day."

Matt's mind flew out the window. *Valentine's Day*, he thought, *that's only a month and a half away. I gotta train, gotta work, I gotta—*

"Listen to me, Matt." Teddy put his hand on Matt's shoulder. "We've got time. We're going to work hard and by the time you step into that ring, you're going to be a machine. There isn't anyone better than James when it comes to footwork and he's going to teach you how to dance. He might be old, but he's sweet."

"I'm dreamin'!"

"You just livin' for once," Mister Jones said.

"Just think of it as an arms race, Matt." James smiled. "You is gonna be the biggest of the baddest. You a superpower. But you got to work hard, harder than you ever have before."

"And if you do that"—Teddy said—"if you give it everything you got, all you've dreamed about is going to be yours for the taking. How's that sound?"

Matt's face hurt from smiling. "So good," he said. "You can't imagine how good."

"That's what I like to hear." James patted Matt on the back again.

"Good." Teddy smiled. "How about we get to work?"

Matt nodded. "Thought you'd never ask."

"Well?" It was evening, just before seven, dark outside, even though it was still warm—still a lie. Tonight, tomorrow, a week from now, the weather would change and then clouds would come dark. But this evening, Teddy leaned against the office wall inside the gym looking down at his old time friend, thinking that James looked tired tonight. Old and tired after a hard day's work. "What do you think?" Teddy said.

James took a deep breath. "He can move." And he let that breath go in a long exhale. "He'll dance too."

"How good?"

"Like Sammy Davis Jr.."

"That good?"

"He'll be sweeter than Mister Bojangles." James looked up at Teddy and the one time Irish Hope knew that it was true. "And it shouldn't take him long either. The man's got the skill and he got a work ethic I ain't ever seen before, but I don't need to tell you that. You was already thinkin' it. And you was confused too," he said.

Teddy loved the old trainer like he was his own father. Only the man was better than Teddy's own. "So what gives? I mean today we see him and he's doing things that...," he said and then shook his head. "Can you honestly tell me that you've ever seen another fighter like him?"

"Only in my dreams." James laughed. "And then it all changed and there was this woman, this beautiful woman. Man o' man, was she somethin'."

Teddy held back his laugh, only the smile on his face couldn't be hidden. "You never do change, do you?"

"I always say"—James smiled—"you are who you are."

"So who's Matt Gore?"

"Honest to God." The old trainer sat back in his seat. "I don't have a clue. We wasn't shootin' no jive out there. He has a chance to be good if he can get out of that head of his."

"That's the key, ain't it?"

"Amen."

"I still can't believe that this man is the same man that we've gone up against," Teddy said. "How many times, James, how many fights have we been across the ring from him?"

"Shoot." James scratched his head. "Maybe four or five. Maybe even six."

"Seven."

"Seven!" The old trainer couldn't believe it. "You sure?"

"Martin fought him twice."

"That's right, Martin lost twice too."

"But they were close fights," Teddy said. "Matt had heart, Martin didn't, that's the final score. We both have come to know his weaknesses, and we both believe we could help him. So, what's the difference with today?"

"How do you mean?"

"Between the fighter we've been across the ring from and that man we saw in the gym today?"

"That—" James breathed out. "That is one of them million-dollar questions. Being truthful here, honest to God and everything, I don't know."

"Well"—Teddy shook his head—"we better find out quick."

It was an evil-looking thing with tubes and cords and a mouth that beeped every now and then. The machine stood next to Johnette, looking down on her tired body, waiting for the inevitable moment with its hand over her mouth. Johnette's chest rose and fell, and the clear hand fogged with her breath.

"Teddy and James." Matt sat at the bedside, holding Johnette's hand. He still couldn't believe everything that was happening. "I mean they're the best trainers in the world and now they're training me. Me"—Matt pointed to himself—"Matt Gore, I'm just the sixth ranked contender in the world. And you'd like them, Johnette, especially James. He's a little bit like you. And Mister Jones." Matt smiled. "He got me my own apartment!"

"It's got a bedroom and a bathroom that you wouldn't believe. A big tub and a nice shower. *And* I don't got to share it with nobody. I don't think I've ever had my own bathroom. And the kitchen, I know you'd love the kitchen. I ain't ever had a place I could call my own.

"When you're better and everything, don't worry. I know you don't got no place to stay, but you can stay with me. You can have the bedroom and it ain't no thing. The kitchen would be all yours, just like you like it. I can't cook, anyway. And don't worry about me being loud 'cause…" Matt stared down at the floor between his feet. "'Cause maybe it's better this way."

Matt turned and looked out the window.

"I mean I miss them and everything, but they're probably better off, you know? Art, he's tired and Margaret, well…" Matt breathed. "Margaret's got Mikey and her job and everything. She's got a lot more important things than me to worry about. But I ain't got no hard feelings. I just—"

"Mister Gore?" Matt looked up, a nurse stood in the door. The woman dimmed the lights without even asking. "I'm sorry, visiting hours are over," she said.

Matt nodded. "Okay."

The nurse smiled, a thing rehearsed ten thousand times, and walked to the next room where she said and did the same damn thing.

Matt looked around the darkened room. "I'm sorry that I haven't been by, but I will be by more often now." He kissed her hand as the machine loomed over Johnette's body. Matt stood and said, "Good night, Johnette. I'll see you tomorrow." And Matt walked out of the room.

In the dark, Johnette's chest rose and fell. The machine beeped and beeped though the room was empty.

By the time Matt climbed the stairs into the building, it was half past eight. The day had finally caught up with him. Mister Jones, Teddy and James, the gym, the training, the unbelievability of where he was as compared to where he had been had sucked every ounce of his energy. *And Douglas,* Matt pulled the door open and stepped into the lighted hallway, *I'm fighting Dogulas in a month and a half.*

Maybe because he was tired, maybe a little of the old Matt stirred in him, nevertheless he suddenly felt scared. Real scared because this fight, Valentine's Day, would set the tone for the rest of his life. Every morning after February fourteenth, Matt would stand in front of a mirror and see the direct results of that fight. That he could live with. But what he couldn't live with was everyone else.

One more look from the corner of any man's eye, the look that said, 'You ain't nothin'.'" Matt couldn't live with the realization that they were right despite all his believing otherwise. It was the same old fear that had twisted his guts after his first loss.

It had been a close fight, a split decision that should have split Matt's way. He beat Harris good, but Harris was a showboat. He was nothing but a Bolo Puncher who jumped in and threw a wide uppercut that was supposed to be a feign, a setup for a combination. All Harris could throw was a flurry of punches that never landed. Matt stalked him fifteen rounds, cornering him, landing good shots, but nothing that ever connected square. But what Matt didn't do was work Harris's body, beat his bread basket until his legs were gone.

Instead, he had stuck with the game plan until the twelfth round, but by then it was too late. There was enough in Harris's tank to carry him through three rounds, enough to keep him dancing to the end of the fifteenth when Matt had put the showboat on his back just before the bell. But the officials at ringside just didn't see it that way; it was a two to one split. In fact, in every fight Matt had lost, all four of them, it was always a two-to-one split. One official in his corner, the two other birds in the nest that counted.

Matt could still hear the boos, the heckles and jeers from the crowd. He could see the faces of men as they shouted at him; men who had urged him on. And then there was the look on Art's face, the disappointment Matt could clearly see in his eyes, that old, wrinkled hand patting him on the back without an ounce of feeling. It felt like sandpaper. But even more than the look, even more than the heartless pat was what Art had said to him after the fight.

Matt couldn't remember the words Art had spoken, but he remembered the tone, the hollowness of it all. Looking back, Matt knew that it was at that moment that Art stopped believing in him. In effect, it was all over between them.

*What if I do that now? What if I lose to Douglas? What if it's a two-to-one split decision? What if I disappoint Teddy and James and Mister Jones, then it'll be just like Art—they won't like me.*

Of course it was ridiculous, but as Matt walked down the hallway to his new apartment, as he pulled the key from his pocket—the one that hung on the white rabbit's foot—and unlocked his door, Matt felt that old familiar fear beat around in his brain. Things had changed for the good man, his thoughts were better, he had walked out of that old burned-out building on his own, knowing just who he was, but Matt Gore still struggled with the same old triggers. To Matt, love and acceptance were and always would be conditional. *Win and I'm somebody, lose and I'm—*

Nothin'.

Matt turned the handle, opened the door, and took a step inside before stopping dead in his tracks. She was fine.

F-I-N-E.

Fine.

Donna stood in the kitchen, a dishrag in her hand, staring up at Mister Matthew Gore. A moment, another, just the two of them standing there looking into each other's eyes. "Welcome home," Donna finally said and Matt closed the door.

The hallway lights dimmed and somewhere up or down or all along that red casino carpet, a laugh track played.

And played.

Matt couldn't believe it. "Donna."

"You remembered."

How could he ever forget. "Yeah." All his worry, all his fear just washed away. "Of course, I remember."

"So this is…" Donna looked around. "This is your place?"

"As of yesterday."

"It's nice."

"Thanks," Matt said, still dumbfounded.

Donna smiled wide and gave Matt a little wink. "Ain't you the lucky one."

God, he loved Mister Jones. "Yes I am."

"It is all right if I call you Matt, isn't it? 'Cause if you prefer Matthew, or Mister Gore, or something else, that's just fine with me seeing how I work for you."

Of course, he was smiling. Who wouldn't smile? "Whatever is your pleasure."

"Matt." Donna touched her face. "Matt fits you just fine."

"Then Matt it is," Matt said. "Why don't we sit down."

Donna nodded and they sat at the table. Matt across from Donna and those long legs of hers. Legs that he just couldn't take his eyes off of. "So tell me, Matt." Donna almost laughed, knowing just what Matt was looking at. "What do you want?"

Matt looked up, up every inch of her body. "What? What did you say?"

"I said"—she smiled, beautiful—"what would you like?"

Matt pointed to himself. "Me?"

"Yes, you." She laughed as Matt grew hot under the collar. "You know, your favorite food, favorite meals, those kinds of things."

"Oh." Matt felt relieved. "Well…I love homemade macaroni and cheese."

"Really?"

"Ever since I was a kid."

"What else?"

"I never"—Matt sat, staring at her—"I never thought you'd be here."

"Why's that?"

"'Cause you is…" Matt groped for the right word. "You're different."

Donna's eyes narrowed. "Different how?"

"I mean"—Matt shrugged—"why would you talk to me?"

Donna sat back in her chair. "You're serious?"

"Yeah," Matt said. "People talk to me, you know, tell me things like hit the damn bag or how I should train, or they talk at me about themselves, you know? But you, when we met outside the grocery store, you talked with me."

"Well, I'll be." Donna stared at the man in a whole new light. "Tell me, did you ever get that jacket of yours fixed?"

"Nope."

"You know, my mother was a seamstress. She made the finest threads. I'm talking the best clothes you ever saw, Matt. She even made a suit for Carry Grant, you know, the movie star. After that, everything she made was gold though she only charged what she thought was fair. She never got rich, didn't care to be rich either, she just loved sewing. We was close, me and my mother."

"Now cooking." Donna looked into the empty kitchen. "I got that from my father. He said that there was nothing better than sharing something you made with other people, and he was right. Between my mother and my father, that's me in a nutshell. People is just people, and as long as they is good to me, well, I am good to them. And all I've heard is good things about you, Mister Matt, good things. So of course I would talk with you. I ain't nothin' special."

But Matt thought she was special. "Sounds like you grew up good."

"I did." Donna nodded. "I miss them both. Now, how 'bout you Mister Big Time Boxer? What do you love to do?"

"I love boxing," Matt said.

"Mmmmhmmm."

"Boxing is"—Matt sat back in his chair—"it's getting up early before anyone else and running before the sun comes up and watching the whole sky light up. You wouldn't believe how quiet the city is then, but it is. It's so peaceful and all. And training, I love training 'cause that's all you got to think about. I mean, just think about doin' what you're doin', if that makes sense. And"— Matt stopped and looked at Donna—"I'm boring you, ain't I?"

"No." She meant it. "Not at all."

"I love it, that's all." Matt shrugged. "I love every part of it. I guess it's just me, you know?"

"I do." Donna smiled. "We is more alike than you know."

Matt grinned. "Is that a good thing?"

"You better hope so." Donna crossed those long legs. "So, Matt, what do you want?"

"Back to that, huh?"

"Yes, sir." Donna smiled, her face soft, something that wasn't lost on Matt. "We're back to that. Tell me how would you like your place kept?"

"Believe it or not, I ain't ever had a place of my own," Matt said. "This looks fine to me. But if you see somethin' that would work better, go ahead."

"You're easy."

"So I've been told."

"By who?"

Matt winked. "A gentleman never tells."

"Oh, really?"

"Really." Matt smiled. "Haven't you ever heard that?"

"I ain't ever met a gentleman," Donna said. "Not in this part of the city."

"Well, now you have." Matt stuck out his hand. "I'm Matthew Gore."

"I thought you liked Matt?"

"I asked you what you preferred." Matt grinned. "Remember?"

Donna reached out and took his hand. They felt it, something between them, and neither of them let go. "I do," Donna said, her voice soft just like her eyes. "Welcome home, Matthew Gore."

"It's nice to be home," Matt said and their eyes touched. "Thank you."

Finally, they let go.

"Margaret, you'll never guess." It was late, well after eleven, and Margaret was already in bed. Of course, she wasn't wearing a thing except cotton sheets. Cool cotton sheets and a heavy blanket on top. But Mister Jones walked right into her room and sat smack dab on the edge of her bed; Margaret never felt a thing. "You'll never guess who I ran into today," Mister Jones said.

Margaret looked away from the crack in the window. She really didn't care who Mister Jones had seen, she was too busy listening. "Who, Roy?"

"An old friend of yours."

"Angie." Margaret looked back at the crack. "How is she. Did you two get along?"

"Nope, didn't see her." Mister Jones smiled. "Guess again."

"Kate, you saw Kate again?"

"How come you always got to guess that I ran into one of those women friends of yours, Margaret?" Mister Jones scowled. "You ought to know by now that I don't go running into your friends unless there's a reason to. Please, Margaret."

Margaret pulled the blanket up high above her breasts and sat up in bed though her backside was bare. "Mister Henderson," she said.

"Now who the hell is that?"

"James Henderson." Margret almost looked at Mister Jones like he was stupid, but of course she knew better than that. She turned all sweet. "You know, Roy, my boss down at the grocery store."

"Now why would I go runnin' into him, Margaret?" Mister Jones just shook his head. "You know what a game is, don't you?"

"'Course I do, Roy."

"You sick or somethin'?" Mister Jones eyed her. "'Cause you actin' all funny like you been up to somethin', even though I know you ain't done nothin' the whole day."

Margaret tugged at the blanket. "I'm fine."

"Then play the game like you always do, Margaret, or we ain't gonna have no fun tonight." Mister Jones scolded. "Now I ran into somebody, someone who was real close to you there for a while, and you was real close to them too. And you liked them in that odd way of yours, even though you kept tellin' yourself all them ridiculous things that you do. And don't tell me you didn't do none of that 'cause I know everything you do. Just like layin' here listenin' to that damn crack."

"Roy, please." She was a child. "Be nice to me."

"That there is the magic word." Mister Jones smiled. "Fact is, that word will get you just about anything you want. Okay, guess, Margaret, and if you can't tell, I'm askin' real nice—all sugar-and-spice-like."

"Thank you."

"You're welcome." Mister Jones patted her leg. "Now guess."

"Hummm." Margaret put her mind to it. "This is a tough one, Roy. I don't know. Was it"—her brow knit—"was it Debbie?"

"Margaret." Mister Jones moved his hand from her leg. "That there is a woman. You ought to know by now that I didn't run into one of your women friends like I just said two minutes ago. Are we clear on that?"

"Yes, Roy." Margaret pouted, and if he wasn't nice, she was just gonna shut off. "Crystal clear."

"Who got you that nice fur for Christmas?"

She didn't want to say it. "You."

"And who gave you a wish? A gold ticket wish?"

"You did."

"And who put that nosey brat of yours in his place on Christmas Day?"

"Mikey! You ran into Mikey!"

"I certainly did not," Mister Jones said. "I know where that punk ass brat is and where he's gonna be tomorrow. Why would I want to run into him?"

"It was a guess, Roy."

"It was," Mister Jones said. "And at least it wasn't a woman. Now guess again."

"Roy, I'm tired."

"So am I."

"You sleepin' out on the couch like you always do?"

"Margaret"—Mister Jones smiled—"you ought to know by now that I never sleep. Not a wink ever."

"Ever?"

"Never ever."

"Give me a hint, Roy."

"A hint."

"Yes, a hint," Margaret said. "And a good one too."

"Hummm." Mister Jones put his finger on his lips. "A hint. The woman wants a hint. A good hint that will help her guess who I ran into today."

"A real good hint, Roy."

"Okay." Mister Jones smiled—gold. "I got one. Here it is, ready?"

"Ready."

Mister Jones smiled and said, "Dishes."

Margaret looked like a doe caught in headlights. "Dishes, Roy?"

"That's right, dishes. Washing, scrubbing, dishes, Margaret. You love to do them dishes almost as much as you love smokin' them cigarettes of yours."

"That ain't a hint, Roy! What does washing dishes have to do with someone who you ran into today? Please, just tell me."

"Margaret." Mister Jones breathed. "How are you ever gonna learn if I just tell you everything? I mean really, Margaret. You just can't keep goin' on through life waiting to see what comes to you. You got to choose. You can do that, can't you?"

"Roy, just tell me."

"Guess you can't, but I knew already, even though I keep on givin' you chances." Mister Jones smiled. "All right, I'll tell you. Matt. I ran into Matt." And Margaret sat back in bed. "You okay, Margaret? Cat got your tongue?"

"Yeah."

"Which one, cat or okay?"

"I'm okay." Margaret stared down at her bed.

"You sure now? 'Cause there is another part to this whole game," Mister Jones said. "It's called Guess Who He Was With?"

"Art." Margaret's voice was flat. "He was with Art, training."

"Nope. He ain't back with that fool. Matt's got himself two new trainers and the best damn manager in the business, if I do say so myself." Mister Jones's mouth split at the corners turning up into a big fat grin. "I won't ask you to guess again 'cause this one is gonna be a cake topper. The one and only Mister Matthew Gore was with a fine woman," Mister Jones said and now Margaret looked up. "I think her name is…" Mister Jones looked up at the corner of the room, acting like he was thinking hard, real hard. "Donna," he said. "Yessiree, her name is Donna. Fine-lookin' thing that woman is."

Margaret looked to the crack in the window. "So?" Her lip quivered. "I don't care."

"Really?"

"Yeah." she bit, her head turning, her eyes meeting Mister Jones—fire. "Really."

"Well"—Mister Jones patted her leg—"I must have been wrong this time, Margaret. First time ever. I thought you'd care. But seein' how you don't, I'll just leave you be."

"What were they doin'?"

"Gettin' to know each other," Mister Jones said. "Donna, she works for Matt now. He's got his own place and she keeps it. She does the cookin' and the cleanin' and she even does the dishes. Can you imagine her just washin' all them dirty dishes? Wash, wash, washin'. Must be hard work. She even makes the bed every mornin'—his bed, that is."

"Great, big thing that bed is," Mister Jones said it like it was gospel truth. "Big enough for two, maybe even three people if you did it right. But like I said, they was just gettin' to know each other." Mister Jones stood and walked to the window. "You want me to close this for you before I leave you be?"

She stared at the window, cold seeping in. "No," Margaret said. "Leave it open. I like it."

"You the boss." Mister Jones walked to the bedroom door. "Yessiree, you is the boss, Margaret. Goodnight now, sleep tight, and don't you worry about me none, I got to see somebody, have a talk. But don't worry, it ain't one of your woman friends."

And the door closed when Mister Jones was halfway down the hall.

Margaret sat in the dark, staring at the window, at the crack. She could feel the cold crawling on the floor, making its way to the bed, slipping under its posts. *I wish,* Margaret thought, *I wish that Matt...*

No.

*I wish that Donna...*

And Margaret breathed out.

She laid down in her bed, letting the sheet, the blankets fall where they may. For a minute, she tried to close her eyes, but they opened on their own and found their way back to the window and the crack. *I wish...*

*Oh, I wish, I wish, I wish.*

# NINETEEN

For the past two and a half weeks, every day had felt like magic. It didn't matter if it was morning, or if Matt was out on the road running, or in the gym training, or lying in his bed at night utterly exhausted: it was all magic. Even his sleep, deep and filled with the kind of dreams that men will dream, was magical. Today was no different.

Like the sky that stretched forever up into the stars, it seemed that there were endless possibilities for Matt. It didn't matter that clouds hung over the city or that the wind had shifted to the north and come nasty with bitter cold, Matt felt as if anything could happen and would happen. The world was big again; its possibilities infinite. Inside the fighter, Matt felt something stir that had been lost to him so long ago—Matthew Marvelous Gore felt hope.

It was 1975. The year 1974 had passed without notice, though if Matt had acknowledged its passing, he would have been grateful. The year was done: here's to hope and '75. Outside, snow fell on dark streets and the alleys where bums lay half-drunk or dead; forgotten party hats covered their heads. Life seemed almost perfect, almost.

There was still Valentine's Day, still his fight with Douglas in four weeks; still Margaret, Mikey and Art. One day he would see them, come face to face with each of them in turn, and then a reckoning would come. Douglas was no different. But he would fight that man with his fists. Margaret, Mikey, and Art? His hands were no good against them. And there were things that Matt did not know.

For example, Matt did not know that deep down, the man-boy hated him. Mikey was jealous of Matt and he was glad that Matt was gone so he could take his place. Only it had not worked out that way for Mikey. He was still living on the streets, still bumming floors to sleep on, working hard for food to eat. Tonight as the snow fell, Mikey wondered if he could go home. Somewhere beyond him, there came a laugh and the boy knew he couldn't.

And Margaret, how could Matt know that the woman needed options, that she could not live without a backdoor. The woman was always thinking, seeing the future in terms of what-if, creating scenarios because of her past. She would always have alternatives, different avenues of escape once things went wrong. Matt was just another one of those options for Margaret, a tool in some ways. Even now she used him as she sat in a bar crying over a drink, Angie holding her hand. Lastly, there was Art's hidden feelings.

The old trainer truly loved the kid, only Matt was a man now. Even parents fail to let their children grow up. In Art's old and clouded eyes, Matt would forever be that quiet kid who did everything he was told to do. A good kid, the best kind of kid, a child that Art never had. Honestly, the old man loved Matt. Only, age had blinded him—age and tiredness.

It was all of these things, complicated and twisted, felt but not understood, that disturbed Matt during this time of magic. Like Margaret, it was the ghost of things that had been and could have been.

This, of course, was Matt's thinking, his own plowing and seeding, the nurturing of fear that grew and festered in the recesses of his mind until that malicious disease sprang up in his heart. On nights like this when he was utterly exhausted, when he was most susceptible to that beast named fear, Matt found himself not wanting to be alone.

And every day Donna arrived before noon and let herself in with a key that hung on a white rabbit's foot just like Matt's. The key had been presented to her by Mister Jones. Donna wasn't so sure about that man, he was all smiles, all teeth, and Donna knew that anything that came from him would come at a price.

But the work was good: easy in fact. Matt wasn't like most men who talked the talk and walked the walk and called at women as they hustled by. Matt was a quiet man, a man who was respectful and not some wolf with a whistle. In the short time that they had spent together, Donna realized that Mister Jones wasn't quite right about Matt. Outwardly yes, he was quiet, but the man was a thinker. Behind those arms, that big, muscular body of his, behind the beard and that handsome face, there was a mind both keen and quick. Donna could see it in his eyes. It was the spark of interest that led to Donna's own lingering around Matt though the woman was unaware of it herself; tonight was no different.

The dishes were done, the counter had been cleaned, leftovers had been wrapped and set inside the refrigerator, but Donna had left the laundry unfolded. It was a thing she could have done earlier in the day only Donna didn't consciously know that she had left it for later. And later meant when Matt was home, and dinner and cleanup were done, and Matt was sitting in the oversized chair like he was doing now at this very moment. It was a purely unconscious act by Donna, something that only her soul understood because life just works that way—sometimes.

Still it was hard to start a conversation with a man who's quiet. If Donna had known it at the time, it was harder yet to exchange words and feelings with a man who had grown up in utter silence. But that didn't stop her from trying, and it never would.

Donna walked from the kitchen to the sofa where the laundry sat in a basket. She took a towel, folded it, took another and did the same thing. "So," Donna said. "How long we been doing this?"

Matt was taken aback by the question. "Excuse me?"

"You heard me." Donna set the last of the towels folded on the stack. "I asked you how long we've been doing this?"

This was just the type of blunt sincerity that sent Matt reeling. He felt his cheeks grow hot, his world spin. Furthermore, Matt wondered what the right answer was. "What do you mean, what are we doing?"

"Nothin'," Donna said, and Matt was somewhat relieved because nothing wasn't bad, right? But Matt's feeling of relief only lasted for a moment. Donna set the laundry aside and turned squarely to him. She said, "Every night for the past two weeks we been doing this: me finishing up my work, you sitting there watching me, I ask you about your day, you ask me about mine. I tell you, if I didn't know any better, Matthew Gore"—secretly Matt liked it when she used his full name—"I swear we was an old married couple."

Of course, this old married couple comment sent Matt reeling again. His mind threw questions both left and right. This wasn't anything like he had experienced with Margaret, or anyone else for that matter. No, not even once. There was only one thing left for Matt to do, something that a cornered fighter might do. "You forgot," Matt said with a smile and turned the tables.

It was Donna's turn to look confused. "Forgot what?"

Matt smiled the way men would do when they dangled bait in front of a woman's nose. If he had had a newspaper, he would have started reading it. "Nothin', I guess." Matt shrugged. "Thought you would have remembered if it was important to you."

"Remembered what?"

"Nothin'," Matt said again. "Guess you didn't mean it."

Donna found herself helplessly caught. She sat on the edge of the sofa near Matt—their legs almost touching. "Mean what? Tell me."

Again Matt shrugged, which only ensnared Donna further. "It's nothin'. You were just makin' nice, that's all." Matt casually looked away. "So, how was your day?"

Matt didn't expect what came next, but Donna reached out and touched him. And by touching him it meant that she smacked his arm. "Matthew Gore." Again, the smile from Matt. "If you don't tell me what you're talking about, you'll get yours."

Matt liked where this was going. "Really?"

"Yes, really." Donna meant it too. "If you don't tell me what you're talkin' about, you're gonna get more than a smack on your arm."

Matt smiled almost as wide as Mister Jones. "I don't know," he said. "That could be fun."

This comment left Donna with no other option: she hit him. Doubled her fist and hit Matt on the arm. The punch did not have the desired effect that Donna had intended. Then again…

Maybe it did.

Matt lifted his hands in mock surrender and laughed. "I thought you were going to fix that jacket of mine?"

"Well, I don't see no jacket here."

"That's 'cause I threw it away."

Donna hit him again and inexplicably found herself attracted to the man. She took him in: his smile, his eyes, his hands, and then her ears heard his laugh. Donna found a man who was even more handsome than she had thought before. She couldn't help but laugh.

Maybe it was her openness, maybe the warmth in her eyes, or the way she was looking at him that caused Matt to say what he said next. "Your eyes. I noticed. You do have nice eyes."

Donna brushed her hair from her face. She hadn't expected it, not at all. He was a quiet man, a thinker, but there was also a part of him that she had just seen, a part that others never knew existed in him. It was there, somewhere in that man, it was there. She could feel it. "Thank you," she said and looked into his eyes.

Magic.

Art sat under a single lightbulb that hung down from the ceiling, staring down at a pile of bills. Electric, water, sewer and garbage, most of the gym's bills were paid. But there were other bills that loomed over Art's head. Things the gym needed, like new speed bags and heavy bags, and the ring needed a new canvas floor too. And then there was the water heater that was all but dead, and the windows on the south side that some street hoods had broken because they were bored. These things added up, even the small bills, and then came death and taxes.

Art had just paid December's property tax to the wonderful city that had forgotten all about this side of town, and in three months he would pay his gratitude to the great state and Uncle Sam. Art looked up from the pile of bills to his little ledger and the small column that was labeled savings.

His nest egg was about the size of a robin's egg. Until recently, it had been enough for Art to retire with, but that was during the Great Gore Era. Art's dream, Matt taking over the gym, Art working with him, making a little on the side because it was still his gym, had gone up in smoke in December with the mention of Barns. No Matt, no fight with Barns meant no incoming revenue for the foreseeable future unless you counted the measly fees that Art collected from his current crop of fighters. The year would end in red unless…

Matt came back.

But that wasn't going to happen, and Art knew it. For the foreseeable future, Art would spend every dreary day here in the gym surrounded by crumbling bricks, telling boys and men alike the same thing he had preached for so long. Only Art had preached those words so much that he hardly believed in them anymore. The trainer sat back in his chair and washed his knuckles over his face. He was tired.

He breathed; the gym was cold because the old trainer had turned the heat down low, his breath steaming in front of his face. Somehow his eyes found the door and ran out into the dark. He could still see the ring, its shape, the ropes around it, the hard corners, a spit bucket that was left in the far corner, and above it all were the banners where men hung dead.

He was there, Art's cloudy eyes instinctively knowing just where he hung. He could almost make out the outline of his body, his stance, his gloves out, his chin tucked, the hard look in his own eyes, and the big cursive letters that painted his name in gold. Art's eyes fell from his banner to the pile of bills on his desk. The old trainer pushed them away.

Cold, stiff legs walked out of the office door to ringside where the trainer crooked his neck back. Art stared up at the banners. Life was so different back then; men lived their dreams every day, fighting two, sometimes three times a week, more if they could get it, just so they could eat. Art's brow bent—

*No, that wasn't right.*

*We fought two or three times a week because we loved it. We were fighters, and fighters fight. It didn't matter if your nose got broke the night before, if there was a fight, we would take that fight at the drop of a hat. Night after night, week after week, all year round because we loved it. We were born to fight.* And in the dark, Art felt something very odd, very strange, something that he hadn't felt in years; a smile stood on his face.

He could see them back in the day, all the men who hung above him on those banners. Boys he had trained, boys who had grown into men, men who had become champions like Art had done himself. He had almost forgotten. Forgotten that he was a fighter, that when he was forced to retire, when he lost his belt and never got it back, when he couldn't go toe to toe with the best fighters in the world anymore, he became a trainer because he loved boxing. The bills, the ledger, call it your books, they didn't mean nothin'. In his heart, Art was a fighter.

The tears still came as he stared up at the forgotten. "I'm sorry, kid," Art said. "You should be hangin' up there too. Kid, I miss you. I'm so sorry. You got to believe me, I'm sorry."

Art was alone, but words spoken were always heard. It didn't matter if those words were spoken in an empty church where a mouse lived under a pulpit. But these words were spoken in a gym where the gods of the ring hung on dusty banners. As he stood there, as Art remembered who he was and what he loved, as the realization of what he had forgotten came crashing in on his old head, a knock came at the door.

At first, Art didn't hear the door, though he turned and looked around him. His skin pricked, shadows stood dark; the knock came again. The old trainer's legs forgot their stiffness, and Art hurried across the gym to the front door.

"I'm comin'," he hollered, wondering just who was knocking at his door so late at night. "Keep your pants on." The knock came again, louder, the door rattling with it, the old trainer got a little perturbed by it all. "I said keep your pants on!" Turning the dead bolt, freeing the door lock, Art opened the door to Mikey. The kid stank. Flat out smelt like a bum in an alley, looked like it too—skinny, dirty, even his face looked sallow. Art was confused. "Mikey?"

The kid looked embarrassed, or maybe it was shame that smeared his face. Maybe it was a whole hell of a lot of both. "Hey, Art."

"You okay, kid?"

"Yeah," Mikey said like he would have said a few weeks ago, only there wasn't so much bite to his voice. "I was wondering if I could, um…" And now the kid looked away, looked up and down the street, not wanting to meet the old man's eyes. "I was thinking…maybe if it was all right with you, I could maybe stay here?"

Art could have put his arm around the kid and just let him in, but the old trainer remembered something. Something very important. "Why?"

To say the least, Mikey was surprised. He looked at the trainer. "Why?"

"That's right." Art nodded. "Why?"

"'Cause I need a place to stay."

"So do the bums in the alley," Art said. "Why should I let you stay in my gym?"

"'Cause I been thinkin'."

"I'm listenin'."

"I was thinkin' maybe I don't know everythin'."

"That's a start." Art smiled inwardly. "Is that all the thinkin' you've been doin'?"

"No." Mikey's head fell. "I been thinkin' I don't know nothin'. I'd like to learn how to fight, coach."

"Coach?"

"Yeah, coach." The kid's eyes met Art's. There was something new in them that Art had never seen there before. Something he had seen in other kids who were serious about fighting.

*Maybe*, Art thought, *maybe I can teach him something.*

"I'll work hard, train hard too. Do all them things Matt used to do when he was here. I'm sorry too." Mikey said.

Art was hearing all the right words, but anyone can say the right things. The difference came in action. "Tell me, what you sorry for?"

"That I didn't never listen," Mikey said. "I had you, I was trainin' with Matt every day, I wasted all of it. Leonard too."

"Leonard too, huh?"

"Yes, sir." Mikey nodded.

"Why should I believe you?"

"'Cause I listen now, I see things too."

"Tell me what you see."

"I don't want to be on the streets no more. Don't want to be cool either. I want to be..." The kid meant it, Art could see that he meant it. "I want to be like Matt, like you and Leonard," Mikey said.

"One week." The old trainer lifted a crooked finger. "I'll give you one week. You prove yourself, you work hard, do everything I tell you, you get another week. You work hard that week, do everything you suppose to, you get another week. We clear?"

"Thank you, coach." The seventeen year old man-boy was crying. It was something that no one had seen him do since he was twelve. "Thank you so much, you won't regret it."

"Come on." Art stepped aside. "Let's get the heat on and you showered. We got work to do tonight, kid. You don't mind me callin' you kid, do you?"

"No, sir, I like it."

The door shut behind them, banging on its frame before the dead bolt held it still.

Art had gone but not before turning on the heat. Mikey stood at the top of the stairs wearing gray sweats, his feet bare and cold on the old wooden floor. At least he couldn't see his breath in front of his face anymore. Mikey shut off the lights.

The kid was halfway across the floor, the boards groaning under his feet, halfway toward the cot where he would sleep, when he stopped. The radiator hissed and popped. It was his, Mikey thought, it was all his. The refrigerator, the cot, the folding chair with the alarm clock that wasn't there anymore, even the wool blanket, they all had belonged to him—Matt. Even the darkness and the cold.

This was Matt's room, Matt's things, even though he wasn't here anymore. None of it belonged to Mikey. He felt like a stranger again, a kid who was living on the streets, borrowing the concrete and blacktop because they were safe. The gym, this room, the cot that he would lay in, none of it was Mikey's. They were Matt's. Mikey couldn't say that about anything in his life. Not the gray sweats he wore, not his room back home, not anything he had ever had in his life was earned. He was all mouth, all blown up reputation with a bad attitude to match.

And the man-boy realized it.

But the bottom of the barrel didn't come because he was living on the mean streets, it wasn't even the humiliation he felt when he had begged Art for a place to stay. The bottom of the barrel had come when Mikey realized what he was. Seventeen and nothing to show for himself; eighteen coming soon.

No one told Mikey that though; he had heard it on the streets. Heard it yelled from the mouths of old men and women as he ran away, but that didn't mean a thing. In fact, their words had, at first, been a source of pride for the man-boy. What stunned him, what shocked Mikey into looking into himself, was the voice he heard in his head. He recognized it, of course; it was his own voice, though he thought it was older and deeper. It spoke to him as he stood around a burning barrel, his eyes fixed on the licking flames.

*Punk.*

*No good.*

*Punk.*

Over and over again, bottom of the barrel, his own voice calling him names, stinging his soul. He couldn't laugh and run away, not like he did when he stole something from some old man, he couldn't get angry although he tried; the truth had set him free. Free to know, to see, to understand just what he was and what he would be.

Eighteen, nineteen, twenty-three, twenty-eight, forty-two and living on the street, stealing from old people, stealing from his mother when he could. He would be a street punk, a hood one day without a job, an old man with white whiskers and a brown paper sack that hid his bottle inside. It was all his, and Mikey was already paying its price. That night, the voice had driven him away from the barrel, back to his home though he had never stepped foot inside his old place.

He could see his mother's window. The light was on in her room. As the man-boy got closer, he could see inside the room because the shade wasn't drawn. Like always, the window was cracked. She was in bed, lying under the covers, but something struck Mikey as he looked in on her, as she stared at the crack in the window. He had never seen that look on his mother's face.

It was jarring, confusing, and it made Mikey step closer to the window. He knew that he was safe; it was light inside, dark outside. Mikey had learned that trick a long time ago when he had first started prowling the streets. Still, he was careful, even though the snow on the ground muffled his steps. Just inches away from the glass, Mikey stopped and stared.

He tried to discern her thoughts, tried to figure what that look might mean, but he couldn't. It was as if he did not know the woman who lay in his mother's bed.

Mikey bent down and looked through the small crack. Warm air mixing with the night's cold—bending, twisting the woman's face like it was a mask in a potter's furnace. Mikey found himself backing away from the window, turning and running up the street as fast as he could though his empty gut wrenched in pain. That night, though he did not understand it, Mikey knew that his home was lost forever.

After that night, Mikey had spent three more nights on the street alone. He never went back to that burning barrel or that group of "friends." But the memory of his mother on the other side of the window haunted him. When he closed his eyes, when exhaustion overcame the cold and the hunger in his belly, Mikey would dream that he was a young boy again.

He would stand in front of his mother, seeing only her legs that seemed so tall, so high because he was so small. The sun was shining in his dream, falling through the small side window in the kitchen, lighting it warm. And then Mikey would hear his mother's sweet voice calling gently to him. What child would not look to their mother when called? And so Mikey looked up. Up those familiar legs, up her torso to her face only to see a stranger who had stolen his mother's skin.

Again and again the dream would replay in his sleep. Now, as Mikey stood in the dark and stared at the cot, he wondered if he would sleep. And if he did, would he dream again? *Please, God, don't let me dream.*

He walked to the cot like a shambling corpse. Tired, exhausted, cold, and half-starved to death. For the rest of his short life, Mikey would always hate the cold, though he would be buried in winter. He lay down, the last vestiges of the man-boy that was in him fleeting into the dark, and Mikey pulled the old wool blanket around his shoulders. For the first time in a long time, Mikey felt warm. It didn't matter if it was Matt's blanket, didn't matter if it was his cot, or that the gym belonged to Art; he would make this home.

Home.

Tomorrow he would get up, train hard, even if that meant getting his clock cleaned by a bigger, stronger fighter. He would listen to Art, listen to Leonard; the kid smiled—*Leonard.* He would do everything they told him to do and keep his mouth shut. And when the day was over and he lay down to sleep, he would thank Matt for the cot. Mikey's eyes closed, his breath slowed, the young man slept.

Mikey dreamt that night. Only he did not dream of his mother. Instead he stood on a rooftop, blue skies above him, a warm wind from the southwest, and the sun on his shoulders. Mikey turned, around and around, following the flight of a hundred pigeons or more as they circled him again and again—the whole world a whir. Even in his sleep he felt it, it was something that the young man had not felt in a long time,

Peace.

At his birth, his mother had chosen a Christian name—David. David, the King of Israel, who was said to be both strong and wise, a man of great faith who was God's beloved. It was precisely these attributes that the child's mother wished to instill in her newborn son. But there was something that Rula forgot about King David, something that was of vital importance: David lost the Lord's favor.

And so did her son.

Just like the biblical man, David had killed a man, but unlike the King of Israel who sent Bathsheba's husband to the front lines, David used his own hands. In all fairness, the fight was started by the other man, notwithstanding the fact that David had slept with the other man's wife.

It happened in a bar on the wrong side of town. There was a switchblade, and when it flashed, so did David's temper. Without a thought, he charged the other man who promptly made David eat his blade, but the monster of a man never felt that metal's sting as it sank into his belly, his fists were already flying.

The six-foot-four man's hands were literally the size of boxing gloves, mittens that were as big as the other man's face; and when those fists hit, there was a crunch, a bone-breaking snap that everyone in that dark and seedy place heard over the music. The other man's face looked like a pumpkin with teeth poking out its stringy flesh.

But the punch did not kill the man—not immediately. In five, six hours when the man's brain had had sufficient time to swell, he would have passed into that great oblivion, but the man never got those hours of suffering because the second punch was already on its way. It was deemed by a jury that David's second punch, an uppercut that came up from the floor, a shot that caught what little was left of the man's chin and drove the bones in his face up into his brain, was only manslaughter. David got five years of hard labor.

The man did his time, all six-foot-four of him, 220 pounds at the time. Working on farms, bailing hay, throwing 150-pound bales twelve feet up to the top of a flatbed truck where a ferret-faced fool named Barkley struggled to arrange all the bails. And if David wasn't bailing, if he wasn't pounding rocks in a quarry, he was swinging an ax, clearing swamps, wading though the muck in leg irons and all of it made him stronger. No more drinking, no late nights in smoky dens, three squares a day, and David's legs, his chest, his back, and those arms of his grew. At the end of his sentence, David had swelled to a wonderful 243 pounds.

He would have gone right back to jail if he hadn't stumbled across a "Wanted" sign. David was in need of money and at the time, being an ex-con, there were only a few options for such a man. There was a war in Vietnam and though he had a record, the military always found a way to bend the rules. But David could never take orders except from his momma, so he took a chance on the sign and found himself standing in a boxing ring.

He was hired as a sparring partner, a man used by another boxer for practice. And as it happened that day, David knocked the number four heavyweight contender out. The ex-con—the man with a temper and a liking for married women, a man with a loud mouth—found himself a career.

In boxing.

David went thirteen and zero in eighteen months, all of them knockouts; eight of the men never fought again. He was set for an upcoming date with Herns, set to take the Heavyweight Championship of the World when he ran into a hiccup by the name of Matthew "Marvelous" Gore. Fifteen rounds, a broken nose, and a deep cut over his eye later, Douglas found himself in a place that he had never known before, the world of split decisions—two to one.

Yes, he had won, but his ascension to the top was halted by a man who wouldn't go down. Shot after shot, uppercuts, hooks, heavy jabs that landed like so many sledgehammers on stone, Douglas had never fought such a man, and the Herns's camp pointed their finger and laughed.

Laughed so damn hard that all David "King of the Ring" Douglas could think about was revenge. He wanted to kill Matthew Gore, put his fist through his face and turn it into stringy pumpkin and teeth. So when the call came in, when the Gore camp approached him with a rematch, there was no hesitation on the bad man's part.

And now Douglas stood in the ring, staring down at the sparring partner he had just put down. The poor man did not move, not even his chest, but Douglas didn't see the man's broken body. All the bad man could see was a face, the face of Marvelous Matthew Gore.

# TWENTY

"You ready for this?"

"No." Teddy and James stood just off from the boxing ring in the shadows where they couldn't be heard. Matt had climbed through the ropes and into the ring for his last sparring session before his fight with Douglas. "Are you?" Teddy asked.

"Nope. Fact is"—James looked down at his friend—"I'm scared as hell."

"Do you think he's scared?"

"Matt?"

"Yeah."

"I know he is," James said. "You could see it. He knows this is important, he knows what we doin' here, even if he don't understand it exactly. The man's got instinct, let's just hope that head of his follows his gut."

"Let's hope." Teddy breathed.

"You ain't havin' second thoughts, are you?"

"Maybe." Teddy turned to his old friend. "Are we asking too much of him? Did we wear him out?"

"Maybe." James stared at Matt. "Maybe it wasn't enough."

"What do you mean?"

"We could have pushed this man to the ends of the world and he would have gone there without question. The man's got a work ethic like I ain't ever seen. But…" James hesitated. "We should have done more. We should have burned that doubt out of him before today."

"But that's what this sparrin' session is for."

"I know, I know, we planned it, but it is an awfully high ledge, Teddy. If he falls, if he gets busted in that ring today…" James just shook his head. "It's an awful long drop, Teddy. An awful long drop. We won't have time to rebuild him, you know that, don't you? Douglas is two weeks away. Maybe we should have done this weeks ago."

"He wasn't ready." Teddy looked up to the ring where Matt loosened up. "If we had thrown him two weeks ago, all we would have been doing is rebuilding. Like you said, this is the only way."

James breathed out. "I hope we was right."

"It's too late to be wrong."

The old trainer laughed. "Ain't that the truth."

"Did you talk to Leon?"

"I did." James nodded. "Me and him had a long talk too."

"What'd he say?"

"Just what he promised," James said. "He won't hold nothin' back in there today. He's gonna go in like a bull and give Matt hell. He owed us and he knew it. We can count on that at least."

"Good."

"To be honest with you, I think he'd like to knock Matt out. He's still got it, Teddy," James said as a matter of fact. "I can see it in him, he's dangerous. Lord knows why he ever stepped down."

"You know why. It's the same reason both me and you stopped, the same reason most great fighters stop, the fire was gone. He beat everyone, there wasn't nothin' left to conquer."

"Until today."

Teddy nodded. "Until today."

"He's playin' with that fire again, he's thinkin' a little, you know? One of them maybe things, Teddy. He's seeing a mountain before him."

"That's good." Teddy smiled. "That's real good 'cause I want to see what happens to that fire of his once Matt hits him with one of those hooks."

"You foreseeing here a little, Teddy? Imaginin' what Douglas is gonna feel?"

"And what he'll think."

"So what do you think?"

"I think"—Teddy folded his arms and breathed out—"I think we'll see."

James, that old, chopstick thin man, watched as the one-time heavyweight champ climbed through the ropes and into the ring. It looked as if Leon hadn't lost a thing. Not only was he in shape, but the man looked strong, solid and quick. It was as if he was still the Champion of the World. "Yes, we gonna see a lot of things today, Teddy," James said. "Gonna know a hell of a lot more too."

It felt like he was sailing right across the concrete sidewalk that dreary night. Soaring so high that Matt never even noticed the dark on the way home. He was on top of the world, a million miles high, and nothing could bring him down because…

*I knocked him cold.*

It was beautiful. So damn beautiful, so damn great that Matt could hardly believe it, but it happened. Just as sure as day is day, it happened. Third round, two minutes in, Matt landed a hook that knocked Leon down. There was no getting up for the former champ, no eight counts either. Matt had seen the opening, used one of the ten thousand or so combinations that James had worked with him to exploit, and then all he did was let that hook of his fly—magic.

Beautiful magic.

For the first time since Matt was a younger man, since he was twenty, twenty-one and quickly climbing the ranks of the heavyweight division, he felt that he could do anything, that the world was big again. Bring on Douglas, bring on Joseph. Bring on the Dancing Man from Detroit, Mister Herns; tonight it didn't matter who Matt fought, he would beat them all just like he beat Leon tonight.

Leon who had never lost a title bout, Leon who held the belt for three years and a day while Herns demolished the ranks beneath him, Leon who retired a day before Herns was ranked the number one contender in the world.

Matt wanted to tell the world, shout it from the mountaintops, walk right in his door tonight and lay the good news on Donna. He could see it, imagine it in his mind, see the smile on Donna's face after he told her just what he had done. And what was more, it felt so damn good to Matt; the fantasy of that imagined moment felt like nothing he had ever felt before. Maybe he would take Donna out, celebrate or something, talk the night away until the sun rose on a new day.

Three steps at a time, Matt flew up the concrete stairs that led to his apartment and hurried inside. Down the hall, closer and closer to his door, the excitement growing stronger and stronger as he pulled his key from his pocket. The white rabbit's foot hung from the key chain.

Magic.

Matt kissed that foot, kissed the dead, and stuck the key in the lock, turned the handle, opened the door, and Matthew "Marvelous" Gore stepped inside his apartment with a smile on his face, only to find that Donna was not there.

Not in the living room, not in the kitchen, not anywhere Matt could see. Still he called to her, but the fine woman never called back. He looked in the bathroom, looked in his bedroom. Matt even turned around three times before looking in his closet. His heart was sinking.

Sinking so damn low that he double-checked the bathroom before walking back down the hallway to the kitchen and the living room that was really one room separated by a counter island; still, there was no Donna. Matt stood there, staring at the sofa, at the oversized chair, at the kitchen chairs that stood around the table—they were all empty.

It fell, like dirt from a grave, loneliness buried the man black. The utter emptiness of his childhood, the realization of his life, crushed the fighter. Even Margaret, even when they had made love, he had woken to find his cot empty. Tonight would be no different.

An empty bed, void of words, of laughter and shared dreams. He sat silent and buried his face in his hands. And now Donna was gone too. Just like his parents, just like the apartment building, just like the little girl from the fourth floor.

*All my life…*

"Hey."

*I've been…*

"Matt?"

*Alone…*

"Matt?" A hand on his shoulder. "Are you okay?"

He looked up, the big man lifted his head and found Donna looking down on him. She was worried, concerned, and beautiful. He almost cried, a big man who felt like crying.

From the very first moment he had seen her, that early evening outside the grocery store when the world was so dark, so cold, when she looked into his eyes, when her first words passed from her lips—words he could still hear— Matthew "Marvelous" Gore had loved her. Only now, he realized it.

The light that shone so brilliantly inside, the warmth that swelled every time he thought of the most beautiful woman in the world, it was all because he loved her. Hurrying home on nights like this, on other nights when the world was cruel, it was all because he wanted to be near her. That was why he sat on the sofa while the beautiful woman finished her nightly work, that was why he ate his dinner so damn slow every night: to hear her voice, see her face and her smile, to feel the touch of her voice inside—it was love.

Donna's voice was soft. "You okay?"

Matt had never smiled so wide in all his life. "Yeah."

"You had me worried there for a minute." Donna left her hand on his big shoulder; it felt nice. "Somethin' happen today?"

"Yeah." Matt nodded. "A couple things."

She could feel it, staring down into his eyes, she could feel it. "Care to share?"

"Maybe."

"Maybe?"

"Yeah, maybe."

"What's a girl supposed to say to that?"

"That depends."

"On?"

"If I tell you or not."

"Can I bribe you?"

That smile of Matt's turned to a grin. "I certainly hope so."

"So"—her hand still on his shoulder—"what do you want?"

"What will you give me?"

"That depends."

"I think I said that."

"I know." Donna turned to smile. "It still depends though."

"On?"

"What it is you want."

And now Matt turned, letting it all sink in, nodding, liking what he heard, feeling brave in the moment because there was something happening here. Something he had never felt before—not even with Margaret. Matt turned and looked back up at the beautiful woman. "I want to kiss you."

With cheeks flushing, Donna was even more beautiful, if that was possible. "So if you kiss me, you'll tell what happened today."

"Somethin' like that, yes."

"Why?"

"Why what?"

"Why do you want to kiss me?"

"Because I've wanted to ever since I met you outside the grocery store."

Donna melted. "Really?"

"Yeah." Matt's voice was deep, but soft. "Really. You still want me to share?"

She didn't know that she was nodding, she didn't know that her eyes, her pupils were wider than the world, but Donna did know what she felt. "Yeah," she said. "I'd like that."

Matt stood and turned toward her. The sofa between them, Donna leaning towards him, Matt took her in his arms and lifted her over the sofa. Donna loving the feeling of his arms. "Tell me," she said. "Tell me what happened."

"I knocked out the former champ," Matt said.

"Oh, yeah?"

Matt leaned down and kissed her, pressed his lips against hers, touching, loving. Their love imprinted in a moment. "Yeah." He breathed. "But that ain't nothin'."

"Then what? What's got you so wound up tonight."

"You," Matt said. "I want to spend every moment with you."

She couldn't describe it, but everything inside of Donna said yes. "I bet you say that to all the girls."

"I've never said that to anyone before." Her body in his arms, her heart in his hands, Matt leaned down and kissed her again; Donna floating on air. "I've never felt like this before."

"Matt?"

"Yeah?"

Donna leaned back. "I'm so happy"

"Me too." He smiled, so much emotion in him, so many things he had never felt in his long quiet life. "Me too."

It was two, maybe three in the morning. The middle of the night. Matt woke, the dream fading from his memory; the dream of Donna in his arms. Matt didn't even bother to feel the bed beside him, he was alone, and it was cold. Pulling the blankets aside, Matt got up from his bed and walked to the window.

It was snowing outside.

There were footprints in the snow; in his mind he could see them again. Footprints that disappeared in the dark. Tonight was no different. It was just a moment, just a memory, nothing but a footprint that would be covered by time. Nothing had changed.

Just like when he was a child, a young boy on that fifth floor who looked down from an empty window on high. Day after day, year after year, people passing by as bottles broke in an alley—the kingdom of a fool. And still the people walked, never seeing the eyes that looked down upon them, lonely eyes that wondered why those people never looked up. Not a wave, not a wink, never a hello to the boy who lived above the world in a forgotten kingdom of shattering glass. The big man breathed.

Heavy, deep, letting his life go in a breath. He turned, the room dark, the door to his room open, shadows lying on his bed. A pile that moved up and down like a breath. A beautiful breath that lay asleep.

Still, his eyes played their game as he walked to his empty bed. And as he climbed under his covers, his ears joined his deceitful eyes as breath soft and warm touched him. He was dreaming, or so he told himself, he had to be dreaming. Matt turned and reached out: soft skin, naked, breasts rising gently. "Matt?"

Tonight was different, Donna was different, he knew it. Forever.

"Yeah?"

"Am I dreaming?"

"No."

"Promise?"

"Forever."

Her hand touched his arm. "Hold me." Matt pulled her close, their bodies touching, warming. "Stay by me."

"I will." Matt smiled. "I will."

Margaret slipped from the bar stool and strutted across the room in that red dress of hers. Her hips, her backside moved from side to side like some old grandfather clock that was ready to strike. High heels clicking on the floor, up two steps to the old wooden door that weighed as much as the tree it came from. Her hand on the brass handle, her mind anywhere but home, one last look, Margaret turned back. The old barkeeper smiled down at the bar, touching its wood like it was the skin of some naked woman; a bum sat alone at a table, crying over a half-empty glass of gin; Margaret breathed out.

Just a cracked window at home.

The door opened and Margaret stepped out into the stairwell. Flakes fell from a speckled sky, swarming down the steps, bowing before the woman's feet—red polish. Margaret put on her jacket, fox fur hiding her mouth, her nose, just eyes peering up from a high collar. Eyes that saw everything.

It was like a grave, dug deep in the earth, left open for men and women alike, Margaret walked up the stairs from the underground bar and stepped into the world. It was cold. Tall buildings halfway seen; gusts of wind blowing shapes that looked like scattered men. Margaret could still see all their faces.

She took off her heels and walked through the snow in her bare feet, passing under a window where some figure had been standing moments ago. The curtains just now hanging dead. Margaret never felt the cold on her feet, even though the snow was already up to her ankles, already up to her shins because of the drifting. Her red toenails never turned blue.

There were blocks to walk, things to think as she walked home, wishes to consider, one that could change everything. A wish that she knew would come true. And what would she wish? What would pass between her red lips? What would change because she wished it that way? She was here, wasn't she? Beneath his room, beneath the sounds that came down from above, sounds that only three people heard. Sounds that Margaret knew to be love. Is that what she would wish for? Death? And with death came birth: pains both deep and great. Pains that would gush from open mouths and flooding eyes.

Under that high fox collar that hid half her face, Margaret could feel her breath under her mask. Or would she wish for something else? Something like a spark, a smolder of flame that would soon scorch the ground, level the earth, eat the trees that were just now nurturing their young fruit, burn the whole damn building down? Margaret stopped and looked behind her.

The wind blew, white curtains hiding the way she had come, her footprints nowhere to be seen. Or would she wish something else? Something that didn't come to mind yet, but a thing that would come in a growl of anger, with gnashing teeth? The woman smiled, but it was never seen. The dead fox hid her mouth. She could wish for anything, and it would come true.

She turned, heels hanging in her hand, bare feet in spotless white, never cold or frozen in that snow; Margaret walked home. It was nice to have options. So many options, so many things to have, to hold, to swirl around her because she was the eye of the storm now, like her feet, like the sun. The whole world revolving around her.

There were footprints now, not just one pair, but two. Long legs stretching, teeth shining gold, snow never touching Mister Jones. "Are you ready, Margaret," Mister Jones asked. "You ready to make that wish of yours?"

She never stopped walking though she did look up at the man. "You do love me, don't you, Roy?"

"Oh, Margaret." The shining man laughed. "With that fine jacket, you seem like a ventriloquist, though I can see that mouth of yours. Yessiree, you are one of my favorites. Top of the class."

"Thank you, Roy."

"And you always hear just what you want to hear too. So tell me." Mister Jones's teeth flashed—sharp. "You ready to make that wish?"

"If I wish, it'll be gone," Margaret said. "And you'll go too."

"Ain't that what you want?"

"I want lots of things, Roy."

"Don't I know."

"I wish…"

"Yes?"

"I wish…"

"Say it, Margaret," Mister Jones said. "'Cause I already know what you gonna wish for."

"I wish…" Margaret looked up, so many flakes. "I wish I had another wish."

"I know, but you know the rules."

"Then I use my wish and wish that I had just one wish."

Mister Jones's head fell back, his neck breaking in half, his mouth splitting open like a crack in the earth. Not a flake fell in that bottomless pit as a laugh stilled even the gusting wind. "Granted," Mister Jones said. "One wish just for you, Margaret."

"One that will come true," the fox smiled. Of course Margaret was alone, walking down the street through the deep snow, high heels on; her feet freezing cold. But the woman didn't mind, didn't care if those expensive shoes were ruined. Nosiree, not at all, because she had that wish, and Margaret held it close to her heart like a special love that would keep her alive. And it would. Day after day, the knowledge of her wish would hold her up until she uttered the words of her heart. Words like breath that would slip carelessly through her lips and turn the rose black. One breath, one wish, life in an instant. Margaret could imagine the moment, imagine the power, the desire as she spoke it. But it wasn't time to make a choice. The wind blowing, a blinded city—snow.

So much snow.

It was an hour before sunrise. The snow fell heavy, lighting the dark world. Every now and then as Matt was running, he noticed footprints in the snow. They were misshapen things, blown and distorted by the wind, footprints that seemed more animal than human. An animal that stalked its prey, a thing ready to strike, to rip the flesh of another and devour it whole. A thing that needed to kill to live. But after last night, after he had woken this morning to find her arm across his chest, Matt didn't care about footprints.

He didn't care that his feet were soaking wet, or that the thin cotton sweats that he wore were drenched and cold. All that mattered to Matthew Gore this wonderful morning was Donna.

Before he had left for his run, Matt had leaned down and gently kissed her forehead. She woke and asked him to come back to bed as her hand touched his face. Matt promised to hurry, he promised that he would climb back into bed with her and hold her before the sun rose. Donna had nodded. She understood who he was, what he needed to do. And that understanding, that acceptance, it was magic to Matthew "Marvelous" Gore.

In fact, right now his life was nothing short of magical. Ever since he had left Art, ever since he had been able to walk out of that burned-out building, from the moment he turned his back on the shadows and ghosts of the past, Matt's life had turned. Not only for the better, but for wonderful, fantastic… magic. Day after day, week after week, for the past month, today, February First, life kept getting better and better. Yesterday didn't matter, neither did tomorrow, not even his fight with Douglas; it would come when it came. All that mattered was this moment—living in the now, this very moment, feeling that happiness that Matt felt. For once in his life, all Matthew Gore wanted to do was live. Feel the cold in his lungs as he breathed in, feel the sting in his legs, feel the warmth inside his chest every time he thought of her lying in his bed. It was beautiful.

It was the falling snow, it was the city, it was the alleys and lumps that buried the bums, it was the black barrels that held cold fire; they were all a part of this moment. And they were beautiful. Why hadn't he seen it before?

How could he miss it? How could he not see the beauty that was all around him? His whole life, it had been there, he had seen it, and yet he had never seen it. The gray clouds; the black asphalt streets that stretched a county mile; the whites and pale browns of concrete pads; silver windows that shone when the light was just right; metallic girders and beams that held up the sky; and the reds and yellows, the greens of stoplights that shone on the wet street—they were all beautiful. Like the falling snow, white and perfect, the beauty was all around him.

He had been blind, but it didn't matter anymore. He could see, he felt that warmth inside his chest, that swelling that made him feel like he could fly. Like his nickname, life felt marvelous, perfect...magical.

Just like the weather around him, like the unseen fronts that lifted water from a distant sea and drove the laden clouds a millennium of miles to the city where snow fell on a perfect morning; magic had made the conditions for Donna and Matt. Magic and Mister Jones.

The world, the universe, shining glorious as Cupid draws his magnificent bow. For the first time in his life, Matt felt a strong sense of validation. Who he was: a boxer, a fighter, he was all right. He was what he was and a fine woman loved him for it.

It was the oddest sensation he had ever felt. And he wanted to feel it forever. To fight, to train, to work hard in the gym and come home to Donna, to spend day after day with her, just the two of them, talking, laughing, making love, lying in bed at night together. Matt wanted life to always be like this. And it could be.

No more cold nights above a gym alone, he was realizing that life could be more. It could be something that lasted beyond the falling snow, beyond the seasons that stretched to the very end of his life; Matt could love her and she would love him. He would never be alone, not again, not anymore.

Matthew "Marvelous" Gore rounded a corner and turned toward home. The snow fell, blowing behind him, covering his tracks, hiding the beasts.

# TWENTY-ONE

If there had been a man, young or old, married or a lonely bachelor, if there had been a dozen of those men, every single one of them would have stared at her. Donna with the nice eyes, nice other things too, Donna with a smile on her face as she walked down the aisle of the grocery store. She didn't need groceries, the shelves at Matt's apartment were fully stocked, but she wanted to make him something special. What was it about watching a man eat, anyway?

Digging into something good, something special made by her own two hands, Donna could sit there night after night and watch him eat. Bite after bite. Tonight, homemade macaroni and cheese, she was going to do exactly that. And just as she had done for the past week, Donna was going to enjoy him.

It didn't matter that the snow had melted, that the rain had come cold and wet, the kind of air that soaked right through to your bones, the gray world washed away every night when the door opened and Matthew "Marvelous" Gore walked in with that smile.

It did something to her, deep inside, something more than the warmth, the relief she felt when he was with her. Donna felt safe, she felt like nothing could hurt her, she was home. Home with a big man who would take care of her. A man who made her laugh, a man that actually held her in his arms, a man that, when he kissed her, Donna could feel it beyond her lips. Rounding the end of the aisle, Donna stopped.

Between the bottles of wine, between the pull-top cans of beer, Donna saw her face in the open refrigerator's mirror. It was her mother's face. The same look, the same feeling, the same expression in her mother's eyes when she talked about Donna's father.

Donna could barely remember the man, only that he was good, kind to her. That he bounced her on his knee and called her "Love." Love because she came from love. They had lived somewhere else then, somewhere dry, without water. Her momma had told Donna that Daddy was bringing water to the desert— water from a rock. Only this rock was in a place called Nevada. Drilling holes in the bedrock, dropping old, sweaty sticks of dynamite down deep, lighting the fuses, blowing the earth away, moving mountains, just so a sprawling little town in the desert could get more water: Las Vegas. As Donna now stood and stared at her face between the bottles, between the pull-tab cans, she remembered the pain in her momma's face.

She understood it now, Donna knew what her momma felt when the desert and dynamite took her father away. There was nothing left of the good man, only love as momma used to say. Love, who sat on momma's lap and sewed and sewed and sewed because Love and momma needed to eat. Momma, who woke up every morning and sat at an old table with two cups of coffee like she and daddy used to do. Momma, who talked to a man who wasn't there no more.

Leaving that house, that little one room thing and moving here to the city, far to the east, it was like the day daddy left them again. Momma took the table, took their two cups, took their bed and left the rest to rot. And when her mother had passed, Donna found her with her hand across the table, lying there like she was holding a hand. And maybe she had been.

As Donna stood at the end of the aisle, as her eyes stared back at her, something funny happened to her, something rose to the surface that she had never felt before. *I can't lose him.*

If she had heard such a thing from a friend, she would have thought them crazy. But she wasn't crazy; the thought, the feeling, the whole entirety of it scared her. Because she could lose Matt. She wanted to be with him now, today, tonight, tomorrow and the day after that for the rest of her life. In that moment, Donna understood her mother, knew her father again. The strong, beautiful woman was discovering the name her father had given her—Love.

It was more than just being together, more than just coming home and living with someone; it was two lives becoming one. *Me and him*, Donna thought, *ain't ever gonna let go.* She saw the smile on her face. For the first time in her life, that beautiful woman thought her face looked pretty. Donna pushed the cart ahead, the pretty face between the bottles and the pull-tab cans disappeared.

Sharp cheddar, milk, fresh eggs and a whole hell of a lot of elbow macaroni, Donna wheeled her cart to the front of the store and stood in line at the checkout. The line moved fast, but it wouldn't have mattered if it had moved slow, Donna was someplace else. His arms, their bed, him lying close the whole night.

"Don't tell me that smile's for me." Donna woke from her daydream, looked up to find the line empty and Margaret Jones looking right at her. "How you doin', Donna?" Margaret said.

"I'm good, thanks." Donna pushed her cart forward, trying not to look at the other woman. "How are you?"

"I'm here." Margaret's voice was cold. "Workin'. At least work's still work for some of us. Looks like you makin' macaroni and cheese."

Donna nodded. "I am."

"Matt sure does love it," Margaret said. "It always was his favorite. Tell me, how you like workin' under him?"

"It's good work."

"Don't I know." Margaret punched in the price of the eggs. "Be good to him 'cause it's gonna be hard on him."

"What is?"

"When he loses the fight." A wicked thing spread across Margaret's face. "I tried to tell him, but you know how some men are, they don't ever listen."

"He ain't gonna lose."

"You just keep tellin' him that too." Margaret's face looked like a mock of sympathy. "He'll love you all the more."

"Excuse me?"

"Nothin'." Margaret rang in the price of the macaroni. "I was just talkin' to myself. Funny thing me talkin' to myself. I do it all the time. In fact, if you heard me, why, you'd think I was downright crazy. You ever talk to yourself, Donna?"

"Sure."

"Really now?"

"Don't everybody?"

"I don't know." Margaret shrugged. "I ain't everybody. Tell me, when was the last time you talked to yourself?"

"It was here at this grocery store, actually."

"You kiddin'?"

"Nope," Donna said. "It was right out that door there."

"Tell me 'cause I'm dyin' to know what you was sayin' to yourself."

"Well, I was rehearsing something I was gonna say." Donna nodded. "See, there was this good-looking man standing out there waiting 'cause he had a date. So I see him, and I'm thinking to myself what I should say 'cause he's pulling open the door, holding it for me."

"So you said thank you."

"'Course, but that's not what I was rehearsing."

Margaret folded her arms. "I bet."

"What I said was, 'Treat her good now 'cause she deserves it.'" Donna looked the other woman straight in the eye. "Tell me, Margaret, how's that husband of yours?"

"Fine, thanks." The cash register rang. "Nine forty-three."

Donna paid the price, dropped her bills, her change in Margaret's outstretched hand. "My regards to Mister Jones. It sure was nice running into you. Bye bye."

Out the door, across the parking lot, that woman crossed all those cracks in the blacktop and walked down the street. As Margaret watched Donna, her mind flooded with ten thousand wishes.

Big wishes, little ones, wishes that were full of pain and hatred. And they would all come true. It didn't matter which one she chose, once those black words passed by her lips, they would come true.

Margaret stood beside the cash register, the wicked thing smiling on her face. A thing so evil that the woman next in line left her cart full of groceries and hurried out the door. But Margaret's eyes were fixed on Donna, though the woman was now far from her sight.

"I wish…"

Her wicked smile grew.

"Oh, I wish…"

Mikey spit out his mouthpiece, and walked to his corner where Art was standing with that look on his face, the one that said, 'I've told you a million times.'

"I know, I know." Mikey sat slumped on the stool; his chin hurt. "I don't know why I do it. I'm sorry."

The old trainer laid a cool, wet sponge on the back of Mikey's neck. "Did you feel it?"

"Yeah." Mikey stared across the ring at the other fighter in the opposite corner. He was a little older, a little bigger, an amateur champion who was ready to step up into the professional ranks. "I felt it."

"And?"

"Just like you said, I'm gonna lose my head."

"So what you gonna do, kid?"

"Coach"—Mikey turned and looked up at the old man— "when I'm in there, I'm thinkin' about it, I'm doing just what you told me, but it just happens. I throw a punch, move, and *bam!* My chin's stickin' out with a big bulls-eye on it. I don't know what to do."

"Relax." It had been a good month, been a damn good past couple of weeks. Mikey was changing little by little, learning how to bite his tongue, doing everything that was asked of him without having to be asked twice. The most important thing was the fact that the kid was changing. Art patted Mikey's shoulder. "Tell me, how long we been workin' now?"

"Today?"

"Tell me how long you think you've been working hard? I mean really hard."

"Probably since I started livin' here," Mikey said. "Really hard the past two, three weeks or so."

"Do you think you've improved?"

"Yeah." Mikey nodded. "I can go twelve rounds of sparring now, couldn't do that before. I can run five miles. Yeah, I'm better, I'm in shape."

"What about your skills, I'm talkin' about handwork, footwork, even that big old chin of yours, do you think they're better than before."

Mikey thought about it, really thought about it. "Yeah, a little. I know my hands are faster, feet too, body feels good and I know my punches are harder. Against him"—Mikey nodded to the other fighter in the opposite corner—"They don't do nothin'."

"Don't worry about him," Art said. "We talkin' you here. Tell me, is your head better or worse?"

"About the same, and that ain't good."

*Amazing*, Art thought, *not only was the kid being honest, but he was being honest about his faults.* "Believe it or not, kid, that head of yours is a whole hell of a lot better than it used to be. It ain't stickin' out like it used to, and it's better outside the ring too. You doin' right by yourself. What you got to remember is that it takes time. Your chin, well, it's a little slower than the rest of you, but that ain't nothin' different from any other fighter out there.

"Every fighter's got strengths and they got weaknesses. But here's the thing, kid: a good fighter relies on his strengths, but a great fighter works to overcome his weaknesses." Art looked at the kid, in his eyes. "*His* weaknesses, Mikey, not his opponents.' Today, here, right now, that's what you doin'. We ain't talkin' about James over there, we talkin' about you.

"You is learnin' all about yourself, we seein' your strengths, we seein' your weaknesses, and we seein' what you is gonna do about them. You facin' them, kid. Takin' them head on. That shows who you are, what you gonna do. A bad fighter tries to hide his weaknesses from himself, but a man like that never makes it far in the ring. Seein' your fears, facing them"—Art shook his head—"that's the hardest fight of 'em all, kid. If you win it, if you don't quit, there ain't nothin' you can't do. You hear me?"

Mikey had never really thought about it before. "So you're sayin' that I can do anythin' no matter what?"

"If you face all them fears of yours, if you work hard and never quit, then yes." Art pointed at the kid. "Only if you want it, only if you're really doin' what you want to do. I'm talkin' about livin', dreamin', breathin' boxing. If that's what it is, if that's what drives you, then yes. You follow?"

"Yeah." Mikey nodded. "It's got to be it."

"Why couldn't I just say it like that?" Art smiled and then said, "You got it, kid. One last thing."

"Okay."

"Tell me, if you could be anywhere right now, anywhere in the whole wide world, where would you be?"

Mikey hadn't been anywhere but here: the city, this part of town, the neighborhood school he went to, the gym, these were the only things he had ever seen. This was all he knew. Mikey shrugged. "I don't know, coach. I ain't ever been nowhere but here."

"Then do me a favor."

"What's that?"

"When you find out where you want to be," Art said, "you tell me, all right?"

"Okay."

"Good." Art took the sponge off the kid's neck and dropped it in the bucket. "Okay, we got three more rounds here. You know what to do, so just relax and let it happen. Don't force it, make it part of you. Remember, keep your chin down, your hands up, and keep that head of yours movin' like you was some drunk, all right?"

Mikey laughed and stood before turning back to the old trainer. "Coach, did you ever ask him that?" he said.

"Ask who what?"

"Did you ever ask Matt that question?"

Art nodded. "Yeah, I did."

"What'd he say?"

Art smiled, an old memory of a thing. "He said he wanted to be here, in the ring."

Mikey smacked his gloves together and met his opponent in the middle of the ring. He did well, moving like he should, hands up, avoiding most blows, taking others straight on. But halfway through the round, Mikey's chin popped out like a bulls-eye.

It was something even a blind man could see. The older fighter with the longer reach let a straight jab fly, a shot that connected square with Mikey's mark. The man-boy's head snapped back, and by the time Mikey set his head to rights, an uppercut jumped up from the floor.

The sky filled with staggering stars.

Steam ran through that old building, traveling through red rusted pipes that crisscrossed like so many veins hidden behind the walls. As Mikey laid in his cot in that room above the gym, he listened to the dull crack of the radiator. He could hear the boiler in the basement, hear the clicks as that beast tried to ignite its flame. But it failed. Time and time again it tried to heat that cold pool, but the steam in the body of the radiator was already condensing. Great drops fell back down to the basement and pooled in a cold dark vat as the heart of the beast fluttered. Mikey closed his eyes.

In all his life he had never imagined such a world had existed. There had always been his mother, his room, the city and the streets, the laughter of his so-called friends. Friends who were friends no more. There was more than just dirty jokes, more than being cool, more than a jaw that hurt like hell, not to mention the crick in his neck. In the dark, in the quiet of that otherworld, Mikey found peace that he wished could last forever.

Night after night, lying here in the cold dark where there was nothing but the sounds around him. Sounds without smiles, without ears, without faces, sounds that never expected to be heard, sounds that didn't care if they were answered. *This*, Mikey thought, *this is where I want to be.*

*No place else, not even with a girl—well, almost. But if she was here, if we were together,* he thought, *me holding her. No talking, maybe a whisper, the sound of lips touching now and then, and we'd be warm. So damn warm in the cold dark that the streets, the city, nothing else would matter.* But as Mikey thought about that moment, as his mind played with the idea of love, it slowly slipped away because love didn't matter right now.

He felt good, content. For the first time in his life, Mikey let the moment be. He didn't try to change it, didn't wish for something in the future, something he thought would be better because this moment was good. In fact, it was more than good. Mikey felt so damn good that he wished that the night would never end. That he could lie here and listen to the otherworld around him and feel its quiet peace forever. Moment after moment, time slipping in an empty mind, a soul so filled that it was satisfied.

But there was a shadow in that room. A shadow that knew of the otherworld, a shadow that could discern the thoughts of a man-boy who had found his first moments of peace. Change never does come easy. Not when one must walk in the daylight. And Mikey would walk.

He would wake up, find the common world bristling around him, a world that challenged every man, a world that called every woman to the bar, a world that faced every living being with its temporality. The shadow knew this and so much more.

In the basement, the boiler ignited. The monster's heart beat again and again as fire turned water to steam. Steam that rose hot through the unseen veins pumping into the radiator in Mikey's room. It cracked, the snake hissed in the dark.

The shadow laughed.

# TWENTY-TWO

Both fighters stood on opposite sides of the room, staring at the other, their jaws flexing, temples flaring like billows that fanned the fire of hate. It was nothing short of a classic weigh-in, a precursor to a Bloody Little Valentine that the press had dubbed.

Douglas Gore-Fest II.

"Mister Douglas." The official stood next to a perfectly balanced scale in a blue shirt that had fit three sizes ago. "If you would step on the scale."

The sea parted and David Douglas walked through the masses. His eyes never once left Matthew "Marvelous" Gore. He stepped up on the scale and undid his robe. As it fell to the ground, the room gasped, cameras flashed, trainers and cut men alike stood with their mouths agape. Douglas was bigger than before.

There was a stab of doubt that cut Matt. He could feel it in the pit of his stomach where it grew. Deeper and deeper, more black than shadows, thoughts formed in his mind. Thoughts that began to chatter with the murmurs of men all around him.

They stared at him with wide eyes filled with both pity and gratefulness. After all, they weren't stepping into the ring with Douglas. And they would watch, wait for the massacre and then cheer when it happened. In the far corner of the room, one reporter was already writing his headline on a pocket-sized notepad. A thing that would read: "Gored in the ring."

"Mister David Douglas weighs in at the weight of..." The official slid the scale with his sausage-like fingers until it balanced at "Two hundred and sixty two pounds and one quarter."

Matt could feel his own jaw drop as Douglas stepped off the scale. But before his mind could take its little trip, Teddy leaned close and whispered, "You remember what to do, right?"

"I remember."

"Not a word." Teddy kept talking, wanting to take the edge off his fighter. "Nothing. Don't talk to the official. Not even when he asks you to take off your robe, okay?"

"Okay." Matt still felt the pit in his stomach.

"I want you to do one other thing for me." Teddy put his hand on his fighter's back. "Call it a favor of sorts."

"What's that?"

"When you get up on that scale, don't take off your robe." Matt turned and looked at Teddy like he was nuts. Teddy winked and said, "Trust me, leave it on."

There was something in that man's eyes, something that Matt saw and recognized even if he didn't fully understand it. Matt smiled and for a moment forgot all about that fear in the pit of his stomach. "You're the boss," he said.

Teddy and James laughed. A laugh that had been secretly planned by both trainers before the weigh-in. It was a gamble, of course, and it all depended on Douglas's reaction, but it worked.

The more Douglas stood there and watched them, the more Teddy and James laughed and patted their fighter's back as they watched Douglas out of the corners of their eyes, the more it made Douglas forget the Marvelous in Matthew Gore. They were making fun of him, or so the big man thought.

"I'm gonna kill you, fool!" Spit flew out of Douglas' mouth. "I'm gonna beat you so bad that your momma ain't even gonna recognize you no more!"

It was a funny thought, the kind of strange thought that only comes at a time like this. *My momma's dead*, Matt thought.

"You ain't nothin', Gore!" Douglas raged. "You hear! Nothin'!"

"Mister Gore," the official called. "If you would please step on the scale."

Matt walked through the crowd as Douglas went on and on like he was the sole member of an asylum. Matt stepped up on the scale and stood quietly. "Mister Gore," the fat man said, "your robe?"

Matt just shook his head.

Fat fingers slid the little weight, the scale balanced; "Two hundred twenty-five," the official announced, "and one-half pounds."

"You ain't nothin'!" Douglas laughed as Matt stepped from the scale and turned toward the other fighter just like he and Teddy and James had planned. Douglas's eyes flared like voodoo. "That's right, fool, look at me! Get a good look too 'cause this is the last face you're ever gonna see! After tomorrow, you ain't even gonna be! You ain't nothin' but a has-been, Gore! You ain't even a fighter! You just a stupid sucka who I already beat down before! Gonna do it again, fool. But this time"—Douglas shook his head—"this time, I ain't gonna leave nothin' behind."

Calm and cool, Matt walked toward Douglas—just a machine.

"That's right! Come on, sucka!" Douglas moving, hands up, head bobbing ready to go, both fighters separated by a sea of officials and reporters. Douglas's trainers grabbed their fighter, holding him back, telling him to wait for tomorrow as Teddy and James reached Matt and did the same damn thing. Still, Douglas raged. "Let's do this now!"

"Come on." Teddy tried not to smile. "The fight's tomorrow."

On cue, Matt turned his back on the other man.

"Don't you turn your back on me." Douglas spat. "Don't you ever turn your back on me!" Douglas yelled as a team of men dragged him through the door. But as the flashbulbs popped, as a herd of men dragged Douglas out the door, Matt couldn't help but look back—voodoo. Sweat poured down Douglas's face, running around the big man's eyes, eyes that were wide and white, eyes that belonged to a man possessed. "Tomorrow"—Douglas laughed—"you hear me, Gore! I'm gonna kill you tomorrow!"

# TWENTY-THREE

Matt wished it would rain. Just a breath of air, just a push of wind, something—anything—that would stir the atmosphere. But nothing came. There was only the sound of his breathing, just his feet on the concrete, shadows all around as he walked under that black sky. Even the clouds didn't blush tonight. It was just dark and cold, a stale breath that felt like death. Matt walked down the street, going nowhere, just walking down a street he should never have walked down; he would never sleep tonight.

In his mind, he could see Douglas stepping on the scale, see the fat man slide the weight past 250, past 260 to 262 pounds. Matt could feel the big man's punches, feel the gut-wrenching shots, and Matt knew that this time, they would be worse.

But he had to win, he had to beat Douglas, he had to become the Heavyweight Champion of the World. He just had to. Nothing else would satisfy him. Not just beating Douglas or facing Herns in a title bout: Matt had to win.

But as he walked down that street, as he came to its end and rounded the corner that led to Art's gym, Matt never saw the shadow that watched him. He passed by it, feeling its cold, shivering, walking to the gym door where he looked in through the small glass window at his past.

From the rafters, the men still hung on banners around the ring, looking down on that old canvas where their feet had once danced. Feet that now rotted in the grave, all but Art. Matt cupped his hands and pressed his face against the cold glass. The more he stared at the banners, the more he came to realize that there was no room. No space, no empty place that had been reserved for Matthew "Marvelous" Gore.

There never had been.

"Matt?" He turned and found her there: smoky eyes, perfect lips, Margaret looking up at him. He didn't know what to say, and even if he had known, there wouldn't have been time to say it. Margaret stepped close, stepped into him, wrapping her arms around him, standing on her toes, pressing her lips against his. Margaret let her mouth linger on his, tasting him, even though Matt didn't kiss back as much as Margaret would have liked. But he did kiss back and that alone made her smile. "I'm so glad I found you," Margaret said. "I've been looking for you for forever."

Douglas, Valentines Day, it all washed away, forgotten.

Matt could only say, "What?"

"I've missed you, Matt." She tried to smile, but there was a sadness there that Matt had never seen. "I've missed you so much."

"But you—" It felt like he was on his back, looking up at the lights from the middle of the ring. The man who had never been knocked down felt the world spin. Matt shook his head. "You didn't want…"

"Mikey." Margaret looked into his eyes and Matt felt her searching his soul. "Mikey told me that you needed some time to yourself to—"

"Mikey?"

"He told me everything, Matt. Told me 'bout the fight between you and Art and that Art wanted you to fight that no-good boxer. Told me you said no and stormed out. Mikey said that you needed time to figure things out and that I shouldn't go mixing you up any more than you already was. I guess he knew about us after all somehow." Margaret looked away. "But I miss you, Matt. I miss us. Miss us so damn much." And now there were tears. Tears that slipped from her eyes and rolled down her cheeks where they fell through the cold night air onto the ground and froze—ice. "I've been waiting for you, hoping you would come back. I've been sleeping with my window open, prayin' that I'd hear you runnin' down the street like you used to. You remember that, Matt, kissin' me at my window?"

"But when I…" Matt couldn't think straight. "When I came over that night, you said that you couldn't—"

"And then imagine my surprise when I ran into her at the grocery store." Margaret looked away. "It killed me, Matt. I thought that we had somethin'."

"Her?"

"She told me she was workin' for you now." Margaret's voice grew bitter. "Is it true, Matt? Is Donna working for you?"

"She is."

Margaret's body shuttered. "I knew it. I knew something like this was gonna happen. Nothin' good ever happens to me. It's always like this. I should never have listened to Mikey. I mean yes, I knew he was jealous, but I didn't think he'd do this. But you can't blame him, Matt. Growin' up in your shadow, them are big shoes to fill. And after tomorrow, everyone knows you gonna win, it's just gonna be harder on the boy."

Matt couldn't believe it, he turned toward the door and the little window where the banners hung inside; there was no room for him. There had never been. Everything that had seemed so certain, everything that seemed so good, crumbled before him like a house built of sand.

"You're tellin' me"—Matt turned to Margaret—"that Mikey did this?"

"I'm sorry, Matt." Margaret dabbed her nose with a tissue that appeared out of nowhere. "At first I didn't want to believe it, but he took your place."

"He took my—" Matt shook his head. "What do you mean he took my place?"

"He's livin' here, Matt, he took your room. Moved in just as soon as you left. If the truth be told, I know Art was glad to have him; he's always been lonely. Oh, Matt, I'm so sorry. This is such a mess. I wish..." The tears came again, only it seemed there were more of them. Tears that glittered like diamonds on her face. "I wish that..."

"What, Margaret? What do you wish?"

"I wish that things could be how they were."

And somewhere behind her, a laugh track played.

From the window above the gym where Matt had stood so long ago staring out at the tracks in the snow that had led away from the gym door and into the night, Mikey now stood.

He had seen his mother wrap her arms around Matt, how she kissed him, how Matt had barely kissed back, and the tears that had come to her eyes. Tears Mikey had seen throughout the years. And as Matt had walked away, Mikey saw her smile, the one that was still painted on her lips.

Mikey stared down at her, perhaps seeing her face clearly for the first time. Anger rose in that man-boy as the shadows stretched behind him. More than anything in the world, more than Matt, right now Mikey hated his mother.

As if she had known that he was there, Margaret turned and looked up at him. He could feel her eyes as they met his, feel his heart stripped bare before her. One by one, his secrets poured from his soul as that smile on her mouth formed into something familiar. Mikey felt as if he was looking down the barrel of a...

Finger gun.

Margaret blew him a kiss, waved goodbye to her son, and crossed the street where she disappeared under the streetlight. Mikey could still see her as she walked on that crumbling sidewalk. See her today like yesterday, like tomorrow, like she had and always would be.

Mother.

Matt was only a block away, just a jog from home in the rain; all he could think about was Margaret. The wind whispered in his ears. The scene played out in his mind again: Margaret's eyes, her hands, her arms around him, the woman stretching to meet his mouth, her lips. He walked down the dark street and passed by an alley where trash whirled around an unseen devil.

Fragments that were lost in a blur: his cot in that room above the gym; the light from the street that fell in through his window; early morning when he'd knock on Mikey's broken window; afternoon training sessions with Art; watching film with Leonard and eating pizza; Margaret and the dishes—Margaret and those perfect lips. And the more Matt thought about all those bits and pieces, the more he found himself suddenly longing for yesterday.

There was a strange comfort in his old life, a peace that came from knowing his place. Things would always be the way they were in that gym—yesterday, today, and forever. Just like the rising sun, Matt could count on Leonard, count on Art; he could know that when he went for a run in the middle of the night, Margaret would invite him in for cake. Matt turned from the devil, blind to the blur, and walked through the rain toward his steps.

The night was cold, but Matt never felt it. Instead, he looked through the rain at the sky. Matt saw nothing. Not the clouds, not the raindrops that fell like bombs; Matt only felt a sudden, unexpected reverence for the way things used to be. *Maybe*, he thought, *maybe I should go back.*

"Shine, sir?" Matt stopped dead in his tracks. An old man with pale eyes stood in front of a wooden step. At his side, brushes and cans full of black and brown polish sat in a carry-all—a little wooden thing with a handle that the man had made himself.

"Those shoes of yours sure do look like they could use a good shine. How 'bout it, sir, shine?" the man said.

Matt looked down at his shoes. They were scuffed, dull, and scratched around the toes. Matt wondered if he was dreaming. Why would anyone stand out here at night when it was raining and…only it wasn't raining anymore. The wind had died too. It was suddenly quiet. Up and down the street, it was too quiet.

"It's late," Matt said. "You need some help?"

"No, but thank you, sir. But how 'bout you? How 'bout a little help for them shoes of yours?"

"I swear we've done this before. You know, I met you before."

"You mean something like déjà vu?"

"Yeah, something like that."

"I don't believe in them kind of things."

Matt stared at the man. "You do know it's late, right?"

The blind man looked around as if he could see. "It is?"

"It is."

"Then that explains it."

"That explains what?"

"Why business is so slow." The shoeshine man smiled. "For me, there ain't no night and day. There is only now, and right now that now is tellin' me that your shoes need a shining."

Matt couldn't help himself, he laughed. "Sure," he said. "Why not."

The man reached down, feeling for his stool like a dog who sniffs with its nose. Only now Matt fully understood that the man was blind. The man sat on his stool and patted the little wooden step in front of him like he did day after day, year after year. "Your shoe, sir."

The man went to work, washing Matt's right foot, drying with a towel that was as white as snow before reaching in his carry-all for a toothbrush. The man dipped the brush in the brown can and Matt wondered how the blind man knew that his shoes were brown.

"I got a feeling about you, sir."

*Here comes the line, a little bit of prattle for a little more money.*
Matt smiled and said, "Really?"

"Yes, sir, I sure do." The man's eyes wandered. "You know, I'm gonna let you in on a little secret, a trade secret, the secret to perfectly shined shoes."

"Oh, yeah? What's that?"

"Spit." The blind man smiled. "Spit makes shoes shine like you can't imagine. Believe me, sir, I know. Fact is, I've tried everything from oil to water, but nothing works half as well. If you wouldn't mind, sir, may I spit on your shoes?"

*I must be dreaming,* Matt thought, *it's all just a dream—Margaret.* "Sure," Matt said. "Why not?"

"You won't regret it." The shoeshine man spit and buffed Matt's shoe with a heavy brush. "And don't worry none, I'll have you to bed and dreamin' soon enough. You got a big day tomorrow. That's why you so nervous."

"Nervous?"

"I can feel it." the shoeshine man smiled. "In the soles of your feet, of course. You got a big day tomorrow. Tomorrow night, I mean."

"How'd you know?"

"When you've polished as many shoes as I have, you get to know people," the blind man said. "Tell me, in your words that is, what's tomorrow all about?"

"Got a fight."

"That explains it." The man smiled and shook his head. "Your feet, I mean. I knew you wasn't no dancer, though you could be one if you wanted to. You got real sweet feet. They is jumpin', even now." Matt looked down at his dead dull shoes. "But let me tell you something, sir, from me to you." The blind man looked up, his pale eyes locked on Matt's. "You can't dance around right now 'cause you is all inside out."

"What?"

"I know who you are." The man smiled and Matt thought maybe he imagined what he had heard. After all, he was dreaming. "You is Matthew Gore, the Marvelous. It is a pleasure, a real pleasure to meet you, Mister Gore. I listen to all your fights, every single one of them. I even got to see me one of them, so to speak. I sat right up front, ringside, or so they told me. But I could hear your punches, Mister Gore." The blind man shook his head. "Those punches of yours, they sound beautiful. Say, did you hear that wish tonight?"

Chills ran down Matt's back. "What wish?"

"Other foot if you would, Mister Gore." The blind man said and Matt set his other foot on the wooden step. It was washed and cleaned—pristine. "I got good ears, Mister Gore, I hear things other men can't. I'm telling you, these shoes of yours here will last forever if you just clean them every now and then."

The man's nuts, Matt thought, certifiable. "What you talkin' about?"

"Oh, no, Mister Gore." the blind man shook his head. "I ain't. I assure you that. You see, when you is blind like me, blind since birth, mind you, well, you know things other men can't. I can see you, clear as day, see you, even though some would say I can't even see black. But I can, Mister Gore, I can smell it, taste it, feel it creep up my skin. The whole world is like water and I can feel the ripples in the pond."

And the blind man spit.

Matt felt sick, felt like running away, but he didn't. For some reason, he stood there as the blind man buffed with bourbon and used coffee grounds.

"We almost done here, Mister Gore. Just you hold tight for a minute more," the blind man said. "I think you gonna be pleased with these here shoes. They could almost shine white. Can you see that, Mister Gore? White shoes."

Matt could somehow see them shine—snow white.

"Good, good, that's real important. Just you remember that." The blind man smiled and put his brush away. The man stood, his eyes wandering. "It sure was a pleasure, Mister Gore, this shine's on me. It's not every day I get to shine shoes like yours. Now hurry on, time's going by and she's waiting for you."

The blind man pointed to the stairs; they were only a step away.

Matt thanked the man as the wind kicked cold and drops of rain fell like bombs. He was halfway up the steps when he stopped, music playing beneath him in TJ's bar below, Matt turning back to the blind man. There was no wooden step, no stool, no carry-all filled with cans both black and brown. The sidewalk was empty.

So was the street.

Matt lay and stared up at the ceiling. He was a million miles away, a million more to come; so far away he didn't even notice Donna next to him.

It was already past midnight, tomorrow was here, and good old Valentines Day, Matt wished it was gone and done, but it wouldn't go away with a wish.

No, not ever.

It wouldn't have mattered if the big man was looking up into a sky filled with a million stars because there was yesterday and tomorrow for the rest of his life, and it all hinged on tonight. All Matt had to do was kiss Douglas on the chin. Butterflies.

Moths.

Matt felt like throwing up. But this is what he had wanted: a chance, a date, a fight with a top five opponent! Matt had begged Art for a shot. When the old trainer declined, when Art offered him a third-class chump, Matt had up and left the man who was more like a father than his own. All for a night just like this, a moment under the stars.

But the time had come, the wish had been granted, Matt was going to get his shot with a 262-pound gorilla. Deep inside, Matt knew that this was it. No more tomorrows, no more chances, come win or lose, Matt's life, his future was now. The magic that he had felt, the serenity that he found with Donna's face, it hung dead in the air around him.

Matt could have gone on like that, his mind whirling, his gears spinning, getting nowhere. But instead, he did something that he had never done before. Matt turned over and touched Donna.

It was odd that Matt reached out to her, he was so used to being alone. When he was a child living on the fifth floor where mom had sat reading her love stories and dad drank on the fire escape, there was nothing but the sound of breaking bottles – alone. And when he was a man living in that room above the gym, the night before a fight, Matt would lay on his cot in the dark and stare up at the ceiling. Sometimes he had wandered around the ring, staring up in silence at the dead men who hung from the rafters—banners. But not tonight.

Tonight, Matt gently touched her arm. Maybe he should ask her tonight, give her that present he had hidden in his bottom drawer.

Donna turned, her eyes even brighter in the dark, her voice soft. "You okay?"

What could he say?

*Tomorrow, everything that I am is on the line. Win and I'm somebody, lose and I'm nothing'. And by the way, the reason I was so late tonight was because I needed to think so I went for a walk and ran into Margaret. She kissed me. I didn't kiss back.*

*That much.*

*But here's the thing, they all replaced me with Margaret's kid. Mikey's livin' up in my old room. You know, I thought me and him was close, but I guess that ain't so. And then I ran into the guy who shined my shoes.*

The big man breathed out. "Talk to me."

"Matt?"

"Ever since I can remember, since I was little, it's always been quiet," Matt said. "I hate the quiet. Please, just talk, about anything, I don't care. I just want to hear your voice."

For a moment, Matt didn't think that she would say anything, but then he heard her breath, the intake, and Donna spoke to him.

# TWENTY-FOUR

"He ain't gonna get up." Art just shook his head. "It's over." They were sitting up high, sitting right close to the nosebleed seats, but neither Art nor Leonard minded, even if Mikey did. They stared down at the blue ring and the lone fighter on his back. The referee counted, "Three...four...five..."

"The kid could have won," Leonard said. "He's got better skills, a better punch too."

"But he ain't got no heart," Art said as the referee waved his arms. The bell rang, the fight was over, the losing fighter's corner poured into the ring. "Too damn bad too 'cause you're right, Leonard. He certainly gots the tools only he don't like gettin' hit."

"Who does?"

"You." Art laughed. "Both you and that other knucklehead."

"You talkin' Marvelous." Leonard smiled, missing front teeth. "Ain't you?"

"The one and only."

"Tell me, Art, how you think he's gonna do tonight?"

"Good." Art turned to Old Forty Two. "He's gonna do good like he always does."

"How good?"

"You know them banners above my ring?"

276

"That good, huh?"

"Maybe."

"I hope you're right." Leonard looked back down at the ring. "I surely do."

"Tsk." Mikey wanted to puke. "I hope he gets whooped! I hope Douglas beats him so damn bad that he can't never fight no more again!"

Leonard wanted to kill the kid. "You do, huh?"

"Yeah." Mikey's face looked like he was sucking on something rotten. "I do. Don't you?"

Leonard shook his head. "Not in a million years."

"Amen." Art chimed.

"That's stupid." Mikey just shook his head. "I can't believe it! He left us, hooked up with them other trainers! I hope he gets beat good."

"Kid"—Art met Mikey's eyes—"you're forgettin' somethin'."

"Oh, yeah?" Mikey looked away. "What's that?"

"It's Matt," Leonard said. "Matt."

"He did good by you. Did good by all of us," Art said. "Don't ever forget that, kid. Not ever."

Mikey turned and stared down at the ring, the man-boy nodded.

Not such a stupid kid no more.

Light from the locker room seeped in through the door. The bathroom was dark. At the end of the room, leaning against a cold concrete wall, Matt stared into a mirror that hung over a dirty sink. The man was nervous, his gut was full of butterflies and moths, his mind full of wishes and wants. *Please, God, please.*

*I can't be a step, can't be a nobody no more. I've worked hard my whole life for this moment, please help me win. Let me throw that hook just like I did. Please, God, help me.* The room was quiet.

There wasn't an answer, there wasn't a voice from on high either, there was only that face in the mirror. The one that stared back. Only Matt could see the face. There were shadows like coins that covered the eyes.

"Matt." James stood in the bathroom's doorway, but Matt never saw him. There was only the face in the mirror. "Matt? It's time."

They were on the couch, sitting side by side; Angie was already holding Margaret's hand, even though the fight hadn't started. "Oh, Angie." Margaret stared at the old black and white television set. "I'm so scared."

"It's okay, Margaret." Angie patted Margaret's hand. "Matt's gonna do just fine. I know he will, you'll see."

"I hope you're right," Margaret tried to smile. "Oh, I hope you're right. He deserves it, Angie, he's a good man. A good man. I'm so lucky to have him. I'm glad we patched things up."

"Me too," Angie said, like a good friend should. "Is that Matt?"

On the television, Douglas appeared at the top of a tunnel surrounded by a myriad of men. There was hate in his eye, murder in his heart. Margaret reached for a cigarette.

"I'm scared for him, Angie." the strike of a match, Margaret sucked in, smoked seeped from her mouth as she exhaled. "It'll kill him if he loses."

Douglas danced down the aisle toward the ring, pointing up at the crowd, nodding his head, calling for Gore. All the way to the ring, dancing and shouting, laughing like a madman until Douglas's eyes met Mister Jones's.

He was there, standing at his seat, smiling at Douglas with those sharp gold teeth. Douglas's mouth suddenly shut. The big man stood there stupid, his trainers looking at him, confused looks on their faces, and the cling-ons around him getting scared. Mister Jones laughed.

Laughed long and hard as his head tilted back and his mouth stretched like a rip in the earth. And then Mister Jones said something unheard by everyone except Douglas. But Margaret read his lips as she crushed her cigarette.

Douglas's trainers pushed him towards the ring. They never saw Mister Jones, neither did Angie. The big man climbed up through the ropes. In a moment, maybe two, Douglas was his old self again. Dancing, pointing, never looking Mister Jones's way again, calling for Gore.

"Relax, Margaret." Angie patted her hand. "It's gonna be all right. You'll see."

"You remember, don't you?" There was a fire in the old trainer's eyes. Teddy and James stood with Matt just outside the locker room in the rear of the tunnel. Matt could hear the crowd, hear the music, see the light at the end of the tunnel. James put his hand on Matt's shoulder and said, "What we're makin' tonight?"

History." Matt looked up at James. "We're gonna make history."

"With a capital H, champ." James smiled wider than the world as Teddy stepped to his side. "Hear me now. Tonight, every person out there is gonna remember what you did. They is gonna see just how sweet your feet is, how smooth you move, and when you throw that hook of yours, mothers are gonna cover their kids' eyes."

"Listen to him, champ." Teddy was nodding his head, agreeing. "He's speaking nothing but the truth."

"Every man, woman, and child is gonna have the wind knocked out of them tonight. There ain't gonna be a sound, champ, not one. Fact is, it's gonna be so quiet that you could hear a pin drop. Even the referee is gonna stand there like he was struck dumb by the good Lord Himself, but then he's gonna start counting and his voice is gonna beat like a drum. A deep drum calling out history, counting the marking of time, announcing the coming of a new champion."

"You," Teddy said. "You. After tonight, you're on your way."

"Tonight, you is like a thunderstorm comin'." James could have been a pastor, maybe he was in another life. "There's gonna be a charge in the air. They gonna know history has come, and then you gonna feel it."

"Feel it in their voices that roar like thunder, speeding down to the ring, sweeping over you as you stand above Douglas. When it comes, champ, when you feel it, when you hear it, you take it all in 'cause then you know you made it. You made history."

Teddy smiled. "Amen."

"This fight"—James searched Matt's eyes—"is your fight. Believe it and it's yours, champ."

Donna could see him coming down the aisle. She stood up from her seat and tried to look through the crowd. Matt moved in and out of her sight as he walked by. "Don't you worry none." Mister Jones looked down at that fine woman. "You gonna see plenty in a minute. Yessiree, even if you don't want to."

The ring was full of trainers and cut men, and there were officials and judges who all milled around in the middle. Somewhere lost between them, the referee stood waiting. But Matt never saw any of them.

Nothing felt right: not his arms, not his legs, Matt's whole body felt like Jell-O. He stood in his corner, trying to stay loose, trying to dance, but all he could do was bounce on his toes. Even his punches were weak. Matt didn't even hear the bell that called him to the middle of the ring, but he felt Teddy and James's hands on his back.

The two trainers escorted their fighter to the center ring where Douglas waited with a smile: just a little Valentine that said, "I'm gonna kill you." The two men stood face to face. Matt looking up at Douglas, the gorilla looking down as the whole world stood by and watched. There was a charge, a surge of energy everywhere as a microphone fell from the sky.

"I want a good fight, a clean fight," the referee spoke into the microphone. "You both received your instructions in the locker room. Remember to follow my commands at all times. In case of a knockdown, go immediately to a neutral corner. I will not begin my count until you are in a neutral corner. Remember, men, I'm firm but fair. Now touch gloves and come out fighting."

Douglas raised his gloves, Matt met them with a thud—the softest blow either man would feel tonight. The crowd broke and gave a roar as the two fighters backed away, neither man taking their eyes off the other. Both corners gave their fighters some last-minute instructions. Even though both fighters nodded, neither man heard a word.

"Gentlemen," the referee called. "Get ready!"

"History, champ!" James yelled. "History!"

"Remember, Matt"—Teddy leaned close to Matt's ear—"just like we did in the gym. Just like sparring. This is no different."

The referee waved both men forward and stood between them at center ring. He was an old veteran of too many fights. Douglas moved forward, smacking his gloves together, hitting himself in the head. Matt stepped closer, flatfooted.

"Loosen up, champ," James yelled. "Relax!"

"Okay, gentlemen," the referee called. Eyes locked, hearts pounding, the two fighters waited. "Let's dance!"

And the bell rang.

They circled, both fighters out of reach of the other, getting a feel for the other man, trying to get into the rhythm of the fight.

Neither man heard the crowd. There was only the pounding of their hearts in their ears; only the sound of a laugh track that looped in their minds. Douglas moved in and threw the first jab.

It was just a meaningless thing that missed. But it brought both fighters closer to the other. Douglas danced, circled to his right and let one fly. The jab connected, Matt could feel its bite, feel the sting, feel that old familiar rush of blood. Matt tried to counter, but Douglas stepped back.

Matt pounded his gloves together as Douglas laughed. The gorilla touched his nose with his glove before dropping his chin. Douglas moved in: a left, a right, both measuring jabs. But both punches caught Matt square. Behind his gloves, Douglas smiled.

He could throw it, he knew his uppercut would catch Gore square. The gorilla moved in, he was Kind David now, King Kong, and the King was going to make his old hiccup pay. The man who had stopped his ascension to the throne was going to die. Douglas threw jab after jab, waiting, watching, smiling all the while.

"He ain't thrown it." James shook his head. "Matt ain't hit him with that hook."

"Move! Move! Move your head!" Teddy pounded his hands on the ring's mat. He stood with James in the corner, both men looking up through the ropes as Douglas measured Matt up. "Throw a jab, Matt! James, he hasn't thrown a punch yet!"

"He's tight."

"Well, if he don't get loose real quick, there isn't going to be another round!" Teddy pounded the mat again as Matt took another left. "He's measuring you up, Matt! Stick and jab! Come on, for hell's sake!" Matt stood flatfooted as Douglas unloaded a hook. "Look at him, James." Teddy couldn't believe it. "He doesn't trust himself!"

"Give him a minute," James said. "He'll get goin'."

"He ain't got a minute." Teddy shook his head. "We're in big trouble. For hell's sake, Matt, move!"

There was mouse, a little bump swelling above Matt's left eye, a little something that could blind him—end the fight. Matt was taking shot after shot, moving flatfooted, steered back by King David into the ropes.

Jab after measured jab, Douglas smiling all the while, waiting, watching, measuring his hiccup with a few combinations. The crowd screamed for blood. Douglas was only too happy to oblige. A straight right, a hard sledgehammer of a thing, Matt tried to swat the cross away, but it caught him in the mouth. Matt tried to counter, but nothing felt right. His arms were lead, his feet felt like they were in cement; he had to land that hook. But the faces, there were so many faces in front of him. Still he tried, he moved, came in close and threw it: his shot, that hook, and Douglas ducked under the punch.

It was there, right where Douglas thought it would be, an opening so wide that any fool could have driven a truck straight through it. Douglas dug under the punch, cranked his right tight to his body, and let that uppercut explode straight up. People that night said they could hear the ring in Matt's ears.

Matt's head jerked back with the force of the uppercut's impact. Blood gushed from his nose like a fountain. Matt fell back against the ropes only to rebound right back into Douglas. He was open, defenseless, Matt was nothing but a slab of meat hanging right in front of King David.

A left jab, a right cross, a hook followed by another sledgehammer. Matt was staggering, wobbling like a top, there was nothing he could do as Douglas dug down and drove up. The punch connected square, the crowd roared.

Matthew "Marvelous" Gore fell.

"I knew it." Margaret grabbed Angie's arm and dug into her friend's skin with her nails. Matt was about to go down. He was taking shot after shot, wobbling like a broken top, ready to take the fall. Margaret sobbed. "I knew somethin' bad was gonna happen. I just knew it."

Angie stared at the television set and patted Margaret's hand as Matt hit the ropes. She never felt the sting of Margaret's nails as they sank into her skin. She never noticed the little dots of blood that beaded up on her skin, but she would. Tonight, when Angie lay in her cold bed, she would feel Margaret's sting all over again and wonder what had happened to her arm. But now, right now as she stared at the black and white television set, her mind was too caught up in the moment to notice. "Don't give up yet, Margaret," Angie said. "It ain't over. There's still plenty of time—"

Matthew "Marvelous" Gore fell.

*This can't be happening*, Donna thought, *it just can't*. In the ring on a knee, Matt sat slump. His head drooped down as if his neck was broken, his arms hung stupid at his sides. Quickly, the referee escorted Douglas to a neutral corner and told the gorilla to stay there. *He can't lose*, Donna thought, *he just can't. He's too good of a man. He deserves this*, Donna thought, *he deserves to win*.

Donna clasped her hands together and stared up through the ropes into the ring. Her eyes were fixed on Matt. "Get up," she whispered, hoping to instill her strength into him. "Please, Matt, get up. You can do this. I believe in you. Get up."

The referee stood over Marvelous and began the count.

"One…"

There was bell, ringing sharp, ringing clear. A sound that slowly faded as a buzz filled Matt's head. Only Matt didn't understand what was happening. He didn't know who he was or where he was for that matter, he just was. His world was as small as a mouse.

"Two…"

A shoe, there was a shoe. Matt didn't know why the shoe was there, or why he was looking at it either. It was just there, just a shoe, the first thing that was outside of the buzzing in his head. But nothing made sense. Not the shoe, not the bell he had heard, not the buzz that clouded his mind. There was only the shoe, only a buzz,

*Get up.*

The shoe was white.

"Three…"

A rhythm formed in his mind. A slow, methodical thing that beat like a heart. Only this heart wouldn't keep beating, it was destined to doom, and none of it made any sense to Matt. The shoe, the buzzing, the ringing, the blue ground beneath him…

*Get up.*

*My shoe. It's my shoe.*

"Four…"

*A white shoe. My white shoe. Where am I?*

*Get up.*

There was movement. Movement that Matt caught in the corner of his eyes. Like a shadow seen skirting just out of view. Something that flashed with the building rhythm. Something like,

"Five…"

*Fingers.*

*It was a hand,* Matt thought, *a hand. Flashing fingers, heartbeats, one, two, three…counting. My white shoe,* Matt thought, *Mister Jones gave me white boxing shoes.* Counting, white boxing shoes, buzzing. *Oh, God, where am I?*

*Get up!*

"Six…"

*Six, I heard six. Someone said six. Five fingers, one finger—a finger gun. Oh, God, Douglas. I'm fighting Douglas.*

*Get up!*

*He caught me with that uppercut and I'm—*

Matt's mind jumped, into the ring, into the last moment he remembered, his head snapping back as Douglas's fist drove up into his chin.

*I'm down!*

"Seven…"

*Get up!*

Matt turned and looked, the referee stood at his side, his hands out, fingers up—seven. *I'm just a step, just a nobody, Douglas knocked me down. It's over. Twenty-eight and all washed up. Ain't ever gonna be Big Time. But a fighter fights.*

*Get up.*

*You're nothin'.*

*A fighter fights. Get up.*

"Eight…"

*A fighter fights—a fighter never stays down—I'm a fighter.*

It cut through the buzz in Matt's head. The truth, what he was, who he was, who he had always been—a fighter.

*I ain't ever gonna stay down, not ever.*

*Get up!*

*No matter what, no matter who's tryin' to keep me down, I ain't ever gonna quit. Not ever. I'm gonna stand, I'm gonna win—no matter what. These white shoes are gonna dance! I am!*

"Nine…" Matthew "Marvelous" Gore stood—the crowd roared.

# TWENTY-FIVE

"You okay, Matt?" The referee grabbed Matt's gloves, feeling for strength, stability, looking into his eyes. Douglas stood in the neutral corner, shaking his head. Nobody had ever gotten back up once he had put them down—nobody. "You want to go on?" the referee asked Matt.

"Yeah," Matt said. "I'm fine."

"You're sure now?"

Matt met the man's eyes square and saw the face, not his, not the one that changed again and again, but the other man's. Matt smiled. "I wanna dance."

Across the ring, Douglas's heart sank; Gore was smiling.

"Okay." The referee shook his head—*unbelievable*—and turned to Douglas. "Let's get it on, men. Fight!"

"Look at him!" Leonard stood, staring down at the ring— unbelievable. Matt moved, he danced, he threw jab after jab, right crosses, left hooks, and a flurry of combinations only a humming bird could see. And all of it was landing square on Douglas' chin, his body. Thunder shots. "Look at him move!"

"I'm lookin', I'm seein', but what I'm seein', unbelievable." Art stared down at his boy and saw something in his eyes. "Just unbelievable. Come on, kid, you can do it!"

"I mean I'm lookin' at him, I see Matt." Leonard went on, his eyes soaking in the fight in the ring. "But I'm askin' myself who that bad man in the ring is?"

Matt threw a left hook. It wasn't his strongest shot, it wasn't thrown with his dominant hand, but it was a good shot, a hard shot that made the crowd gasp—a shot to the body. Douglas stumbled back, his hands dropping to protect his body, his ribs, his mouth hung open. King David gasped for breath.

"He's yours, Matt! He's all yours!" Art yelled. "Knock that bum out!"

They were white shoes, beautiful shoes that danced, shoes that never touched the ground. Matt moved smoothly as silk, throwing hard left hooks, brutal right crosses that snapped Douglas's head back. He was a trainer's dream and an opponent's nightmare. Inside that man, something had woken up: a fighter that fights.

Matt was working him, hitting his head, moving to the body, taking Douglas's legs out from under the 262-pound gorilla. Douglas's mouth hung open like a cave. Matt threw a jab to the head, Douglas's gloves rose up just like Matt knew they would, but their rising was slow. The shot connected, stunning Douglas momentarily. Matt dug down, aiming for Douglas's body, driving an uppercut right into his ribs.

A crunch, cracking, bones breaking—Douglas's knees buckled and Matt saw it all. He moved in, unrelenting, measuring Douglas up with short jabs. In Matt's corner, Teddy and James leaned under the ropes into the ring, pounding the mat as they yelled. "Finish him!"

Matt led with a left jab that kissed Douglas's chin. His distance was perfect, his opponent was open, and Matthew "Marvelous" Gore threw it, a right, a hook.

A shot heard around the world.

Maybe it should have been the other way around, but as it was, Margaret sat back on the couch, staring at the black and white as Angie sat on its edge. Matt threw shot after shot, catching Douglas cold, setting the man up for the coming fall. Angie yelled and cheered and threw punches right along with Matt.

"Knock him out!" she screamed.

But not Margaret, no, she just sat quiet and cold. Maybe Margaret was in shock, or maybe she just couldn't wrap her mind around the fact that Matt had gotten up after getting knocked down, or that the flow of the fight had changed so dramatically. In fact, it could have been ten thousand things of a similar sort that whirled in that woman's mind, but it wasn't. Not one of them. And it wasn't shock—not by a long shot.

*I wish,* Margaret thought, *I wish that things were how they were.*

Matt threw jabs and crosses that pushed that other man back, and Margaret wished her wish again. And she wondered, a troubling thought, a thing that might keep her up that night, if her wish didn't come true now—right now—how could things ever be like they were if…

If he wins?

As she stared at that television set, as she wished and thought, the black and white image became a blur. *How? He can't win. How? I wish,* Margaret thought as her fingers strayed for a cigarette, *I wish I could—*

*Finish him.*

It was all Margaret heard as her mind pulled back from the smoke. Angie stood inches from the television set, Douglas stumbled like a broken record after eating an uppercut. Angie screamed. "Finish him! Finish him!"

A right, a hook.

A shot heard around the world.

Angie turned and lifted her friend from the couch and danced, spun around and around, holding Margaret. "Oh, Margaret." The smile stretched across Angie's face. "I'm so happy for you!"

Margaret cried.

There wasn't a breath, not a word spoken or shouted in that arena. Just eyes seeing, believing— Matthew "Marvelous" Gore. Donna stood with the crowd, time slowing down for her as Matt threw an uppercut. King David's hand rose, but too slow. The shot connected and Douglas's head snapped back. *I knew it*, Donna thought, *I knew it.*

*From the first day we met, the first time we talked outside the grocery store, I knew who he was. I could feel it. He's a good man, a one-in-a-million man, a man who listens to me. Who really listens to me. A man who gets up after getting knocked down. He's a fighter,* Donna thought, *a marvelous fighter. I'm not ever going to let him go. Just me and him, just the two of us—forever.*

A right, a hook.

A shot heard around the world.

*It's over,* Donna thought, *it's over. I know it's over. King David began his fall. Even if Douglas gets up again, it's over. Matt is going to win. And tonight,* Donna thought, *Matt's going to be sore, his body beaten, bruised from the fight. I'll take care of him, I'll be there for him. Tonight, tomorrow, just like last night, I'll be there 'cause he'll always be there for me. He'll sit out on that couch and listen to me and care. Care what I say. Tonight I'll fill the tub and sit on the edge behind him, drape my legs around him and put my hands on his broken body. I'll touch him, rub him, feel him because—*

Donna's breath caught.

*Because I love him.*

There were tears in her eyes. Tears that ran down her face and fell from her smile. *It's over, it's done,* Donna thought as Douglas fell. *He's won, he's won, we found each other.*

*We won.*

"It's over, kid, it's over." Art stood and watched as Douglas fell toward the hard canvas. At his side, Leonard stood frozen for a moment, he had been jumping and dancing, screaming for Matt. "Put him away!" Art felt something swell in his chest.

"You won." The old man stared down at the ring. "You won, kid. You did good, so damn good, I'm proud of you. Can you hear me, kid? I'm so proud of you."

And the old trainer cried.

All the way through his glove, Matt felt bone breaking, shattering as his fist drove through Douglas's jaw. Matt had never thrown a hook like that. Not ever in his life. The bad man's eyes rolled up in his head as he fell and hit the mat. Douglas's head bounced on the blue mat. His body flopped like a rag doll.

Quickly, the referee fell to Douglas's side. There was no count, no neutral corner—Douglas was out cold. But as the man lifted his hands to call for the bell, to call for the ringside physician and Douglas's corner, time slowed…

To a stop.

Matt stood over the sleeping giant, the world dead around him, no cries from the crowd, no man, woman, or child jumping up and down. It was as if Matt was deaf and dumb, but he could see. See just as clear as day as Mister Jones stepped right through those ropes, his long legs stretching halfway across the ring, his body bending like an unnatural thing. Mister Jones stood over

Douglas, shaking his head as if he was looking down on some fool. And then his head lopped back, his mouth parted like the Red Sea.

And he laughed.

Laughed as the whole wide world spun around him. But the spin, the world, everything that had been, everything that was, slowed to a stop. But there was a sound, faint but unmistakable, rolling across a distant hill, but it was coming closer. The thunder grew louder, stronger, until it cracked magnificently!

"Life sure is beautiful," Mister Jones said. "Isn't it, Matt?"

Matt couldn't answer back. He just stood there, staring at his manager, his eyes fixed on Mister Jones's mouth—gold.

"What's wrong?" Mister Jones asked. "Cat got your tongue? You just won, champ, you should be jacked. In fact, you should be runnin' around the ring, beating your chest, tellin' the whole world what you did. And what did you do? I'll tell you what you did." Mister Jones winked at Matt. "You just did what no man has ever done. You just knocked out one mean gorilla. I'm talkin' nobody, champ, not Harris, not Smith, not even Big Time Joseph could do what you did here tonight. I'm telling you, Matt, nobody gonna stop you. Nobody could." But Mister Jones smiled. "Well…almost nobody.

"I should let you in on a little secret. Just somethin' between me and you for right now." Mister Jones leaned down, put his mouth right close to Matt's ear, but not even a breath came out of that man's mouth as he spoke. "There's a part of you, a part deep down inside, a part that just achin' to beat your chest." Mister Jones leaned back. "But it's only just beginnin'. Oh, Matt, is it ever gonna come at you now! But don't you worry none. Nosiree, not one bit 'cause I'm gonna make sure you get it. I'm gonna make sure you get everythin' that's comin' to you."

Mister Jones opened his mouth. Matt knew he was laughing, but he couldn't hear a sound from that man's mouth. Instead, a laugh track played somewhere in the ring. Mister Jones pointed his finger at Matt.

Finger gun.

Then he turned and walked right through those ropes, legs stretching out through the crowd, disappearing in the thick of it all. The faces were gone.

The whole world broke in Matt's ears. The bell rang; Teddy and James rushed into the ring as Douglas's corner poured through the ropes.

"You did it, champ!" James hugged his boy. "You knocked that fool out!"

"Best damn punch I've ever seen!" Teddy put his arms around Matt, around James too. They all were smiling, but Matt stared down at the crowd where Mister Jones had disappeared to. "Watch out, Herns, here we come!" Teddy said.

Herns.

Matt heard it, heard the Dancing Man's name, and woke from his stupor. A smile broke like a wave across his face, stretching farther than ever before—smile wrinkles in the corners of his eyes. "I can't believe it!"

"Believe it, champ!"

"We did it." One after another, waves of joy swept over the big man. Matt's eyes shone. "We did it!"

"You did it, Matt." Teddy smiled. "You."

"You sure damn did!"

"Thank you." Matt hugged them. "Thank you so much!"

"No, champ." James patted his back. "Thank you."

And then he saw her, tangled at the ringside, thronged on every side by the crowd. Matt ran to the ropes, thanking men and women, kids who now looked up to him, and pulled her into the ring.

Matt held Donna in his arms, held her tight right there in his corner where she had always been. In front of the whole wide world, televised, Matthew "Marvelous" Gore kissed her.

Kissed her long.

They parted and looked into each other's eyes—both of them smiling.

"We did it, Donna! We did it! We won!" Matt said,

*I'm not ever going to let him go. Not ever.* "I'm so proud of you!"

# TWENTY-SIX

"Roy!" Margaret was waiting for him at the door, foot tapping, arms folded, cigarette hanging between her fingers. "Where you been?"

It didn't bother Margaret when she found herself staring at nothing. Nothing but an open door—rain on concrete. Margaret closed the door and walked right down that hall to the living room. Of course he was there, sitting on the couch, his long legs stretched out through a sea of brown bottles.

"I said"—Margaret's voice was as cold as a winter day—"where you been? It's been weeks since I've seen you! It's March."

"Oh, Margaret." Mister Jones laughed and the black and white television set flickered to life—snow and a quiet hiss. "You should see yourself. I mean, really, go have a look at yourself in the mirror 'cause that look of yours could kill. Well"—Mister Jones smiled—"almost."

"Roy." Margaret's hands found her hips. "Answer my question."

"Which one?"

"Where you been?"

"Margaret, please," Mister Jones said. "I ain't in the mood for twenty questions. I know that ain't what you want to ask me, so how 'bout you being a big girl and speakin' your mind for a change. Just straight out, Margaret. If you can, that is. No beatin' around the bush, woman, straight from the hip, shoot."

"You mean my wish?"

"If you do."

"Tell me, how come it ain't come true?"

"Now it's time to play." Mister Jones rubbed his hands together—sandpaper. "Tell me, Margaret, how come you think it ain't come true?"

"What do you mean?" Margaret's brow dug deep. "Things ain't the way they used to be."

"They ain't?" Mister Jones looked around. "It sure looks like they is 'cause things look just like they always have around this here place. Yessiree, home sweet home."

"Roy, Mikey ain't here, is he? And..." Margaret remembered her cigarette and breathed in. You could see that smoke move through her body. For a moment she calmed. "You is just playin' me, Roy. I know it too. It's what you always do."

"Margaret, I would never, ever in a million, billion years *play* you." Mister Jones put his hand where his heart should have been. "Boy Scout's Honor."

"You promise?"

"I just did."

"This ain't a game, right?"

"It's always a game, Margaret." Mister Jones smiled. "You of all people should know that. It's how you play the game, remember?"

"Not today." Margaret begged. "Please, Roy. Just answer me straight. Can you do that for me after all we've been through?"

"Margaret, I've already done so much for you. No, I'm afraid it's my way or the highway," Mister Jones said. "You don't have to play, it's always your choice. All you got to do is choose. That's it. Just like you did with Mikey, make a choice."

"Fine." Margaret walked to the ash tray and crushed her cigarette. "I thought we was closer than that."

"We as close as the sun and the moon." Mister Jones smiled. "We both right up there in that sky, spinnin' around this here earth. We like night and day, me and you. Ain't it beautiful, Margaret?"

"I'm the moon."

"Of course you are."

"Tell me, Roy." Margaret turned to him. "How come my wish ain't come true?"

"I can always count on you." Mister Jones laughed. "You always do play. Now then, tell me how come you think that it ain't come true."

"Like I said"—Margaret huffed—"nothin' is the same."

"You here, ain't you, all alone, the world out there spinnin' around you." Mister Jones looked her straight in the eye. "I mean you got things out there, but they always at an arm's length. Even when you was kissin' on Matt. Be honest, Margaret, you like things like that, don't you?"

"But he ain't at the tips of my fingers, Roy! He's with her." Margaret almost spat. "And Mikey, he's with Art! Ain't seen Leonard neither!"

"Leonard, huh?" If possible, Mister Jones almost looked surprised. "You just throwin' him out there, ain't you?"

"Nothin' is the same, Roy. You promised me a wish." Margret breathed. "A wish that would come true."

"I did." Mister Jones nodded. "Mikey's come by, so has Art, and Matt. Well, he ain't changed a bit now, has he?"

"But he won!"

"Was that hard on you?" Mister Jones looked into her eyes, into her soul; Margaret batted her eyes. "I mean the whole world got to see a man with a dream rise towards the top. Ain't nothin' can stop him. Well, almost. But did that eat at you, Margaret?"

"No." She sounded like a child. "It didn't."

"Could have fooled me." Mister Jones's eyes rolled like a roulette wheel. "How 'bout that kiss in the ring. The one with that damn fine woman. What's her name?"

"Don't, Roy."

"Donna."

"I said don't!"

"How come?"

"'Cause it hurts."

"Does it now?"

"Deep down."

"Don't lie to me, Margaret." Mister Jones scolded. "It didn't hurt you a bit. You smash through it all: paper, rock, scissors too. Ain't no stoppin' you, Margaret. You is a regular A-Bomb."

"Thank you, Roy."

"You're welcome."

"Please, Roy." Margaret got down on her knees and reached out to the tall man. Her hand laid on his knee, her eyes were just as wide as the sea—a sea of sand. "I'm beggin' you, I want to eat cake in the middle of the night, I want..." Margaret breathed. "I want..."

"Just say the word."

"It don't matter if it's Matt or some other man as long as he's fine," Margaret said. "Even Leonard would do."

"Go on."

"And I want Mikey to come home." Margaret never blinked. "And Art could live here too. I mean he's lonely, Roy. Almost as lonely as me."

"Ain't you the charitable kind. Tell me, you've already asked him, haven't you?"

Margaret blushed. "I did."

"And the old fool said yes, didn't he?"

"He did. We're gonna be family." Margaret dreamed. "The best kind. And me, I'm the moon."

"Now, Margaret, both me and you know that ain't gonna happen as long as I'm here. You can't have your cake and eat it too." Mister Jones lifted his long finger. "Not on this one, Margaret. It's either all of them, or me."

"Both me and you know that you is leavin' soon, Roy."

"I don't know." Mister Jones shrugged, except his shoulders never moved, and his head dug down deep as if he had no neck. "I was thinkin' maybe I'd stay."

"You never stay anywhere."

"Is that all you want, Margaret? Just things like they was, washin' dishes, late night showers, cake, that old fool comin' over?"

"Or someone new."

"And Mikey, him here again, hangin' out on the streets. And you, dear Margaret"—Mister Jones reached out and touched her face—"you, the little lamb with teeth, is that all you want? Same old, same old, with a new face or two?"

"That's all."

"Not even another fur coat?"

"I already got the best one."

"You sure do." Mister Jones nodded. "Yes, you sure damn do. Just think of all them little foxes runnin' out in the woods, all them lives now hangin' dead on you. How many foxes do you think made that coat of yours, Margaret? One? Two? Maybe three?"

"A forest-full."

"I couldn't have said better." Mister Jones's hand recoiled. "Like I always say, everything comes with a cost. Yours is just a forest-full of foxes. Well, you know what to do. Until then it's till death do us part."

Margaret's head fell, her eyes stared down at all those caramel bottles. She could see her face in one, see it in another, see all her faces staring back at her—faces littered across the floor. "This is hard on me, Roy," she said.

"I know." Mister Jones patted her head, "I know. But you know that there ain't nothin' I can do until you tell me. Just say the words, Margaret, and you'll be on your way."

"Will you come back?"

"Does the postman ring twice?"

"I don't know."

"I'm sure some woman does." Mister Jones smiled as if remembering something. "Go on now, I'm waitin', listenin' too. Listenin' close like I always do. The story ain't over, it's only just begun."

"I'm sorry." Margaret's voice cracked, even though there was moonlight in her eyes. "I'm going to have to ask you to leave, Roy."

There were no bottles on the floor, no faces either. The television sat dark in the corner; yellow light hung from the ceiling. Margaret sat on the floor with her hand on the empty couch—a smile on her face.

"Thank you, Roy. Thank you," she whispered. "I love you."

"Well, well, well." Mister Jones smiled. "How is we today, champ?"

"I'm good," Matt said.

"Just good?"

Matt smiled, a sheepish thing. There was something in his face, a shine to his eyes, a little something that had never been there before. "Really good."

"Come on, champ." Mister Jones tempted. "Just say it."

"Great."

"Yessiree, great! Yes, you is too. I'm tellin' you, Mister Matt." The tall man shook his head. "I'm tellin' you the whole wide world is openin' up right before you. And just between you and me, folks are callin' night and day about you. Seems like everyone wants a piece of you. It's comin', champ, you gonna get what's comin' to you. All of it. Big-time lights, banners hangin' on high, and ladies, well…" Mister Jones smiled. "You get to choose. But me, I'm gonna be leavin' for a while. Don't you worry none 'cause me and you is connected. Hip to hip, so to speak, till death do us part, and even then I'll be there, so don't you worry none. Tell me, how's that new woman of yours, Donna?"

"She's fine."

"She sure is." Mister Jones licked his lips. "The world spins fast, Matt, if you let go, you might just spin off. I never did ask you, but did you like them dancin' shoes of yours?"

"Wouldn't wear anythin' else in the ring."

"Neither would I," Mister Jones said. "Not for all the gold in the world, or in my mouth, whichever's more. Between you and me, I'm bettin' on me. Now them boxin' shoes of yours ain't ever gonna lose their shine as long as you believe. And you do believe, don't you?"

Matt looked around him, blue skies, southern wind, warm air pumping in—March. "Looks like spring is comin' early."

Mister Jones stood tall and this time his smile was something different. "Well said." He nodded. "Well said, Marvelous. I guess you really is the Magic Man."